'Sally Emerson has Heat
she has restored pa l ...
and takes it and its y as
Emily Brontë did. has
dared to do, to re the
Yorkshire moors and place it in a long, hot Washington summer.

Washington, which Emerson knows well, and makes utterly convincing and immediate to a reader who has never been there, is as much a character in the novel as Egdon Heath is in *The Return of the Native* or the seedy streets of London are in Graham Greene's *The End of the Affair* – one of the few English novels of the last half-century to make sexual obsession a central theme as successfully as Sally Emerson does here.

This is a compelling novel, permeated with an eroticism that has no longer anything to do with what we recognise as love, an eroticism which takes possession of people in defiance of all reason' – Allan Massie, *Scotsman*

'Quite simply, brilliant. The power of Eros to make and unmake us has rarely been better portrayed. *Heat* is a daring highwire act, perfectly executed' – Josephine Hart

'Quivering with subtle erotic tension and sparkling with observation ... hypnotically menacing, emotional thriller' – Celia Brayfield, *Mail on Sunday*

'An enticing novel made chilling by the juxtaposition of happy family life and undefined terrors' – *Express on Sunday*

'Brilliant ... economy and style' – David Robson, *Sunday Telegraph*

'A creepy thriller of Hitchcockian dimensions ... Permeated with eroticism and danger ... A really gripping book that captures perfectly the seesawing state of mind of its heroine' – Gillian Fairchild, *Daily Telegraph*

'This is a cunning novel about sexual obsession – when the author has us hooked, she begins to turn the screw, and we realise this haunting novel is a thriller' – Susan Crosland, *Literary Review*

Sally Emerson is the highly acclaimed author of several novels, including *Fire Child, Separation, Second Sight* and *Listeners*. She spent some time in Washington DC and now lives in London.

Also by Sally Emerson

Firechild
Listeners
Second Sight
Separation

HEAT

Sally Emerson

A *Warner* Book

First published in Great Britain in 1998
by Little, Brown and Company

This edition published by Warner Books in 1999

A CIP catalogue record for this book
is available from the British Library.

ISBN 0 7515 2700 9

Typeset by Solidus (Bristol) Limited
Printed and bound in Great Britain by Clays Ltd, St Ives plc

Warner Books
A Division of
Little, Brown and Company (UK)
Brettenham House
Lancaster Place
London WC2E 7EN

To my daughter, Anna

1

The first time she saw her old lover again was at a bookshop, up in Rockville.

Rockville was a nightmare area to the north of Washington DC, a suburban wasteland of low-lying carpet shops, pizza parlours and bed shops, all of which transmogrified into something else even as one watched. Everything was temporary there.

Susan speeded up, turning up the radio. And there it was: Janis Joplin's 'Mercedes Benz', one of the tracks she used to listen to years ago.

As a teenager, she had no particular feelings about the past. All she'd wanted was future; life was by and large a serial process. The door slammed on the last minute as soon as it was over. Life had been like living in Rockville, somewhere without a memory, where nothing remained for long, where adults could return to the streets of their childhood and find absolutely nothing the same; not a shop, not a church, not a tree.

But now life had a novelistic structure, a shape and some themes and some interweaving characters who made appearances at various stages of her life and theirs. The chief characters had been refined down to just a few, mostly people who'd turned up early in the novel of her life.

There was a new supermarket; there was a baby shop which wouldn't last long; there was a shop selling ski things.

Making a left, her car drew up outside the bookshop with its friendly green front.

She had first lived in America for a few months, at UCLA in California when she was twenty-four, and it had always been to her a place of sanctuary from England, where she was born. Her husband, Jim Stewart, was American.

She sniffed and grimaced. Their car had recently been valeted and smelt pungently of wet dog.

She kicked off her driving shoes and put on a pair of high heels, wondering why she was bothering.

As she walked into the shop, she felt a little nervous, as though sensing what brought her here, for these ties of ours are far stronger than we think, and draw men and women over oceans, round corners, through doorways.

She walked to the biography section past the psychology section which always attracted a group of cross-legged women reading tomes on 'How to get love back in your life' or 'Make him love you forever'. It was too embarrassing to buy such a book, and even more embarrassing to keep a copy on a bookshelf. Thus they were mostly read in snatches by women nervous that the object of their affections, or just a friend, might catch them at it.

Even more difficult to manage was the trick of

browsing nonchalantly through the sex books full of incomprehensible instructions and horrible drawings more suitable for a mortician's manual.

Bookshops were a great solace. When she thought of dying, it was leaving behind books which upset her most of all, particularly a battered copy of John Donne's poems, with 'The Good Morrow' underlined in places. At least the relations with those she loved would continue, in that they would continue to love her, while her death would terminate all relationship with these books.

A man in a wheelchair watched a squat lady in shorts balancing a pile of books in her arms. Close by, an overweight man chewed at an unlit cigar as he examined New Age titles.

Susan began to flip through the biography section and read something about Freud's cocaine habit, and about how Elizabeth I had been pregnant with Robert Dudley's child, and also she flipped through a biography of Lewis Carroll arranged in thirty-seven fragments, then moved over towards her area of study, the natural history section.

It was then that she saw Phillip over in fiction, an appropriate place.

He met her eyes, then glanced down as though he hadn't seen her.

She spun round and marched out of the bookshop, nearly knocking over an elderly lady. Outside, under the glare of the hot skies, she tried to find her car.

She'd spent thirteen years avoiding him, checking out every room and every party before entering it.

Whole continents had been eradicated from her

world picture because of Phillip. India had become a no-go area. Africa (he had written a piece from there) had been eliminated. The former Soviet Union was somewhere he had said he wanted to visit so she couldn't go there. Although, even on visits to London, she had never bumped into him, she had been doubtful about the Eastern half of the globe, as though he might pop up in a temple, head shaven, as a monk, or be the beggar her group gave money to, or be a businessman at a Hong Kong hotel.

She stood in the car park twisting her silver bracelet round and round.

She focused on her car, and hurried to it, fumbling for the keys.

2

Of course, this is the age for old lovers, once people have settled in the pattern of their lives. It happens to most people. Those you have thought never to see again appear at parties, in the street, at dinner parties, and while you discuss your child's homework you recall his taking you down on the floor of a concrete office room, and you blink and ask if he understands equations and how old is his son now and which school is he at. And all the while the comedy is there, at the corner of his eyes and yours.

'Oh yes, that's supposed to be a good school.'

'And your children, how are they?' he asks.

All your old loves come back, in the end, in dreams or in reality.

They dream of you now their lives are mapped out. Oh – that is the woman or man who could have taken me to another life. I could have been someone else. I remember her gaiety and the way she seemed to understand and the kisses, hot and fluid from the wide mouth. And to be unfaithful to my wife or husband – well, that doesn't really matter. After all, I met my old lover first, when I was very young, when we were both young, how could it be wrong to do as we did in the past, when her nails dragged over my skin? Maybe my life would have been better if it had been with her.

Even now a father, who has just moved back to the area after many years away, is on a school zoo trip as an accompanying adult. One of the mothers helping the teacher was his girlfriend years ago, when he was seventeen and he was tall and handsome. But now he has a fat stomach and a sadness around the parallel lines of his forehead. Whenever they look into a cage, the animals start making love feverishly. The father keeps nervously clearing his throat. The mother walks away from the cages and makes conversation about the school's PTA, and he kicks at the path with his heels, thinking how beautifully her hair drapes her forehead, just as it used to when she was seventeen.

And when you look at each other, you see the old selves. Choose lovers carefully because you'll have them forever.

It's thirteen years since Susan and Phillip split up, but of course old lovers never go away, they crowd round, watching your every action, coming between you, stroking your thighs when you make love to your wife, laughing at you as you eat your suburban breakfast, help you to pull on your socks in the morning, with lowered amused eyes. They watch as you drive out from your well-kept house – oh, they whisper, and you had such hopes, they say.

For thirteen years she had kept away from Phillip.

3

'I wouldn't mind staying in tonight,' said Susan softly as Jim hurtled from the bathroom. 'Sometimes these huge functions can get a bit much. You know, with everyone you know in Washington there.'

Susan, with her dark brows and vivid eyes, had an air of calm while Jim was racing against time, but time was getting to him all the same, shading his temple slightly grey, whipping off some of his hair, digging gentle furrows in his forehead. A few years older than Susan, he rushed around as if shoring up the mansion of his life against the floods that might try and get it. 'I haven't achieved enough,' he would say, dashing from one room to another. 'I haven't time,' he would say, checking his watch. 'I must do another book,' he would say, hurrying past a bookshop. 'The stories – where are the great political stories?' he would exclaim, as he did up the buttons of his white high-collared shirts which supported his thin, clever face like decorative frills round meat. 'It isn't enough. What I've done isn't nearly enough,' he would say.

In the morning he downed his vitamins: his ginger, royal jelly, ginseng, vitamins E, D, B, cod liver oil, zinc, magnesium – time capsules of all sizes and shapes. Then he would leap on the exercise bike as if, were he to pedal hard enough, he would defeat time. When dressed, he would speed down to the kitchen and seize the newspaper as though trying to shake the information out of it. His life was spent hurtling around – often in restaurants he would hover like a bee over his seat, and sometimes Susan would be convinced he never actually sat down. It was as though he were playing some kind of baseball game – racing from base to base at top speed. Even on his television appearances (he was a journalist on a weekly magazine who did some television work) he looked ready to leave at any second. At first the producers had remonstrated with him, but eventually had got used to it, indeed rather enjoying his air of coiled sexual energy. He even spoke too quickly, words falling over each other, and at parties flitted from one side of the room to the other like a restless moth.

Food occasionally calmed him; although thin, he ate and ate, as if half wanting it to weigh him down, to anchor him in place and make him enjoy the moment instead of plunging from one moment straight into the next.

From the beginning Susan had liked his energy and sense of fun, although sometimes it seemed he was hurtling by her and she would have to catch him by the sleeve and say, 'Oh Jim . . .' But his enthusiasm for everything interested her. 'That is *brilliant*,' he would say. 'I *love* that woman/man.' He never disliked anyone.

In any spare moments Jim poured over the eleventh edition of the 1911 *Encyclopaedia Britannica*: 'The climate of Washington,' explained the *Britannica*, 'is characterised by great humidity, long-continued and somewhat oppressive heat in summer, and mild winters. During a period of thirty-three years ending December 1903 the mean winter temperature (December, January and February) was 35°F and the mean summer temperature (June, July and August) 75°; the mean of the winter minima was 27°, and the mean of the summer maxima 85°. Extremes range, however, from an absolute maximum of 104° to an absolute minimum of –15°. There is an average annual precipitation of 43.1 in, which is quite evenly distributed throughout the year. Although snow-storms are infrequent and snow never lies long on the ground, the average fall of snow for the year amounts to 22.5 in.'

'We've accepted,' he said, buttoning up his dress shirt. 'There'll be a place with your name on it.'

'There are too many dinners,' said Susan in her lilting voice, putting her feet into black heels.

In the garden, trees twitched in an edgy response to the weather, which was about to change, as the weather in Washington DC was so often about to change. All day it had been on the threshold of perfection: sun adorning everything with light, turning rows of houses and smashed-up apartment blocks into gorgeously atmospheric film sets, transforming ordinary houses into New Orleans mansions.

But now it was darkening outside and the trees surrounding the house were uneasy as the weather grew close.

'Come on, darling,' said Jim, grappling with his bow tie. 'No one is ever late in Washington.' He looked round for something which he clearly expected to be waiting behind his back – perhaps a handkerchief, perhaps a comb, perhaps time standing there with its arms crossed like a quirky grandfather clock. Jim tried to flatten out his hair but it sprang back.

All over Washington DC people, preparing to go out, were beginning to argue. In Adams Morgan a man took his gun from the drawer and shot his girlfriend because she admitted to seeing another man. In Falls Church two men gunned each other down over a drugs deal.

The Washington area was divided between those who had guns and no air conditioning, and those who had air conditioning and no guns. Without air conditioning, the heat and humidity of a Washington summer build up until it is hard to imagine not killing someone if pushed an inch too far. Why, the day before, a twenty-year-old named Malice had taken out a 9mm handgun and killed a twenty-two-year-old because he refused to sell him his black Pentel pen. Later, chased by the police, the killer shot himself in the head. This kind of thing happened all the time. It was a game. Those in the game usually hung out in the streets. The violence was young man's violence – the violence of people living in the present tense, without a past or a future.

Susan watched Jim as he adjusted his shoulders in the mirror. Soon the black dinner jacket would be unbuttoned and one of the jacket's shoulders would have slipped down.

'Oh – this weather,' she said in a voice full of anticipation as the humidity clung to her skin. There was something momentous about Washington weather and she shook her head, as if to shake off the warm air. From the day she arrived from London with Jim and their daughter Rebecca four years ago, she had loved the treacherous quality of the climate. Washington pretended to be so sedate – with its monuments like wedding cakes, its shopping malls, its air of high endeavour presided over by Lincoln pronouncing about freedom – yet the weather was out to make a mockery of it all, snatching roofs off buildings in hurricanes, plunging houses into darkness with dramatic storms, chucking snow on the roads so everything stopped, making people throw their hands up in dismay and claim they couldn't go to work, to school, to the shops. And in the summer the heat brooded and betrayed, and made people behave in ways they didn't intend to behave.

Susan drew lipstick onto her lips.

With customary decisiveness, rain suddenly collapsed from the skies and the huge trees became shapes in the mist. The water beat against the window and on the roof and on the streets, sending fountains of rain splashing back into the air.

Susan stood watching the rain, and when Rebecca joined her Susan put her arm around her. Rebecca wore pyjamas covered in red hearts, with the air of someone who wouldn't be seen dead in pyjamas with red hearts over them. Eleven years old, clever, with the air of a startled pixie, she had a fringe like an unruly ski-run sticking out at the front. In the ante-room between childhood and adulthood, she was tapping her fingers, looking both backwards and forwards, looking for answers, ways of interpreting the confusion she felt. She had until the last few months been very close to her mother but was beginning to edge out now, away from her. Skinny and a little gawky, with too many elbows and knees, she had dark eyes which blazed from her pale skin, and her black hair curled into a tight undergrowth on her head.

'Will it be a big party?' said Rebecca.

'Oh – huge,' said Jim, opening a drawer and flinging handkerchiefs on the floor as he searched for cuff links. The whereabouts of his cuff links was of importance in what he seemed to see as the entirely abstract world of material reality; whereas his life took place in the mind, in books, in the black and white paragraphs he shifted around or the commentaries on politics he gave for the television. He treated real life as though it were a somewhat comic and entirely bizarre creation of some remote South American fabulist. 'Do you know where my cuff links are?' he cried out, as if the very idea of cuff links was both implausible and ridiculous, then grabbed at a bottle of aftershave, turned it upside down leaving its imprint on the top of his finger before dabbing his finger behind his ear.

'I might organise parties *and* sing at them when I'm older,' said Rebecca thoughtfully, who spent much of her time inventing illustrious careers for herself. She picked up one of her mother's lipsticks. 'Nice colour,' she said, and glanced at herself in the mirror as she drew two red smears over her lips, then screwed up her face in dismay before wiping off the lipstick with the back of her hand.

Outside, in the street, the houses and the road were darkening. Every so often a desperate light flicked on, and a person could be seen at a window, for this was a neighbourly little cul de sac, where people knew each other by name and shared the street like a garden, except for two couples a little further down the road who lived next door to each other and loathed each other for historic reasons which everyone but they had forgotten.

Eventually Susan and Jim swept out, through the storm, to their car which glistened with raindrops like mercury on glass.

Their house spread out behind them, grey and odd, with its grey-blue tiled roof shimmering in the rain, a French country house dropped at the edge of Washington DC.

As their black station wagon swished down wide, amiable Wisconsin Avenue towards the British

Embassy, people were entering and exiting cinemas, the ones exiting blinking somewhat at how suddenly the rains had come.

'A teenage girl was stabbed and critically wounded last night outside McKinley High School, just as about three-hundred people were leaving a basketball game . . .' announced the radio.

The radio shop they passed, the pizza restaurant, the bookshop, all the shops scattered along the wide thoroughfare looked surprised, as if the buildings had turned up somehow at the wrong party, in the wrong street, and didn't recognise a soul but would make the most of it.

Wisconsin Avenue was flanked by the glittering glass of department stores interspersed with low-lying restaurants, drug stores, even a pet shop. The water-logged street carried them down to the Cathedral, and there they turned left, towards Massachusetts Avenue, and the embassies which lined the street like dowager ladies.

Back in their garden the cicadas had begun to cry out again through the hot, thick air and an undocumented white moth hit against the window of Rebecca's bedroom, and Rebecca heard the thud as she lay awake listening to the sounds of the night, unable to sleep.

At the British Embassy residence Susan and Jim gave their names to a cockney at the gate who seemed to have just walked out of a 1950s British comedy.

Footmen in grey bowed gently to them as they walked up the steps and into the hallway.

On the walls of the ladies' cloakroom a honeysuckle wallpaper wrapped itself round and round, and in the mirror Susan's green eyes stared back at her from a face Susan didn't know. We carry our faces around all our lives, she thought, and we don't know them, don't understand them, stare into mirrors for clues as to who we might be.

Her dress escorted her body out into the hall.

They walked up the red-carpeted stairs watched by portraits of British royalty dressed in pearls and ermine. Queen Alexandra gave them a particularly perceptive glance.

'It's wonderful that an England like this exists somewhere, even if it doesn't happen to be in England,' said Jim.

She took his hand, such a bony hand enveloping hers.

They reached the top of the stairs and there was a marble-floored corridor and a smell of roses, and the smell was lingering and delicate but dense and old too. She stopped and touched one of the roses, and looked at the richness of the petals, the way they folded together, going back and back forever somehow, as if part of some other time yet part of this time too.

Jim waved to an elderly couple in front of them, and surged forward to the receiving line to greet the ambassador and his wife and the guest of honour, the British Secretary of State, a man who looked as though he'd had something very heavy dropped on top of him; he was unusually short and wide, and had a surprised expression as if the accident had only just happened.

In the ballroom to their right, innumerable white-skirted round tables seemed to be dancing with each other, glittering with the jewellery of candelabras and cutlery, filling in the time until they were needed for dinner.

Tonight, most women were in long dresses heavily sequinned round the bosom, and few were young, for Washington didn't have the turnover of wives which characterised the west coast of America. The Washington men, apart from Jim, usually had a military bearing even if they were in fisheries; they were so tall and reasonable whereas British men always seemed on the verge of committing some moral abomination.

'Hello,' said Susan to the elderly couple, and the woman brightened, and they chatted, and the man watched. He had one of those long faces which seem about to drop to the floor at any moment but is just about held up by the twinkle in the eyes.

In the receiving line the ambassador, with pale brown hair like dust, bent discreetly down to kiss Susan while his wife gave a cry of delight and snuggled her warm cheek against Susan's.

'Welcome to Washington,' Jim said to the Secretary of State, who smiled a Play-Doh smile. One of the man's plump hands moved a little, anxiously, by his side. Jim, although not quite anchored in the world of cuff links and black ties, was highly sociable. It was as though those he spoke to might disappear at any moment so he had to make the most of them while he could. 'What are you *doing*?' he would say. 'We *must* get together,' as if that particular person standing in that particular place were quite the most engaging person in the world. Indeed, people in the diplomatic, journalist and Government areas of Washington DC did disappear constantly, to other countries, back home, to jobs elsewhere, so that life here in this relatively small community became a never-ending round of leaving parties. But not everyone enjoyed these formal functions.

Only a few months back a politician's wife had had a nervous breakdown in the ladies' cloakroom of the Embassy, her face falling into the basin, in tears.

About fifty people had already arrived and were scattered about the room. The blue curtains swept expansively to the ground. The residence was the British house of other people's dreams: slightly faded carpet, perfectly tasteful chalky paintwork, grand drapes, silver photo frames, and flowers everywhere, breathing out sweet summer smells.

Here in Washington exiles from England soon became more and more English, eventually achieving a curiously hybrid Britishness, characterised by a pronounced accent, an aristocratic sense of superiority shared even by the most working class of the exiles, and an affection for British food and drink not displayed when actually inhabiting their dark and curiously lonely island.

The only vulgarity in the room was the photographs of the ambassador and his wife with the American President, not dissimilar to those pictures taken with cardboard replicas of American presidents. But these were in old silver frames, and scattered among family photos. Apart from that there were some uncomfortable, valuable chairs, a few oil paintings, and lumps of semiprecious stones on the coffee tables – personal possessions of the ambassador and his wife to suggest they were in fact real people.

'Darling,' said the adulterous voice of a British journalist. He kissed her neck, and Jim dashed off, winding his way through the party, and within moments was examining a plate of canapés as if asked to choose any one of a number of precious gems. The waiter maintained a courtly posture as Jim chose.

Jim loved food and during the course of an evening at home would make a number of forays to the fridge, opening the door and gazing into it, his face illuminated by the light inside, as if taking part in some private act of worship. He would get out food – a piece of cheese, a hunk of bread – with reverence, and assemble it carefully on the table like a still life being prepared for Rembrandt to paint, then he would pull up a chair and slowly and ecstatically eat his snack.

'Having fun?' said Jonathan to Susan.

Jonathan had the voice of Gollum in *The Lord of the Rings*, tender and wheedling, but his body was thin, made of sticks, and his head nearly bald.

'Yes, I'm having fun,' she said, turning her bracelet round and round.

Jonathan dropped ash from a cigarette on the carpet. He picked up a decorative chunk of amethyst from the table by him and weighed it in his hand.

'You know who's here?' he said.

'Who?' she said.

'In Washington,' he said. 'An old amour of yours, I believe. Phillip Jordan.' He paused and stared at Susan. 'At least it's good to have someone else in DC who *smokes*,' he continued. 'People like Jim are so *healthy*.'

Susan waved at a stately woman she knew by sight, who smiled back at her. A portrait of a young boy alone in a rural landscape gazed at her from the walls.

'How's your film script going?' she asked Jonathan in a high-pitched voice, taking off an earring then putting it on again.

'Screenplay, darling,' he said, watching her wide mouth. 'You call them screenplays. Actually, I believe he's coming here tonight.'

A tray of canapés went by: bits of smoked salmon crouched on black bread; marinated cucumber loosely clinging onto another kind of bread; some kind of grey pâté decked with a bit of black olive collapsed over a biscuit.

'Did you hear,' said a loud female voice, 'one of the wives in Paris found the embassy circuit so difficult she held a dinner with rolls in the shape of frog's legs! They never forgave her!'

'He went up and shot himself in the mouth while his family were downstairs. But he was very ill,' said another woman.

'Of course, his approval rating has gone up a few points . . .' said a voice far away.

'Gun control is always an issue . . .' shouted someone in her ear.

Back home, Rebecca pushed off her duvet, for it was growing hot again. On her wall were her versions of the planets, one after the other, the earth a particularly gimcrack place of blue and scraps of brown.

Out in the wet garden, a little brown garden spider (*Araneus diadematus*) was remaking her broken web with all the considerable brilliance in her possession: dropping a drag line, making sure it was held tightly to the twig below, testing its strength, then making more lines of silk, carefully measured, each radius of about ten or fifteen degrees, darting up and down its slender ropes.

The babysitter Maria watched a television programme selling food mixers. As Maria watched, she ate crisps from a giant bag. She didn't hear Rebecca slip out.

At the party, Jim listened bright-eyed to a pompous politician, nodding respectfully while all the time standing on the balls of his feet as if about to race off at any moment. Sometimes, even he wondered what it was he was in such a hurry to find. Whatever it was, he hadn't found it. Meanwhile, his jacket was trying to slip off his shoulders. Every now and again he would wrench it on again before dancing off to yet another politician. His route through a party seemed almost choreographed, as though he were the lead ballerina in a dance of manners.

The voices of the party continued to rise and fall and Susan made her way through the people, stopping to talk to a friend here, an acquaintance there, watching the golden clock on the mantelpiece, which kept saying the same time.

She had half hoped she had imagined Phillip in the bookshop.

Over in Anacostia, in south east Washington, the young men were out on the streets again, their hands in their pockets, having slept most of the day. On one particular corner a police car drove by and the young men turned and stared at the policeman with an expression of hate tinged with fear.

And in Susan's attic study, where she kept her collection of insects and spiders that she painted, the creatures lay, embalmed in their mahogany trays, lastingly beautiful: a bilious yellow locust, a beetle shiny as new shoes, a moth with gossamer wings, a scarlet fly. Ravishingly intricate, each one of them, with their eyes like pilots in goggles.

Every now and again the ambassador, the host, would pop up above a group of people and join in, and then would pop up somewhere else.

'Jim,' said Susan, 'I think I feel sick. I'm going.'

'What's up, sweetheart?' he said, his face close to her.

'Nothing. Just feel sick. Can I take the car?'

'Of course,' he said, and then the words rushed out. 'But what's the matter? What is it? Are you OK? I'll just come with you at once and see how you are . . . and . . .'

'No. No.' She smiled. 'You stay. I'll go. Someone will give you a lift?'

'Of course.'

'Good. You stay. I'll be fine. You stay. Please. I want you to stay.'

Some of his hair was nearly standing on end from where he had run his fingers through it.

'Sweetheart. Are you sure you're OK?'

'I'm great,' she said, somewhat shrilly, car keys clutched in her hand. 'Great. I just . . . apologise for me, will you?'

'I'm really sorry I dragged you here. You should have said. Did you say? I didn't know you weren't feeling well,' he said, opening out his hands crowded with knuckles and lines and veins.

'That's OK,' she said softly.

'I want to come with you,' he said, bouncing from foot to foot like someone warming up for a big race.

'No,' she said, raising her hand lightly to touch his cheek. 'You stay.'

She swept away along the endless marble corridor, down the stairs, watched by gracious kings and queens in gilt frames, through the hallway and out down red steps into the still outside world, where the trees stood motionless, and the cars raced by in the street beyond.

She searched for their car among the rows and at first couldn't find it, couldn't recall what it looked like, although she remembered the car Phillip used to have, a black mini with rust up the left side, and she found she was looking for this, as though if she found it she could just drive off into the past and all this confection of buildings, these white wedding-cake embassies, would dissolve.

Eventually a black Volvo looked recognisable and

the keys matched and the mess in the back was hers and as she started the car she thought how obdurate physical objects were, really, the way that on the whole they just stayed as they were while human beings expanded or contracted or grew to hate each other. The building overlooking Fulham High Street where she and Phillip had lived – why, she had passed by there on her last visit to London and it had been just the same, a Victorian red brick construction with a dirt-encrusted design of flowers and plants in the brickwork between each of the four storeys. They had lived in the top two.

Seeing the windows to that flat had, even then, made her somehow imagine that her life with Phillip was continuing there, unseen by her, that she was in there boiling eggs, making love, organising bills, buying new plates when the old ones cracked in the dishwasher.

Back home the spider has almost completed her web; such a beautiful web, deep in the lush green undergrowth.

The babysitter has fallen asleep, her head in the packet of crisps.

And all the while Phillip Jordan is getting closer and closer to the embassy, down Massachusetts Avenue, the trees above his car spreading out in fluorescent green from the rain. His girlfriend, Sandra, sits neatly beside him, with her well-cut fair hair, her shoes so well polished, her handbag sitting on her lap like a dog.

Phillip Jordan drives his car fast into the parking area and flings it, braking heavily, into a far corner before he unravels himself out, unreasonably tall. And as he gets out, Susan sees him and she drives quickly off, with a roar of the engine. He turns and watches the car go.

4

At first, after Susan and Jim had left for the party, Rebecca was unable to sleep. It was still light so she got up and wondered whether she dared creep round next door to see Ivana Fischer, the next-door neighbour who taught her the piano. Maybe Ivana would show her some old photographs of Poland, where she had been born. When Rebecca thought of Poland she saw turrets, and countesses with long white gloves.

A bug flew noisily round her head.

Rebecca closed her eyes tightly and stroked the ribbon edge of the blanket she'd had since she was a baby, in a final effort to get to sleep. Upstairs, in her mother's attic study, the photograph of Rebecca as a baby on the pink and blue blanket sat on the desk in a tarnished silver frame. Rebecca felt very young tonight, as she often did at night when her parents were out, more like an eight-year-old than an eleven-year-old. Rebecca preferred to play with boys rather than with girls. She tried to play football, only she had brittle little stick-like arms and legs and sometimes she feared they would break. Her father played football with her in the garden. 'You're as good as any boy!' he would shout, but really she knew somehow he wanted a little boy with broad shoulders and big knees and round glasses like the pictures of her father when he was small.

Rebecca was not especially popular at school. She was always on the edge of things, a thoughtful, quirky child.

She heard one of the boys in the street shout out and wished she was up, out playing in the street instead of trapped here between sheets with their cleaner babysitting downstairs. She liked Maria, who cleaned for them twice a week, but didn't like her standing guard.

Rebecca decided that if she were to slip out she'd have to go out through the back door and through the garden otherwise Maria would see her. She opened her eyes. She tried to make faces out of the Sanderson flowery curtains, but grew bored. All her life she had made faces out of those curtains, back in London and here.

She wore a T-shirt emblazoned with the word 'Hershey' they'd bought on a trip to the Hershey chocolate factory up in the Amish country where boys and girls rode about in horse and carts and didn't have television.

She got out of bed and sat on the side of it.

She crept down the creaking stairs, through the hall, past the kitchen where Maria was watching television, and to the French windows which led out into the garden.

The moment she was outside, the sound of the cicadas grew deafening and everywhere there were insects batting into her face.

She ran over the harsh dry grass to the fence and climbed over, then ran to the back door of Ivana's house and beat at it.

The door opened.

'I couldn't sleep!' said Rebecca. 'You said I could come over whenever I liked!'

'Come in, come in,' said Ivana.

'My mother's out and Maria was watching the television at top volume.'

Ivana put her arm round the shivering child with her pointed chin and blazing eyes like her mother's.

'Is your husband out?' said Rebecca.

'Yes,' said Ivana.

'He's always out,' she said.

'Gustav's an important man. He'll be an ambassador one day. He has things to do.'

'When my mother left for an embassy party the atmosphere was . . . very still and quiet, like being inside a ghost.'

'I see,' said Ivana, thinking how articulate Rebecca could be. It was as though Rebecca could understand far more than she should at her age whereas she, Ivana, struggled in a kind of darkness.

Ivana gave Rebecca some chocolates and they looked at some of Ivana's photographs of Poland. 'One day maybe your mother would let you and me go there together. Just the two of us,' said Ivana.

'Oh yes,' said Rebecca. 'She says she wants me to be more outgoing.'

Ivana took Rebecca back after a while, to the back door, and Rebecca slipped up to her bedroom without Maria noticing.

Soon Rebecca lay with her knees curled up tight, dive bombing into her dreams.

5

Susan drove off alone and fast up Massachusetts Avenue where the trees waited on either side in their flamboyant green uniforms.

It was not having the other child, she told herself, as she turned into Wisconsin Avenue. Everything was beginning to go wrong because the next child hadn't come.

The grey street slammed into her face as she drove fast back towards home. The streets which had been so easy on the way to the party, so casually scattered with shops and restaurants, were now entirely malign. She turned up the radio, and heard an old Janis Joplin song. The car seemed too big, and too empty.

'Oh Lord, won't you buy me . . .'

Nearing Chevy Chase, she passed the Neiman Marcus department store confidently bestriding the street, and turned down into Chevy Chase village, which really was a village, well forested, with village greens and tranquil houses taking their time.

Her house was standing there just as it had been before she left when it should have had a crack down the middle, or at least no roof. It spread out before her, comfortably, augustly, intransigently, with its creamy stucco walls, its sea-green paintwork, as though the last few years of her life there really had happened, as though Rebecca really were there, up in her bedroom, breathing softly, as though all that time since leaving Phillip really had passed.

Susan didn't really want to get out of the car because the car represented a sort of timelessness, the state of being between things. She leapt from the car, slammed the door shut and marched with shoulders up as if against a wind although there was only the everlasting heat of a Washington summer. The cicadas cried out.

She wondered where Maria was. The house was unusually still. She walked into the kitchen where Maria slumped, head down, fast asleep, on the red Formica table they'd never got round to changing. Under her head, for a pillow, were the open pages of a book on accounting, for some banking exams she was hoping to take.

She looked so peaceful, with her sleeping face turned towards Susan and the whirr of the fridge making an odd lullaby.

On the television a man confessed to his mother he was a transsexual.

The immense fridge-freezer was skewered with bits of paper held on by magnets: a circular about a karate club, a list of Rebecca's schoolmates' telephone numbers and addresses, the number of a pizza delivery service, the local cab number, a rather bad picture of a hedgehog painted purple ('They like us to do animals ridiculous colours,' Rebecca had said gloomily, chucking it on the dining-room table) – the awesome detail of family life.

Rebecca had stuck her class photograph up on the wall above the kitchen table with Sellotape. In it, among the rows of children with their hands resting on their legs like Egyptian statues, Rebecca glanced warily out. The only one who looked equally suspicious was her friend Jenny who spent most of her time at school inventing ways to blow it up, and at recess sat frowning and refining her maps of the school in an effort to discover the best places to leave the dynamite. Rebecca, who was obsessed by English history, had won Jenny's friendship by telling her about the Gunpowder Plot.

'You see,' said the man on the television, who was dressed as a woman in a short black skirt, 'I feel this is really me, Mother.'

Maria lifted her head from her bookish pillow.

'Hi Maria. I'm back,' said Susan.

The fridge whirred. A fly buzzed repetitively round Maria, as though it could think of nothing better to do.

'Oh yes. Susan. You're back.' She yawned.

Susan paid her, as the mother on the television wept and the son, with a girlish gesture, patted his mother's head, and Susan wished you could switch off life as you could switch off a television when it became too much to stand, switch it off then switch it on again later. Perhaps that was why people committed suicide so much nowadays; they were used to being able to switch things off which inconvenienced or disturbed them.

Languidly, Maria picked up her banking book and browsed to the doorway, looking from side to side like someone at rather a good yard sale. Susan said goodbye and shut the heavy wooden door behind her.

As Susan stood by the fridge, she found her hands were shaking.

The fridge shook too. Large, stately, avocado green, it was an ungainly presence in the kitchen but Susan could not bear to swap it for some discreet white fridge which merely received and gave out food. The fridge was some kind of earthly companion on evenings like this.

The house calmed her. The house was Susan – the attic her head, and the walls her skin, and the little piles of dust in the corners like the dirt under her nails. When there were holes drilled in the walls to put in new electricity circuits, it was as though she were in the dentist's chair herself.

But of course she had chosen somewhere with the past tugging at it constantly – the ivy, the old paint colours.

In the drawing room, she ran her fingers over the wooden bench that sat behind the sofa. How expert I've become, she thought. How very grown-up to know it was wise to put a bench behind the sofa so a guest wouldn't see the back of the sofa: a back like someone being rude at a party.

On the stripped mantelpiece rested a frameless painting of houses in snow, slightly right of centre, rather a good picture she'd bought from an auction. The drapes were ideal too – red and gold damask, elegant, exotic, judicious. The tall windows went up to the ceiling, and flung down their drapes of wine-red damask. Susan pressed the button on the CD player.

She began to move the furniture around in the drawing room; she put the coffee table closer to the sofa, and the armchairs a little further away from each other. The footstool needed to go closer to the blue armchair which rocked repetitively, irritatingly. She tugged at the Afghan carpet with its reds and blues and flashes of gold to move it a few inches to the right. The sofa she managed to push forward a little. I must get it right, she thought, adjusting the dimensions of her life, the gap between things.

Susan went up to Rebecca's room and as she saw the child lying there she was startled, as though it wasn't what she expected. She realised she had half expected Rebecca not to be there, as though Phillip's presence would somehow remove Rebecca from her. Rebecca lay spread out like a starfish, bedclothes on the floor, as always, wearing a white T-shirt. The child's hair was stuck to her forehead with sweat and her mouth was just a little open, as though singing a hymn in a choir.

Susan moved the bedside table closer to the bed.

6

After Susan had left the embassy party, Phillip Jordan introduced himself to Jim Stewart. Later, Phillip introduced Jim to Jane Meadows, secretary to one of the southern senators, saying that she very much wanted to meet him. She was there with one of the young Republican advisers.

'I've seen you on the television,' she said, in a southern voice which was at odds with her rather dull appearance; she wore a mouse-grey, knee-length dress which hung limply over her as if someone had run it up from a dish-cloth. But she wore very high heels and had a way of concentrating absolutely on the person she was talking to which made her at times arresting. A little fake pearl necklace twirled round her neck.

'You look surprised,' he said, moving from foot to foot, adjusting his bow tie, throwing a glance round the room to see what else was going on. Like all journalists, he loved gossip and intrigue. 'Are you puzzled how someone as ugly as me can be on television?' he laughed. 'So wizened! So jittery!'

'It helps to make you memorable,' said Jane Meadows. Her back held her straight, holding up her dull grey dress, slightly broad hips, the features which somehow hadn't quite got together to make a face. Her eyes were faint and vague, her hair a faded brown and there was a sulky curve to her mouth, but somehow all these items were not in agreement about how they should behave; only her mouth suggested someone who knew where they were going.

'I hear you got the job because you *weren't* like the usual commentators,' she said.

'Ah yes,' he said, watching the white plasterwork over the other side of the room.

Yesterday, when he was playing tennis, he had lifted his racket and for a moment hadn't known who he was playing with or why or who he was.

'Where are you from?' he said.

'Alabama,' she said. 'Your voice sounds quite British, but I imagine you're American – one of the Anglo-Americans.'

'I don't know whether to be offended or not.'

'Oh,' she said. 'Be offended, if you like. I don't like the British.'

'Too southern?' he said.

'Maybe.'

Although she was little, she stood firm, like some tiny, still warrior.

7

Susan felt shivery and sick and went to bed. She lay there trying not to think about Phillip, but instead she thought back on her first day in the Washington house.

'Don't stay out too long, Rebecca!' she had called through the open doors. 'It's hot. You might burn.'

It had seemed a long time, the wait on that day in late August, for the movers to arrive with their furniture from London. Susan had walked from room to room, through the heat, past bugs the size of her fists which watched her with their alien, swollen eyes. This was a wild place, she remembered thinking. Before she came, she had assumed it would all be shopping malls and diplomatic dinners. Of course, she had known about Washington's drugs and death and poverty, but she knew America well enough to know that they would see nothing of all that unless they wanted to. This rabid life – the humid heat, the insects, the dirt – was more like the Far East. Neighbours turned up at the front door with gifts of cookies, and flowers, then withdrew.

Jim had been slouched – back leaning against the wall, his face red from the heat, legs sticking clumsily out – typing into his laptop computer on the slate floor of the room that was to be his study. In a sweat-stained white shirt with the sleeves messily rolled up and khaki shorts, he was a curious amalgam of British and American styles, which was one of the things she liked about him. He was a hybrid: both messy and neat, confused and well-organised, hovering in a no man's land between America where he was brought up and England where he had spent the last few years of his life. He had sat, radiating hard, concentrated thought, looking old for a moment. She loved him: the hairs on the back of his hand, the grey tracing its way through his dark hair; the way when he worked papers became spread everywhere, a steadily increasing circle around him; the dome of his head furrowed and the hands typing furiously into the machine. Everything he did was an event.

'Quite nice without furniture,' Susan said.

The back of Susan's neck had been blissfully hot.

'The heat,' she said. 'I've got used to getting it from radiators or holidays. But it's all around. We're here. We've got out of England.' She shook her hair.

He glanced up, and then looked down again. 'You're right. So right,' he said.

She walked to the window which looked out onto the little cul de sac where they were to spend the next few years of their lives. The street was green and clean and dazzled in sunlight. The slate floor felt cool on her bare feet.

'We've left the dirt and the gloom and the shop assistants who hate you for asking for help. We've left day after day of darkness, like being in a parcel being sent somewhere but never getting there.'

'Look, darling, I'm just trying to finish this story. I have to file it.'

'I must have loved you very much to live with you in England.'

'It's your country,' he muttered, pushing his hand through his hair.

'No. But England. To put up with England. I suppose I thought it couldn't be as bad as it seemed. I thought that most mornings. No, this can't be as bad as it is. Impossible.'

'It's fine. England's fine. It's a civilised place.'

'No. It's at the end of civilisation . . . Whatever people say of America, it is still innocent.'

'Darling. Please,' he said, opening out one of his hands, 'I have to write about these missiles.'

She crouched down, put her head on one side and was overcome by a desire to pull out the plug of his computer.

'I'm going to do what I like here.'

She stood up, and stretched, a big luscious stretch.

He looked up at her seriously and frowned.

'Funny about the heat,' he said, and grinned a great U of a grin. 'The erotic qualities.' His shirt had a tall collar which seemed to keep his head propped up. As for his eyes, they weren't especially big or interestingly shaded, but they were avid, and a little desperate, perhaps because even then, four years ago, there wasn't time to do all the things he wanted to do, and to the same extent that he loved life, he feared its passing.

'Well?' she said.

He shook his head far more vigorously than necessary. One day, she thought, his head will spin off. 'My piece. Our child. The movers.'

She shrugged. He looked at her desperately again – her cotton dress, her grace, her lips, the bare legs.

They had left a Victorian terraced house in Kennington in south London which was tall and thin, an upright coffin surrounded by rain and people who walked along staring at the ground, scanning the pavements for an escape hole. But here in Washington the few people they had seen in the neighbourhood seemed to bounce along the pavement like men on the moon, and they smiled as they bounced past, and often they even greeted you. It was almost as though they liked you. She had become used, during the last years in London, to being hated for taking up space on pavements, in shops, on tubes. Only the dogs hated you here, in Chevy Chase village, and barked by their houses.

'Do you want a walk with me in the garden?' she said, trailing her finger over some dust in the woodwork. The shoulder strap of her dress was slipping off.

'Darling,' said Jim, in an agonised voice, 'I have a deadline.'

Susan liked the way the sun tried to get through the curved window of Jim's study. The window was dusty but the sun still tried, sifting its way through any sections of clear glass and throwing itself onto the stone floor. She touched the wooden panelling.

Jim looked up at her seriously.

'That dress suits you,' he said.

'Shall we have lunch? Will you come and have lunch with us? We'll call for a pizza . . . a nice, fat pizza overflowing with cheese and we'll eat it with Rebecca in the garden with cold Coke. She'd like that. A pizza picnic.'

His forehead creased into a frown; sometimes he reminded her of Gandhi without the peacefulness, other times of one of those outsiders of Jacobean plays, diminutive imps.

She smiled at him, then leant down and pulled the plug out of his laptop.

'You . . .' he said. He grabbed her ankle, and she lost her balance and fell, laughing. He kissed her neck, rolled her over and began to kiss her lips. She pretended to struggle a little.

And then, all of a sudden, there was Rebecca, standing perturbed at the doorway.

'Mummy and Daddy . . .' she said.

Susan leapt up. Jim straightened himself, and lurched for his computer as if for an alibi.

'I'm hungry,' said Rebecca, seven years old. 'I came to tell you. I'm hungry.'

'I know. I know. I'm just about to order a pizza for us all to eat outside.'

'Good. Now.'

'Yes, darling. Right now.'

Rebecca stood glaring at her father while Susan made the call. 'You were fighting with Mummy,' she said.

'Playing,' said Jim, back in his position against the wall, towered over by his small inquisitor.

'Playing then,' said Rebecca, as though this were worse.

'The pizza's on its way,' said Susan, dipping down and picking Rebecca up and kissing her. Rebecca put her arms around her and hugged her.

'Come for a walk with me, round the house, while Daddy finishes his article. Will you?' said Susan.

Rebecca nodded grimly.

'It's so big I'll never find my way around,' Rebecca said as they climbed wearily up to the attic room which was at that time even hotter than the rest of the house. But the view at the back was ravishing: the dreaming garden and beyond it the blazing green trees of the country club which spread themselves out as if to express how glorious it was to be them. A couple of squirrels scurried over telephone wires, tightrope walkers.

'When I work,' Susan said, 'I'll work here.'

'You might be lonely. It's a long way down.'

'Oh, I won't be lonely.'

Rebecca opened a cupboard – it was lined with cedar and the room was for a second full of the hot smell of cedarwood.

'I'll be at school all day, remember,' she said.

'I know.'

Rebecca jingled some pebbles in her pocket. Rebecca collected pebbles wherever she went: round ones, jagged ones, any ones.

'I know you'll like the school. We can walk there. You'll have local friends.'

'I like being at home with you best . . . I hope we don't have singing at school.'

'Well . . . you . . . might have some.'

Rebecca scratched a mosquito bite and flung her mother an anxious glance.

When they looked out of the first-floor window, there the pizza man was, turning the corner into their road as he was to do so many times over the next four years, on his motorbike with his red helmet on. He was a wholly implausible sight as he drew up alongside the sleepy houses, with their porches and air of having been forgotten somehow, left behind in the 1950s while the rest of the world sped forward.

Susan hurried to open the door and from nowhere Jim came and put his arm round her shoulder as though he too were part of this other, earlier period, one of clapboard houses, cosy nuclear families and grandmothers on the porch.

With a grin, Rebecca took the pizza and ran off down the hall through to the garden. For her, living in the present, this was it: pizza, the sunshine, the red cardinal waiting for her on the lawn . . .

'It's the movers!' called Jim a little while later.

Susan leapt to her feet clutching her hat and ran in, across the hot grass.

Rebecca had already run round the front and was standing there watching the men opening the door of the thirty-foot container.

The leader of the team was a tall, stately man who regarded Susan with interest and respect. In England he would have been a manager of a bank. He strode up the path towards Susan and Jim and shook their hands. 'Mr and Mrs Stewart. My name's Joe Brett. Welcome to America,' he said.

'Thanks,' said Jim. 'In fact, I'm American myself. My wife is British.'

Joe Brett took them in to deal with the forms, while Rebecca remained outside, watching intensely as the men began to take out some of the cardboard boxes and furniture packed inside like a puzzle.

Two of the four men were overweight, about three times their ideal size, the Tweedledum and Tweedledee of removals. But they and Mr Joe Brett and the rather spindly fourth mover were all men of incredible strength who moved in and out of the house carrying beds like ants carry fragments of leaves.

The men nodded to Susan shyly as they went by.

The possessions trundled out: the antique furniture, the chest of drawers marked with candlewax, the Afghan carpet from Liberty's, the crates and crates of books, all disgorged out onto a green lawn in front of this European house in the heart of America.

Tweedledum was carrying a box marked OLD ESSAYS, one of the boxes Susan had packed herself, being too embarrassed to allow anyone else to do so. She watched another of her boxes go by marked PERSONAL LETTERS in blue biro which contained old letters, some from Phillip. She had stopped herself from reading them all these years but had not had the strength to throw them away, just to chuck out the past, pretend it never happened. She never thought of her last terrible encounter with Phillip in London but she dreamt of it over and over again.

Months later, she was to find bathroom equipment in the dining room, and the dining-room plates right at the back of the attic, behind OLD PHOTOGRAPHS PERSONAL.

'Got some iced water?' said one of the fat movers, who had sweat flowing down his face. Three drops perched at the bottom of his chin about to drop.

'Good idea,' said Susan. 'Rebecca, do you want some iced water?'

She nodded. Rebecca's little figure took up very little space beneath the wide skies of America.

Everyone gathered in the hot little kitchen with the red Formica counter and the monstrous avocado fridge which had already attained the status of a flawed friend, someone you love because of their faults. It towered over them all as though desperately trying to make conversation. Every now and again it shook a little.

'This is some house,' said Tweedledee.

'Sure is,' said Tweedledum.

They both shook their heads.

After a while Susan began to direct boxes haphazardly, feeling at least she must appear to know what she was doing.

'Where's this one going, ma'am?' said a tall man.

'Oh . . .' she said, pushing back her hair. 'What does it say?'

'It says twenty-three.'

'That's a code. I coded everything.'

'Where should it go, ma'am?'

It was eighty degrees outside, and extraordinarily humid. The house had no air conditioning yet and every movement was like moving though some kind of see-through jam.

'Upstairs,' she had said gaily. 'I'm afraid it's right at the top. Third floor.'

'Thanks, ma'am,' he said, and began to trudge up the sweeping wooden stairs.

There were packing cases everywhere: piled up against the walls, half opened on the floor, all over the garden waiting her instructions.

'That'll go on the second floor, please,' she said hectically to a man whose face was obscured by a brown box.

Rebecca was playing a game out in the garden.

Some furniture was taking its rightful place: the chaise longue was in the drawing room. They'd bought it in England especially for this room, this grand high-ceilinged room more reminiscent of that of a French manor house than a street in suburban Washington.

Those first weeks she had found it hard to imagine being much happier. They'd done it. They'd got away from England with its coastline which throttled, and were actually here, looking over a miraculous garden, full of roses, far more English than anything they'd had in England.

The blue velvet armchair which rocked disconcertingly was put by the fireplace.

'Ah!' she shouted. 'Here comes the bed!'

And here came their old bed which had dutifully kept its place in a room in Kennington – providing sleep for many years. It was comical to see the steady old bed coming up the garden path in this tropical heat. She felt like turning it back, crying out, 'Oh no! Not here! Certainly not here!'

The movers negotiated the bed up the stairs to the main bedroom, where the old lady who used to live here had slept.

'There!' she said, and wondered where Jim was.

She still could not quite comprehend this was happening to her. The house seemed to have been waiting for her all her life: the pattern carved on the doors, the black and white tiles of the bathroom, the scratches on the stairs up to the attic – they were all a part of her.

'Where does this go? It says thirty-four,' said a skinny little fellow.

She stared at a pinky-beige sofa she'd bought from an Oxford Street department store years ago. It had never been comfortable, and she'd soon disliked its shape; nevertheless it had accompanied her through a large portion of her life, and was obviously going to continue to go with her, with the peculiar tenacity of certain large pieces of furniture which are expensive to buy and difficult to get rid of.

'Over there, by the window,' she said.

The two men plonked it down, and marched away, down the stairs, back to the van. She hurried down behind them.

Susan turned and kissed Jim as a bookcase bought from an antique shop in Hythe one rainy Saturday walked past them.

'I'm so happy,' she said.

'So am I,' said Rebecca fiercely as a mahogany dresser went by. She stood looking up at them, and frowning. Susan quickly let her arms drop from round Jim's neck, and put them round Rebecca.

Rebecca's skin was warm from the heat.

Rebecca gazed up at her mother with a troubled expression, her forehead that of Mussolini. 'I was lonely out there without you. And hot. I really was very hot.'

'I have to make sure all the boxes go in the right places otherwise there'll be toys in the kitchen and saucepans in your bedroom.'

Rebecca didn't smile.

'I'll help,' she said grandly and walked slowly off to the front door, where she did indeed manage to direct a box marked TOYS to her bedroom before bursting into tears and being taken to lie on the main bed, where she quickly fell asleep in spite of the steady current of men bringing boxes and furniture back and forth through the long, easeful rooms.

'Rebecca wants to possess you,' Jim had said afterwards, as he finished off some cold pizza out in the burning sun.

'All children want to possess their mothers.'

Jim had torn off a gigantic piece of pizza like someone tearing off a leg of an oversize chicken.

She smiled, and leant over and touched his hand.

'What?'

'We're here. We made it.'

'Yup.' He looked up into the blazing sky.

In those first days everything had seemed so simple, and so funny. She had drifted around in light summery dresses, bare feet and a straw hat. She spent her days standing on the front step directing workmen somewhere in the garden or into the building. And the neighbours had all seemed so pleasant, slightly unreal but pleasant. She'd never really had neighbours in the sense of families before. The house next door to them in London had been divided up into five flats, one of which, the garden flat, belonged to a rock group called Satan's Friends. They used to wear white make-up, have black Munster hair, red nails and to look rather embarrassed when caught doing anything like clipping the hedges, which they in fact did rather more attentively than the elderly couple on the other side.

She grew fond of the various builders who came to the house – painting the windowsill, putting in air conditioning, repairing drainpipes. Throughout their stay Susan was unable to make out whether Americans were appalled by the house – with its dark panelling, draughty windows and intense atmosphere of past lives – or impressed by it.

Early on, a plumber stood in front of the boiler and said, 'Boy, this boiler sure has got some age on it.' And she wasn't sure whether age was considered something vile which accrued on naturally new objects, or whether the men were to some extent applauding the size and scope of the boiler.

Susan was irritated by the hint of criticism of her house.

'Yes,' she said firmly to the plumber, fighting off her fringe which kept falling over her eyes like hot seaweed. 'It is an amazing house, isn't it? It was on the market for three years. Empty for three years, can you imagine? Nobody wanted it. And look at it – backing onto the country club, why, it's heaven on earth.'

'It's an unusual house,' said the plumber. 'It has *atmosphere,*' he continued, dubiously.

'A man could get lost in it,' said the plumber's mate, who looked as though he could get lost anywhere.

That was four years ago.

'Hi, darling,' said Jim, back from the embassy, as he hurtled into her study, showering limbs and arms and the atmosphere of parties all over the place. She grinned at him, and got up to hug him.

'Phillip Jordan asked after you,' said Jim, removing some hair from her forehead.

'Oh really?' she said.

'I told him you left early because you felt sick.'

'Well, that's right.'

'Great. He's very elegant, isn't he?'

She shrugged. 'I can hardly remember.'

'You OK now?' said Jim. 'Not sick? You don't think you're pregnant?'

'Unfortunately, no,' she said, twisting on her chair.

Jim dug his hands into his pockets. 'Phillip Jordan was very friendly and wants us to have dinner soon,' he said watchfully. 'I said that would be great. His girlfriend Sandra is charming.'

'Sandra?' queried Susan.

'He didn't choose her for her name, presumably.'

'You always like everyone,' she said.

'Well, Susan, you *love* people,' he said.

Jim smiled that steady, innocent smile.

The following evening, as she began to undress in her lighted room, she sensed someone watching her out in the garden, in the dense blackness. She took off her bra.

8

The week after the embassy party, Susan was woken up at 2 am by voices in the street, unusual in this quiet cul de sac. She closed her eyes tightly, and turned over, pulling up her bedclothes to block the noise. One of the voices she heard sounded a little like Phillip's, and she thought vaguely, sleepily, how crazy she was becoming, as her hand caressed the lacy surround to her pillowcase.

She heard the front door slam shut – oh yes, she thought, of course, Jim is home tonight from the Boston conference – and she fell back to sleep.

To one side of the bed was a metal window which didn't quite shut, and the night seeped through it.

'Hi!' said Jim, at 3.05 am.

'Hi,' murmured Susan, frowning as she tried to open her eyes.

'You awake?' he asked.

'Sort of,' said Susan, trying to sit up.

'Sorry to be so late. We were delayed in Boston.'

'I don't understand.'

'In Boston. We were there for the conference. You remember.'

She frowned again. 'It's late,' she said. Her eyes were growing accustomed to the dark and she could see Jim.

'Anyway,' he said cheerfully, as he wrenched off his buttercup yellow tie, 'Phillip's here.'

'Yes.'

'No. I mean he's right here. He's *here*.' He flung the tie onto a wicker chair and it seemed to swirl through the air like some magic scarf.

'I just want to sleep. It's late,' she said.

Jim burst out of the bedroom into the bathroom and started brushing his teeth with an electric toothbrush which sounded like a drill. He then leapt, naked, back to the bedroom and into bed.

'Mmmm . . .' he said, 'warm bed. Good conference.'

Susan turned away from him, her white cotton nightdress coolly touching every fold of her body.

'Yes, tell me about it in the morning. You smell of cigarettes.'

'The whole house smells of cigarettes. Phillip smokes heavily.'

She turned round to him. 'I'm sorry?'

'I told you. Phillip's here. He lost his keys. He had nowhere to sleep. So I said, well, why not stay here? We'd talked about you and him, you see, about how you two really had just to be friends, and I thought, why not?' He put his head down on the pillow. 'Anyway, I didn't have a choice.'

She sat up. 'I don't believe this. I know you wouldn't just bring him back.'

'Well I did. They're sleeping in the bed in the guest room.'

'They?'

'He and his girlfriend. Sandra.'

'Girlfriend?'

'Yes, you know he has a girlfriend.'

'Now? You mean right now they are?'

Jim yawned. 'Look, Susan, it's three o'clock in the morning. Let's get some sleep. I'm exhausted. I've got to leave for work real early tomorrow.'

'I really cannot believe this,' she said.

Beside her, Jim's body lay as if it had been outlined too firmly; it was all elbows and knees tonight and she wanted it to get out and leave her to the warmth of the solitude she'd had before he'd burst in like an automated pipe-cleaner man, all sharp wire arms and legs.

'I'm tired,' he said, moving around, his limbs digging into her side of the bed. 'But it was a great visit. Look, they'll be gone in the morning. He has to be at a meeting at seven. They'll be gone even before we get up. You won't even see them.'

'I—'

'I only told you in case you were wandering round naked and you bumped into him. It might have been embarrassing.'

'That was considerate of you,' she said.

'Or you might have bumped into her.'

'You shouldn't have done this.'

'What else could I do? His apartment is only down the road. It seemed the obvious thing to do.'

'Hotels are down the road.'

'You're suddenly wide awake.'

'You shouldn't have done this,' she said again.

'Everything seems exaggerated at night,' he said.

'Besides,' she said, 'the sheets are dirty and I have nothing for breakfast.'

'Well . . .'

'Oh God,' said Susan.

'There's cereal,' said Jim.

'And I need a pee. Supposing I bump into them? And what about Rebecca – she's down the end next to them, *she's down the end next to them*. Supposing they start making love . . .'

'Susan, they know she's sleeping right by them.'

'There aren't any towels out.'

'They'll manage.'

Susan lay awake. Soon she heard Jim's breath move into the rhythmic pattern of sleep. She closed her eyes tightly. His body was heating up the bed. She thought of how Phillip's body used to lie next to her, curled up like a question mark, not tall at all, as he lay in bed.

He had a large brown mark on his back, just under his right shoulder blade.

Her hands were clenched into a fist.

The years had separated them, of course, crowded with the days they hadn't shared, the sights they hadn't seen together, the decisions they hadn't made together.

Phillip's body had always been too restless, and too hot, as they lay together, the cars in the street outside fighting each other down below.

She gathered herself tightly together, fearing her thoughts would wake Jim, who at that moment gave a startled little snore.

A little red cochineal beetle, which had snuck through the slightly open window, buzzed as it flew around the room looking for the way out, like an elderly man who has lost his memory.

The walls were a kind of rough white surface, and there were alcoves all over the room where the previous owner had kept her collection of Asian art – golden buddhas and bowing gods.

She tried to find a cool place on her pillow. The bed in the spare room was a small double. She wondered if his legs were even now lying over his girlfriend's body and if he still spoke in his sleep as he used to.

The wallpaper in the guest room was a dingy washed green silk, unchanged since they arrived. A few people had stayed there already.

And now Phillip lay there, his body too long for the bed, waiting until the morning, while outside, in the street, the night life emerged, and racoons sauntered down the road, an owl plundered a mouse, and the flying insects threw themselves against the street lights.

I can hear his breathing, she thought, although there are a number of doors between him and me, doors and years. He is thirteen years away from me, and it is someone else, someone I hardly know, who lies on the bed. Maybe his arm is flung over Sandra now as he used to fling his arm over me, not protecting but to keep her in place.

When she first got into bed when she lived with Phillip the sheets were white and cool because he had a cleaner who ironed them, and put on clean bedding every day. Susan used to long for him never to come to bed. She just lay there staring up at the ceiling wanting to escape but she couldn't escape, although at night sometimes she'd go for a walk alone, looking into the lighted shop windows.

As she lay on the cold sheets, sometimes she would look at a picture on the wall, hanging at an angle, of a few children gathered round a tree, and she never asked him where it came from because it was the only thing in his flat which had reality and she wanted to imagine it came from his bedroom at home in Wales, from when he was a child, yet feared he'd tell her he picked it up from a junk store or had been given it.

The floors all had grey carpet and from every window she could see nothing but sky. Sky and traffic; not a twitch of a tree, only the occasional plant she would bring in, which would soon die in the over-heated flat, and the garden at the top of the flat, the roof garden where once he made a heart in the snow, and looked at her with those grey eyes of his, as though that heart were the entire world – Africa, India, the Americas – and he were giving it to her.

There were other old boyfriends she could happily have seen, and indeed had met. But Phillip was the one whose face she'd got used to seeing in passers-by – his nose there, his eyes there, his hands over there. She'd segmented him, chopped his memory into bits and scattered the bits through crowds. Even their moments together had become fragments.

By the side of Susan's bed, as she tossed through the Washington night, with Phillip down the other end of the house, a photograph of Susan, Jim and Rebecca stood on a side table, in a silver frame, but tonight they all looked separate, as though they were nothing to do with each other but had just by chance been snapped together. Susan picked up the picture, then put it face down.

She thought she heard the sound of someone moving downstairs but didn't go down.

A beetle is flying round and round Rebecca as she tries to sleep. She puts on the light and watches it; its vivid red colour, its goggle-eyes.

It flies to the window and bangs against it, and Rebecca gets up to let it out, into the hot night air full of the cry of cicadas.

Susan has a photograph of her mother by her bed too – sitting stoutly, legs apart, overflowing the Dralon armchair. Behind her, wallpaper erupts in small bubbles but Susan's mother sits resolutely, with a gentle smile skimming the surface of her powdery face.

I should go and wake Phillip now. Shake him. Throw him out. Say, this is not your period, your life. Go back to the past.

It was after the death of her mother, all those years ago, that she'd fallen in love with Phillip.

The council flat, in Wimbledon, south London, where her mother had brought Susan up, had been small and dingy, but she had been able to run up and down the steps of the block of flats and up and down the corridors, feet echoing on the floor, the terror that some man or woman would thrust out of a doorway full of complaints always a delightful possibility. Compared with her former life, Phillip's had both elegance and mystery, with his slow, tangled smiles and cat-like eyes. His mother had died of cancer when he was four and his father had gone on to live with a number of women, none of whom he cared about or married. 'He only ever loved my mother,' Phillip would say.

Susan's mother prepared copious teas: Marmite sandwiches, jam sandwiches, Kit Kats, Penguin biscuits, doughnuts, angel cakes, iced buns, sponge cakes filled with jam all served on delicate china plates decorated with soft green weeping willow trees. Susan's mother would preside like a burial mound over the tea, which was always served on a white lacy tablecloth.

On the walls were prints – The Blue Lady, The Haywain – and in Susan's bedroom the wallpaper was covered in pink daisies and the bedcovers in a shocking pink nylon. Her knickers were all made of pink nylon too. Mrs Price (as she called herself though Miss Price in fact) liked Susan to wear pretty dresses and have ribbons in her hair but Susan would take out the ribbons the moment she could no longer be seen by her mother. The only books on the sitting-room shelves were Reader's Digest volumes, although Susan had quite a collection of books in her room.

The smell to the block of flats, the sort of adult, corrupt smell, Susan and her friends found nearly as enticing as going up and down in the lift which took them to Susan's sixth-floor flat, and running as fast as they could along the glittering stone corridors.

For Susan's twelfth birthday party, her mother had taken six girls to the cinema, which she couldn't really afford (Susan was on a scholarship to the school), and afterwards put on an inept little magic show. In the past many of Susan's wealthier friends had magic at their parties. Susan had heard a friend called Melanie – with pigtails and big hips – jeering at her mother's surprise show. Afterwards, Susan had grabbed Melanie's arm hard. 'If ever,' said Susan. 'If ever I hear you say anything about my mother again, I shall hit you so hard I'll be expelled and you will never ever forget me.' Melanie had pursed her lips and vanished. Although on the whole quiet, there was a hint of savagery and ruthlessness in Susan Price which made the other girls respect her. Even her amazing, luminous smiles, which so charmed boys and teachers, were not exactly soft.

The communal gardens were huge, although badly kept and balding in places. But the children liked the scraggy lawns and the climbing frames with chipped blue paint and the sense that somehow there was more weather in these grounds squatted like an island on the intersection between two major roads than in their suburban lawns. Occasionally she and her friends would knock on doors on the floor above, then run away.

When she didn't have a playmate round, Susan would stand in the scratchy grass and examine insects which passed by just as Rebecca did now, had always done – the beetle with the antennae held proudly over its head like a skipping rope, the stag beetle with its mighty weapons, the lazy ant who pretended to help his fellows carrying bits of grass but never actually did anything, the glamour of a beetle hurrying over a paving stone wearing a stripy red and black waistcoat, the bravery of a drab brown ant who raced, zig-zagging from side to side like a soldier on D-day, across a pathway in spite of having seen one of his companions executed by her foot only seconds before.

When Susan began to bring insects back into her pink emporium, Mrs Price was horrified. It had begun with a school trip to a pond where Susan had caught various waterboatmen and come back bitten all over by insects and exultant, with her jam jar of water and watery creatures in her hand, her wellington boots in her plastic bag. The next day she came back with a book about insects from the library. Susan curled up in the armchair.

'It says here,' she told her mother, 'that ethyl acetate and tetrachloroethane are best for preserving insects although they can turn grasshoppers and crickets pink.'

'Oh really?' said her mother, who was immersed in studying one of her magic tricks, the only really odd thing about her.

Susan hugged her legs to her. 'I do like the wings of insects, don't you, like lacy tablecloths?'

'Tablecloths?' said Mrs Price, and blew her nose. She adjusted her reading glasses. Sometimes Susan loved her mother so much it hurt. Perhaps because there was no father around, she knew she had to be her mother's solace and protection, and to earn a living. Her mother would have liked her to be a lawyer or a doctor but in breaktime at school Susan would go to the playing fields at the back of the school and sit in the grass waiting for a quiver in the grass as a beetle passed by.

'Do you have bedbugs?' she asked a boy as he tried to put his hands between her legs at a dance.

'What?' he said. 'Do *you* then?'

'No. But I'm doing a scientific paper on the subject.'

The boy, who had the face of a Roman emperor, aquiline and a little cruel, backed off into the darkness. The next boy who asked her to dance looked altogether more benevolent, with a baby-face smile, and she didn't have the heart to ask him her question, although she did a few days later when he took her to the cinema.

Susan always took the bus to school and tried to keep her skirt over her knees and her hat from falling back, and not to notice the men staring at her – she was a startlingly pretty child – while her mind swarmed with bulging eyes, with moths like ghosts, with the plodding legs of caterpillars, with the touch of daddy-long-legs in the night, sweeping over her face. She would drum her fingers against the window.

And at school she would do her sums, move the decimal points to the right or the left, study her geography, write essays about the Hanoverians, but long for the smell of the biology laboratory with its wooden benches carved with initials, for the small dirty windows looking over the street. Slice – they would cut up a frog. Slice – they would dismember the insides of a rat. And they would watch and record the life and death of caterpillars, presided over by the black TV-screen glasses of the biology mistress who, like all the science teachers and the Latin teacher, was a lesbian.

Susan, from the age of about fourteen, had a healthy interest in the male sex, if a little over-scientific. The first man she had sex with was at first flattered then put out by the inordinate time she spent examining his penis, as though at any moment she might whip out a knife and carry her biological interest still further.

In her spare time she read about the male *Serianus caroleinensis* scorpion who deposits his sperm bag after meeting a female. He then spins two rows of silken threads to form a path down which the female walks. The path is wide at the beginning and narrows to the spot where the sperm bag stands. He spins her a silken path leading to conception.

She learnt how, after the female ants have laid their eggs, their wings drop off and the rest of their lives are entirely devoted to tending the eggs. At the heart of the ants' nest is the nursery where adult workers tend the larvae, turning them, checking them, cleaning them, like pre-feminist women.

Susan spent most of her time with the bodies of dead insects and the stories of living ones, the ants with their hour-glass figures and spindly, old-ladies' legs, the cockroaches fat, monkish and brown.

Susan still dreamt of the tiny, the minute, perfection under a microscope, the copulation of flies, the dance of dragonflies.

Even when she first met Phillip, Susan was at first more engaged by the strange, silent world of insects and spiders – a whole other empire within our human empire, compared to which human beings are of little consequence, born only to be food for the host of maggots, flies and beetles who scamper and soar over the planet and burrow down under the gravestones. So we see ants, so they see us.

At seventeen, she had won a scholarship to Oxford reading biology and went on to do a study at London University and to work at the Natural History Museum in London. Her favourite studies were tarantulas, especially Mexican red-kneed spiders which combined furry beauty with menace. A boyfriend once said she reminded him of a beautiful spider. In her white lab coat, with her wide sensual mouth, china skin and intemperate black hair, Susan would watch as she introduced a male tarantula in with a female. It was the stillness of the female as she waited which always unnerved her. It was like being in the bottom of some crevasse, with no sound around. And sometimes the male would make a clumsy movement, and the female would attack the male. But even if she chewed off one of his legs, he would still lumber towards her on the legs that were left, eager to try again. The combination of rawness and finesse astounded her.

Unlike her daughter, Mrs Price had never given any sign of much intellectual activity going on. Susan suspected her mother wrapped herself up in plain clothes and fat to avoid any more trouble in life, like packing something well so it doesn't get bumped and broken on the journey. It seemed to work well. Laughing, sensible, Susan's mother never seemed to be troubled as Susan was so often troubled. Until one day, shortly before Susan met Phillip, she had a heart attack and died on the stairs, going up to her flat, surrounded by that strange, corrupt smell of the old building, a smell of cigarette smoke and mothballs, of loneliness.

Susan had needed someone after her mother's death and Phillip, with his alternating boyish exuberances and savage rages, had been a big enough personality to fill what was an immense gap made by such a small person – Susan's mother – and sometimes the gap seemed so huge Susan felt like a vast shell, and couldn't get out of bed in the morning, because there was too much emptiness inside her. Odd that someone who was really just a mass of details and habits – her way of warming her teapot, her way of bending stiffly to pull on the thick socks she wore with sandals, her manner of patting her hair, her fumbling card tricks – could combine to fill Susan up with a whole universe of emptiness and grief. Love, of course, was what it was, and it was from her mother Susan learnt about love – how immense love can be even if expressed only in the silly little details of daily life. From the happiness of her life with her mother, she valued family life. A few friends had on occasion decided that Susan's devotion to family life was because she'd lacked a conventional family upbringing and therefore hankered after it, but that was not so. Her interest in the family was because she had had from her lone parent, and had valued, the most important part of the family equation: the tidy, cosy moments of transcendent love.

When she and Phillip met, at a lecture, he was living with another girl, and their affair began in hotels; at first it had been rather mysterious and agreeably overblown. It was to do, she supposed, with his habit of treating life as a series of performances.

They had made love in a two-bit hotel in Bayswater, on a rainy November day. The day gathered round the hotel, packing it up with the dank air, as though ready to be sent off to some Dickensian establishment, perhaps Nicholas Nickleby's boarding school.

They met outside the hotel, called the Lancaster Gate. He signed his name in the book and climbed the narrow stairs to an attic bedroom.

'Why are we doing this?' she had said.

'It's what we want,' he had said grandly. 'Surely you know that?'

She'd worn a purple silk dress buttoned down the front.

'I don't know,' she said, 'if this is sensible.'

They stood at the end of a double bed covered with a lime green candlewick bedspread.

'Oh, I think it is,' he said.

She looked away, at the tarnished mirror which hung lopsidedly. There was a print of a church in a cheap gold frame.

'I'm not sure. It seems odd. Couldn't we just . . .'

He ran his fingers over her huge mouth, then pushed them in.

'Everything is odd. You should know that,' he said. 'You're too intelligent not to know that.'

She could hear the traffic in the distance.

'I just . . .'

He pressed his lips against hers. But she quite enjoyed his sense of drama.

There were other hotels, in other towns, where they'd met restlessly and each time he'd be slightly different and she would find herself being different too, as though her personality were contingent on place. In a hotel you could walk into another person's time, and make it yours. You could be the person who last left the hotel: the travelling salesman's girlfriend who'd left her mood behind in the bare bedroom of the Reading hotel; the chic wife who left a smell of her perfume in the Ritz; the sadness left behind in a hotel by the seaside where Phillip and she had lain in a bed overlooking the sea and heard the seagulls endlessly crying out through the grey sky.

And each time, at each of these encounters, she had thought that at last she would get to know him and after each meeting would be glad that she didn't, that there was only this incompletion, this confusion, this attempt for their bodies to understand what their minds wouldn't.

Most people searched for some kind of package – let's be like this forever or let's get married or something to gather up experience, pat it into shape, but Phillip seemed to make no attempt. It was just her and him meeting somewhere at his instruction and always the experience being different, even the way they made love being different, as though the shapes who carried these names bore no relation to those with the same names which had made love so scrupulously at a hotel the week before. Each weekend she'd look for words afterwards to describe his body and one week it was strong, muscular and the next very tender while the week after it was the texture of his skin she recalled so acutely.

Always she would come away exhausted, aching, vowing never to see him again like this but always after a few days the phone would go and she would acquiesce to yet another of these meetings.

He was rich, or perhaps he just spent the money he had. He often claimed an aunt or an uncle had just left him money but she never quite believed him. He seemed to make up life as he went along, and she seemed part of his fabrication. He claimed to have been married at eighteen but wouldn't talk about it. He claimed to work as a showbusiness journalist for a tabloid, but showbusiness pieces in the paper came out under another name. Once – at Claridges – on a solemn, cool evening, he told her he loved her. But she didn't take that seriously either. He was a series of positions. Even the flat where he lived, and where she eventually lived, was unlikely. He claimed he owned it but it had the air of somewhere just rented. It was temporary – with only a few books on the shelves, no grater in the kitchen, only a couple of saucepans, and plenty of unpacked boxes. Besides, the place was a stage set. At the top was a roof garden overlooking Fulham High Street. He would stand up there alone when their relationship – whatever that was – was becoming even stranger. He would look out at the buses, at the old people, at the tramps and teenagers. He took pictures of her up there when it snowed and she was touched but afterwards she found there had been no film in the camera.

9

Susan finally managed to fall asleep around four in the morning and didn't wake until ten when she found the house was empty, Rebecca having made her own way to school. The bowl that Phillip had eaten from was still on the table, the spoon lying by it, with just the same pool of milk that he used to leave all those years back, and the glass was half full of orange juice, just as he used to leave it on the pine table in the flat in Fulham, with the traffic roaring outside.

Up in the bedroom, the bed was ruffled and tumbled, and she bent down and smelt the sheets, and it all came back – the way he used always to watch her as they made love, recording every moment of her desire, every frown, every gasp, every smile, every moan, as though he were compiling some definitive study of her for future generations. She smoothed the creased sheets. There were a few hairs in the bed. It was odd listening to the thump of her heart.

In the wastepaper basket there was a condom wrapper and she thought, Why is he using condoms?

Who else is he screwing that he needs one for Sandra? Or perhaps she wasn't taking the pill. Did he really need to leave it there, with its shiny little wrapper?

A rumpled paper handkerchief sat on the chest of drawers. The patchwork quilt lay scrawled on the ground, its homespun cosiness discarded, and the curtains were only half closed as though Phillip didn't care who saw him through the windows. The archaeology of love, she thought, piecing together the remains of the night. And where do the voices go, the voices which cried out or murmured? Is there any evidence of them now, as the morning squeezes its bright light through the gap in the curtains?

This was the study in which Dr Stephens, the man who used to live here, died, shooting himself one summer night when his cancer got too painful. The double doors of this bedroom were once to keep the cry of his children from his thoughts, to keep the sound of the gun from his wife's ears; now they were to keep out the cry of desirous guests, making love in the heat of a Washington June.

From the pictures of him, Dr Stephens looked very ordinary, just a man with mild eyes in a suit, but he put a gun into his mouth and pulled the trigger . . . the same handgun that was left behind in the attic crawl space, the same handgun she still kept hidden up in her cupboard. He was a clever man, an atomic physicist. And five years later the son shot himself too, in the same room, yet the house had a good atmosphere. The wife of Dr Stephens, now in a nursing home, said that she and her nurse had often sensed the ghost of Dr Stephens, like a cold wind ruffling the bedclothes. She had called from the nursing home in Ohio to welcome them to her house, and to tell them that her husband still lived there.

'Oh good,' Susan had said. 'I assume he's benevolent?'

'Of course,' Mrs Stephens had said huffily.

'I thought so. Ever since I arrived here, I felt something here was on my side,' said Susan.

Susan liked to think that the house still belonged to those who lived there before, as well as to her: the upstairs family room still with its 1930s green walls, the scratched wooden floor, the curved staircase which twined down to the main drawing room. The metal staircase rail was made of up a tangle of fruits and plants, some leaves with jagged edges which sometimes stuck into Susan or Rebecca or Jim as they hurried down the wide stairs to the heart of the house, with its fireplace where nymphs and men endlessly chased each other over the mantelpiece. When Susan first saw the house an invalid's stair lift had clung to the wall, and although it had been taken away it still remained in her mind, along with everything else about the old lady who had lived here before, with her magazines and books piled all over the rooms, and buddhas from India gesturing in every alcove, glittering in the dust. In the tiny hall off the downstairs bathroom, which used to be a maid's room, were the names of children marked in pencil with their heights and dates. Susan had added Rebecca's heights and dates and hoped they would never be covered over with vanilla paint. Everywhere in the house was an intense sense of lives lived and she wondered, sitting there, how people managed to live in the present, and what the present was, constantly touched by the hands of the past.

She thought she could make out the outline of Phillip on the wrinkled sheets.

She lay down on the bed and looked up at the ceiling. She was glad she had the gun upstairs.

Every few moments Susan felt as though her stomach were slipping out of her body. She wished humans could climb out of their skins every few months, like spiders, and leave their former bodies behind, crumpled legs, fluffy little bodies, in some corner of a room, to step over.

She'd like to be unrecognisable – 'Oh no, Phillip, it's not me! Good heavens no. You're quite mistaken.'

She had been in hospital after leaving Phillip. In those days she didn't dare look at any window in case she saw the face of the German boy she had met that last day, the day she left Phillip's flat and never came back. Even now she saw in her mind the boy's eyes, blue like the sea far out, where it's deep. She saw him sitting on the sofa in the flat, his knee against hers, talking in halting English, and leaving her afterwards with fear. He told her he had come from Cologne, on the Rhine. But she tried not to think about him. It was too long ago. She tried never to think of him.

If it hadn't been for the German boy, she might still be with Phillip.

She had begun again to have nightmares about that day.

She wished she'd never met Phillip.

As she lay on the bed, the bed where Phillip and his girlfriend had been lying the night before, one hand played with her gold chain necklace. Phillip had bought her the chain in Bangkok.

Sometimes, looking back, it seemed that after that visit to Bangkok her relationship with Phillip began to get more violent, and he began to look at her differently, as if he were startled every time he saw her, but even then he couldn't leave her alone although he seemed to want to. They'd gone there on the first anniversary of her mother's death, and in a way it was their most romantic time together, until they went to see the fortune teller.

'The fortune teller's supposed to be accurate,' Phillip had said in the car, his arm around her, his long legs stretched out, just like any young man. He drummed his fingers on the armrest. 'I wonder what he'll say. It'll be entertaining, at worst.'

Phillip was missing the cats which roamed all over his flat: a grey one, a tabby one, a black one and a ginger one, folded in on themselves like Phillip, confident like Phillip.

They had driven bumpily through the streets of Bangkok which made central London look peaceful. It lacked any trace of Oriental calm: cars, each one filthier than the next, jammed against each other, blew their horns, fought their way through the streets. The fumes were so bad that if you opened the car window you choked. On the pavements the people behaved as the cars did on the roads, jostling, shouting, packing every inch of space. Just occasionally there would be a glimpse through a courtyard to a group of saffron-robed monks who stared out with all the arrogance of humility. Shopkeepers had their wares on the street too: washing machines, vegetables, dead sucking pigs, and a quantity of shops selling plastic buckets and bowls in white, grey or red. Curious she could remember all this, but right now couldn't clearly remember Phillip's face, only his tall figure and the troubled atmosphere around him.

She remembered the things they'd bought together: the stone face of a woman from Palmyra, its features mostly washed away by time, just the eyes left on the grey stone; also what looked like a child's hand, throwing a disc, from the temple of Angkor Wat.

'See,' he said, 'isn't this great?' His hand waved out of the window. 'Next year we'll go to India. You'll love India.' Freckles sprinkled like pepper over his white skin, his limbs long and graceful, his voice with an upper-class lilt to it. Always he took huge steps as if he possessed seven-league boots.

'The furthest my mother ever travelled was Cornwall. She loved Cornwall,' said Susan.

'Cornwall!' he said. 'Look at this! We'll tour the world together. Your mother never lived.'

'She was all right,' said Susan, turning away. 'She lived a decent life.'

'Better than writing about showbusiness?' he said, and laughed. 'I don't know.' His long white trousers, his white shirt, his slow, wicked smile – today he seemed to have mastered life. Perhaps, she had thought, he is OK. One of his feet tapped up and down on the rubber mat.

In Chinatown the driver turned into a courtyard with newly built flats on either side and a few desultory female workers encased in dust polishing a floor here or there. Only one flat appeared inhabited, and then only just, a ground-floor one with a tiny terrace, on which figures of Chinese gods in golden robes were arranged like an altar. At the front of the flat was golden lettering.

Phillip craned his neck, the excited schoolboy.

'There it is,' said the driver, who was also their guide. 'Chung moved here recently. One of his clients bought him this place after Chung's predictions made him a fortune on the Hong Kong stock exchange. He used to live in a real hovel.'

'And this isn't?' said Phillip.

In the courtyard a group of mangey young dogs tussled over which would eat the dead rat that lay with its purple and dark-red innards exposed. Two barefooted Chinese girls, about five years old, watched them from a pile of grey rubble. One wore a dusty red dress, the other a dusty orange dress. Susan threw them a smile but they didn't smile back.

'I've got a great feeling about this,' said Phillip, crouching to get out of the car, and then unravelling himself up and up to the stony-eyed interest of the two urchin girls.

'For someone who claims to be a rationalist at heart, you're very superstitious,' said Susan. In a white dress, she stepped out of the car. But I have no one now my mother has gone, only this stranger here, with his long steps and his efforts to disassemble me, she thought.

'I want answers!' he said. 'That's why,' he continued as he strode forwards, his head high. 'I want answers to the central questions! Aren't you curious?'

Together they passed the effigies of Chinese gods, through sliding doors into a small room where the blind fortune teller sat behind a desk. One eye was just a pleat, the other, white one stared upwards as though trying to escape onto the ceiling. His skin glowed a morgue-white as he sat behind a desk scattered with some sticks of incense, the shell of a small tortoise and a pot of vapour rub for colds.

I should get out of this now, she thought, but Phillip stood there, his head tilted back, aeons away, his hair long, his eyes slanting, one hand caressing his other hand, avidly watching everything.

The stone-slabbed room was bare except for a table and the fortune teller in a thin white nylon short-sleeved shirt and greasy hair swept back from his forehead. The mouth took up most of his face. At first he was fidgety. Phillip sat down.

The driver spoke to the fortune teller in Thai and then asked Phillip the date and time of his birth. The information was relayed and at once the fortune teller withdrew into himself and started muttering to himself and seeming to count with his fingers. His arms and hands looked oddly small, stuck onto his body as his head tilted upwards.

Phillip turned brightly to Susan.

The sliding doors to the next room opened and the blind man's wife wandered in, fixed herself noodles and ate bunched up on a chair, as though sitting on the ground, her limbs pressed together.

The blind man seemed to smile as he spoke, his mouth opening unnaturally wide, a clown at an amusement arcade.

He rolled back his eyes again, and the driver explained that the fortune teller insisted Susan leave.

'But I want her to stay,' said Phillip, pushing back his hair and smiling vividly at the blind man. 'We're going to be married.' The driver translated but the fortune teller shook his head. And then he said – or rather what he said was translated as – 'The girl has a great sense of life.'

'What does that mean?' said Susan, who was standing by Phillip, one hand on his shoulder.

The fortune teller continued to face in her direction until she was led out by the man's wife. As she waited she watched two women filling in the cracks in the stone floor of the flat next door – one had a child clinging to her as she worked; the other woman's hair was tied in a handkerchief. They worked slowly. Elsewhere, a man cut through a pipe, sending sparks flying.

Susan's mouth was dry.

Eventually Phillip emerged, white, and stumbled, as though he didn't know where he was and what to do with his hands. He seemed to have lost control of his long limbs – his legs and arms and head all, for a moment, as he stood there in the heat, seemed dispersed. The child on the back of the woman stared.

'He told me about what would happen to one of us in a high place. But he wouldn't say which of us it would happen to. Just that we'd both be there.'

'What would happen?' said Susan. 'He's just a fortune teller . . . I'll go in now.'

'No,' he said roughly, moving away. 'We're going back now.'

'But I want to see the fortune teller,' she insisted.

Phillip took her by the arm and she shook it off but still he shoved her into the car. On the way back to the hotel Phillip sat, quiet as a cat, completely different from how he had been on the way there.

'What was it?' she had said. 'What did he say?'

'I told you,' he said, looking out. 'I don't want to discuss it.'

'You must,' she said. 'You're trying to scare me.'

'Am I?'

'Anyway, I don't believe in him. Stop it,' she had said.

'You do love me?' he said, in a staccato tone.

'Yes, of course,' she said.

Once they were back in the hotel room, he took her by the shoulders and dug his tongue into her mouth but a member of the hotel staff knocked on the door and entered bringing their nighttime chocolates, which as usual came with a little message, and Susan and Phillip jumped apart.

The message, written in black calligraphy and placed on Susan's pillow, was, 'You can be in my dreams, if I can be in yours.'

After the visit, their relationship changed.

'You lie to me and to yourself,' Phillip told her once, standing there, his hands clenched, his eyes watching her, his hand raised to hit her.

'What a *child* you can be, Phillip,' she had said, 'a silly child.'

She had spun round, waiting for him to hit her.

She lay on the unmade bed in the guest room a little longer, looking up at the crack in the ceiling. It was curious how strong the smell of Phillip was. The smell of people doesn't change over the years, just as the voices stay the same.

After she had run away from Phillip's flat, all those years ago, she had missed his voice. Susan had lived for a few weeks on the top floor of a hotel in Bayswater, under another name, not that that had mattered much. She hadn't known who she was.

The room had two thin single beds, each with an off-yellow candlewick bedspread. There was a sink in one corner. She had bad dream after bad dream, always about cats and blood. Sometimes she dreamt of the room where she'd met the German boy, and in one dream the faces of everyone there – all the men, the women – were the faces of cats.

It was this sink which she threw up in once she began to feel sick.

On the first day she went to the linen department of Harrods and stared at the immaculate piles of white sheets, with their sharp edges. She opened packets of pillows and touched the cool white linen.

In the food department she stared at the hanks of meat – the blood, the sinews, the muscles, the agony in the turn of a foot – and the men in white marked with red behind the counter, smiling and chatting with their red mouths.

Up in the women's fashions she examined the designer suits: perfectly moulded arms, immaculate shoulders, a skirt to encase a body like armour.

Insects too have their skeletons on the outside, not like humans, all soft flesh capable of pain, the only protection a few bones way inside – and even ribs let in daggers, bullets, poor stuff really, ill-fitting blinds.

She couldn't stop thinking about the German boy, and how he had cried out that night, like a child. He crumpled so easily. She wished she knew his name.

A scratch on human skin and there's pain, a touch and there's pleasure. How much better to be a beetle prowling the floor of the forest, waving its antennae, encased in black.

Different kinds of armour, she thought, tracing her hand down the linen suit. In the mirror she saw a girl with untidy dark hair, a garish cheesecloth skirt and a loose blouse – someone altogether too unprotected, with loose clothes, and sea-green eyes. She wore sandals. The face, with its pointed chin, smiled likeably into the mirror. And then she let the smile die down.

She was sick in the evening that day in the London hotel, sick until it seemed there was nothing but bone left in her – all the tissues and muscles she'd seen that morning in Harrods seemed to be coming out of her mouth over and over again. Someone banged on the thin wall, and the framed photograph of the Houses of Parliament wobbled on its hook.

She wished her period would come.

The room was bare except for the framed photograph, the beds, the chest of drawers which leant to one side as if on a tilting ship at sea, a wardrobe, the sink, the mirror. She didn't like looking in the mirror because she didn't know who it was who looked back at her. She knew she should go to the police and tell them what had happened that last day between Phillip and the German boy.

The next day she walked to the local police station, in the glittering light, and stood outside but couldn't make herself go in. In the library she looked up books on Cologne, where the boy had said he came from. One photograph showed a picture of a cruise; had the boy ever been on a cruise ship like that on the Rhine, had he stood in that square, seen that tower?

She tried to go through her qualities as if that would help her fabricate a person, herself – take some felt, some buttons for eyes, some old stockings to stuff the body with . . . If she thought of enough qualities maybe a real person would take shape in front of the mirror. She was born about 23 years ago. She was clever. She was hard-working. Men said she was beautiful. Sew all those things together and what do you get?

She had been losing her personality. Now she needed to get it back. Perhaps she had imagined what had happened that last day. Yes, that was it. It had all been in her imagination.

She continued to look into the mirror, which had a cracked turquoise frame. It was peculiar how substantial even rickety physical objects were – why there was no *doubt* about the mirror. But a person . . .

It was curious to stand there, by a mirror, the cars racing round below, blaring their horns, and not really exist. She turned and touched the candlewick bedspread and was surprised that it felt soft and rough as candlewick bedspreads always felt.

I could die, she thought, and it would continue to have that texture.

She sat down and put her head in her hands and the clock on the wall took hours and hours to take one minute of time away from her and it seemed she would be here forever, stranded, waiting.

Mentally she was spending all her effort slamming doors in her mind which kept swinging open, and perhaps that was why she was so tired, she thought. Every time a door swung open there was Phillip slumped in a chair.

Phillip had never introduced her to his father or friends. She had friends, of course, but no family except a married aunt in Scotland, who was childless. Phillip had wanted her all alone, all to himself, to devour at leisure. Love is only one of its names, she thought.

She wished her period would come. She could not cope with a child. After what had happened, she couldn't go back to Phillip. She did not want to bring up a child without a father, and couldn't have brought herself to give a child away.

'I'm afraid of you,' he had said once.

'What, because of what that fortune teller said?'

'I don't know,' he'd said, and shrugged, and laughed, as if it didn't matter.

The pregnancy test she bought at the late-night chemist that evening was positive.

A few days after the abortion she started to shake, and shake, and was admitted to hospital where, after another few days, she was moved to a mental ward.

'I think, young lady,' said a bearded young doctor in a white coat, 'that you are having quite a nasty nervous breakdown.'

'Oh good,' she said. 'I thought I was dying.'

There was a goldfish bowl at the end of the ward and she used to stare at that for hour after hour.

A few months later she had her things shipped to Los Angeles, spent a day shopping, and flew over the Atlantic in a perfectly fitting beige suit.

Most days, when she came back from work in Los Angeles, she bought herself some flowers, and put them on her dressing table, and looked at them, and their untidy, crazy beauty, before going round and straightening the small apartment by the beach.

She had heard he had been looking for her, of course. Eventually she read his byline as a correspondent in Africa, then India, then the Middle East, and bit by bit her memory of Phillip faded and the nightmares more or less stopped.

*

As she lay on the bed where he and his girlfriend had slept last night, she ran her hand over the soft down of her bare legs and up to the inside of her thigh – he used to like the softness of the inside of her thighs, and cover her with tiny pinches like kisses.

Maybe he hadn't slept last night – maybe he'd lain staring at the crack in the ceiling. Maybe he'd thought of her. He used to sleep on his side, hunched up, like a child, his skin as smooth as a child, soft as warm milk. The sheets lay over her bare legs, up over her tummy. Sometimes all morning she used to lie in bed thinking about him and he'd phone and her voice would be smudged with sleep and desire.

She looked round the room, to see what he had seen last night, to look through his eyes. On the floor by the window was an ink stain; the marks other people's lives left behind, the scratches here and there on the floor, the ink stains, the water stains in other rooms.

When Susan swung her legs round, onto the wooden floor, she saw a laptop computer just sticking out from under the bed.

I should leave it. I shouldn't touch anything that belongs to him, she thought, leaning down and bringing out the laptop.

For some while she sat thinking then she picked up the phone and called directory enquiries for the number of Phillip's office, then dialled. A drawling woman's voice answered and Susan said, 'I have a message for Phillip Jordan.'

'Oh – he's here – won't be a moment. Who shall I say is speaking?'

She shivered, from the air conditioning on her bare back.

'Tell him it's Susan Stewart,' she said.

'Hello,' said Phillip's voice, after a while, and his voice was just the same, nervous and cold at the same time. It was curious to hear it after all this time. The walls of the room were crooked and shaky. 'So you call yourself by his name?'

'Your computer. It's here. You left it behind,' said Susan. 'Or I assume it's yours.'

'Oh – yes. I was wondering where it was, Susan.' The word 'Susan' lay cradled softly at the end of his sentence. 'I wondered how long it would be before you phoned.'

Her insides were like the room – crooked and shaky.

'I have to go out. I'm ready to go out right now. I'll leave it out for you.' Susan's body sat still on the edge of the bed, her hands resting on her thighs.

'How are you, Susan?'

Phillip's voice was as intrusive as ever.

'Great,' she said. 'But I'm busy. I have a lot to do right now. I can't talk long.'

She wondered where she had put the coffee-table book on Cologne and looked down at her small, white feet, with their red nail varnish.

'Look,' said Phillip, shoving his words into her head, crowding the entire room. 'I'll be there in minutes. Minutes. Really. I have to have it. Wait in.'

He had a soft way of talking.

The cats had all loved Phillip; he had stooped down to stroke them, lifted them into his arms, whispered into their twitching ears.

'I have to go out.'

'Please, Susan,' he commanded.

Susan put down the phone then stood up and left the room, and in the hallway a darkened Madonna wrapped in blue swathes of material gazed down from the wall.

For a few minutes she couldn't find her keys, and then, there they lay, sprawled on the coffee table in the drawing room, and she held them tightly, the rings on her fingers sticking out like knuckledusters, as she slipped on some old shoes waiting in fifth position by the door, as if their owner had recently disappeared in mid-plié. Some of the old cork tiles were loose, she noted, as she tripped on the way to the door.

Abandoning the computer by the front door, she ran to the car and took off, actually passing a yellow cab on the other side of the small roundabout at the end of the road, but she didn't look to see if Phillip was in it.

She parked at the nearest shopping mall, a spectacular glass and steel structure packed with perfect shops, fountains, immense palm trees made of metal, and topped with a health club. There was no litter anywhere, no dirt, no sense of time accumulating.

The Washington malls were cathedrals worshipping the pleasure of perfect things, before time got to them: new CD players, new slimline TVs, new computer games, all piled high in silvery rooms staffed by smiling assistants. Here nothing fades, the shop assistants are always pleasant, you never see anyone sick, there is no past, no grief.

The assistants didn't talk to each other – they waited eagerly, at attention yet at ease, in casually smart clothes. Music called out from other shops; inside one were silk waistcoats, silk dresses, flowing trousers, in another uniforms for the elegant Washington lady, chiefly well-fitting suits in assertive colours.

She stopped in front of the toy shop, and noted the watchful pyramid of soft toys which towered to one side – the lamb, the tiger, the fat teddy.

In the next shop bright clothes fluttered from the rails like butterflies.

'What about this one?' said a red-haired girl to her plainer friend, who was dressed entirely in black. The red-haired girl held up an emerald jacket.

'No,' said the plainer one, 'I don't think green's your colour.'

'What is my colour, do you think?' said the other, carefully putting back the linen jacket, stroking it for a moment.

The redhead watched herself in the mirror, and smiled. But the smile was too friendly and childish. She delivered something cooler but even that was unsatisfactory. Behind her a woman flitted past carrying hangers of clothes.

Susan moved out, through the marble halls, past shops full of gadgets, past cosmetics counters. She stopped and put her fingers in a gold-rimmed jar and smeared the cream on the back of her hand. The lady at the counter was serving someone else. Soon Rebecca would be smearing cream on the back of her hand.

As a teenager Susan would go to London department stores and try perfumes and creams until an assistant stopped her. The jars had been smooth, round, gorgeous, witches' pots, magic mixtures served by women with alabaster skins and too much lipstick, versions of Snow White's stepmother, women with masks. It would have been easy to have leant over and torn off their faces. But they were tempting all the same, with their cajoling voices and luscious wares.

Susan turned away, and walked back to the elevators, and as she went she saw the two girls gazing through thick glass into the toy window at a display of defiant dolls in white lace and ribbons.

'I like that one,' said the red-haired girl.

'Oh yes,' said the other, a little sadly, before they both turned away.

When she arrived home, the laptop was gone, and their next-door neighbour Ivana Fischer appeared from nowhere, her eyes inquisitive, her rings glittering, her perfume overwhelming.

'A rather handsome man was here looking for you, Susan. Phillip Jordan,' she said, searchingly. 'You left his computer outside, he said. He looked angry.'

'Thanks,' said Susan, and disappeared into the house.

Inside, Susan felt again the presence of the other child in the house, the child she hadn't yet had. For just as the past has its presence, so does the future, waiting round some corner not yet turned.

When Susan collected Rebecca from school the trees waved their branches above them and a moth with black wings struggled in the grass.

'I've just started *Gone with the Wind,*' said Rebecca. 'And I'm going to live a life like Scarlett O'Hara,' she said. 'But I'm *never* going to get married and have a child.'

Ivana Fischer was at the window to wave as they went by, as usual.

10

The cul de sac where the Stewarts lived had five houses on each side of the road. In the mock Tudor house to one side of them lived a frail couple who looked as if they'd been pressed between the pages of a book, but drove a large white Cadillac and behaved with unfailing politeness. Always there was the wife's round face at the window, with thinning hair dyed an odd shade of lemon and always there was her husband taking his stroll, greeting passers-by with a considerate nod of the head, an occasional invitation for a glass of sherry. The smell of their rooms was that of grandparents – decent and clean with a hint of mothballs.

June Brown from the house opposite stayed at home with the children while her husband worked for the navy. They appeared to have perfect family lives: they had garage sales and barbecues, the husband ran the local school's Parent-Teacher Association, and the wife did voluntary reception work at the school. Susan felt sometimes that she'd dreamt them up to reassure herself that life could be a simple matter, but didn't spend much time with them in case they disappeared, leaving just smiles behind.

Next door to them, in a miniature house, lived an overweight family, who would roll out at weekends to play baseball in the street. Only the husband was thin. His son Joe would yell at him in the street when he missed the ball, and the father's shoulders would look sad, his red hair wispy, as if remembering a time when fathers could spend their weekends with their feet up, getting fat.

Susan seldom spoke to this family either, as she found the mother far too overpowering – she feared she'd be mowed down by her – and the husband too nervous.

'One more time, little Joe,' he would say, standing in the middle of the road, as his son threw another ball at his baseball bat.

But Susan felt it was absolutely right that the plump family should be where they were, in the little house with the blue door, that each part of this cul de sac was crucial to the whole, that somehow they were all acting out some drama, the finale of which she would eventually know. Sometimes, during the hot turbulent summer days, she would stare out of the windows and listen to the silence.

Further along, a man with a beard, a cigar and a dalmatian helped his dying wife take the occasional walk in the cul de sac, during soft sunlit summer evenings. Each day the wife grew thinner as if she were being carefully rubbed out. And indeed, one day, he would be walking along the cul de sac with an empty space behind him.

The only person who didn't seem fixed in some predetermined role was their other next-door neighbour, Ivana Fischer, the Polish woman married to Gustav, the Swiss diplomat. She pottered up and down the street in pale green suits with her black hair in a bun. She had no children.

Ivana paid great attention to the man with the dying wife.

'This street is just full of wonderful people,' June had said on their first day.

'I know,' said Jim.

'And terrific kids.'

'I know,' said Jim.

'It's true,' said Susan.

And June smiled a smile of infinite sorrow and disappeared into her blue house which was the colour of the sea before a storm. Through the window Susan could sometimes see June hoovering around her bright yellow sofa.

As the temperature rose, Susan went around rearranging the furniture in the house, thinking if only she could get just the right positions, everything would be all right. In the shops she stocked up on food, filling the cupboards and the fridge until they could take no more, counting the tins and packets as if checking an armoury. And she made soups, all kind of soups, as if those too might help defend the house. Cucumber and lemon, bean and tomato, turnip and orange. And she washed everything she could in the house, and ironed it, until everything was in straight rows, piled high. With a pile of ironed sheets, their folded edges sharp as knives, she felt far safer, but still the windows didn't fit in their frames properly and the hot air crept through into the house.

Meanwhile their next-door neighbour Ivana plays patience, taking out the cards, making circles, playing the ace of spades, the queen of hearts, the jack of diamonds, and watches from the window, watching the children play.

It is fortunate that the rest of the people in the cul de sac – the tall, striding woman with glasses who throws back her head when she laughs, the soft-spoken June with her endless hoovering and gardening probably warding off other sorts of attacks, the plump lady who is always off on some school committee meeting – are on the whole, it seems, benevolent. And when Susan looks out of the window she sees the bright colours and deep shadows.

11

'Phillip's a pleasant guy,' said Jim. 'I see quite a bit of him now we're both in the press building.' He brushed his teeth ferociously.

'Oh really?' said Susan, who stood with her back to him, doing her make-up in the long mirror. Painted what the tin called caterpillar green, the bathroom, with its cracked black and white tiles and old white bath, still looked like something from before the war.

He spat out and began to hum.

The mirror she was looking into was stained at one side.

'What were you like when you were young, Mummy?' said Rebecca, at the door. 'Were you very pretty? The way he looked at me at breakfast after he came to stay that night a while back – as if I were you. You must have been very pretty. I wish you'd tell me about him.'

'You're overreacting, Susan,' said Jim. 'Since you found out he was here you've been wandering round like a zombie.'

Rebecca, who wore the pyjamas speckled with red

hearts, moved from foot to foot. The hair at the top of her head stood up in spikes from when she'd been sleeping.

'He's just very ordinary,' said Jim.

'Sure,' said Susan, wrapped up in a white towelling dressing gown, applying pink lipstick.

'You're being British, Susan. Caught up in the past and so on,' said Jim. Even now, with a razor in his hand, he moved restlessly from foot to foot.

'Oh, I'm sorry to be so British. That must be a drag for you.' The belt on her dressing gown slipped off.

Jim wrenched the razor down the side of his face.

'He's just an ordinary guy, Susan.'

'I know. Sure.'

She wrapped the dressing gown tighter around her.

'Presumably it's important for you to build him up. But let me tell you – he's nothing special. Rather polite. Interested. Pleasant.'

'I didn't think he was that . . . polite,' said Rebecca. 'Remember I met him at breakfast. He lounged. When he was eating breakfast – and you weren't up – he lounged. I thought he was handsome. I think he thought I was pretty.'

'Rebecca – I'm trying to talk to your mother.'

'Jim, I've been a bit thrown, that's all,' said Susan.

Susan turned and leant against the wall. Jim continued to shave.

'Well, I think we should all meet. Have a meal,' said Jim, in a stifled voice as he pulled his mouth to one side to get a better stretch of skin to shave.

'I don't want to do that,' she said.

'I know he meant a lot to you, but it was years ago,' he said.

Rebecca's dark eyes and pointed chin had an elfish quality but Susan stood, uneasy, cocooned in the voluminous dressing gown. Her skin shone slightly, like parchment.

'I've been thinking – maybe one day we really should go back to England,' she said.

Jim's razor stopped, then continued its precarious course round his nose.

'We've been here a long time – and it's great. But maybe, for Rebecca . . .' she said.

'I thought you didn't like England,' he said.

'From the point of view of my work, though, it would be better. That's all. I mean, English spiders are my speciality and I'll get more commissions to draw and paint them there.'

'You like tarantulas though,' said Rebecca. 'And they're not at all English. They come from hot countries.'

'I don't know,' said Susan, flattening her hair at the back in case it had spikes like Rebecca's. 'There's something wonderful about English spiders – small, of course, but extraordinary . . .'

'You can't be chased around the globe,' said Jim. 'You have to face your fears.'

'*Face your fears!*' said Rebecca. 'You sound like our personal counsellor at school. She makes me want to *throw up*.' Rebecca flung a wild grin over her face. Her curly hair had such energy it seemed it could carry her off, out of the window into the air. She dug her hands into the pockets of her pyjamas.

'Thank you, Rebecca,' said Jim grandly. The statuesque tone of his voice was belied by his skinny, naked body so covered with body hair it seemed a hopeless task to try and remove that which covered his face.

'I thought I asked you to leave,' he said to Rebecca.

She checked her watch, not in the least afraid of her good-natured father whose attempts at sternness always seemed faintly ridiculous to her.

'It's not late,' she said cheerfully. 'School doesn't start for ages.'

'Christ,' said Jim to Susan, 'you hold the most horrifying spiders and yet you're scared of some journalist from a middle-brow magazine.'

'If he were from a high-brow paper, he could be scary?' said Susan making herself stand up a little straighter.

Outside, through the casement window, the tall trees of the country club stood green and glorious.

'Look, what actually happened?' said Jim.

She leant against the cold mirror.

'I think I should go,' said Rebecca, and backed away.

Jim took a towel and wrapped it around him, a Roman emperor in a toga.

'Maybe you just don't want to be disappointed,' he said.

She grinned. 'You're so romantic, Jim. You think you're so down to earth but you're romantic,' she said, passing by him, back into the bedroom.

12

Early the next morning Susan put her key in her pocket, closed the front door, and jogged down the pathway for her daily run. She ran first to the end of the cul de sac. A dead mouse lay by the bank where daisies grew.

She passed the conventional clapboard house where June and her husband Ben lived. Ben played baseball with his nine-year-old son continuously. Although Susan's car was pit-holed with the balls Ben hurled, she thought of his tall figure, tossing the ball at his handsome, blond son, with affection. Like his wife, he seemed to have wandered out of a Norman Rockwell picture – part of an America you can discover only by living in it. They always greeted Susan and Jim with warmth and interest.

The grass grew wild on the banks opposite the good people with their daughters who baby-sit and sons who mow the lawn on Saturdays in the eternal sunshine of a Washington summer.

Often when she jogged she greeted a policeman here, a resident there, happy to be part of a past that wasn't hers and yet in some indefinable way belonged to her – the tilt of the oak tree, the slope of the sidewalk.

When she lived in London on some days she could hardly move.

In the cul de sac the small detached houses sat in their gardens, surrounded by trees, at the mercy of the roasting sun.

She ran past the mock Tudor house lived in by the thin couple who had lived there all their lives; she saw the wife looking through the window, and waved, and the woman's face brightened and she waved back. And this again seemed to be the place she had lived all her life, the place she grew up in, and all these other memories, of streets as intricate and desolate as the human brain, seemed entirely irrelevant.

Up the hill, by the long white house with the summerhouse, past the house with the dalmatian, past the basketball area, up to Cedar Parkway, lined with stretching cedar trees by the side of the country club. There was a smell of newly mown grass.

Susan ran past little silver birches gallantly spreading out their arms from which hung just a few delicate leaves, past vast camellia bushes, their leaves dark green and glossy, past sprightly oaks, tidily mulched, by the side of the street, waiting expectantly to turn into grand old trees protected and admired by the committee which ran the village – the oldest, most traditional and most costly of the villages which made up the area of Chevy Chase.

Susan waved hello to Officer Mitchell, a jowled man with mismatched ears and sandy hair, who beamed at her.

Nothing much happened here in the village, and Officer Mitchell spent most of his time drifting around in his police car. He was always eager to stop and talk – usually his conversation was full of cryptic comments about weather: 'The storm in Virginia's gathering strength', 'They say we're due hurricanes this summer', 'You want to be careful if there's lightning tonight. You know it can travel down metal pipes?'

A few flowers gamely stood there, among the trees and bushes; some Black-Eyed Susans, Impatiens, but all seemed to lack the air of prosperity and longevity which surrounded the bushes and trees. In this area there were no tract mansions – overbuilt houses with too many immense bathrooms covered with marble and heated under the floor. This was the old America, solid, with good values and few swimming pools, a place which had a Christmas party for the local children and an Easter hunt every year. It lacked a community pool but there was one over in the next 'town' of Somerset over the other side of Wisconsin Avenue, and anyway it was thought most people could afford to join the Chevy Chase club, where the joining fee was in thousands.

Behind bushes she heard the laughter of children, high-pitched, carrying sharply through the air.

She ran faster, feeling her heart begin to pound, enjoying the thud of her feet on the road, the sweep of the trees above, the clapboard houses with their turrets.

And then, as she turned down a long stretch of road, she thought she saw Phillip facing her, tall and lanky, wearing an old white shirt and jeans.

Behind him, as a backcloth, stood a vast cream clapboard house with brown awnings. It seemed almost as though he were waiting there to welcome her into the house. Even from where she was, she could see his grey eyes and his tense smile.

She turned and ran away from him.

'Susan!' he called clearly after her. 'Susan!'

13

'Shall we have lunch?' said Jane Meadows, when she phoned Jim up in his office in the press building.

'Bit busy for the next few weeks,' he said, rearranging his papers on the desk. There was another call waiting for him. A tower of magazines lay on the floor by him. Although efficient, he was often so dazzled by the sheer range of information in the world that it threatened to overwhelm him. It was one reason he had done well in his profession but had never reached the top; he didn't concentrate on any one thing to the exclusion of all else.

'Oh, I'm sorry,' she said.

'Maybe in a couple of weeks,' said Jim.

'I might have a story for you,' she said, in the warm southern voice which was much more beguiling than her appearance.

'Well . . .'

'A very good story,' she said.

'Look . . . really . . .'

'A business lunch. I promise you you'll be interested in what I have to say. I promise. You need a good story, Jim.'

'We all do,' said Jim.

'Oh yes,' she said, 'of course.'

It was over a Chinese meal that Jane Meadows told him she had been secretary to one of the leading southern senators – Senator Spalding – for over ten years.

'And I've been having an affair with him for eight years,' she said, dabbing her mouth with the white linen napkin. The waiters stood far back in the vast half-empty restaurant.

'Is he married?' said Jim.

'Yes.'

'With kids?'

'Yes.'

'Is he going to leave his wife?'

'No. He's just broken off his relationship with me.'

'In itself,' said Jim politely, 'your affair isn't the kind of thing I would write about. I presume you don't want me to write about it.'

'That isn't what I wanted to talk about,' she said.

In the distance some waiters were pushing a trolley towards another couple, and he wondered why that couple was there.

'I have found out things about him you would like to know,' she said, brushing some fluff off her crisp white blouse.

'Would he like me to know?' he said.

'He would hate anyone to know, I assume.'

'What kind of thing?'

'Money paid to him by drug barons. Various bribes. Money paid into Swiss bank accounts.'

'Why choose me to tell it to?'

'I trust you. You seem trustworthy.'

'And why tell anyone?'

She shrugged. 'He's ditched me. Besides, I want . . .' She leant forward. 'A little glory.'

'An affair with a senator isn't enough? I couldn't pay you.'

'We could do a book.'

'But what you're talking about is a news story.'

'It's more than that, I promise you.'

'Maybe first we do the news story, then the book. I'm a journalist, after all.'

'Maybe.' She put back her spectacles.

'Your wife, how is she?' she said, blinking.

'Fine.'

'I saw her at the embassy party. She seemed very on edge. Beautiful though. That big mouth. You have a child too?'

'Rebecca. She's eleven. But my wife's usually not on edge. She's a calm person. Very calm.'

'Lovely name . . . Rebecca,' said Jane.

14

Susan climbed out of bed leaving Jim lying there, curled up on their brass bed with the patchwork quilt. How American she'd become, she thought. She drew the drapes a little and the green day swelled out before her, the house-high fir trees spreading their limbs, the plane trees towering into a blue sky. And beneath the trees lay her garden, tumbling with phlox, lilies, white trumpeting hibiscus, spilling out of the beds.

Her feet bare on the wooden boards, she watched a spider scurry over the window ledge. There were spiders and insects everywhere: a family of crickets lived in the basement playroom and washroom, and sang arias day after day, sometimes one sitting on the pile of dirty washing, watching her. They studied her, as though knowing she was the intruder, the newcomer, the oddity, whereas they or their relations had been on the planet millions of years before the first man staggered around, shoulders bowed.

Phillip had told Jim he was house-hunting in the area and that had been why Susan had seen him standing there in front of the house. He had informed Jim that she had looked quite terrified at the sight of him, and had asked if everything was OK with her.

Spraying herself with scent, she got a little in her eyes and wondered if it killed you in the end, all these sprays of perfume and deodorants and insecticides.

She turned the silver ring on her finger round and round, then her hand went up to her neck and felt her gold chain.

She drummed her fingers on the window ledge, which was rotten where the rain had got through the intersection with the window. It was hard to keep out the weather. In summer the heat smacked unremittingly against the window, crawling through every crevice, relaxing in the house like some loafer from New Orleans, hanging out. Only immense quantities of air conditioning fought back the lazy heat. And when the air conditioning went down the heat took over the house, organising passionate rows, turning the place into a Tennessee Williams play.

Even the rain when it came bucketed down as if the skies had never wanted to do anything but this, had been made for this ecstasy, throwing out lightning, chucking out thunder, filling the streets and basements with waterfalls, lakes, streams.

Jim emerged from the bedroom as Susan began to dress, and the minute he entered the room something changed. The curious brooding atmosphere disappeared and an air of conviviality took over. He had rosy, well-washed cheeks, and smiled at Susan as if he hadn't seen her for days.

'Come and talk to me while I shave,' he said, for Jim always needed company.

On the window ledge behind the bath stood a row of shampoos, conditioners, offering body and shine, and blocking out some of the green beyond. He spat into the basin.

'I had a bad dream,' he said, blinking at his own face. 'As you know, it's not like me to have a bad dream. I dreamt we went to China to look for a baby and we were sold one who couldn't see. You said he was the one. You were sure. But he couldn't see.'

He splashed cold water on his face.

'There are worse things than not being able to see,' she said.

'Well, maybe, but it was a nightmare. Brushing your teeth can seem a nightmare in a nightmare. You look nice. Sort of awake.'

Susan, still naked, was playing with the gold chain round her neck.

'We looked through child after child, baby after baby, all in hospital cots, mostly crying, some holding out their arms, some just pleading with their eyes, like dogs at Battersea Dogs Home.'

'Horrible,' she said.

'It was just a nightmare,' he said, walking to the built-in closet and opening the door. His ties hung there forlornly, his shirts waited attentively. He had dark hairs running down his back.

'I still think I'm going to get pregnant. I don't think we'll adopt,' said Susan.

'Oh God,' he said. 'Now I have to decide what tie to wear. How can I be expected to make these decisions every day? I really don't feel good today. It's not like me.'

Susan switched on the television, and the weather news informed them it was going to be hot.

Rebecca was already downstairs, busy sticking bits of rock together with glue. Rebecca was endlessly creative; egg boxes transformed into cities, shells into necklaces, dried pasta into engaging pictures which blocked up various cupboards in the house. 'You're not going to throw *that* away?' Rebecca would say.

'One of these paperweights is for you,' said Rebecca, as she stuck a varnished piece of stone to another.

'How lovely,' said Susan, now dressed in shorts and a white T-shirt.

Susan got the milk out of the immense fridge, and placed three cereal packets in front of Rebecca. The cardboard vouchers had already been cut out by Rebecca. Included in her collection were about twenty vouchers for a cream to treat vaginal yeast infections.

'Look,' Susan had said, 'you don't need those.'

'But why don't I?' she had said, then paused, and peered up, her dark eyes peering out of her narrow peaked face. 'What is a vaginal yeast infection?'

Sometimes it seemed that Rebecca examined the adult world as if it were a giant jigsaw puzzle she must solve. Sometimes she seemed too clever and too lonely. One reason Susan and Jim wanted another child was to provide Rebecca with companionship.

'I don't want to go to that self-esteem class with that counsellor Mrs Ruth. I hate saying, "I love myself – I'm worth a lot." And she's always asking me about myself, with an understanding frown,' said Rebecca.

'Oh, she probably thinks you're repressed,' said Jim, studying the picture of the orange monster on the cereal packet. He took a mouthful of oatmeal cereal.

Jim started to study the *Washington Post*.

Susan glanced at the clock. 'It's time for you to get to school,' she said.

'Will you walk with me?' said Rebecca, anxiously.

'Of course,' said Susan, and laughed that crystal laugh, and Rebecca looked at her mother with wonder.

That night, Rebecca fell asleep on the sofa at a neighbour's party and Jim carried her home, cupped in his arms. As Rebecca slept, she looked younger than she was – with her rosebud lips mouthing something. They undressed Rebecca together, Jim taking care of the socks and shoes while Susan tenderly unbuttoned the dress.

'How deeply children sleep,' she whispered to Jim.

'Yes.'

'She's beautiful, isn't she?'

'Yes,' Jim admitted, 'she's beautiful.'

She took his hand.

'I feel happy,' she said. 'It's all going to be fine.'

The room was hushed. When they first moved in, the rest of the house had remained unwrapped except for the books but they had busied themselves to get Rebecca's room straight so that it looked as though it'd been lived in for years. It still looked much the same: white now instead of pink, with curtains displaying the same Sanderson flowers, a small white wardrobe, a white chest of drawers, a poster of two puppies, loose at the right corner where things always come loose first, pictures of the planets, a clock, a bookshelf crowded with soft toys. All the darkness draped itself over the furniture, covered up all the twentieth-century bits and pieces, and left just an extraordinary stillness.

Rebecca clenched and unclenched her fists and murmured something soft and sweet in her sleep.

Jim pushed hair from Rebecca's forehead, and Rebecca stirred.

He lifted her and with Susan's help put her under the sheet where she made a shape like a white stone. The room smelt of her.

Susan sat on the bed for a while listening to her breathing while Jim, standing by the door, watched both Susan and Rebecca.

Later, looking out of their dark bedroom window at the black garden, they saw a racoon blunder across the lawn. They saw stars too. In London the sky had seemed a tiresome addendum to a perfectly workable city. They had simply never bothered to look up at it. But here – the sky and the stars seemed to spread out forever.

15

Guests from England arrived to stay with Susan and Jim now and again and with them, more often than not, their children, usually for some reason boys. The adults would watch with doting expressions while the boys rioted over the garden – running over flowerbeds, knocking over pots, stamping on ants. Meanwhile the poor parents sat, weary, a little joyless, polite, allowing their real selves to live it up. As the adults became wearier, it was noticeable that the children became wilder, and Susan often observed a glint of pleasure as a parent profusely apologised for some malevolent action of a child.

A friend from England, Louisa, came over with her boys and had dinner with Susan, looking over the garden with its rose bushes, and beyond that the country club through the wire fence.

'You don't find it tame being here?' Louisa said over burnt crab cakes.

'Tame? Oh no.'

'I always think of you as wild – at university you were impossible. The men! You used to seem so wicked – and now, here you are with your lovely house, a child, and a perfect husband.'

'This is paradise,' said Louisa, the next day. 'You are so lucky.'

She and Louisa sat under the sun shade in the garden while Louisa's two young sons dismantled a wooden bench over in the corner.

'The roses, the day lilies, the sun, the wine . . . it's perfect . . .' said Louisa. 'Sometimes it must seem so perfect you feel you've invented it.'

She dipped a tortilla chip into hot salsa, and closed her eyes with the pleasure.

Rebecca was crouched by the wire fence at the back of the garden, gazing at a spider's web, and she was a big figure somehow. For a moment Susan could imagine Rebecca out in the garden there as she'd been the first day they came here, just seven years old, standing stock-still and talking to herself. In those days her knees had been round and plump and the backs of her knees the part Susan like to kiss most; they were secret and soft ecstasy.

As a baby Rebecca had been made up of a series of circles: the head, a fat top arm, fat tummy, miraculous fat knees which sometimes made Susan so weak with longing she could hardly bear it.

But that was long ago. Only yesterday, when doing the washing, Susan had picked up a white T-shirt of Rebecca's and thought how big it was, as it hung limply from one hand.

Susan stood up, leaving Louisa with her face

tipped back to soak up the sun, and wandered over to her rose garden. She could hear the sound of the fountain in the back yard next door, and she plucked off one of the roses which was dying, and smelt it, and realised that it smelt of gasoline. Each of the roses smelt the same, and she crouched down and found that the mulch was covered in it too.

'Louisa!' she said. 'Come over here.'

Louisa ambled over, in straw hat, her shirt rolled up into tight doughnuts above her elbows, hair tied back in a pony tail.

'What is it?'

'Gasoline,' said Susan. 'Petrol. There's some all over the rose bed. The old lady who sold us the house made us promise to keep the rose garden and – I don't know . . .'

'Maybe someone spilt it by mistake,' said Louisa, adjusting her sunglasses.

'I don't think so.'

'Are you sure it's petrol?'

'Yes.'

'Probably it was your gardener or something. There's always an explanation.'

'Maybe the ghost did it!' said Rebecca.

At the sink Susan washed her hands over and over again as she used to when she was ill in hospital all those years ago.

Susan heard the roar of Ivana's lawnmower next door.

That night Jim told Susan he thought he might have spilt some when bringing some from the shed to his car, but Susan thought he was probably lying, to keep her calm and stop her worrying; to humour her.

'Of course I'm not,' said Jim.

16

For someone so thin, Jim went in for very fat books: biographies of Dickens, Wordsworth, Tennyson, Abraham Lincoln, Tolstoy, Washington – all big people with big lives and achievements. Their books' shiny covers gleamed from his shelves like jewels. 'Ah,' he would say, 'Mozart, Raphael and Byron – all dead by the time they were thirty-seven. But what they had achieved!' He would tap the end of his black fountain pen on the table in the garden where he sometimes worked, and jump up. 'I feel like a game of tennis. Wanna come?'

After tennis, he would swim length after length as if he really thought he was swimming somewhere.

'Come on, Becky, dive!' he would shout and Rebecca would dive. 'Race you!' And she would race.

'What shall we do next?' he would say as he emerged from his last swim, looking over to one side or the other, ready to be off. He and his father before him had been fast sprinters. His father, another wiry figure, had thought of being a professional sportsman but had drifted into banking where he stayed for some while. His mother had learnt to fly a helicopter at 50 years old. Sometimes his parents would come and stay the weekend but no one would sit down. Each of the three adult Stewarts would wander anxiously from room to room like caged animals occasionally darting out for a jog. Only meals would briefly unite them. His father, like Jim, showed inordinate interest in food, but his mother hardly ate, listlessly moving lettuce around.

'But the interest rates must go down!' Jim would say, emphatically beating the table so the plates and cutlery sprang up in the air. Or he'd announce, 'The Federal debt is a catastrophe!' and his father's eyes would spin like the insides of a fruit machine. But for all his parents' movement, there was something oddly insensate about them, as if all their action never got them anywhere, and Susan suspected this is what Jim feared, that all his brilliance and curiosity was leading him nowhere. In the last few weeks he had begun to sport emerald handkerchieves and jaunty bow ties, and change his little round spectacles to contact lenses.

She never quite knew why he seemed to love her.

'Your gaiety!' he would reply. 'You always seem . . . so abandoned, yet strong. So strong.'

Perhaps that is all it is, she thought sometimes, sex. He finds in me briefly the end he is seeking while all the rest of his life is incompletion, incomprehension.

Sometimes she saw him looking up at the huge biographies, and he looked like a little boy.

Only if he has a son will he grow up properly, stop being a little boy himself, she thought.

'Come and play baseball, Becky!'

'Come and play football!'

'Come and play.'

She'd first met Jim in a London Soho café, close to the British Museum where she was doing some research into the mating habits of English garden spiders. Now she specialised in drawing and painting insects and spiders. Susan had been sitting at the table reading when a dark-haired man entered, glancing quickly from side to side, and rushed to the glass counter, under which was displayed an array of different gateaux: a cheesecake scattered with redcurrants and blackcurrants and dusted with sugar, a chocolate cake which rose up threateningly, glossy with icing, an apple strudel from which plump sultanas oozed at the sides, a slice of bakewell tart which had the advantage of looking puritanical compared with its decadent companions. There was also lemon meringue pie with its meringue frothy above the sharp lemon filling.

The man leant over the counter intently like someone examining a pornographic magazine. His hair was black and wavy. It was attractive hair, she thought. His trousers were dark blue corduroy and baggy at the knees.

She went back to the article she was reading, about the sale of arms to Iraq.

While the man pursued his lengthy study of the cakes, clearly weighing the virtues of one cake against another, the café filled up with the usual immensely varied mixture of Soho people, from advertising executives to Italian shopkeepers, most of whom sipped strong coffee and held slim, silver forks. A few dug non-committally into their cakes, others chose to crouch low over their plates to wolf down the food more quickly, some pushed the cakes aside for long periods while they read the newspaper.

Susan was having a coffee, and had not yet decided whether or not she would have the cheesecake.

Finally, the man made his decision, she noted over the top of *Newsweek*. He pointed to the apple strudel, then nodded, presumably accepting cream, she thought. He turned. She looked back at the magazine. As there was no other seat now in the whole café, he came to sit next to her.

For a while he just sat looking at his strudel, with tenderness. She tried not to smile. He adjusted the plate a little as though wishing to examine the confection from all angles before proceeding further. He wriggled on his seat. A waitress in a black dress and white apron brought him coffee but he hardly looked up. Susan thought perhaps he was having an epiphany or some such religious experience. Or maybe he was a poet and was about to write a poem about the strudel. He glanced quickly up at her; she looked down at her article. He grasped his silvery fork, and allowed it gently to enter the strudel at the far right corner. It slipped down the soft fruit, and a fragment of the strudel broke away. He stuck his fork in and popped it in his mouth.

She found herself hoping the experience was every bit as wonderful as he had hoped.

'Aren't you having anything?' he said, incredulously. His voice was American and soft.

'Well, no,' she said primly. 'Not quite yet.'

'Quite yet! How can you stand it? How can anyone not want to go and gorge themselves on every one of those tempestuous cakes? How can they not?'

She smiled quickly, and returned to her article.

'Is the article good?'

'Yes, thank you,' she said, her eyes still fixed on the words, which she had some time ago ceased to read.

'Good. I wrote it,' he said, with his mouth full.

'Oh,' she said, putting down the magazine slightly. 'Did you?'

'Yes,' he said grumpily. 'I did, as a matter of fact.'

'Well done,' she said. 'I thought it attacked all the points well.'

'Thanks,' he grunted. 'It should do. I've been writing this kind of thing for over ten years. Should be able to do it by now.'

'Yes.'

'Are you really not going to have a cake?'

'I might do.'

'I recommend this. If you want pure pleasure, this is it. The rest – love affairs, complete dinners, aunts, Christmas, newspaper awards – they are all insignificant compared with the pleasure of this particular strudel.'

'Well, you made the right decision then.'

'That I couldn't say. I suspect the lemon meringue pie might have managed to surpass this strudel.'

He stared at her.

'I don't suppose you would allow me to buy you a piece of the lemon meringue pie and I would just have a little of it?'

She shook her head.

He sighed.

'I know it'll be delicious. I wonder if I should try it.'

'No. It won't live up to your expectations.'

'Are you sure? How can you be so sure?'

She shrugged, and sipped her coffee again, and folded up her magazine to go.

'Well,' he said. 'Can you remember anything about the article? The kind of machine guns sold to Iraq, for instance?'

'Allegedly sold,' she said.

'Good. But I think you're wrong about the lemon meringue. You ought at least to try it. You ought not to turn your back on clear, superb pleasure.'

'Oh really?'

She leant down to get her briefcase.

'Are you a lawyer?'

'No. Why?'

'You look a bit like a lawyer. You give out an air of terror. I mean, you look demure, but you give out an air of terror.'

She frowned. 'You look exactly like a journalist.'

His head weighed over to one side. 'I take it that's not a compliment.'

'I don't know.'

He screwed up his nose. He had nice eyes, big and brown.

'Some journalists are OK. I am, for instance,' and he grinned for the first time and his whole troubled presence suddenly altered for an instant.

'But you eat too much cake.'

'Yes,' he said, raising his brows at her moment of teasing him. 'I eat too much cake. But is that a big fault in someone who is skinny? I mean, in the whole panoply of possible faults a journalist can have, is eating a bit too much cake the worst?'

'No,' she laughed. 'Of course not.'

'What are you then?'

'What do you mean?'

'If you're not a lawyer, what are you?'

'I'm a naturalist.'

'Oh?' he said. 'Any special area?'

'Insects and spiders.' She checked her watch. 'I'm late. I should go.'

He scraped what was left of his strudel onto the fork, so that his plate looked as though a thousand chariots had careered over it.

'This place is emptying . . .' she said.

'I know. These people just gulp down their food. No quality left in eating nowadays.'

'I must go.'

'Really?'

She nodded.

'Are you in love?' he said.

She stood up. 'Yes.'

'Ah. That's it.'

'That's what?' she said.

'The manner. Terrified. Slightly patronising, you know. Happily in love?'

'Unhappily, actually,' she said.

She began to leave.

'What's your name?'

She turned back. She smiled. 'Susan Price. My name is Susan Price.'

She closed the door of the café and walked out into the cool street, wanting to look back to where the curiously attractive man sat, whose name, she knew from his byline, was Jim Stewart.

It was a year later, after breaking up with Phillip, when she saw Jim again at a wedding reception.

The reception was under the glass roof of the Orangery in Holland Park in London. It was raining, and the drops slid down every pane of glass.

There was an avid quality to Jim, standing before her in a black suit, holding his glass of champagne, his bow tie pink, an American in London.

'You arrived late,' he said.

'Yes,' she said, glancing quickly round the room.

'We've all been here for days, it seems. And then you walk in.'

Susan shivered. 'I'm a little jet lagged,' she said. 'I've just come back from America.'

She wore a chiffon dress of brown and red, with a high waist, and when she moved, the dress swirled around her.

He dipped his fingers in the canapés as they went by, and popped a pastry into his mouth, which looked as warm as an oven. 'Mmm, these pastries are good,' he said. 'Full of goat's cheese. The others are sun-dried tomatoes.' His tongue flashed quickly round his lips. 'Don't you want to have one?' he asked incredulously.

'No, thanks,' she said.

'So, why were you in the States?'

'I had some work to do at UCLA.'

'What kind of work?'

'The sexual habits of insects.'

'Ah. How exclusive.'

'Not really. Insects are the most dominant species on the planet, by far.'

'In terms of what?'

'Numbers. Proliferation. Variety. And remember malaria and plagues. They can wipe out human beings far more easily than we wipe out them.'

'Is it . . . erotic? The sexual habits of insects.'

'Sometimes,' she said. 'All that frenetic mating.'

'Ah. They have a reputation for coolness.'

'Quite false. They're enthusiastic. Why, earwigs are some of the best mothers in the natural world. Devoted creatures.'

'You changed the subject.'

'You've seen dragonflies mate – it's beautiful – mating on the wing in the sunshine by a lake. And wasps – you've seen them fighting together, having rumbustious sex, and then soon afterwards the males become tired and stagger around and die, and their bodies end up all over the floor.'

'Is that erotic?'

'It's not passionless, anyway.'

'It's pre-programmed.'

She shrugged. 'Well, does that make it any less passionate?'

'I would say so,' he said.

'I disagree. You overestimate the pleasures of free will. Giving way to your most base and instinctive desires undoubtedly provokes great passion. It's virtually a definition of it.'

'I thought entomologists were skinny women with big glasses and huge shoes.'

'You're mixing us up with our subjects. But I am skinny.'

'Slim. I had no idea the sex life of insects could be so . . . inspiring to anyone . . . I shall have to check out the back yard.'

'Garden.'

'What?'

'In England we call it a garden.'

'Oh yes, I know.'

'Where do you come from?'

'San Francisco, originally.'

'How wonderful. I love America.'

'And I love England.'

'What can you possibly like about England?'

'Everything. I like everything. And what do you like about America?'

'The same,' she said, as the waiter filled her glass. She sipped some more champagne as the rain ran down the windows.

'The bride looks nice,' she said. 'Like something off a cake.'

Someone was playing the piano.

'Would it be sudden of me to ask you to leave with

me now to get a meal?' said Jim.

'There's a meal here.'

'Yes, but you're shivering and the piano music is strange, and besides I've drunk a lot of champagne and would like to sit with you in a warm restaurant and talk about dying wasps.'

'It's beautiful here though. It's cold, but it is beautiful.'

The windows were covered with condensation.

'Can I take your number then?'

'I don't really have a number. I'm between lives, you see. I think I'm going back to the States.'

'Where to?'

'Maybe to do some research at Denver University.'

'But you must be living somewhere.'

'I'll stay in a hotel tonight. I love hotels.'

'Which one?'

'I haven't decided.'

'The Savoy is a good hotel. Let me take you to dinner there.'

'No thank you,' she said, and began to walk away from Jim. He followed her, and held her arm.

'I'm not letting you go,' he said, 'now that I've found you again.'

Suddenly she found the room overwhelming, with the women chatting and laughing with their hats on at an angle, and their smiles on at an angle, and the men so stubborn in black.

He took her arm and they went to the cloakroom, collected their coats, and slipped out of the reception together, walking through Holland Park in the rain, talking.

They walked to his rented mews house nearby. There was a woman's coat in the hallway, a bottle of nail varnish remover in the kitchen. But in the mirror she caught sight of a dark-browed young woman with questioning eyes, who seemed at home.

He had slumped in the armchair facing her.

'You know,' he said, 'I find the way you tilt your head very cheering.'

'Thanks,' she said.

A copy of *Vogue* lay on the sandy-coloured carpet. On the front cover a model swirled in a white coat.

A cluster of dead roses sat in the vase on the mantelpiece.

'When can I see you again?' he said.

'You're seeing me now.'

'But I want to see you again soon.'

'I shall be away,' she said, looking at her watch.

'Are you married?' he said.

She shook her head.

'You have a boyfriend?'

She stood up. 'I must go,' she said.

'But it's still raining,' he said.

'I really must go.'

She left but the next morning he rang, having got her number from the newly married couple on their wedding morning.

She laughed when he told her what he had done, and they had lunch together a few days later, in a Soho restaurant, and a few days after that he told her he loved her.

'I'm not in the business of being in love at the moment,' she had said. 'I'm rather avoiding it.' And she had left the next day for America.

When she was back in London and she picked up her post from a holding address, she found a pile of postcards from Phillip from India:

'Found a book of yours amongst my things. There are tears in things, and the world touches the mind . . . Virgil . . . *sunt lacrimae rerum et mentem mortalia tangunt*.'

She spent most nights with Jim in his mews house, and the postcards and notes continued, always short, with something mournful about the time and date ink marks on the stamp, as though all she and he shared now were times and dates. A postcard of the Taj Mahal, on cheap card with a too-bright blue sky, a picture of a temple in Jaipur, a postcard of a smiling monk in yellow, torn at the corner, which had first been delivered to an address in Halifax, in error.

There was also a 1950s postcard of the street where she and Phillip had lived together, in Fulham:

'See the building
Where whilst my mistress lived in
Was pleasure's essence
See how it droopeth
And how nakedly it looketh
Without her presence.'

And after that the postcards stopped, and soon after that she married Jim and was at once pregnant with Rebecca.

Jim worked as a foreign correspondent for *World News*. He was always at all the parties – the Russian embassy, the Swiss embassy – darting around like a clockwork toy then returning home or to the office to tap out acerbic prose. But he was well liked. In those days, he never took himself seriously.

He came hurtling home at night and rushed into bed and made love feverishly as though not wanting to waste a moment of life.

She never told him any of the things that had happened between her and Phillip, in particular their last day together. She put it out of her mind. She could no longer think about it. But he kept asking.

'When was the last time you saw him?' he would say. 'What happened? I know something happened.'

It was as though Phillip Jordan were in some way part of their relationship from the beginning.

'You always seem . . .' he said, kissing her, 'I don't know. As if there's some secret behind you.'

'Being female, darling. Men think it's a huge secret. And of course being British. You think I know something you don't. Which I do.'

'When I make love to you, sometimes I think I'll find it out, whatever it is, but I never do.'

17

Up in the attic cupboard Rebecca was looking for the spider she was fond of, whom she called Sillea, but couldn't see her anywhere. Rebecca had given the spider the name Sillea because it seemed a good name for a spider. She found a cardboard box marked PERSONAL LETTERS in big, rather childish writing, which looked like her mother's. She wondered if there were any letters from Phillip Jordan in the box.

Ever since Phillip Jordan had stayed the night, Rebecca kept thinking about him and his girlfriend and the things he had said.

The morning after they had stayed the night, Rebecca had padded down the wooden stairs in her bare feet and pyjamas covered with hearts and found them there, and it was a shock to see him there and to find out that he was an old boyfriend of her mother's. Rebecca had heard someone moving around downstairs during that night so should perhaps have been prepared for something strange, but wasn't.

Phillip was sprawled at the breakfast table, arms and legs all over the place as if his limbs had been separated and dumped in the wrong places. He ran his hand over his hair and it sprawled too, this way and that. Although he must have been quite old, as old as her mother, he looked younger somehow, not quite finished, and he seemed made up of angles; elbows, knees, limbs spread out all over the room. He had a soft manner and was eating corn flakes. Around him were the remains of the rest of his breakfast: crusts of toast, an open pot of marmalade, a smear of butter on the side of a plate. He offered her a slow, interesting grin, and she found herself momentarily confused.

'Who are you?' she demanded.

'My name's Phillip Jordan,' said the man. 'I stayed the night.'

'Oh I see,' Rebecca said.

'And this is Sandra, my girlfriend,' he said.

Sandra emerged from the kitchen. She had pudding-basin blonde hair and a way of walking as if watched by a vast crowd of admirers.

'Hi,' said Rebecca. Sandra smiled graciously, then seemed to remember it was a good idea to be nice to children in front of men.

'Why hello . . . aren't you lovely?' she said, sitting down in Susan's place.

'I'm an old friend of your mother's,' Phillip said, and dipped his spoon in his corn flakes, loaded with white sugar, again. 'Do you breakfast?'

He smiled. He had a charm quite different, for instance, from the creepy charm of Ivana's husband, who looked as though he wanted to pin you on a sheet like a dead butterfly. The smile sort of bowed before her, yet teased her for allowing herself to enjoy its graciousness, and at the same time it suggested it liked her a great deal, and admired her for exactly the qualities she wanted to be admired for, although she was not quite sure what they were. But most of all the smile suggested its bearer was a great deal of fun, and considered that Rebecca was a great deal of fun, and told her that, after all, that was the point of life, to have fun, whatever anyone else said, and Rebecca liked the way the smile colluded with her, made her and the man friends.

She shrugged and reddened and tried not to stare at Phillip, who created some kind of reaction in her she didn't understand as he watched her so slowly.

'Do I breakfast?' said Rebecca, looking down at her bare feet. 'You mean, do I eat breakfast?' She thought for a moment, as he'd offered the question in a serious manner. 'Yes, I certainly do eat breakfast. I like breakfast.' She sat down at the table. 'It's the best meal of the day.' She stared at the corn flakes. 'Especially corn flakes with lots of sugar. Can you pass them? I thought grown-ups all ate muesli for their health.'

'I don't,' said Phillip, eating, and reading the *Washington Post*. The plastic bag it had come in lay on the table, still wet from the morning dew.

'It's early,' said Rebecca.

'Only six o'clock,' said Phillip.

'Do you always get up early?'

'I do really. I can't imagine why. I don't particularly like mornings. All that dew and the birds croaking away at each other.'

'That's silly,' said Rebecca, regarding him closely.

'What is?' said Phillip.

'Not liking mornings.'

'Why?' queried Phillip.

'I'm sure you know why,' remarked Rebecca.

'You like dew?'

'I like mornings – with no one around.'

'And what is it,' he said, leaning towards her, 'you like so very much about mornings?'

'The way the colours look all new. I like that,' she said.

'It's because they're wet from all that dripping dew . . . Pass the corn flakes.' Phillip checked his watch. 'Sandra, could you get me some orange juice?'

'Are my parents up yet?' said Rebecca.

'No. Are they usually at this time?'

'No.'

'I imagine your father gets up first, is that right?'

'That's right.'

'And your mother is rather slow in the morning, a little like a snake?'

'I don't know about that. But she certainly doesn't get on the exercise bike like Daddy does. Daddy loves to exercise and eat vitamins.'

Outside, in the garden, the red cardinal was wandering over the lawn and birds called to each other from tree to tree above the emerald grass.

'We're leaving in a minute – I've got a meeting,' said Phillip.

Rebecca spooned corn flakes into her mouth. He watched her carefully.

Since his visit she had felt older, had been thinking differently, feeling differently.

'You do look a little like your mother,' he said.

'Do I?' said Rebecca, pleased.

'She was my . . . girlfriend once.'

'Oh,' said Rebecca. 'You were my mother's boyfriend.'

'You adore her?'

'Yes, she's my mother.'

'And she adores you?'

'Oh yes, she does. Very much.'

Phillip finished off his mug of coffee, and wiped his mouth with the back of his hand. 'I used to write to her a lot. I expect she's kept the letters. She always kept things. They're probably somewhere in this house – curious to think that.'

He checked his watch again and stood up, with a graceful movement which made her think of cats. He thrust out his hand to Rebecca.

'You should look at them sometime when you've nothing else to do. You'd be interested. No doubt you and I will meet again before too long,' he said.

She didn't take his hand, pretending she didn't know why he stretched it out to her. Instead she continued to eat greedily, childishly, as if to weigh her down, to keep her where she was.

He shrugged.

'Your name's Rebecca, isn't it?'

She nodded.

'Well, bye, Rebecca. Say bye to your parents. Tell

your mother I'm so sorry to have missed her. Tell them we got a cab on Wisconsin.'

'Yes,' said Sandra. 'Do thank her for having us.'

Rebecca nodded, and the couple let themselves out.

After they had left, the house felt very empty, and Rebecca let herself out, into the garden, and found a glass-beaded spider's web, and she kept thinking of the unshaven man with the empty eyes.

The silver air-conditioning unit whirled and roared beside Rebecca as she knelt down on the bare wood in the cupboard, looking at the box marked PERSONAL LETTERS. Still some of the things they had brought from England had not been sorted out – some boxes, a few bags of old toys – and Rebecca wondered what was in this box. The words 'personal' and 'letters' both sounded intriguing, especially after what Phillip Jordan had said. Rebecca carefully stripped off the yellowing Sellotape which was securing the box shut.

The first thing she saw in the box was an old stamp album, entitled *My Stamp Album*, and she remembered how her father teased her mother about never throwing anything away. Rebecca opened the album reverently, and found some pretty stamps emblazoned with the words MONACO stuck in rather haphazardly. After the first four pages, the book was empty. The air-conditioning unit gave one of its louder roars and Rebecca started.

Maybe I shouldn't be here, she thought, but the box smelt different from anything she had smelt before, old and mysterious. She saw a letter addressed to Phillip Jordan, in her mother's handwriting, with a London address; it looked as though it had never been sent. She wanted to open it but she didn't, feeling it would somehow be wrong.

She heard a sound downstairs and quickly closed up the box and hurried away. She wondered why he had mentioned the letters. Maybe he liked life to be dramatic, like she did.

18

'Oh Susan!' called Ivana Fischer as she stood on the front lawn watering the plants, looking as if she hardly had the strength to hold the hose. 'Your friend Phillip Jordan was round here while you were out. With his girlfriend.' Her hair lay piled up on her head, but tendrils fell down as though her bun, too, wasn't strong enough to hold anything. Her skin had the translucent quality of fine porcelain, and was perfectly made up, like some figurine who should never have been released into the real world. Ivana wore pale colours: white, pale pinks, pale yellows, as though anything strong would be too heavy and make her collapse from exhaustion.

'Of course you probably know,' said Ivana, 'that he's trying to rent something in this area. I showed him our house just out of interest, and he wanted to see the garden. He looked over and was surprised how good your garden looks. Said when he knew you well you didn't like flowers much.' Her voice was soft as if she had been trapped in a room for months and was dying of thirst and starvation. She managed a smile but it was an effort. She liked to take fixed positions; the figurine watering the garden, the figurine at the piano, the figurine on tip-toes kissing her husband goodbye in the mornings.

'Did he actually come over here?' said Susan.

Ivana smiled, her lipstick pink and tragic under the glaring sun.

'Why yes . . . I believe maybe he did wander over . . . I think . . . of course I was busy.'

'I found some gasoline spilt on my roses – just a few days ago,' said Susan.

'Really?' said Ivana. 'How weird.'

'They haven't recovered yet,' said Susan sharply. 'I thought I'd just mention it.'

The next afternoon, in a day as jubilantly green as the day before, the fat postman waddled to the door. Through the letterbox came the usual friendly collection of letters and catalogues, including an outrageously early Halloween catalogue. Susan sat and read it disconsolately, flipping through pictures of fancy dress, of Batman costumes, witch costumes and a spider costume which she was quite taken with. Maybe I'll dress up this Halloween and be a spider, she thought.

The boy who cut their grass arrived with his truck of lawn mowers. He had curiously full lips and a way of talking which made Susan uncertain whether he was doing it or not – she half expected him to produce a ventriloquist's puppet and explain that the puppet was talking and he was only pretending. But he did the lawn well enough.

She took a cab down, into DC, to work in the Library of Congress. She stared out of the window at Washington disgorging itself onto the pavement: women in shorts and trainers, people jogging, restaurants and cafés everywhere, with tables out on the pavement.

And everywhere the heat like a presence – dripping down their foreheads, shimmering over the pavements.

'Are you English?' said the cab driver.

'Yes,' she said.

'I can tell from your accent,' he said proudly, as if he had recognised early Swahili.

On the seat in front of her, covered in yellowing plastic, was a photograph of a child with the words 'Have you seen this child?' beneath. The child was smiling long-sufferingly, as if wanting to get on with playing his GameBoy or watching cartoons rather than have his photograph taken.

'You got any kids?' said the cab driver.

'Just one little girl.'

'You want another?'

'Yes. We should like another child.'

'We *should* like another. That's cool. I think that's really cool.'

On the way back she took a yellow taxi driven by one of the enraged drivers typical of the area. After he'd taken her money with a silent malevolence he roared off, fumes spewing from his exhaust.

That night Jim's body curled up in a foetal position; at night Jim was always surprisingly compact.

Susan dreamt she gave birth to a sand-coloured form, about the length of her little finger. The form had a big, perfectly shaped head, tiny arms and legs, and fingers as slender as grass, webbed as they were in the *Life* magazine pictures, a little insect of a creature, but the ears were fully formed, miniature versions of Rebecca's. The creature reminded her of the embryo bees, white amorphous shapes growing in their own chambers, their honey cells, and those fed with enough royal jelly forming female sex organs, curious ghostly outlines in their white bodies. But of course this embryo was more developed; this was a human baby. Susan pulled the embryo's arm and watched the shoulder joint move.

Proudly, in her dream she carried it downstairs, filled up a plastic sandwich bag full of warm water, and put the embryo in it to simulate the womb.

'There,' she said to it in her dream, 'you'll be fine now.'

The dream took her to the hospital where she handed the baby in to the receptionist who had the face of Ivana; the receptionist took the baby, opened the bag, and peered in.

'Lovely baby. It'll be fine. Just fine. But do you really want it? Can't I have it?'

Susan woke up streaming with sweat.

19

Susan and Jim read together – he thumbing bright-eyed through pages of documents while sitting on the black leather sofa they'd found on a skip in Kennington, she curled up on a chair. Curious, she thought, how words of a language looked the same on a page whatever they were saying . . . even if they were describing abominations, still they lay there in black and white, in straight lines.

'Apparently Sandra – Phillip's girlfriend – is trying to install him somewhere more family-centred. They are still looking seriously round here,' continued Jim. 'I think she's determined on marriage.'

'Lucky her,' said Susan, in a voice suggesting the opposite.

'You'll run into him all the time. This is a small town. You might as well clear the air,' he said. 'Christ, I wish he wasn't here. But he is. You have to live with it.'

'Clear the air!' said Susan, closing her book.

'Remember he did me quite a favour. He

introduced me to Jane Meadows, the secretary to Senator Spalding, at that embassy party. It was nice of him to introduce us – I owe him something. Besides, he's smart,' said Jim.

'Certainly he's clever,' she said, frowning.

'That's the first nice thing you've said about him.'

'Where did he meet . . . this girlfriend of his . . .?' said Susan.

Like most journalists, Jim, for all his high-mindedness, was a good collector of information on people's lives.

'Sandra used to run a watch shop in New York. He went in to buy one and she sold him a gold one, but it's already stopped,' he said.

Do other people forget? she wondered. When it becomes clear that life is after all a narrative, with people turning up here and there from the past, do women and men properly remember the person they used to know – the one who used to tie them up, or who never washed up his own plates, or the woman who left open pots of nail varnish all over the place, or the one who said she would jump from the window if he came an inch closer? And when they are all playing bridge in old age, or bumping into each other at their children's school or at parties, or buying butter by chance side by side at the supermarket, do they then remember that person as he or she actually was, or is all that gone, transformed, the old skin long ago discarded, the new person standing there virtually unrecognisable, unremembered?

'Look. Let's just pretend he's not here,' she said, 'I . . . I'm really . . . please . . . let's just ignore him. And please, don't trust him.'

'Darling,' said Jim, 'what exactly happened between you and him?'

'We lived together. I told you.'

'We should talk about it.'

'No. That would not be a good idea. Besides, I can hardly remember.'

'Maybe when I've finished this story we should ask to go back to London, as you suggested. What do you think? After all, in London you got pregnant with Rebecca.'

'I don't know,' she said.

As a child she had wanted to live somewhere no one had lived before – in some rainforest, in a desert. Instead they had lived in a council flat and worn old clothes – the jumper with the hole in the elbow where she'd fallen that day from the kitchen table, the stain where she'd spilt strawberry jam that Christmas breakfast, with the frayed sleeves from so many washes. Time wore things down, bit by bit. What her mother could never see was that time wasn't on their side. Time is against human beings, Susan had told her mother as she sat knitting. But she hadn't understood.

There was another kind of past here in America: the geological past of giant mountains, of grand canyons, of immense waterfalls. And that was why Americans could cope with the future – in America there was a sense of so much raw, glorious past time they didn't have to hoard it for themselves, in cupboards, in museums, in cities, the way the Europeans did.

Later, Susan painted a jewelled beetle at her easel. The small window overlooked the country club grounds beyond. The attic seemed much further away from the rest of the house than it was; it was just up a few wooden stairs but, with its white sloping ceilings and skylight, it was another world.

She thought of the male desert tarantula who wanders in dim light after sunset or near dusk searching for a mate, then hides by day in abandoned holes or under stones.

She thought of the grumpy thin-legged wolf spider, a grey tarantula, who after the birth of her spiderlings becomes quite maternal and carries them on her back.

Why must we all be expected always to love only human beings, why can't we be allowed to love other creatures on our planet? she thought. Only children understand that properly . . . they don't see the difference between the spider and the human . . . they can love everything, not yet having learnt the class distinctions. But Phillip grew to hate and fear spiders during his time with her, as if they were his real rivals.

They were making love in the shower once and she saw a spider slipping down the tiles; she stopped the shower and fished out the spider and took it to the window while Phillip stood, scared and angry.

'Why do you fear them?' she asked.

'At school I used to get teased for being so skinny and serious and once a boy put a spider down my back. But that's no big deal, to be scared of spiders – Queen Elizabeth I was scared of roses.'

20

Up the stairs of the Capitol building come a number of shoes – that one which is scuffed, that one with a worn heel, that one buffed up shiny enough to inspect your face – all hurrying up to offices and corridors beneath the marble hat of the Capitol, glorious in the sunshine, with the postcard-blue sky behind it, a white marble palace, a Xanadu. Underneath the dome a train shunts senators around underground from office to office, and the teenage children of their friends deliver messages, their tall, well-dressed frames and hopeful faces a pleasure to see, as they sit, bright-eyed on the trains, carrying their messages to the senator from Ohio, the senator from Montana, who rule their kingdoms from their spacious offices.

Senator Spalding straightens his papers on his desk, making all the lines straight, straight as his thin mouth, straight as the lines on his Swiss bank statement. Only his face fluffs out, the fat beneath the skin. He has cancer, but has told no one. He broke off his affair with Jane Meadows because he is ill and exhausted. If he tells no one, maybe the cancer will go away.

He picks up a pile of headed notepaper and taps the bottom against the desk to straighten it, so each little piece falls into place. On the wall is a picture of his wife and children squinting into the camera.

He first met the businessman Riccardo a few years back, on a trip to Colombia. The senator loathed communism, of course, and the businessmen of Colombia felt the same. It was a couple of years after befriending the charming Riccardo that the Colombian businessman mentioned he was in the export business. Later, the senator was asked if he could arrange to keep open certain airports in his state which for some reason certain people wished to close and when the senator, as a friend, arranged this, Riccardo made a large contribution to the senator's political funds. The next payment was paid into a private Swiss bank account for the senator. The drug baron told the senator how very grateful he was for his continual help.

Meanwhile, the drugs poured into Washington from Colombia via the sleepy southern state over which Senator Spalding presides – the crack, the heroin, the cocaine – and helped to dismantle whole areas. Up go the housing projects, down they come: first a broken window, then a needle on a stairway, and soon they are dismantled, discarded, folded up, and the children are left in the evening to look after themselves.

But the senator has grown to hate himself for what he is doing, although liking the idea of the off-shore mansion he will be living in on his retirement. Sometimes he is taken out by the drug enforcement agency men and together they drive through the desolate streets. 'We have to eradicate this problem,' he says. He is afraid of what he has done and yet he is sure he is safe, in part because he is the President's friend, and the President has allowed the airports to stay open as a personal favour to him.

The senator's secretary, Jane Meadows, is clever, neatly dressed, strapped in by her belt, her blouse, her glasses. She sees everything as if written on pieces of paper – straightforward, to be filed in a category. At first she didn't see the lies beneath the surface of black and white, the complexities in the senator's obsequious smile when he laid his warm hand on hers, when his warm hand stole beneath her skirt. He liked her too, with her stifled little moans and the twitching of her sparrow's body.

When he first told her he wasn't going to continue their sexual relationship, she didn't inform on him, didn't rifle through his papers and examine too closely the words beneath his embossed letterhead.

At night she went home to her apartment with its kitchen table, its queen-size bed, its sofa in front of the television set – but there was no table in front of the sofa, so people have to leave their coffee cups on the floor, and it was this unfinished quality that appealed to the senator. He used to pull back the sheets of her bed and pull her down. Sometimes she used to buy a few flowers – expensive in

Washington – and arrange them in a vase. But he never bought her anything, as that would make him feel guilty, as he humped up and down with the vanilla walls of her bedroom standing well back as if not wishing to see.

21

Again, Susan dreamt of cats. Sometimes she became sure that she had only imagined that scene with Phillip, a scene which had changed everything thirteen years ago.

Since that night she'd been a different person but now Phillip was back she was afraid the old self would break out.

She felt guilt, too, for her part in it all.

The following day a dinner at the embassy took place in slow motion. Susan stared into her soup as her spoon cut into its thick texture. The businessman by her side passed her the salt cellar and Susan watched her hand shake it over the soup – and the salt hit the greeny pond.

To her surprise she began to wonder what it would be like to make love to him.

'Are you a resident?' said the businessman in a tight voice.

Susan sat up straight and put her head to one side.

'We're real Washingtonians. Why, we've been here four years now. In Washington terms, yes, we're residents. My husband works for *World News*. He's American.'

She thought – I am doing fine. Just fine. I'm not even seeming agitated. I can cope.

'And you?' said the man drily.

'Oh, I . . .'

'Yes?' Perfectly dressed, neat at the neck, neat at the cuffs, with small hands, he was teasing her now, virtually parodying the role of an attentive dinner companion, as though sensing her absence.

'I'm a kind of artist. I used to be a naturalist but once I had a child I no longer wanted to travel or go out of the house to work. So I draw pictures of insects and spiders for nature books, mostly.'

'You enjoy that?'

'I do. I like seeing the patterns.'

The man coughed nervously. It was always somehow so important not to go too far, to say the wrong thing, the too intimate thing, the thing that would discomfort people, rock the table.

Around the table sat eight people in evening dress, turning and turning and chatting and leaning over, passing things.

She nodded and laughed her rich laugh and asked questions in response to the businessman. She thought of Rebecca left with Maria. Maria seemed a little distant at the moment. Perhaps her banking exams were worrying her.

Facing Susan, over the other side of the room, was a portrait of a mother and child, the mother enfolding the child tenderly. Susan forced herself to stop worrying.

The sound of people talking rose and fell.

'I like the shirt you're wearing,' said the man on the other side of her.

'Oh thank you,' she said, putting down her spoon, suddenly tired of this pond of soup.

And, further over, a little to the right, was someone who looked like Phillip, his back to her, reminding her of the Vietnam memorial, something momentous yet intimate. When she'd seen the man walk in she felt a fall in her stomach, an openness and a hollowing out. But it wasn't him. She wished she understood what she felt for him; hate, partly.

A white frieze fought its way round the top of the walls – flowers and fruit. Sometimes when she looked in the mirror, she thought he'd be there. And at the windows, his face pressed against the glass. 'There's Bill Byford – he's taken over the President's press relations – and that guy over there runs . . .' The businessman ran through the people and the gossip about the people and every now and again Susan glanced in the direction of what she kept thinking was Phillip's long back, far away, the other side of the room, with other backs and fronts making circles round the tables, games of clock patience.

'I have to stop this,' she said to herself.

'If you ever really tried to leave me, I think I'd kill you,' Phillip had said to Susan one day, late in their relationship, and his hands were round her arms so tight it hurt.

They were lying in bed. Clean white sheets. That bare ceiling gawping down at them. His few spare paintings on the wall.

He had just made love to her.

'You wouldn't dare, Phillip,' she'd said, kicking him hard and scrambling free, laughing as she stood naked, watching his narrow face, a face in the mirror, watching her. 'You're far more afraid of me than I am of you. Why is that, Phillip?'

Afterwards they had gone to dinner at an Italian restaurant over the road and she'd wondered how it was possible to be both desperately unhappy and utterly fulfilled at the same time.

When the phone rang Susan picked it up. 'Susan Stewart here, can I help you?' she said, but there was no reply, just somebody breathing.

Over the next few days she could sense Phillip moving round the apartment where he was staying as she moved round her house. She could sense him picking something up then putting it down. She could feel him looking at the telephone.

The telephone rang. It rang and rang but she didn't pick it up. When it finally stopped ringing she found she was shaking.

I am a fool to be afraid, she thought.

I have nothing to be afraid of. It was all a long time ago, another lifetime.

As Susan lay awake she could hear huge insects beating against the window, trying to get in; all that tiny, ferocious incredible world beating at their bedroom window, with exploding eyes and quivering wings. Beside her, Jim tossed in his sleep.

Susan made herself get up and in the dark window for a moment she could just see her own reflection then she saw someone in the shadows by a tree but couldn't see the person clearly.

'Jim,' she said.

'Yes,' he said sleepily.

'There's someone out there, spying on us, watching the house.'

'Darling, someone is probably taking their dog for a walk,' he said.

'No . . . it's not like that. I . . . I sensed there was someone there, and there is.'

Jim rolled over and said in a foggy voice, 'You're just not sleeping well, that's all. It's all this baby business. It worries you.'

'He's there, a kind of dark shape by the side of the tree. Come on. Come and look,' she said.

'I have to get up at five tomorrow to get to Denver . . . I . . . really . . .' he mumbled.

Susan stood over the bed and swept off the bedclothes. Muttering, Jim clambered out of the bed and stumbled, crashing into the bedside table, to the window where, in the street below, he saw the overdressed neighbour Ivana. In a silver coat and high heels, she was taking her dog for a walk. 'Humph,' he said, scowling at Susan, and stumbled back to bed, pulling the bedclothes over him.

Later, unable to sleep, Susan wandered around the house.

'It's your own self who is stalking you,' her friend Carol had told her on the phone. 'Ignore it. There's no one there.'

'I want to do something remarkable with my life,' Phillip had said, turning proudly to her. 'And you will help me do it.'

'You see,' Phillip had said, 'individual existence is a kind of prison, and I want to experience the universe as a single magnificent whole. You do see? To see everything coming together – what will be and what has been.'

Sometimes when Phillip was out she used to try to get on with some work, would get out her lined paper, her well-sharpened pencils, then find herself up in his wardrobe. She'd breathe in the smell of him and touch his ties, which he seldom wore, and try to imagine on what occasion he might have worn which tie in the past – the striped one might have been for lunch at a club with his uncle, the plain red one for meals with his grandparents in Wales, the black one for funerals. And a few for jobs – interviewing film stars, having lunch in grand restaurants, travelling to Paris. By the end she would swell with jealousy for his past life.

When he got back one night she said, 'That walk-in wardrobe is ridiculously pretentious.'

He smiled, and his smile crept slowly up the side of his face, until it was at full, ironic stretch.

That evening the sex started off tender, even gentle, and then something happened, whether it was the music or the scream of the ambulance or something to do with his work. She remembered even the cats seemed alarmed, their hair on end, that evening. There were cats everywhere in the flat.

Jim kept telling her how agreeable Phillip was; 'a decent person', 'a friend'.

22

Susan sat at her dressing table looking into the mirror and tried to see herself clearly. The face had no proper definition; it was as though her past face had somehow been superimposed over the face she had now, and the result was something out of focus.

She outlined the hills of her lips, smothered her face with foundation then blended it in so it hid all the unevenness of her skin texture and some of the fine lines which had begun to slide down her face like tiny rivulets. There, she thought, I can just blend time away, but still the eyes shine out gaudy and inquisitive, containing all the lost days.

Susan applied mascara on the sweep of her eyelashes, and some lashes stuck together, and still the eyes looked out at her, puzzled. If only I could shut them out.

The thick dark hair now had one or two threads of grey.

She smoothed down her hair and tried to feel strong, but her heart was thumping. This fear she had of him, it wouldn't leave her alone.

I'm too skinny, she thought, made of balsawood, too breakable. He said I was breakable. He put his hands round my neck. But now he is mild and polite – or is it all one of his complex games? He used to like to play games. She put a thin black choker round her little neck.

We played so many games.

The sunlight fell like a drunken visitor over her floor.

She turned on the compact disc player and the sound of choirboys filled the air with the hardship in their high voices. Why does Jim like this music? thought Susan; someone as sensible as Jim shouldn't like music like this, full of beauty and betrayal and transience.

She reminded herself that there were far more reasons to be true to the one you love than to be untrue. Susan had not always been as she was now – a loving, warm mother – and in recent weeks some of her old self had begun to nag at her, the desires slipping under the door of the house, through the windows, crawling like snakes over the lurid green grass browning now in patches, torched by the unending sunlight. When she took a bath, sometimes, the desires came rustling through the water, billowing over her like tides, part of time tugging at her, whispering to her that she was hiding from life here in her fortress, with her jumble of objects around her, with her pretty English roses, with her wardrobe of densely coloured clothes, with her love like a flame soaring over her child, her husband, her house, all the soft walls encompassing her and them, keeping them safe and strong, walls which could change overnight to battlements, surely, to keep all the enemies out, all the enemies which waited outside, ready to destroy whatever grew lazy and lax in its own perfection.

In the old days she had let desires overcome her and the return of these feelings disturbed her. After all, if she stepped away from the house, from being there when Rebecca came home, from watching the movement of the trees out there at the back of the house, from calibrating the moods and mysteries of the house, it would be leaving it unguarded for thieves of one kind or another to break in.

She was still concerned by the shadows at night and in the day, by the creaks and whimpers of the house as it expanded and contracted in the heat, by the echoes of its past sweeping like winds through the corridors, dancing over her skin like desperation, reminding her of things inside herself she wished to forget.

But what called women and men out, to leave the families, to leave the houses, was sweet too, and real, another version of love in all its many forms, urgent, strong, redefining the moment with its variable ecstasies – the scream, the shape of a man's body, the curve of his hand, the slow calculations of seduction, the sense of growing close to some other human being for some momentous purpose and afterwards being shaken, changed, absolved. But the purpose was this, this version of ecstasy, this tending of a house and loving and being loved, and this was fierce too.

23

Susan remembered first moving in with Phillip. Somehow making love, living with someone, was a small thing compared to putting your books on their shelves. Phillip had helped her get them from her flat.

'There!' he said, and she didn't know why she stood there, lost, on the endless grey carpet like some sea at the very end of things. The sound of traffic grew harsher as she stood still, not understanding why she felt as though her insides were being ripped out. He went over and put on one of his favourite tapes because he too had heard the traffic growing harsher and harsher. Susan's books were in Phillip's shelves. She allowed her copy of Donne to nestle between his Blakes. Her *Mill on the Floss* next to his Sartre. She could see the books now, in his shelves.

'I . . . I haven't got my . . . name in them all,' she said, and he laughed.

That night she lay in bed early, listening to the rise and fall of the cars and the shout of the tramps who gathered nearby.

He had fixed up a television on a black bracket and came to bed but held the zapper and changed from channel to channel, and every channel that night showed scenes of war, and the windows scowled back at her blackly, and she turned over, away from him, but before they slept they made love, as they always did, and the love was like nothing else that had ever happened to her.

He left her lying beside him on the bed like one of the bodies they had seen on the news as he quickly vanished into sleep. And it felt like this every time they made love – she was caught up inexorably in the war, as though they were fighting each other for something central and significant but not yet in existence. It puzzled her that it should all seem so important when she was unable to comprehend what the importance was.

He went away for a few days and each day she went to her job at the Natural History Museum, and in the evening she drank black coffee and smoked, and read her books, as though by reading her books – the poetry, the novels – she could keep a hold on a self which was being cut to shreds. She wrote notes in the margin, and in each of her books she wrote her name in girlish black handwriting, and after that she felt much better. She began to paint jewel beetles. Phillip used to say she had magic green eyes like chips of emerald.

She didn't see her friends apart from those at work. She was beginning to lose a sense of who she was, therefore it was difficult to direct herself in conversation.

'Some people have a problem with their self-image,' said Derek, an untidy, red-haired young man at work, as he adjusted his glasses and examined her appraisingly. 'Particularly women.'

'Oh really?' said Susan, continuing with her notes, but giving him a slight, grateful smile.

'Although of course,' continued Derek, giving her an adoring glance, 'didn't Fitzgerald call personality simply a series of unbroken gestures?'

'I believe so,' said Susan, thinking how good it would be if she could care for this gentle, considerate young man.

'Everyone, you know, has some problem with their self-image. You know – who you are. I mean, who you actually are, if you're anyone at all. I mean, am I who you see or who I see? And maybe all I see is who you happen to see. Think about it. Before glass and mirrors were discovered in the twelfth century nobody knew exactly what they looked like – and do you know I think that was easier. What is confusing is the discrepancy between what you look like and who you feel yourself to be.' He scratched his head. 'I don't recognise myself in me at all. Not at all. I'm not the person I see in the mirror . . . sometimes I think I'm on the way to becoming someone in particular but haven't quite arrived at that person yet . . .'

'I used to have a clear idea,' said Susan, squinting at the picture of the golden silk spider she was studying, 'but that was a while ago.'

'If ever you need . . .' he coughed again, '. . . need anyone to talk to . . .'

She glanced at his shambolic corduroy jacket and the way when he walked to get a reference book he seemed buffeted by some unseen wind, and felt a kind of distant affection for him before continuing her work.

That evening on the roof garden Susan pruned the plants.

When Phillip returned home she threw plates at him, and mugs, and they smashed against the wall.

The next time he went away she organised a flat for herself and the day she was leaving he returned. He made love to her on the floor, her suitcase by her, her books in their cardboard boxes, and in the night, as she slept, he put them away for her, the books back in the same places, her hairbrush back on his chest of drawers.

24

'You're more like you were when I first met you,' Jim said. 'Kind of somewhere else. You're so beautiful.'

'You belong to me,' Phillip used to say.

'The weird thing is,' said Jim, 'sometimes Phillip reminds me of you. He walks quickly and silently. Do you know what I mean? Even his voice, the way it sways, and his curious air of bewilderment as if he doesn't quite understand what's happening to him. Do you remember? I think it's one reason I like him. He reminds me of you. And he talks about you – what you were like in the past.' He watched her intently. 'Curious. Your skin . . . recently it's as though you've got a lamp inside you. It glows.'

She closed her eyes and heard Phillip's voice: 'Einstein said, "All our knowledge is but the knowledge of schoolchildren." The real nature of things we shall never know, never.' But she couldn't see his face.

Jim's tongue was in her ear, his hands between her legs. Jim had always been an ardent lover, as if trying to create something which would last forever. But afterwards he would turn away from her, as if disappointed that in the end it had just been another act of love.

'Susan,' said Jim, 'what's her name?'

'Who?' said Susan, draping a soft cream jacket over her shoulders.

'The person we're having dinner with,' he said, in a high-pitched voice.

'I don't know – Marjorie?'

Jim flung both hands through his hair.

'No. I'd remember that. It's my grandmother's name. Is it Matilda?' He moved anxiously from foot to foot.

'Matilda?' said Susan, laughing her rippling laugh. 'Nobody's called Matilda nowadays. But more importantly, how do we get there?'

'No idea.'

Jim's shoes shone black and twitched as if about to shimmer into some tap dance, the Fred Astaire of journalism. His hands collided together then he tugged them apart. Susan's hands lay by her side. He took a step towards her to be calmed by her, his head to one side, but she moved away.

'How long do you have to train to be a tightrope walker?' asked Rebecca, gliding through the door.

'I'm not sure,' said Susan, turning away to look for the map, and all the time the windows around watched her and creaked.

Rebecca walked, stared straight ahead, arms balancing her on either side as she crossed the floor.

'You know you have blood on your collar?' said Rebecca, tilting up her head at her diminutive father.

'What?' he said, jumping back and rushing over to his chest of drawers where he started to knock back vitamin pills.

'Are you going to change your shirt?' said Rebecca. The tall white collar propped him up. He examined a pill containing ginger. 'Will you dance at the party? Ivana always used to dance at parties. She loves dancing,' said Rebecca.

'The senator will be there,' said Jim to Susan. 'The one I'm investigating . . . the one who had the affair with the secretary.'

'What? Ah yes,' said Susan.

He bent down and pulled up his socks.

'You're investigating the fact that she's having an affair?' said Susan.

'No,' he said. 'The affair's over. She's . . . well . . . informing on him.'

Susan ambled to her dressing table and applied more red lipstick.

'I don't know,' he said, lowering his caterpillar-sized eyebrows, shaking his head, 'it's a big story. Amazing. But I don't like it. I don't think I like her. She has a sort of preternatural calm.'

'Who?' said Susan.

'This girl Jane Meadows.'

'Who is Jane Meadows?' said Rebecca, with blackcurrant eyes.

'Just someone helping me with a story,' said Jim, and checked his fat watch.

'What's his name?' said Susan.

'Who?'

'The host tonight,' she said.

'His name? You know his name.'

'I don't,' she said. Susan glanced at the embossed invitation on her dressing table. 'It doesn't say. It just says General Simons.'

'I have lunch with him frequently,' said Jim, frowning. 'But I can't remember his name. I know his face. I don't know what's the matter with me. It's this story. I can't think about anything else.'

'At least you remember the General's face,' she said. 'Call him darling.'

'I can't call a General darling,' he said, holding the invitation up in front of him as if it might somehow reveal the Christian name of the General if he held it in the right light.

Downstairs Maria sat in the drawing room, studying her books, and hardly looked up as they said goodbye and went out to the car.

On the way Washington flashed by confidently, and Susan tried to feel happy. She wished that Maria, who had worked for her as a cleaner for four years, was not beginning to make her uneasy. Maria was no longer looking her in the eye. Perhaps it was Maria who kept moving the photographs into different positions. But Maria had denied it, and looked at Susan oddly. Susan kept missing bits of clothing too – a scarf, a hairband, little things.

Jim turned up the air conditioning and it blew cold air in their faces.

'You know,' she said, hectically, fiddling with her gold necklace. 'One of the things I really have loved about our relationship is the hours we've spent, lost in dark cars. Do you remember that time when we were living in London we went to Tooting and offered to give that guy a lift and we went round and round, each time passing the same bed shop, but I didn't dare point it out because the guy would think we were jerks and he thought you were wonderfully calm and in control? I think he saw the bed shop too. But I don't know. I often wonder about that . . .'

Jim drove too fast down the bland wide Washington streets to one of the area's smartest enclaves – Kalorama – where their host held court with uniformed soldiers as maids, butlers and waiters, in a double-fronted Georgian house with a mulberry door and an air of serenity which wealth, comfort and status provides.

Jim nipped the car into a parking space and darted out while Susan stepped out of the car and looked around, as though taking in every green leaf tilted to her. Jim hurried towards the General's house. A soldier in uniform let them in and showed them into a room of people who turned for a moment to look at them then returned to their conversations. Distinguished portraits stared from the walls. The General saw Susan and Jim and approached – stomach first, an overweight, smiling figure of enormous charm wearing a green satin waistcoat.

'Soldier ants!' thought Susan. 'With big pincers!'

'You've come!' he exclaimed, as if they above all

were the people he wished to see. He dipped down and kissed Susan on both cheeks, before handing them flutes of champagne.

For in Washington people are used to giving parties. Some have done nothing but that, for, after all, that is what diplomacy is about – the giving of parties, the gathering of people to you, the charming of individuals.

Susan sipped her champagne, feeling more at one with the dark corners of the portraits than with the other guests, while Jim just used his glass to steer as he deftly manoeuvred the room as if on one of the motorbikes he used to drive. He sped over to a senator, took a left and braked before one of Washington's grand dames, a sweet-looking old lady with a poisonous tongue. Next he made a difficult turn to speak to the General and his wife.

A shiny-faced man new to Washington was telling her about himself as a straight-backed soldier poured her another glass of champagne.

Susan held her glass with a long white hand and sipped the bubbling liquid. She smoothed her finger over her glass. All around her the voices bubbled up, one after the other. The man's round cheeks look as though they too would at any moment float like balloons up into the air. She thinks of the monumental calm of a bird-eating spider; furry, huge, oddly vulnerable because of her unusually thin outer skeleton. If you dropped her, she'd die. And her poignant red knees at each bend of her eight legs.

'Of course,' he was saying, 'my wife finds all the

travelling trying. You know . . . moving from country to country, finding different dentists, different doctors at each place. It gets tiring, after a while.'

'Of course,' she said, as if understanding utterly.

He moved restlessly from foot to foot and adjusted his tie, a jovial one with red and white stripes, quite daring by Washington standards. A smile tugged up one side of his face, as if trying it on for size. 'One never shows it, naturally. That it's difficult at times.'

She nodded, narrowing her eyes sympathetically. She wondered how Rebecca was, if she was lying awake, her face white in the half darkness.

'And you?' he said, after he had described his last three foreign postings to her. 'Did you have to give up a career to come here with Jim?'

'Not really.'

'Good journalist, Jim. He's much admired. He's making his mark.'

'Really,' she said.

'Did you meet in England? You are English?'

'Oh yes.'

'Jim is from round here?'

'No – he comes from San Francisco.'

'Now,' he said. 'What exactly do you do . . . let me guess . . . an actress . . . or an artist.' He stepped closer to her. He had well-manicured nails.

She nodded. 'An artist.'

Susan noted that Jim was in sudden close conversation with the General, who had a habit of passing on to him excellent defence tips on British strategic defence decisions. Jim naturally knew what was important, or rather what newspapers considered important. It was curious that even this august badger of a general with his straight-backed soldiers for staff had a desire to pass on information to someone who enjoyed it. The desire to gossip is in a way a form of altruism, the same spirit which makes people good hosts.

'My dear!' said the General to another guest, gusting forward, a caricature of a British general.

Dense paintings in golden frames hung on the walls, and fine antique furniture stood with its back to the walls: a little desk, a bookcase, a chair, all in dark wood.

Just as they sat down for dinner, Jim at the other end of the wide mahogany table, a drawerful of cutlery in front of each guest, Phillip entered the room.

A silver candelabra sat in front of her on the glossy, long table. She spread butter on her bread.

Phillip looked round for a moment, as though lost, as though not knowing where he was. Without me. He is lost without me. That's what he used to say. Lost without you.

Susan wanted to leave.

'Who's that woman with Phillip Jordan?' said Susan brightly to the man beside her.

'Sandra. His girlfriend. Sandra. Funny young woman. Pretty. Adores him. Always holding his hand.'

'I see,' said Susan.

Susan saw Sandra giggle and her heart tightened. He doesn't look at me. Look at me. Look at me, she thought.

Phillip turned and raised his eyebrows to acknowledge her presence. His face was thinner than before, a little weary. A tabby cat would lie on the bottom of the bed when they made love, watching with glinting eyes.

'Sometimes,' she told the man beside her, to whom Jim had been talking intently earlier, with that wide-awake look he only sometimes had, 'at these functions, I long to knock over the table, and throw the candlesticks at someone. Do you ever feel like that?'

'Of course, often,' he said.

He was a senator from the south. She couldn't believe he was the Senator Spalding Jim had been talking about. He seemed too wholesome, except he kept disembowelling white bread rolls with his hands and applying layers of butter. Like a child, he left the crust behind. The man sat very close to the table, and tended to grab for things while his wife, who sat near Jim, moved as though she were underwater, reaching out for her glass in a slow impassive motion while her eyes stayed open too wide. At any moment it seemed she might just swim away, one of those see-through fish. Blonde hair lay curled on her head as if it were only this which was keeping her in place on earth; and she had the alarmed air of someone out of their element. She was beautiful too but when Susan had heard her speaking she sounded dull. Her voice had trailed on about her horses. Her eyes were pools of water she didn't want to spill. Jim monopolised the senator's wife.

When Phillip was out, the cats used to watch Susan, and when he was back they rubbed against him and purred too loudly.

'I mean, I know all about good manners,' said Susan and she looked back at Phillip's head and heard her voice begin to sound reckless, as it used to do. She thought of his long limbs and soft tread, and the way he would sometimes make love in a random, lazy way, like a cat washing itself. In those days she'd had long nails, and used to scratch his back.

'I know to pick up my napkin only when the hostess has, and to place it open over my lap and afterwards never to fold it up, but just to put it nonchalantly on the table. I know all these things. I know not to talk too much to the person on my right or my left, and never to be too intimate so that the rest of the table is cut out. I know to start with the outside cutlery and never use one's own knife to take butter. I am aware that I should never cut up a roll . . . one should always break it. I know it is not considered correct to be effusively polite to waiters. And I suppose all this is reassuring. I mean, it's something, isn't it? But I don't know, I don't know if I like rules.'

Susan's black dress dipped low down her front. The senator had crumbs over his mouth, and seemed somehow to have grown in size over the last minutes as his wide shoulders loomed over the table. His eyes were grey pebbles and scanned her bare flesh.

Her memories of what happened that last terrible night had been neatly boxed up. They used only to come out at night, as she slept, and then the figures came back provokingly, terrifyingly, sympathetically. Always there were the three figures: her and Phillip and the German boy. The boy would greet her sometimes in his heavily accented English but his face would be all smashed in like raw meat. Sometimes Phillip would just be standing back, by the window, laughing, the traffic far below, and then he would fall backwards and she would scream, and suddenly she'd be all alone and Phillip's cats would be crawling over her and she would wake up, the bed wet from sweat. But the scenes changed, and sometimes she didn't dream for months and months, and she never thought about her dreams during the day.

But now Phillip had stepped out of the past, out of her dreams, and was here, in Washington, in the place she had been so happy sometimes it had hurt.

'And I know that really you should never take a sip of wine with anything at all in your mouth,' she continued, in her high, clear voice, 'because that can smear the glass and make it look disgusting. You should swallow everything in your mouth, and dab it with a napkin before drinking. Did you know that? There, you did,' she said. She looked at his glass, which was unsmeared, and wanted to run out of the room but she tried to push herself down. Here are my small feet pressed into my kitten-heeled shoes, resting on the floor, and my legs lead up to my black silk dress and on my black silk dress I wear a silver brooch in the shape of a butterfly, and my head is inclined to one side.

Susan clutched at her white napkin.

She drank some more.

'Do you have children?' he said, moving slightly closer to her so she smelt his aftershave. The material of his suit was too thick and she could almost feel it between her hands. Curious how all these desires waited at dark windows, under dark tablecloths, under the thick material of suits while civilised people at civilised parties drank good wine from cut glass which glinted like diamonds.

'You OK?' he said.

She let her smile overflow.

'Of course,' she said.

A portrait of a young boy in a green silk suit, with a dog, a Yorkshire terrier on a lead, gazed down compassionately from above the marble mantelpiece.

Further along the wall was a picture of a bowl of fruit and even the apples and oranges seemed dark, rounded, mournful. And the people, talking, and asking each other about themselves, then turning to the person on the other side. They all seemed to be in shadows, like the fruit, dark and mournful in the sombre room.

'Yes,' she told the senator, 'I have a little girl. But we're trying for another one. And you?' she said.

'Three children. All girls,' he said, and he talked about them a little.

'Your wife, by the way, she's very beautiful. Only she looks terribly sad,' said Susan.

'I don't think she is sad,' he said.

'Why is she so sad?' said Susan.

For ages they all seemed to have been eating tiny lamb cutlets which were tasty but extremely hard work. She had attacked hers from one side then another, and after one particularly driven five-minute attack had emerged with only a half centimetre of meat.

She sighed. 'I haven't the energy,' she said, putting down her knife and fork.

'It does take perseverance.'

'And you? Are you happy?' she said. 'It's difficult to tell, meeting you. You politicians are so good at covering things up, so good at subterfuge.'

'Of course I'm happy,' he said, in a voice which sounded to her like the touch of uncooked pastry, soft and cold.

'What is the matter?' she said quietly. 'There's something the matter, isn't there?' she said.

She saw Jim watching her and the senator, from further down the table, and his eyes were bright.

The Baked Alaska was brought to the table and elicited little murmurs of delight, and she thought, This is the high point of everyone's evening, this folly, this absurd fluffy creation.

She refused the Baked Alaska and then realised she felt sick and stood up, swaying slightly, and stumbled over to Jim. 'Come on,' she said, as Phillip watched her, his grey eyes enclosing her like a blanket.

Jim frowned. 'Susan,' he whispered, 'go back.'

'No. We have to go now.'

'Susan. Look . . .' he said fiercely.

'We have to go,' she said, in a voice which was too loud.

*

'You were sitting next to the senator I'm investigating,' said Jim angrily as they walked to the car. 'Senator Spalding. I needed to talk to him but you dragged me away.'

'Him? Really?'

' "A man can smile and smile and be a villain." You see? I know some literature too. It isn't only Phillip who is good on quotes,' he said, striding forward.

'It seems Senator Spalding may be involved in allowing a drug cartel certain concessions – for instance making sure various little airfields in his state stay open in spite of them contravening safety regulations.'

'Him?'

'That's right ... the charming family man ... helping out the guys who help to lay waste half of Washington.'

They got into the car.

As they waited at traffic lights his hand trawled through his unruly hair and for a moment he looked startled, as if he had momentarily forgotten its presence on his head.

That night, after dropping Susan off, Jim drove to his office at *World News* and worked there until three among the ticker tape from all over the world, some of it pinned in categories on the wall – mentions of the President, mentions of the President's wife, mentions of the various countries or wars. On the top bookshelves were a few unwieldy reference books, clearly seldom opened, and sprawled on a table were some badly bound copies of the magazines, attempts to create something lasting in a job devoted to change.

Amid the snaking piles of ticker tape, various bits of electronic equipment glistened: computers, faxes, gods of the moment. Jim hammered away into his computer, with a brow of Bach, the ballerina fingers of a Margot Fonteyn, as if trying to hit the keys so hard he'd escape from where he was into somewhere more permanent. In the meantime, he rolled up his sleeves, and worked in the empty office, lit by the one artificial light.

He called Jane Meadows around 11.30 to tell her what had happened.

'My wife – Susan – she insisted on leaving,' said Jim crossly.

'Oh dear. That was unfortunate,' said Jane.

Back at home, Susan went up to paint in her studio or study. She was painting in the lilac wings of a grasshopper but couldn't work; the task was too delicate for her tonight. After a while, she left it and went out into the garden where a spider spread out below the fire escape just where the night light brought the little flies. It wasn't a perfect web – though the fine lines which glinted and shimmered in the light made the Golden Gate bridge look like child's play. There was a gap on the display and some flies went through while the spider sat, enormous, unhidden, in the centre, a sandy brown colour, its legs spread out for generations while the strands of its empire tautly braced themselves like hard steel over to the stairs going up. There was nothing soft about the silver web – it was all metal and geometry – but somehow the spider was soft there in the middle, big and lovely and hungry.

Recently, Susan often thought back to her mother's flat. That was safe, with the caretaker at the door, safer than this detached house surrounded by blackness at night, with the windows which rattled.

25

Regally, Ivana approached Susan and Rebecca as they stood behind the hatchback, unpacking Saturday shopping. She glared at the huge bottles of apple juice, immense plastic bottles of milk, vast cereal packets, as though surprised Rebecca and Susan would have to do something like this themselves. Today, in her tailored pink dress, with her Duchess of Windsor face and her tiny body, she seemed unreal, like a nineteenth-century pottery figure.

'Hello, Ivana. We've been shopping!' said Rebecca, a smile all over her face. Resplendent in buttercup yellow shorts, a pink T-shirt she had selected herself and trainers, she seemed to float in the air.

'Ah yes,' said Ivana, squinting slightly as if trying to recall what shopping was. Her white skin was dressed in a gold bangle and her usual collection of rings: a ring with a big turquoise, a ring with three rubies, a silver ring like a snake, a gold wedding ring. She smiled a pink, well-outlined smile at the child.

'We went to the supermarket. It was great!' said Rebecca and slipped her arm through her mother's.

It seemed to Susan that for a moment the smile lapsed.

'Good. How enjoyable,' said Ivana. Then, to Susan, 'By the way, I bumped into your charming friend Phillip at the mall. We had coffee. He sent his regards. He really is so attractive. How did you ever leave him? Even the waitress couldn't stop staring at him. We talked and talked – mostly about Poland. I felt quite homesick by the end.'

'I used to hate shopping, didn't I, Mummy?' said Rebecca. 'But now I like it . . . boy, but I'm hot.'

Ivana kept her eyes on the child and adjusted one of her golden earrings in the shape of a shell.

Adults were often mesmerised by Rebecca because of her radiance, her sense of utter excitement, as though she'd just been formally awarded the whole world for some forgotten achievement, but to children she seemed odd. She ran off to the open door.

The crickets were chatting and Susan noted a huge one resting on the stonework of the house, throwing a shadow, waiting, as all the insects seemed to wait in the heat, as she too at times seemed to be waiting for some unknown event. Only Rebecca never seemed to wait.

'Mummy!' called Rebecca. 'Shall I put them all in the freezer?'

Ivana smiled again and walked away.

Susan and Rebecca brought the rest of the food in, and Rebecca put things away briskly, with her head thrown back, as if she were someone accustomed to making sure items were in the right place. In fact

Rebecca was one of the most untidy people imaginable, and seldom put anything back anywhere, in part because she was far too interested in everything to decide her interest had ended: the drawing paper was always out, the tracing paper, the juggling balls, the jewellery-making set.

She took out the eggs and put them in the special holes in the fridge, as her mother did. She put the cheese in the fridge door, as her mother did. She put the apples in the fridge.

'I much prefer cold apples, don't you?' she said, as her mother had in fact said to her many times before.

All the time, as Rebecca busied herself, there were the cuts on her knees where she had fallen down playing tag, and Susan could still see the child's baby shape: the slight tummy, the little bottom sticking out.

'Where do you want the carrots?' Rebecca asked in the voice of an accomplished new employee.

'In the vegetable rack, please, darling. Thank you,' and she wanted to hug her daughter to her but she knew she couldn't because that would take away all her glory, her sense of her own efficiency, and would suggest an element of pity in her life.

She wanted to tell her she was being a big help but was afraid she'd get the tone wrong and Rebecca would realise she was being patronised. Instead, every now and again, Susan said respectful thank yous.

Susan and Rebecca put away frozen crabs, waffles, maple syrup, peanut butter, three massive steaks, sugary cereals, ice cream, grape-flavoured bubble gum.

'The fridge isn't even crowded,' said Rebecca.

'I do like domestic appliances,' said Susan gaily, swirling off to the sink, her skirt a mass of red and blue.

'Especially the fridge. It's so . . . sad somehow,' said Rebecca. 'The way it just stands there being useful.'

'And leaking. I fear it leaks.'

'Stands there being useful and leaking . . . oh well.' Rebecca spun round, having no time for anything maudlin or depressing. 'I think I'll go outside.' And she strode importantly off.

Susan watched the girl try and fail to stand on her hands. Rebecca's legs kicked up at a paltry 45 degrees.

I could say the other child was for her, and of course that's partly true, thought Susan. But that's not really it. There's an emptiness in my belly, an old, raw longing as old as time, which makes nonsense of tidy equations about time; for this is what time is, in fact, this spinning, desperate, searching need to measure time in generations, in genes, passed on, mutated, carrying time forward in human terms, spinning out into the future, taking the future with them, making the future with them, all expressed in the aching emptiness of a woman's belly.

When Rebecca came in, hot and flushed, Susan wanted to hug her so much that it hurt her; Rebecca saw this particular desperate expression on her mother's face, and she laughed. 'Oh Mummy,' she said, in that competent voice of hers, and ran to her and hugged her.

Later they played chess.

'Mummy,' said Rebecca, as Susan moved her

bishop forward, 'what happened between you and Phillip?'

'That was years ago. Check mate,' said Susan.

That night Susan went round the house as usual, checking and double-checking every window, every lock, keeping the outside world outside.

'So what do you think about the President?' said Ivana, standing too close to Susan. 'Do you think he'll win the next election? Have you seen any more of that handsome man? Phillip . . .'

Susan turned her head away and murmured something acute, something worth saying, something Ivana could think about when she returned home. Ivana gave a little acquisitive smile which sneaked unexpectedly from the side of her pink mouth. Everything about Ivana was charming, from her feet so tiny they were the same size as Rebecca's, to her silky hands, all pervaded by the smell of her, which had some stupid name like Bliss but smelt unexpectedly of tragedy, of something far off and sad and rather more sturdy than anyone would have connected with the apparently pleasantly superficial Ivana.

After lending Ivana a soufflé dish, Susan dragged herself round the house, moving from room to room, looking out at the haze outside, followed around by the mirrors which caught her here and there.

All our lives we look at videos, at photographs. Women are not vain, but anxious that they'll die without ever having seen themselves.

When Ivana had been round, it always took a long time for the house to quieten down. Everywhere Ivana's voice seemed to be echoing, and the blue velvet rocking chair where Ivana liked to sit seemed especially noisy, roaring with solicitude. Susan went and silenced its creaking, holding it until it stopped.

The house had always been totally on Susan's side, waiting since being built to look after her, shield her from the sun, provide her with solace and space, allow her a sense of nature surging all around her as the huge trees in the garden grabbed at the sky and the dark ivy contorted itself at the paned window of the bedroom, pressing to get in.

But now it seemed Ivana – and the whole world of other well-meaning people – had supporters within the house. The chairs seemed to welcome Ivana, sink back so she could flutter comfortably into them, and even the coffee table which was always unaccountably too far from the sofa for Susan to put her coffee on, even that seemed amiably to move close to Ivana so she had no trouble resting her glass of milk on it, or the camomile tea she especially brought round. 'I think it's so important to look after the body,' she would say, screwing up her eyes with their silver eyeshadow as she always did when she thought she was saying something particularly sincere.

Increasingly, Ivana screwed up her eyes. Increasingly, she talked about herself. Emboldened perhaps by the welcoming quality of the furniture, she even began to confide in Susan about her past, to Susan's wide-eyed horror, for the confidences were like unwanted presents, things to sit in cupboards and make the recipient uneasy as time went by.

'Of course,' said Ivana, looking down at her perfectly manicured nails on her white doll's hands. She had the mannerisms of a pretty young woman – the shy glance to the ground, the touching of the hair, the beguiling tilt of the head – although she was actually a good few years older than Susan. 'My mother left my father when I was two. That is the tragedy of my life. And she left me too. I think that is why . . . you know . . . I seek for happiness. You – you come from a stable family; happiness is yours by right, you feel. I have to find it.'

She glanced at the picture of a Madonna on the wall.

'Your paintings, your carpets, they make clear someone who knows what content is. I find that wonderful. Could I have a glass of milk?'

Susan went out into the garden and tended the rose garden. She kept looking round, as though she were being watched.

She had noted how Ivana was always popping out like a malfunctioning weather lady whenever the widowed man from down the road went by.

In the *Roget's Thesaurus* she read the words under the bold title: '**Safety**: safety, safeness, security, surety . . . invulnerability, impregnability, immunity, charmed life, safe distance, wide berth . . .' Next she looked up love. '**Love**: love, affection, friendship, charity, Eros; agapism, true love, real thing; mother love, baby-worship; possessiveness.'

To fight back, Susan spent time organising her

house, as if preparing a fortress for a siege. She called in her builder to put new white countertops in the kitchen to replace the 1950s red ones. She called in Blane's windows to repair the ill-fitting windows . . . a ginger-haired man with a can of oil and an old blue bag full of window fitments came round and spent hours adjusting and shaking his head. 'Victims of the weather,' he said, whenever she went by, 'victims of the weather.'

Susan stood at the door, her hands on her hips, thinking, This is all fine, and Ivana watched her from the windows.

Susan changed the locks too, and had an alarm system put in so wherever she walked in the house red warning lights winked at her.

The phone kept ringing but when she answered it there was nobody there.

She kept not being able to find her clothes. A shirt put down in one place turned up in another. The books she was sure she'd placed in order – Swift, Tolkien, Tolstoy – were shifted around so that Tolstoy was before Tolkien. When she mentioned it to Jim, he just shrugged.

'It would be great to have another baby,' said Susan, standing in Jim's study while he sat at his desk, facing the street, where the little boy opposite was practising baseball with his father.

'Maybe we really should return to England,' said Jim.

'Another baby. Something intense,' she said.

'I always loved England anyway.'

'Maybe it would be a boy.'

'At least the summers aren't baking in England,' he said.

'We could call it after your father. Joseph.'

'England might be good for Rebecca's education.'

'It's odd the way I don't get pregnant. There's nothing wrong, they say. I suppose we'll have to try IVF again. Or maybe adoption is right.'

'Rebecca likes England. She finds it a manageable size.'

'Another IVF might do it. By the way, you've put out more photographs of me,' she said.

26

Wherever Susan went, Jim waylaid her – while she was cooking, while she was out in the garden, while she was trying to paint up in her studio with the light falling from above on her white skin.

'You look different. You're wearing brighter clothes,' he said.

'Oh dear,' she said, as he kissed the back of her neck, 'bright colours attract predators.'

Susan was painting a Red Admiral butterfly – and her clothes were the colours of a butterfly too, reds and browns – leaning over the thick vellum paper, paintbrush in hand, the light spilling onto her paper.

They made love on the rough rug there, in the studio, beneath the skylight.

Her hair fanned out around her and he ran a finger over her breast.

Sometimes Susan convinced herself she had imagined the last crazy evening with Phillip – that it had all been part of her breakdown, rather than the cause of it. She turned the gold band of her wedding ring.

'I just want life to continue as it is,' she said, closing her eyes, feeling him watch the flicker of her eyelids, 'that's all. Just day after day as it is ... Happiness is wanting to be nowhere but where you are at this precise moment. I'm happy.'

He didn't stop watching her, as if she were about to open the curtains to show something he needed to see. Suddenly, he'd sprung up, and in seconds was in the bathroom off the studio, splashing his face with water.

Susan checked her watch. It was two forty-five – time to collect Rebecca from school, which finished at three. She pinned stray scraps of hair back in her bun. Recently she had begun to grow more untidy.

This was the best part of the day. She liked the walk underneath the tall trees by the side of a slight embankment where grass grew wild. Next she crossed over Wisconsin Avenue, waiting for a gap in the fast-flying cars, then running fast and landing on the other side. In front of her was a grass basketball court and as she continued her walk she passed a little red clapboard house, which was the town hall of the area.

Susan crossed the scraggy playing fields, with the grass parched from the Washington heat, to where Rebecca would be waiting for her.

*

Sometimes when Susan drew at her desk in the evening, the creatures from out there, in darkness, seemed to want to get into the house, to be with her. Ghostly moths, bright insects, hovering creatures with innumerable legs, creatures who had come here from the beginning of life, long before mammals, aeons before man, were here banging at her window, visitors from complex societies with complex rules, apparently attracted to the recent settlers on this old marshland who erect their marble monuments.

She sharpened her pencil. She liked to work with a pencil because of the soft texture but also because it was easy to rub out.

We humans think we have such control over our lives but really we too are ruled more by instinct than intellect – the smell of an old lover, the look in someone's eyes, the need to rest, sleep, have sex, have a baby.

She took down one of her trays and in it lay a yellow butterfly, with black round the edge of its wings. As she stared at it she could almost hear its wings, and she began to paint it.

Later, in her blood-red shirt and black trousers, with gold bracelets climbing up her arm, her feet bare on the scarred wooden floor, she climbed down the stairs into the drawing room and looked out into the street. She ran her hand over the soft down of her arm.

She thought, Phillip is out there, out in the street now, looking up at the house, and maybe he's about to cross the road and come up to the door and in a moment he'll be ringing the doorbell.

But no one came.

She watched Ivana walk by, with her dog.

27

'You look pretty peculiar,' said Susan's friend Carol, speaking in her warm southern drawl but looking as cool as milk, with her fawn trousers creased sharply, her pearl earrings, her shirt with tiny round buttons, each one carefully done up. Carol tapped on the table with her pen.

'I saw Phillip at a dinner a while ago,' said Susan. 'He arrived late. I left early. But I was still shaken afterwards. I'd drunk a bit too much. Jim was angry with me.'

'Has he contacted you? Phillip?'

'Not really.'

'Would you like him to?'

'No . . . I don't think so,' said Susan. 'But Jim insists we must all have dinner in a few days – to clear the air, he says. I don't know why I'm going along with it.'

'Don't you?' said Carol.

Susan tore at a piece of bread which the waiter had zestfully told them was made of walnut and cranberries. Susan had scowled at him. The straps of her purple cotton dress kept slipping off her shoulders and she kept pushing them back.

Carol had twin girls about Rebecca's age who were clones of Carol: neat, beautiful children with tiny feet, an advanced dress sense and round faces like sunflowers. Susan called them the haiku children, they were so perfect. Carol managed them, and her job on a New York fashion magazine, immaculately, as if she had been aiming for this all her life, although she was trained as a psychotherapist.

'They're usually quick,' said Carol, who had chosen the café – which was called a café but was really rather an expensive restaurant.

'I used to think,' said Susan, 'that there was a place for everyone. You know – that there was the right place for each individual to live, somewhere in the world. I mean, it might be a remote Tibetan village or it could be Scunthorpe but it was all a matter of just finding the right place, and you'd be happy. It was a silly little theory, really. I never propounded it much but I believed it. I always thought that all that blue bird of happiness stuff was nonsense – you know, that you can search the whole world for happiness but if it isn't in you, you won't find it, and that it's probably waiting for you at home anyway. I still think that Maeterlinck story has a lot to answer for. It makes people stay put. But in fact those who are miserable in Surrey might be happy in Sydney. And I thought that Washington DC – or rather Chevy Chase village – was my place, that it had been waiting for me forever and that if I'd never found it I'd never have been completely happy. But now I wonder . . .'

'It's certainly not my place,' said Carol.

'Paris would suit you,' said Susan. 'New York's too crass for you.'

On the coffee table in Carol's New York apartment were just one or two beautiful books and a glass vase which contained the right number and shape of twigs and flowers.

'It's not so easy to change lives. Besides, I like New York. Are you quite sure you're OK?'

Carol offered Susan a quick smile. It was Carol's intactness which attracted Susan; she seemed perfectly in control of her environment yet open to and interested in the lack of control of others.

'I'm sleeping badly. Getting bad dreams,' said Susan. 'You know, over Phillip, the old boyfriend . . .' Susan took another sip of wine. Carol sipped at a glass of carefully selected water.

'Do the different waters really taste so different?' said Susan.

'Oh yes,' said Carol, studying the menu, then looking up questioningly.

A sprightly waiter turned up behind Carol and the two women quickly consulted their menus, and ordered.

'I'll have another glass of wine and a Caesar salad,' said Susan.

Carol gave a light, disapproving cough.

'I'm just not that hungry today,' said Susan.

Carol ordered some complexly minimalist lunch.

'You realise,' said Carol to Susan after ordering,

'that all love relationships, even ones based entirely in the present, involve misrecognition? You don't see the people as they are and they don't see you. So really you're never in love with the person you're in love with. You're in love with the past or the future or some idea of the other person.

'You know,' Carol leant forward, her voice lowered, 'a few years ago an old boyfriend from my first year at college turned up at the magazine in New York to see me. He was married with four children, said he'd made some awful mistakes in his life and the worst one was letting me go. That gave me bad dreams.'

Susan tore apart a piece of bread.

'In the past,' continued Carol, 'I don't think he even liked me particularly – he was gorgeous and a little irresponsible, while I was sensible, and he found me over-serious. But now he wants someone serious. His pretty, frivolous wife spends all his money and never thinks, so he rifles through his mental files of his past and comes up with me as the person he's always loved. After all, with four children under ten he can hardly go searching through nightclubs for the woman of his dreams, can he? Not with the pressures of work and a mortgage and finding time to play with the children? And you know what he said, as an excuse, when he put his hand round my waist after just one drink – he said that he felt unfaithful fucking his wife rather than me, the great love of his life whom he met first!'

'Ridiculous,' said Susan.

'You see,' said Carol, 'until the late twenties or thirties, life really is not so romantic. But those who have just stumbled out of their twenties or thirties look up in horror at their empty thirties or forties. After that, the real romance in marriage or out of it begins. It's no longer, "Let's have fun together", it's: "Will you make shape of this life of mine?" and "Will you hold my hand through the darkness?" and "Will you and I die together? If we can't have a baby together, at least we can die together . . . it's the next big event, after all." '

They could hear the young bald-headed waiter at another table repeating his list of specials, mostly involving salsas and fish, with too much emphasis on the wrong things. 'The tuna is *delicately* grilled and suffused with a warm raspberry *sauce* liberally flecked with blanched almonds and *served* with a grape salsa and cornbread lightly heated . . .'

'I told the old boyfriend of mine,' said Carol, 'that I was just a figment of his imagination, when he'd finished his avowals of love, but he just squinted and put his hand on my knee rather than my waist. "You were always wonderfully complicated," he said. He used to loathe it when I said that kind of thing in the past. It really pissed him off. I think it was why he left me.'

'I can see that,' said Susan, nodding thanks to the waiter who brought her another glass of wine.

Carol coughed again, and gesticulated to the waiter that she too would like a glass of wine.

'Did you know that Stanley Spencer wrote to his

lover, Hilda, for nine years after she died?' said Carol. 'Strictly speaking, the actual lover is unnecessary, a physical encumbrance. It is one's own love one is addressing. You have to realise that your love—'

Susan frowned, and shook her head, picking up her wine glass.

'. . . or feelings for this guy,' continued Carol, 'are a fantasy. It is yourself you are haunted by – yourself as you were when you knew him. He is, as I said, a figment of your imagination, as all lovers are. I mean, he hasn't even approached you, and look at you.'

'I've seen him in a bookshop, at a party. Then he was at the same dinner.'

'So? That's Washington.'

'He stayed the night.'

'But you told me that he left before you got up.'

'Look, I'm not haunted by him,' said Susan.

'Susan,' said Carol, leaning forward, 'you should talk to Jim properly about it. Tell him exactly what happened.'

'I can't do that,' said Susan. 'I can't talk to Jim about it. He . . . he's very matter of fact . . . in some ways . . . very, I don't know, innocent. It's what I like about him. His innocence.' She looked away, at the picture of a spiky cactus on the wall to her left.

'I still think you should have a proper talk with him.'

'He's so busy at the moment. He's onto some amazing story. He wouldn't want to listen . . . Carol,' said Susan, as the Caesar salad was put before her with a flourish, 'do you think . . . Phillip . . . might be here just by chance? He's a journalist.'

'Washington is where journalists work. There's probably nothing else to it. Look, you should take a break.'

'Difficult to take a break from yourself,' said Susan.

'Oh, a change of place. You're probably getting things out of proportion. There's something else, isn't there? I mean, this isn't just about some old love affair.'

'What?'

'What is it you dream about?' said Carol.

'All kinds of things,' said Susan.

'You should cancel the dinner,' said Carol.

'No. It's too late now,' said Susan.

That evening Rebecca rubbed away at the frown mark beginning to appear on her mother's forehead, as if straightening out a crease in a piece of paper. And she kissed the forehead, a mother kissing a child, and it seemed to Susan that Rebecca had only ever pretended to be a child.

That afternoon the postman had brought Susan a brown envelope containing a bag of what seemed to be dry bones, and a letter in spidery writing.

'It's from Martha. You know, they're in China,' said Susan, as she spread it out on the kitchen table. 'She says it's angelica root and, if slowly cooked and eaten, it massively increases the chance of becoming pregnant.'

'I wish you would have another child,' said Rebecca.

'Yes.'

'I'd like a bright yellow dress,' said Rebecca thoughtfully. 'Really bright. You know, I'm not going to have children when I'm grown up. I'm going to be free – and maybe be a dress designer.'

28

Up in her bedroom, at her card table, Ivana Fischer turned over a queen, then a jack, then a king. She laid out the royal cards with her porcelain hands. Her diamond engagement ring glittered. The walls of the bedroom pressed in on her; dark turquoise dotted with paintings in golden frames, European pictures of fruits and flowers. One featured a black fly, as delicately depicted as the pink rose on which it sat. The paintings were darkly complicated affairs, part of a European tradition of despair.

The bedcover lay perfectly straight, without a ripple, over the bed. The sides hung neatly down.

There was very little on view in the room except for the paintings, her silver brush set, and his cufflink box.

Ivana stood up and went again to the window. Beside her Susan and Jim's huge house spread itself out, with its wide wild garden and the shout of a child's voice.

29

Rebecca creeps out down to the bottom of the garden where a spider makes a web, and Rebecca watches her somersaults in the geometry of ropes. The web gleams in the light from the windows.

Rebecca hoped nothing would happen to the web after all the spider's work.

There is a shiver of wind in the air, and Rebecca is afraid it will rain tonight and damage the web, and the spider has worked so hard on it, adjusting all the weight loads with such skill, measuring each radius meticulously, until she has a perfect web, a silver masterpiece of construction.

But these things are so easily damaged, thinks Rebecca as she watches the agile spider take up its position at the centre. There are so many things that could harm it – wind, rain, time.

30

The dinner with Phillip passed in a kind of dream. Susan and Jim arrived first at the cramped, crowded crab restaurant, where the waiter brusquely dumped some newspaper on their table and spread it out quickly. Then he confiscated their salt cellar as if he'd found schoolboys with a catapult.

'What'll you have?' the waiter demanded, looking over his shoulder as though he hadn't really got time to take their order, and was doing them a favour even asking them for it. He wiped his hands on his white apron.

The newspaper-covered tables all around were graveyards of crabs, with broken claws, cracked bodies, stray bits of flesh soaking into the newspaper, darkening it in patches as people slouched very close to the table and used their hands to tear apart the bodies. Most people were drinking beers, but a few had cheap white wine. The air conditioning whirled hopelessly in the background.

'We'll have a dozen crabs. Our friends will be here soon.'

Susan stared at the newspaper and read that a knife-wielding man in Capitol Heights, quite near the White House, had been slain by police.

'I was on Long Island once, years ago, and there were dead hermit crabs all over the beach,' said Susan.

She read that a sixteen-year-old had been killed and an eighteen-year-old seriously wounded in a drive-by shooting in the Edgewood district of north-east Washington. 'The two boys were standing in front of a house when a late-model station wagon approached and a gunman fired several rounds from a semi-automatic weapon. Officers who responded to the reports of gunfire found the two lying on the sidewalk.'

'I used to catch crabs as a child,' said Jim, 'with a net, at a beach house, and they frightened me when they escaped and scurried over the deck. It was their habit of walking sideways I found most alarming.'

Susan thought of Rebecca lying in her bed, tossing and turning, dreaming in-between kinds of dreams, neither those of childhood nor adulthood.

A man over the other side of the restaurant took up his hammer and hit his crab shell, and it split nearly apart, and he looked at Susan intently. She turned away from his glance.

Phillip strode in, all smiles, still with short, dark curls and a strong nose worthy of a Roman coin. He shook her hand vigorously.

'Great to see you! You look great!'

She knew she had turned white – but he was fine, relaxed, improved by time, seemingly a well-balanced individual.

Phillip had the same slow-motion movements as before. Susan tried not to look at him. Time changes people, she told herself. He is not the person he was. But even when he took apart the crab, he didn't tug as Jim tugged but slowly drew the legs from the body as if gently prying something from a child.

Whenever she glanced at him, his tongue seemed to be licking his lips.

She saw in her mind the grey Persian cat's little tongue licking at the blood which was soaking into the grey carpet.

He dug into the crab with a sharp knife and she thought how skilled he was with the knife.

'You have to realise that your feelings for this guy are a fantasy,' her friend Carol had said. 'It is yourself you are haunted by – yourself as you were when you knew him. He is a figment of your imagination, as all lovers are.'

Throughout the meal, as they all pulled at the legs of the crabs, she thought of the tiny baby she'd aborted. Phillip glanced at her every now and again. But she could hardly see him – he was so far back in the past, in clouds of regret and lost hope and fear.

Lips like hell, he used to say. I am lost in them. Save me.

Of course she was sure the German boy had been fine afterwards. Perhaps she would ask Phillip if the boy had been OK. Perhaps everything was fine, had always been fine.

Phillip's hands were the same, white puppet shapes, expressing some kind of despair as he grabbed the tumbler of wine and drank from it, his lips wet. I was a fool to turn up here, the flesh of crabs everywhere. Death, that's what I fear.

Face my fears, they say. So here I am, facing my fears – this tall man with the thin lips and quick smiles, as if grabbing them back the minute they escape, and the bones of his face. I know them all. All the shadows of his skin. He's wearing a white shirt and tie.

Did it take him long, to decide what to wear today? Did he put on that tie, especially for me? Am I imagining the sweat on his pale forehead, the way the fingers of his right hand tap on the table, the emptiness at the back of his eyes?

Sandra sat bouncily on the chair.

'It's so peaceful in Washington,' she said. 'I love it. But Phillip – well,' and she leant forward towards Susan, 'he's a little uneasy. Jumpy. He's been used to covering wars you see in Africa and the Middle East. I suppose it seems tame.'

He dissected the crab with expert movements, and she thought of her dissecting knife up in her attic studio. She still had to cut up the occasional insect for her diagrams and drawings.

'Rubbish,' said Phillip, laughing gaily, covering Sandra's hand with his as if covering her mouth. (Afterwards Jim said, 'Did you see how he kept touching her? They must be so in love.') 'It's a great place.'

Susan went off and was sick in the toilet and when she came out Phillip was standing there, in the hallway, and he put his hand on her bare arm.

'OK?' he said, and her body started to shake.

When she sat down, Susan said, 'I feel ill. Can we go?'

'Of course,' said Jim.

'You see?' said Jim, in the car driving back after the dinner. 'He's perfectly pleasant. Sandra did all the talking. Did you notice?'

'Yes,' said Susan.

Jim's hand lay on her knee like a crab.

'It was nothing. I told you. He's nothing,' said Jim.

'It's the past,' said Susan. 'The problem is he exists in the past. That's where I see him.'

Susan curled herself up tight in bed, an ammonite, round and round.

'He adores Sandra,' said Jim. 'You can see it.'

'No, he doesn't adore her,' she murmured. 'He doesn't even like her. I know what he's like when he adores someone.'

'Look, Susan.'

'She does what she's told, that's all. He wants her around for that reason. You watch. He'll drain the life from her – day by day. He'll enjoy that. It's what he wanted to do to me. But I got out.'

'She seems happy enough.'

'Nervy. She's nervy,' said Susan. 'As though all this isn't going to last, as though she's afraid.'

31

It was a hot Washington night and Susan's skin clung tightly over the bones of her skull as, inside her skull, thoughts rushed from side to side as if trying to get out. How neatly the skin fitted and yet how she hated it; it encased you, held you in, held you down – the violence of cracked glass. She had become that selfless, maternal person she feared. Maybe it waited for every woman.

She moved her hand to a cool place in the hot pillow but there wasn't anywhere cool. She thought about the gun lying in the cool metal tin up in the attic, its barrel black and shiny.

Sometimes, a long time ago, when she had been in hospital, after the fight between the boy and Phillip, she had wanted to tear off her skin, leave it behind like one of her insects.

The long graceful hand was knotted now into clenched fists as she turned away from Jim's body which lay splayed out beside her as if dropped from a great height. The skin of her lower arms, brown and freckled from too much sun, leading to the ugly mechanism of the elbow, a well-designed but aesthetically unappealing contraption, a cheap Angle-poise. And the breasts, so adored by Rebecca, and admired by Jim – how she hated it all, the straitjacket in which she lived.

Outside the leaves rose up boundless into the sky and the country club behind them spread out. The things in the room – the chest of drawers stoically standing there, its whole body heavy on the floor, the dressing table, the mirror – the whole horrible weight of possessions taking her down.

In hospital she had thought about taking her skin off with a knife. She closed her eyes tightly. But that was a long time ago. She was fine now. The only reason she was disturbed now was just stress over wanting another baby, and then Phillip coming back. That's all it was. She knew if she'd had another baby he wouldn't have turned up here. Phillip knew all about her. Maybe he'd always known all about her. Maybe he'd been following her all those times she had felt he was. Just because when she looked round there had been no one there it didn't mean he hadn't been there. Maybe he had been watching her as she undressed. She touched the skin of her thigh and it felt hot.

And the house too, how heavily that stood on the ground – spread out wide, all its brick, its stone, its roof, weighing down. The atomic physicist, Dr Stephens, who lived here before had got rid of the weight of his life with just one shot. One shot and, like a human cannonball, he was off, into the clear air, leaving his body behind.

It had plagued her, this body – so lusted after,

adored for its pale skin over fine bones. 'I could crack your bones so easily,' Phillip had said.

Jim too, with his humour, his easiness, he kept her trapped here.

In hospital the room had been white and the sheets were too, and the whole place had had a clarity and cleanliness except at night when thoughts tormented her and she occasionally would believe her head was a cage full of something, but she didn't know what. It had got so tiring, being her day after day. If only, she had thought, I could be someone else for a day or two, and at the same time had known this was part of her craziness, this desire to step out of the body and personality she'd been given: the knees, with the childish scars intact – the white mark left by the bicycle accident, the time she fell on glass and cut herself; it was all there, the days of her life, etched even on her knees.

A fly buzzed in a corner of the room.

She sighed.

He had always wanted to possess her, to pin her down.

In London one night Phillip had taken her up to the roof garden of his flat and gestured towards the streets below, with the houses and the necklaces of street lamps, as if offering her it all. She went to the edge of the roof garden, just a little brick wall.

'You should build up the wall. It's dangerous,' she said, and was aware of a sudden sensation of sickness. But a pale green, tiny insect landed on her arm, and its antennae moved around infinitesimally and she was comforted.

He would come and see her as she sat at her desk at the Natural History Museum, where she was working in rooms smelling of camphor used for preserving the insects. She would sit, making notes, squinting at the creatures.

'One of the guardians of the dead,' he said. 'Would you like to be preserved like this?'

'Phillip,' she said, 'I really must work.' She checked her watch, and turned her bracelet round and round. Her overall was green, the colour of the walls and the metal filing cabinets which stored the stacked-up insects.

He whispered in her ear as the other workers pretended not to see them. 'I'd like you preserved like this,' he said. 'Beautiful. With your yellow and black wings – perfect.'

He ran his fingers over the skin of her bare hand as she closed her eyes. 'I'd better go,' he said.

'Yes, you really should,' she said.

At night as she lay in bed the blackness pressed against the window, filling in every corner of every pane, as if there really was no way out, just as the windows had watched her all last night.

Sometimes Phillip cried out in the night.

It seemed that the night was there, waiting to grab them, both of them, as they slept in the high flat overlooking the endlessly busy streets.

A moth would flutter over their bed night after night and its soft wings soothed her. A moth's breath – the comfort of the delicate, the refined, so different from their clumsy passion.

There were moments when it all seemed fine –

when she trailed her fingertips over the palm of his hand and noted the lines, the paths they took, the detail in the pores of his skin. Sometimes when he cooked for her some gargantuan meal, their life together was pleasurable in a simple, ordinary way. And her meals, complex, detailed meals from Indonesian or Thai menus with eight courses and spices and the perfect positioning of the ingredients on the plate, they were good times too, watched by the pictures on the wall, the books in the library.

He didn't like her collection of insects.

'They're ghosts,' he said, 'ghosts of the dead.'

'Nonsense,' she said, curling up one of her lettuce leaves soaked in spicy sauce for the Thai meal she was preparing. She laughed, her laugh like silver, and he was watching her as he was always watching her, almost as though he were afraid of her.

She moved to the cupboard and took down the plates, beautiful fine china plates she had bought from an auction, and touched the white surface of one. Carefully, she arranged the plates on the table.

She liked to see his rows of shabby tweed suits in the wardrobe, where some of the moths came from. He picked them up in junk shops but on him they looked terrific. He either wore the suits just as suits or the jackets with jeans. Sometimes he found things in the pockets of the jackets – a handkerchief, once a dried pressed rose, once a ticket for entry to Hampton Court Palace. Other people's lives and pockets.

She watched as he cut through a black-skinned avocado with a knife and scooped out the centre with a spoon. 'Do you want it?' he said, and the taste when she took it in her mouth, looking up into his face, was complex and bewildering.

Even bread, and the texture of bread, was different in his presence. Everything became exaggerated – the feel of the rough edge of a country loaf, the sensation as her hand pulled at a bit until finally the hard crust broke off and she touched the soft centre and ate it, and her senses couldn't believe the pleasure in ordinary things.

For all her life her pleasures had by and large been intellectual ones with brief spurts of hedonism. This day after day, exhausting, enduring hedonism with Phillip was more than she could bear. Yet her present joy in the physical world she now knew had partly been inspired by Phillip all those years ago. Now she had pleasure in taking in the washing from the drier and touching the textures of the cotton, the wool, in pulling weeds from the moist earth, sometimes with the little albino root left behind, in touching the satin of Rebecca's cheek. It was all part of the same passion.

At night in the past with Phillip she would dream of the coolness of filing cabinets, of cold metal closing firmly, of the pleasures of edges, of things being complete, of a firm shut of a cabinet door at the end of the day. Right angles, straight lines, the satisfying push of steel against steel, the lock of a key.

'You're so fragile,' Phillip said one evening. 'The way your bones are so fragile . . . I could snap them so easily,' he said, running his hand up her arm and to her neck.

'Look, Phillip . . . I really . . .'

She was lying with her clothes on, a skirt and tight top.

They were lying on the leather sofa.

'What is it, baby? What is it?' he said.

'Phillip . . .'

'You don't like my hands round your neck?'

'No, actually. I don't.'

' "Actually" – so ladylike in spite of your upbringing in a council flat in south Wimbledon.'

'Stop it,' she said.

'Sometimes I wish I'd never seen you at that party – your cool green eyes were like floodlights, and they blinded me. I should have stayed with Janet. I understood her.'

'Look, I need a pee, let me go.'

'Pee then.'

'Stop it, Phillip, I said stop it, take your hands from my throat.'

She closed her eyes. An old Stones record was pounding in the background. A moth was circling round and round them as one hand caressed between her legs and the other held her throat.

She began to fight him off but he was stronger than she was and she could hardly breathe.

The next morning she stood at the bottom of the stairs as she tried to leave. In those days she didn't wear neat suits but more flamboyant clothes and today she wore a purple and red dress dotted with purple and red waterlilies, like bruises, and her hair was longer then, over her shoulders and not cropped tight.

He had looked down from above as she left.

She had only got a few steps away from the house, through the people with their food shopping, by a young girl with her baby, past a shoe shop and an antique shop, when she found she had to go back to him.

When she returned he was still waiting at the top of the stairs and he put out his arms to her, and his face was gentle.

She should have known better. It was just that his skin was so hot to the touch and soft as broken promises. And the way he stood, always leaning to one side, as if somehow he were some speech mark as yet uninvented, something suggesting a certain irony, comedy, a way of not taking anything seriously.

A few days later Phillip had spoken to an aunt who was sick in hospital with some wasting illness no one understood, so maybe that was why this time the sex was rougher than usual and went over some kind of threshold. 'I'm leaving you. This time I really am,' she said that night.

'Shhh,' he said, as if she were a child. 'I love you,' kissing her with those warm lips of his.

The next day while he was at work, she packed up her bags, and she called a taxi and she left for a hotel. But as she sat in the hotel room she knew she had to go back to say goodbye.

He was waiting for her on the sofa, and jumped up.

'I knew you'd come back!'

She shook her head, one hand in her pocket, feeling the crisp linen of her white handkerchief.

'Darling. I'm sorry. It was just . . .' He ran his fingers through his hair.

She continued to shake her head.

'You just came to say goodbye, did you?'

She nodded.

'You took some of your books. Oh Susan . . . really . . . look.' His voice sounded so young and boyish. 'We have so much to do together. You can't walk out on me like this. I know I can be moody. But I'll be better now . . . really.'

He jumped up and went over and put his arm round her.

'Let's get out of here. Let's go up on the roof.'

She let him lead her up, through the little door which led to a small conservatory covered over with glass.

He'd planted all the flowers up there, on the roof, and they were all white, and there was a fountain and pond in the middle. She used to go up there early when it was frosty and see the frost cling to the plants. His face was white too, and nervous.

'I think you'll always be OK,' he said, picking a dead rose. 'You're strong.'

'No.'

'Yes,' he said, taking her arm, and he squeezed her bare arm.

'No,' she said.

'The fortune teller told me – he told me about a high place and a death. One of us. He wouldn't say which one. Maybe he didn't know.'

He was holding her arm so hard that it hurt.

Below them, in the darkness, the traffic interwove the streets with their restaurants crowded with people smoking and kissing and flirting and it seemed to her that she and Phillip should be down there too, people seen from a distance, talking at a small round table, a vase in the middle containing a few white spring flowers.

She and Phillip should be far away living a proper life together and the people here on the London rooftop among the white flowers and the smell of lavender were the other part of them, the part she didn't want to be.

'Don't you think you should move from this place?' she said. 'The rock-star roof garden bit is a little passé.'

He gripped her arm tighter. There was grey at either side of his hair, and it looked almost silver in the moonlight.

'You really are trying to get out, aren't you?' he said.

She nodded. A slight breeze mixed honeysuckle with lavender.

The smoke from the cigarette in her free hand trailed up, curving like a staircase, through the night air.

He took the cigarette from her, and pressed the lighted end hard into the palm of her hand, and she kicked him and they began to fight, and as they fought she realised he was dragging her to the edge of the roof garden.

She screamed. He stopped.

'I was just joking,' he said. He held her to him and

she could hear his heart pounding. 'Just fooling around.'

All the while, up on the roof garden, the fountain continued to play, and the shadow fish inside the pond beneath continued to dart up to the surface to gasp oxygen.

It was a month or so later, when he was away, that she met the young German boy. But she couldn't think about that. She didn't want to.

It was curious but whenever she had tried to talk to Phillip about the incident on the roof garden he looked puzzled, as if it had never even happened.

32

At the office Jim behaved with even more vigour than usual. His hand movements were legendary – it was never enough to tell a story; it had to be accompanied by enough hand movements to challenge an Indian god. The main office of the magazine was in New York but this didn't stop him turning his office in downtown Washington into one of the town's meeting places. Other journalists and contacts dropped in all the time, and the long-suffering assistant had to provide constant coffee.

Like most journalists, Jim found it hard to keep secrets. Although he hungered to make this a substantial enough story to hammer his name into the statue of eternity, or whatever passes as eternity, he was constantly tempted to tell other people all about it. Occasionally he had to leave the room and hide in the men's room to escape the urge to divulge everything he had learnt from Jane Meadows the night before.

'Do you know that Jane Meadows made love on the senator's desk?' – he heard the words ringing in his head as his friend Brian slopped into the room, hands in his pockets, low-slung like an orang-utan. The guy needed cheering up, and he knew that such a piece of news would turn Brian instantly from an orang-utan on a bad day to a bouncy young man of the world, eyes alive with interest and humour. It was the joke of it all that appealed to journalists, the whole ridiculous joke, which was somehow at odds with huge worthy tomes written by high-minded writers.

Brian fingered a piece of paper on Jim's desk. 'Anything new?' he said glumly in a voice which seemed to have been dredged from the bottom of the earth.

'No. Just the usual stuff. You know. Decline and fall.' Jim spread a smile like a picnic over his face and Brian squinted at him suspiciously.

'You hiding anything? I've thought for a few days you seem a bit unusual. Kind of spring to your step.' He grubbed around in the bottom of an ashtray and found a stub, which he proceeded to light. 'I know you always bound around like someone who's never been able to get off your fucking trampoline. But . . . you're even more like that . . . and you keep opening up your eyes like cat flaps.' He wrinkled his face in distaste. 'Your vast hopefulness really, truly, gets me down, particularly when I think there might be something behind it. Come on,' he said, moving closer to Jim, 'you can trust me . . .'

The words: 'Senator Spalding – that fat, amiable senator – is involved in one of the biggest drug organisations in Washington, and the President might be implicated' spun giddily around Jim's head while he attempted to subdue them with a bumpy smile. Brian moved even closer as though trying to hear Jim's inner thoughts.

'I don't know what you're talking about, Brian.'

'You know, you get all the best stories because you're so fucking nice. Fucking nice. Who could dislike you? I mean . . .' – he stubbed out his cigarette – 'even I like you and I like no one. I was educated not to like anyone. But I sort of like you. You're not a cunning bastard like the rest of them. You're open. Aren't you?' he continued, lowering his brow. 'What is it, Jim? What have you got? Shall we have a drink?' Brian glared out at the day. 'Looks a great day. We could go for a walk. God, I need a break. We all need breaks. In this town no one keeps anything to themselves, you know. It's not done. You know that. I know you're American and I'm British but you do know that, don't you?'

Brian kicked at the desk a few times.

'You've been seen with that Jane Meadows a few times. Anything going on?'

'She's a friend,' said Jim.

'Sure. We all have time for friends. All of us. You've been seen together a few times. Better take care. Your wife – that Susan – she's attractive. You don't want to lose her.'

'Brian, I should like to make clear there is no question . . .' said Jim, opening out his hands as if displaying a book available to be read.

Brian turned round the calendar so the month was upside down, and gave a grim little curl of the mouth.

'Look, we're working with ephemera here; nothing of any lasting consequence. It's not worth getting damaged for, you know. Losing the respect of friends, that sort of thing. We think it's all so significant but it's nothing really, just a mixture of idle gossip and the manure of history. A poem . . .' Brian leant forward. 'Now a great poem, that's something.' He stood up straight, and shook his head.

'Brian,' said Jim. 'Why don't you fucking leave me in peace? Can't you see I want to get some work done?'

'Tut, tut,' said Brian. 'You swore.'

Elsewhere, in Senator Spalding's office, Jane Meadows was standing at his filing cabinet when another of his assistants came in.

'I'm not sure the senator is well,' said the other assistant. 'Have you noticed anything?'

'No.'

'You used to be quite . . . close . . . I would have thought . . .'

'No. We're not close,' said Jane Meadows.

33

Susan had a note from Phillip. 'Thanks for the dinner,' it said. 'Great to see you.' And it was the same writing as before, the same lettering as up in the cardboard boxes, in the letters of love and hate.

The doctor stared at Susan over his glasses while on his desk the photograph of his five beautiful children gazed at her.

'You seem to be immune to your husband's sperm. The sperm can act as a foreign protein substance and provokes the formation of sperm antibodies. In short, you become immune to his sperm, incompatible on a cellular level. It happens. What can we do?' He tapped the end of his pencil up and down.

'It's peculiar,' the doctor continued, 'but it does sometimes happen in close partnerships. Common, actually. Another man's sperm, and you'd probably get pregnant immediately. It's why more than ten per cent of children aren't by the named father. In certain circles it's much higher. Of course, the women usually don't intend to get pregnant by the other man, it just happens.' He leant back, spreading out his chest a little. 'Nature tends to sort things out for us.'

A calendar featuring a photograph of bears hangs on the wall, with nothing marked on it.

His whole manner was one of sympathetic regret; the thick lips, the quiet voice, the austere white eyebrows, the way his shoulders rolled down. Even his build suggested regret; he was a small man, and he always seemed to be wearing his plastic gloves. The room was subdued; nothing in it suggested energy or money except the five well-dressed children on a perfect lawn.

'So. The point is there's nothing wrong with either of you,' he said. He took off one of his plastic gloves. He sighed.

'It seems greedy, to want another child so much when I already have one,' she said.

'Biological destiny is not to be argued with, my dear, as you should know.'

'I didn't even like being pregnant. I was sick. I didn't like giving birth.'

He glanced at his watch. Behind him on the window sill were disposable gloves, spatulas, swabs, tissues, chrome instruments in an egg box.

'Even in Italy there's more infertility,' she said, fixing her feet on the soft brown carpet. 'Friends of mine say there's an epidemic of infertility there.' The lights glared down on her.

'Ah yes. It is true. It is a problem,' he said, moving on his seat.

'I probably won't come back,' she said. 'We've tried everything.'

'Yes.'

'Maybe the human race will die out, bit by bit.'

He smiled compassionately, and stood up, the five children still staring at her. Wearily, he stretched out the hand which wasn't wearing the plastic gloves.

She stood up.

'At least I'm not seeing you about some horrible disease,' she said.

'Quite,' he said, letting his reassuring eyebrows jump up and down expressively and his blue eyes become merry.

'I'm very grateful for all your help.'

'Not at all, not at all,' he said, in his avuncular manner.

She stepped out into the waiting room which was swollen with pregnant women, and a receptionist called out someone's name in the same regimental, slightly contemptuous voice that doctors' receptionists use throughout the world. A woman in a red and white checked maternity dress meekly rose to her feet and waddled to the desk.

Back home, she went up to the attic and opened the cupboard door.

In the box marked PERSONAL LETTERS there were letters and postcards from Phillip, which she should have thrown away long ago. She was always aware of their presence. Now she was tempted to read them again.

Again, she found some of her things missing. An evening bag wasn't with the others, a collection of Shakespeare sonnets wasn't in the usual place.

'It's called losing things, Mrs Stewart,' said Maria when Susan mentioned it. 'I always lose things when I'm under stress.'

'I'm not under stress,' said Susan.

34

In London years ago, when Rebecca was five, Susan had gone to the doctor and had her uterus checked out, her Fallopian tubes examined, her blood and urine tested. Everything appeared fine. Jim wasn't pleased when she said he had been called in to see the doctor.

'I'm not going,' he said. 'That's all there is to it.'

He was standing at one of the two sink units in the pine kitchen of their London house. The sinks had helped sell the house to them – it had seemed wonderfully luxurious to have something they so clearly didn't want or need.

Behind him, leaves pressed against a window and the grey London light tried to get through.

Jim plunged his hands further into the pockets of his corduroy trousers as though wishing to disappear into them. He scratched the back of his neck. Overhead Rebecca and a friend were bouncing on a bed.

'It's only a matter of checking your sperm count,' she said.

'Sperm count!'

'Other people check their sperm counts,' Susan asserted.

'Not me,' he said, slouching over to the scrubbed pine table and collapsing onto a chair.

He slipped the little drawer of the table out then carefully put it in again.

'It's only been a couple of years. We'll have sex more often. That'll do it,' he said.

'I told you, darling. That's not what does it. In fact it can be unhelpful. The idea is to have sex only once a month but do so at the right time.'

His shoulders had sagged further. He took a drawing pin out of the drawer and placed it on the table.

'I find that impossible to believe,' he said, pushing the drawing pin into the table. 'I don't wish to believe it. I don't intend to believe it.'

He stood up, walked to the fridge, and took out a bottle of white wine. He poured out some for Susan, then poured himself one twice the size and drank it quickly.

They went to the doctor one cold winter's morning. The car wouldn't start so they went by tube, and arrived shivering and out of breath in a waiting room with scuffed lino floors and peeling magnolia paint. Beneath an untidy noticeboard was a sign, 'Sperm samples here'.

Jim sat reading a history of South America and humming to himself, as he did in moments of great stress.

She tried to think of her drawings, as she always did on her visits. She imagined the child's face taking shape, a charcoal ear here, an eye there, the shape of her chin softening as she rubbed away the hard lines of the pencil.

But the child eluded her.

'Let's just forget it,' Jim said.

'But I don't want to,' she said.

'Look, all this masturbating into receptacles, well it gets you down after a while.'

'It can't possibly be more humiliating than being pregnant and giving birth. I'm willing to do that, for the sake of a child.'

'The way that Dr Lindsay – the one with the six fucking children – looked at me sympathetically over his ridiculous round glasses as he told me never to wear tight underpants. Well, really. I wanted to hit him on the nose. I just can't bear being endlessly polite to these patronising doctors.'

'You aren't, darling. I seem to remember you telling Dr Lindsay to fuck off.'

'Well, he'd just given me a coy lecture on the fact that it was no accident that testicles were where they were – they needed to be kept cool, with plenty of air getting to them – and then he asked me for some more sperm. I mean, really.'

'He was surprised, though, about you telling him to fuck off.'

'Yes, he was,' Jim said, blowing his nose conclusively.

Looking back, all the drama over getting pregnant hadn't been painful then. She hadn't really been sure that she wanted a child quite yet. She had such a strong relationship with Rebecca that to have had another child would almost have been like a husband taking a second wife, while still in love with the first, and then expecting them all to live together. Susan hadn't been sure it would be good for Rebecca. It was only recently that she had become more desperate for a child, just in the last weeks.

On her way to the adoption agency a few miles north of Washington, Susan's car swirled through the leafy streets interspersed with village greens which in summer became the scene of Fourth of July celebrations, and which always sported children's bicycles and children climbing trees. She passed the local shopping centre with its fresh bread shop, the two shimmering glass shopping malls which faced each other on either side of Wisconsin Avenue, and she swept up Wisconsin past the Gucci shop, past Saks Fifth Avenue, along the wide stretching road.

London roads always wanted to catch you out, turn you right when you wanted to go left, make you turn back when you wanted to go on, while Washington avenues just led you where you wanted to go, and seemed to allow the very shops to step back to let you pass.

She turned on the radio as she passed the Silver Diner – one of the few places in Rockville which was bearable, not least because there were always pink-flamingo sunsets when she went there with Rebecca, who liked the mini hamburgers served in a cardboard convertible car.

The adoption agency was in an office block made up of a pile of white stones. The building stood sulkily by the side of the road, with the next one some distance away, for America had plenty of space. That's good, Susan reminded herself. Plenty of space is good.

She parked her car and managed to find her way through some glass doors into a hallway with four different lifts, all, it seemed, going to different floors. The hall had a speckled, pebbledash appearance which recalled the exterior of a garage. A temporary-looking blue sign up on the wall listed some businesses and their floors, although there seemed to be no thread whatsoever connecting the offices; they varied from Dial-a-Gift to Auto Accident. The adoption agency just called itself The Adoption Agency, for which she was grateful. As was so often the case in these office blocks, there was nobody in the hallway although a multitude of offices inhabited the place, and she travelled up alone in the lift, staring at herself staring at herself in the smoky brown glass of the mirrors all around.

She stepped out of the lift and found herself in another hall. The Adoption Agency was along a corridor to the right. She knocked and entered.

'Hello,' said Susan warmly. 'My name's Susan Stewart.'

The pretty black girl behind the desk smiled gaily, stopped what she was doing, jumped up and shook her hand.

'Now, take a seat,' she said, gesticulating towards the one chair, with a blue Terylene cover. 'I'm Martha Edwards. We spoke on the phone. Just you ask me any questions you want and I'll do my best to answer.'

Susan sat down. 'Oh,' she said, as though the sound had just drifted in through a window and landed in front of her, rather than come out of her mouth. 'Right now?' Susan was a few inches lower down than Martha Edwards. The walls glared at her, marshmallow white.

'You just wanted a preliminary talk, wasn't that it? I'm one of the social workers here.'

'Social workers?' she echoed.

'Yes,' said Martha. 'As I think I said on the phone, only qualified social workers would be visiting your home and organising the Home Study.'

'What's the Home Study?'

'It's a report we have to have before we can start any adoption proceedings.'

'On my home?'

Martha smiled sympathetically.

'On you, your home, you know. And there's a Criminal Justice Investigation – to make sure you haven't any kind of criminal record, child abuse, that kind of thing. We are looking for the best for the children.'

'Of course,' said Susan.

'There's an initial fee to start the process and of course more once it's underway . . . all the medical and health and criminal checks, you know . . . and then the business of finding a child for you.'

'Oh yes,' said Susan.

The computer at which Martha sat had an eerie green background.

Martha lowered her chin a little, and her voice. 'Of course you have to be prepared that finding a birth mother willing to give up her child isn't easy – I assume that's what you're looking for, a baby. Most people are. A healthy baby.'

'Why yes . . .'

'If you'd consider an ethnic minority, your chances might be better,' said Martha.

'Oh yes. I'm not concerned about that. I wouldn't mind.'

Martha wrote that down.

'I just wanted you to come and look at our books – we've got some photographs of mothers and fathers with their adopted children, and some letters of appreciation. It gives you some kind of context to work in. And then you take away this package here, fill in the application form, send in the money, and we can make a start.'

She pushed a scrapbook over and Susan turned over page after page of smiling mothers and children with letters stuck in beside them, and parts underlined in red: 'My life was empty without her', 'I couldn't understand how God could make me want a child so much when I couldn't have one', 'I couldn't bear to go and see my friends who'd just had babies', 'I'd had one and knew I should be grateful and I was but I wanted another one so urgently and nobody could understand. It was as though someone who belonged with us simply hadn't come, had died on the way, in some accident we'd yet to hear of, and I suffered grief every day, not knowing quite whether he was coming or not, but gradually suspecting he'd never come', 'I couldn't walk past a baby clothes shop without going in', 'I used to think about stealing another woman's baby', 'I became a nanny to be close to babies'.

'Would you like a cup of coffee?' said Martha.

Susan shook her head.

'You can be lucky – it can be easy ... a birth mother takes a liking to your picture ... you know ...'

Susan smiled. 'And – who are the social workers, the people who make these reports?'

'We're all MAs ... in their late twenties at least ... experts in the field.'

Susan nodded.

'Now, your husband's American – a journalist, you say?' said Martha.

'That's right.'

'And you're a ... naturalist ...?'

'Correct.'

'That's fine,' as though the whole business were practically tied up.

'Maybe an Asian child,' said Susan listlessly, looking into the face of a handsome Asian boy.

'And sex preferences?'

'A boy or a girl, I don't mind,' said Susan in a small voice. 'But ... I fear ... you see ... a long time ago I had an abortion, and now I can't get pregnant – and sometimes I worry ...'

'No point in worrying about the past,' said Martha.

When she stepped out back into the car park the sun seemed to retch down on her and she had to sit for a while with her head resting on the headrest before starting the ignition and driving back.

On the way back, she stopped at a bread shop and from behind thought a man was Phillip, but when he turned he was just a man with a moustache, and she didn't know if she was disappointed or relieved.

35

'What do you think about adoption?' asked Susan, a few days later.

'Adoption?'

Jim was in the middle of a press-up.

'That's right.'

'You said your period was three days late.'

'You shouldn't do press-ups. You're too thin already. It is three days late. But *if* I can't have another . . . what do you think?'

Jim was doing his press-ups in front of the television, which dominated the upstairs sitting room. His desire to use every particle of time efficiently amused Susan. Even now, he didn't stop doing press-ups while he thought about adoption and watched CNN. One more press-up. Another press-up. A red face.

The light burst in at the windows, not waiting for morning to come at a dignified pace. It spread itself all over the floor, all over Jim, all over the television screen so that all she could see on it were vague shadows of another world.

'I think it's great for many, many people.'

She took a breath. 'But us. Do we think we should adopt? I did go and find out a little about it – up in Rockville. But I don't know . . .'

Up and down he went, up and down, in his white shorts and white top, his black hair glistening with sweat, gloss-painted like a wooden toy soldier.

'It's been eleven years, Jim. Eleven years.'

Up and down he went again. She wanted to step on his hands. He looked directly at her.

'I thought you wanted the pregnancy, the giving birth, all that.' He sat back, sweat pouring down his face, and squinted at her. 'Would you love a child who wasn't yours?'

'She would be mine. I'd have fed her, and looked after her. She'd be mine.'

'Genetically she wouldn't be. She wouldn't look like you.'

Susan shrugged. 'She might. Would you mind?'

'If she didn't look like me? No. Not at all. Rebecca doesn't look like me. I don't mind,' said Jim.

'You see, it wouldn't *be* somebody else's child. It would be our child. If we nurtured it, took it to the doctor, loved it, it would be ours. There wouldn't be anyone else involved.'

'That's right.' He checked his watch and stood up.

She followed him to the bathroom and he stepped into the shower. She had to shout as he showered. The way he soaped himself seemed to suggest that there was nothing at all wrong with the world, that he was in absolute control of it, and anybody who was worried about anything was quite wrong to be, including Susan. He began to sing.

'What about a Russian?' she shouted.

'What?' he shouted back, soap streaming down his face.

'What about adopting a Russian baby?'

'Russian? Why Russian?'

'Tolstoy was Russian. Dostoyevsky was Russian. Chekhov was too.'

'So was Stalin,' shouted Jim.

Jim could be sure to take the opposing view in any discussion, just for the sake of it, and at one dinner he had insisted on censorship of all books just because someone was being irritatingly liberal, while at another dinner a few weeks before he had argued against any kind of censorship for equally dilettante reasons. To him, it was all fun, this business of words, just a matter of juggling, entertainment, without any reality.

'Well, Stalin was someone's child,' she said. 'Even your own children can turn out vile. Some have bad tempers. Some steal. We have no knowledge that another child would turn out like Rebecca.'

'Sorry?' shouted Jim.

'What about a Salvadorean child?'

'I don't know, darling. Are there any great Salvadoreans?'

'It hasn't been going as long. Anyway, what's all this about greatness? We just want a healthy child, not a genius.'

He towelled himself dry with a vast new towel that left little black bits over him, which served him right, she thought; then she relented and picked one off his shoulder.

He flung talcum powder all over himself and over the floor. After a shower, the bathroom looked as though it had been hit by a soccer team: water everywhere, talcum powder on every surface, towels all over the floor.

He spread shaving soap over his face.

'There are risks you take if you adopt. But if you give birth you might die or the baby might die. It's all a risk,' he said.

He rinsed the soap off.

'Besides,' he said, 'when you consider our family history . . . all our ancestors died, didn't they?'

'That's pretty common.'

'Still. They must have all died of something. It's not as though we're passing on perfect health.'

'What do you think? What should I do?'

'Find out about it.'

'I've been testing myself. Looking at children in the street. Black children. Oriental children. And I'm sure I could love a child who wasn't mine.'

'Mmm. But could you? I could, but could you? I'm pragmatic. I accept what happens. But you . . . for a scientist you do behave like a poet.'

'Like a painter, actually. But I am a painter. Anyway, if I adopted her I'd have chosen her. I mean . . . I know what she should look like. I imagine her sometimes.'

'I know you do.'

'Well . . .'

'It won't work, Susan . . . you have to want *any* child . . . Rebecca!'

Rebecca was standing at the door of the bathroom.

There was something poignant about the serious, dark girl, with her thin shoulders and vulnerable straight body. Susan moved forward to take her in her arms. But Rebecca moved back.

Rebecca's fists were clenched. In the next room the television was on, playing cartoons on the cartoon channel. Susan could hear Tweetie Pie chattering away. She realised it had been on for some while, as they'd been talking, but they'd been too involved in what they were saying to realise Rebecca was in the next room.

'I was curled up with my blanket. You were talking loudly,' she said. 'Arguing.'

'Discussing,' said Susan.

'I'm going to watch TV,' she said grandly and flounced over to the sofa where she sat rapt, apparently having forgotten everything.

36

Rebecca crept up the stairs, and the light from the studio above threw a shadow behind her, and her bare feet seemed to thud like boots over the wooden stairs, with their faded steps.

In the studio the paintbrushes stood on a stand by her mother's easel, and more lay on the table overlooking the garden. In the half light, Rebecca could make out one of her mother's glass-topped cases, containing turquoise butterflies shimmering like jewels, which her mother was painting for a book. Rebecca liked the smell up here, of paint, and colour, and change – the way a blank sheet of paper became a painting, and a dried dead butterfly pinned through its centre a living creature again on the paper.

She hadn't been able to resist the cupboard up here and that unopened letter to Phillip. It was all the piled unsorted things in the cupboard, all the cardboard boxes stacked secret at the back, like the dark thoughts she sometimes had before falling asleep. Rebecca didn't dare turn on the main light, in case her parents saw it, and knew she was up here, and she was a little afraid of the shapes around the room – of the easel, the brushes like odd heads of hair, the crushed tubes of paint filled with worms of colour, and in particular the boxes of insects Susan kept piled to one corner of the room as if at any moment they might choose to break out.

Rebecca reminded herself the insects were dead, and didn't exist any more, that they used to be alive and relevant, but now were part of a past which didn't exist any more. The jewel beetles, and grass-hoppers, and moths the size of her hand didn't really exist, only their shapes existed.

Opening the cupboard door, she heard a noise downstairs, and stopped still for a moment. She switched on the cupboard light and it smashed into her face like a moth; she took a step back and then steeled herself to continue. With her scrawny mop of black hair, the fringe sticking to her skin, her T-shirt far too big for her, down to below her knees, she knelt down and reached for one of the other cardboard boxes marked PERSONAL LETTERS.

At the top she found the letter to her mother and felt she needed to read it, to understand what was happening in the house.

Her father hardly seemed to know where to put himself. He shot like a rocket from room to room with a startled expression and he seemed to be hurling words down the phone or into his computer non-stop, well, when he wasn't grabbing Rebecca's mother and trying to kiss her, which always made Rebecca uncomfortable.

For fifteen minutes she searched through piles of

old letters, and old essays, until she came to what she wanted, the letter she had seen before addressed to Phillip, which had no stamp on it, as if it had never been sent. The letter had been moved around, as if someone else had been looking through the box. She opened it up quickly, then checked the envelope again. It was to an address in London.

'Dear Phillip,' the letter read. 'You should know that I had an abortion last week. Susan.'

Rebecca put the letter back in the cream envelope, placed it back in the box, and switched off the light, creeping down, over the stairs, and back to her room, where she lay awake and unable to sleep.

After a while she sneaked down the creaking stairs, through the hall, past the kitchen where Maria was watching television, and to the French windows which led out into the garden. It was good to get away from Maria and her moods.

The moment she was outside the sound of the cicadas grew deafening and everywhere there were insects batting into her face.

She ran over the harsh dry grass to the fence, then climbed over and ran to the back door of Ivana's house and beat at the door.

'Rebecca! What is it?' said Ivana, as she opened the door. 'Has anything happened?'

'Can I come in?'

'Of course, come in, Rebecca.'

'My mother went out,' said Rebecca. 'I couldn't sleep again. Maria is there.'

'Has she done something to you?'

Rebecca shook her head.

'But can I stay with you a while? She won't know. She's just watching television. Just a little while. I don't want to go back just yet.

'Well . . .'

'Do many people have abortions?' asked Rebecca.

'Some. Why?' said Ivana.

'I just wondered,' said Rebecca.

'Have you seen something about them? Are they talking to you about it at school?'

'No . . . just I think a long time ago . . . I think someone I know very well – a grown-up – may have had one and I just found out and it shocked me.'

'I see,' said Ivana, looking at Rebecca closely with a little smile. 'Now that is distressing. How did you find out? Did someone tell you?'

'I read it in an old letter.'

'I see,' said Ivana. 'I think I know who you may mean.'

'Is your husband here?' asked Rebecca.

'No.'

'Why is he always out?'

'He's busy, that's all . . . I should at least call your babysitter.'

'Please don't. Just wait a moment. She'll be cross with me. If you don't tell her maybe I could just slip back and she'd never know. Nobody would know.'

Ivana's face softened. 'Rebecca . . .' She sat on one of the voluminous sofas. 'Come and sit beside me. Are you OK? You seem alarmed.'

Rebecca sat down.

'I don't know . . . it's an atmosphere in the house. I think my mother's worried about something.'

'Ah. I see,' said Ivana.

'I don't know what it is,' said Rebecca. 'Everything used to be perfect. You know – Happy Families. But maybe we were too happy.'

'You and I,' said Ivana. 'We should take a little holiday away together. It would give your parents some time to themselves. What do you think?'

'Sure,' said Rebecca.

As Ivana made her way to the kitchen area, Rebecca called out, 'Do you have a Coke please?'

'Yes, Rebecca,' said Ivana, smiling.

37

'How *is* your poor mother?' said Ivana when Rebecca turned up for her piano lesson a few days later.

'She's fine,' said Rebecca.

'I know she's a wonderful mother – I can quite see that – but it just seems that that formal quality of hers with other people is going. Do you know what I mean? Every day she seems to be wearing brighter clothes. That emerald silk shirt! She used to wear such muted colours. And her hair! She's wearing it loose. Doesn't it look . . . a little . . . young for her?' said Ivana.

Rebecca frowned. 'Ivana,' said Rebecca, 'you really should try roller blading. It's excellent exercise, you know.'

Ivana allowed her head to lean a little to one side. 'I have no desire to . . . roller blade.'

'You might like it. You don't think you would but you would.'

'The next tune is in E flat . . .'

'I've begun to roller blade up and down this street with a Walkman and earphones,' said Rebecca dreamily.

'I've seen you. You go quite fast.'

'They're all boys in this street. I used to like playing with boys but now . . . I don't know. It seems all they want to do is hit things hard.'

'Rebecca. Please concentrate.'

Rebecca's white T-shirt was splodged with what looked horribly like tomato ketchup. Ivana, on the other hand, wore a pearl bracelet and pearl earrings; her baby-blue trouser suit was pressed to such perfection that the crease in the trousers looked hard enough to cut with.

'You and your mother . . . you're so close, aren't you? I think that's lovely.'

'Yes . . . only she's a little . . . different at the moment. The publishers are getting ferocious about her not having sent in the illustrations for the book about the area's insects and spiders yet. But she's had so much on her mind.' Rebecca yawned.

'That man who was here . . .'

'Who?'

'The one who stayed the night . . . Phillip Jordan.'

'Oh yes.'

'An old boyfriend of course? Someone like that you would never forget. Mesmeric. Very attractive.'

'Yes,' said Rebecca.

'I am quite sure your parents do need some time to themselves. You and I really should go to Poland together soon for a little holiday. It would give them a surprise to have some time alone. Gustav will be able to cope without me. As long as he's got his collection of glass, he's happy,' she said brightly. 'It would be an adventure! A real adventure. You could wear my long white gloves and walk round my country estates. It would be wonderful!'

'Could I really wear long white gloves?'

'Why yes! Of course.'

'You see, although I seem a little bit of a tomboy with my shorts and everything . . . really I like pretty things.'

Over the piano were a number of photographs – including a sepia photograph of the old mansion which Ivana had told Rebecca was Ivana's ancestral home in Poland. In one her husband Gustav grinned, displaying his white, even teeth which were too perfect and too white, as though they'd been manufactured, not grown. When Rebecca played, the teeth watched her intently, white keys, and the bright blue eyes shone as if a jeweller had spent time buffing them up.

Ivana checked her watch after half an hour. 'I'm so looking forward to our visit to Poland,' she said.

'I don't know if my mother would like it, you know,' said Rebecca. 'I would have to ask her.'

'Of course, of course. We'll just wait for the right time to ask.'

Rebecca began to play again and the notes hung plangently in the air. Everything in the room was dark – dark wood bureau, dark paintings, dark brown chairs. Even the curtains were drawn.

'How old did you say you were when you started the piano?' asked Rebecca, her head tilted to one side.

'Six. My parents were very ambitious for me. Both of them. I had to do everything, be good at everything. What they would say now of me – a middle-aged woman with no children teaching the piano . . .' She shook her head.

'Oh no!' said Rebecca. 'That's not how you seem *at all*. All my friends think you're . . . mysterious.'

'Do they?'

'And beautiful. They say you're beautiful and that you have awesome clothes.'

Ivana straightened her back a little. 'I look after them, that's all.'

'When I'm older,' said Rebecca passionately, 'I shall look after my clothes.'

'Maybe after our lesson – if you get properly back to work – we could look at my clothes again, and some of my photographs of the old house. Would you like that?'

'Oh yes,' and she tucked her hair affirmatively behind her ears to signify concentration.

'I always wanted a little girl so much but Gustav doesn't like children.'

Later they went up and Ivana showed Rebecca an embroidered jacket, a black velvet skirt, a ballgown, and Rebecca felt each one, and exclaimed how gorgeous they were, and asked Ivana to tell her when she had worn which one and what had happened that evening.

'Not a great deal has happened to me, really,' said Ivana.

Rebecca looked disappointed. 'Oh, but in the ballgown . . . surely . . .'

'A man kissed me.'

'Really . . .'

'Lots of people kiss one, Rebecca. Lots of people will kiss you.'

'I'd hate to have a tongue in my mouth though . . . I think that's disgusting.'

'Oh – you'll like it.'

'Will I? How funny . . . and look at the embroidery on the jacket.'

'Yes, just look at it,' she said, watching Rebecca run her hands over the swirl of gold.

Rebecca cascaded home, and went out into the garden to see if she could find any spider's webs, and she found one, right at the back, by the hedge, a mottled garden spider presiding over a glistening web of geometrical brilliance, and the spider's position, in dead centre, made it seem for a moment that she was proud of this creation of hers, with one strand attached to a piece of ivy, another to an azalea bush, a third stuck to a twig sticking out of the tree above, and the rest attached firmly as if to nothing, but nevertheless held tight.

Rebecca ran off and started practising her handstands but then returned to the spider. Every time she ran off she found the sight of the web brought her back.

Her mother had told her that spiders were the first animals to make the move from sea to land, 300 million years ago. No webs had survived as fossils because they were too fragile.

At school years ago she'd been read a myth of the Navajo Indians which said that in the beginning of the world there was nothing but a spider in the dark purple light at the dawn of time, and that all life came from her.

Rebecca looked up into the sky and hoped it didn't rain because although the spider's web looked strong it could easily be broken.

An atmosphere had been building up in the house which Rebecca didn't understand but felt it had something to do with Phillip. Her mother was distinctly different – with brighter clothes, more jewellery, a curious kind of bounce to her step, but a distance too. But maybe that was good, thought Rebecca. I have been young for so long, loved by my mother intensely, friends have asked me over to parties, to sleepovers and often I didn't want to go. I preferred to stay home. But now I should go. And I should go with Ivana to Poland for the little holiday. She would mention it to her mother.

But she forgot, and instead she asked her mother if she could put her bed against the wall, and have a new cover, to replace the pink one.

'Against the wall?'

'Yes,' said Rebecca. 'It would feel . . . safer there. And do you think I could have a purple cover?'

'Yes, I see what you mean,' said Susan.

38

Susan made herself go up to the attic cupboard where she knew there were some of Phillip's old letters. She wanted to try to understand why he had come back into her life after all this time.

She was surprised to see that the Sellotape seal had been broken, but assumed Maria must have been looking for something. As she knelt down by the box her mouth felt dry, and as she put her hand into the box her insides lurched around like people in bumper cars. Whenever he went away from her he used to write to her, and the first letter she took out was from South Africa, where he'd been interviewing someone. The stamp was of a flower, and the envelope was thumbed. Curious, she thought, that paper lasts so well; it's so thin and fragile looking yet it lasts and lasts and carries messages, from one decade to another. She supposed she must have read the letter a number of times while she was with Phillip, because she knew she had not done so since they broke up.

Dear Susan, [it said, in his scrawling black writing]

A friend asked me what I loved about you and I found myself saying, 'The way she butters the toast in the morning' and it's true, there is some essence of you I love, not to do with your education, or your looks, or even your voice.

I was just reading Graham Greene's 'The End of the Affair'. He writes that the sense of unhappiness is so much easier to convey than that of happiness because in misery we seem aware of our own existence. Happiness, however, annihilates us: we lose our identity.

There's a commonplace book here at the hotel in which people have scribbled some of their favourite quotations, and I wish you were here with me, sitting beside me in the empty cane chair, with one cane broken, and you leaning over, your dark hair brushing against my skin, and looking with me at the battered blue book, the cover peeling at the corners from the heat, and white in patches where the sun has hit it out on this balcony overlooking the dry brush. 'Love is . . . never lost, just mislaid, like a one-armed doll buried beneath old carpets and empty picture frames in the attic' (John Updike).

My mind is full of words and phrases tonight, but the relationship they have with the real world is something I just don't understand.

Love always,

Phillip

One quality in Phillip she had forgotten was a certain gentleness which came out in the letters. All she had remembered from the past were his moods, and anger, because, she supposed, it had been easier to forget him by concentrating on those things. But perhaps it could be that the anger was the central part of him, that she had forgotten the moments of tenderness because they were not essential to the core of him.

Dearest Susan,

They say that the pleasure of love lies in loving, and we are made happier by that than by being loved back, as if by loving someone else we are relieved of the weight of our self love, but I want to be loved back. Yet however much you love me there is something more I want, some corner left dark, some area of you I have not reached, I do not possess, and all I can think about is that missing corner.

The couple who run this hotel have two children and seem blissfully happy – always looking into each other's eyes and seeing the other person perfectly reflected. I envy them. Funny, really, the unhappy both envy and despise the happy; it's far more of a division in society than mere money or status.

I think you have the ability to one day be happy but I . . . you told me you thought I could never be happy, and perhaps you are right. Women who want money leave men who are poor if they show no signs of getting richer. Women who want status leave men who have no status. So women who want to be happy leave men who have no capability for happiness.

Susan. Sweet present of the present. I shouldn't look to the past or the future.

With love from

Phillip.

Dearest Susan,

I feel crazy tonight, and wish I had you in my arms.

Sometimes I have wanted to kill you, because only by killing you could I possess you. But, of course, even that is false. You'd be even more separate then, in another world, only at least the memory would be intact, and you'd never leave me and you wouldn't make love to other men. You'd be like one of your fine insects, pinned down in the box of my memory. Oh God, it's the heat, I suppose.

I can smell your thoughts, even here, can sense you moving around my flat, touching my things. How long is it now? A year of feeling like this. Unbearable really. But oddly I feel closer to you here than I do when I'm lying in bed with you, separated from you by your white skin, your way of looking away from me.

There's a spider beginning to weave just by me, a tiny busyness at the centre of the web, throwing down a strand, which catches the light. Oh God. I want you.

With love,
Phillip

In another envelope was a letter from Ireland, again dated over thirteen years ago.

Dearest Susan,

I'm sorry. I screwed a girl last night in Dublin.

It wasn't out of love or even lust, just out of curiosity. I want to know, you see, whether all women's eyes grow bright and wide, and if they all shudder.

I thought of you when I fucked her: the way you look at me directly only for the second before you come. It is the only time you are mine.

You say you don't think you could ever give birth to a son. You say you don't know men – but you acquire them, don't you? You like to know how they make love, how they sigh? You are scared of becoming like your mother – steady, certain, plump – and yet you want that too.

I keep that photograph of you in my wallet. Of you on the sofa.

Where are you sitting, as you read this. Curled up on my sofa? One hand lying long on your thigh? I want to make love to another woman tonight, and think of you, as if they are all forms of you. Blonde hair, red hair, with wide mouths, with voices which cry out, each one of them seems closer to me than you. You seem to be editing yourself out of my life; first you remove a comma, then a full stop, then a preposition, and soon whole sentences will have gone, and there'll be a blank page, and then not even that. But at least I possess these girls, these versions of you, with their hot inner thighs, their legs opening and closing like scissors.

I miss you. You should be carved in ivory.

I can still smell the girl's cigarettes in my hair, and the sour taste of her perfume.

Oh God, I miss you. Do you miss me?

Love,

Phillip

PS 'For love is strong as death;
Jealousy is cruel as the grave'
(*Song of Solomon* 8:6)

Dearest Susan,

Just drank too much red wine and talked of you. My friend said that love is either the shrinking remnant of something which was once enormous, or part of something which will grow in the future into something enormous, but that in the present it doesn't satisfy. It gives much less than one expects. I suppose this is why I find I am totally in love with you when I'm away from you, and troubled and bothered by my feelings when I'm with you.

In the flea market today there was an ivory carving of a skeleton of death clinging to a beautiful woman – death and the maiden, I suppose. It was in a curious occult stand. I might go and buy it tomorrow.

I hope you'll be in when I get back. About four o'clock Tuesday.

I keep thinking of your lips.

Love,

Phillip

PS It's the same with love as with everything else. What you have is nothing. It's what you haven't got that counts.

Susan slipped the letter back in its crumpled envelope.

Dearest Susan,

You seem to leave rooms as I enter. I follow you around. I never reach you. I call to you. But you say you love me, and sometimes I think I see love in your eyes. Hate, too, sometimes. You say you are beginning to have no self, to be like Scott Fitzgerald during his crack-up, to find that the sides of your personality are suddenly paper thin, and that, like him, you see the ego as an arrow shot from nothingness to nothingness. You feel I am taking your ego all away, storing it up in some room of mine as if I am Bluebeard. But all I do is love you.

In a way we're lucky. Happy love has no history. Romance comes to life when love is damaged or incomplete. Romance has nothing to do with contentment – and passion means suffering. You should understand that. You want things too easy, Susan. You don't seem to want to suffer.

I like to see the dirt from your shoes on my sofas.

With love,

Phillip

Dearest Susan,

You said last night in London that if you really left me I'd never find you. But I would. I would look for you and find you.

You said you would vanish, that you would be happy, that you wanted to be happy.

Love as always,

Phillip

Dearest Susan,

To know oneself is to foresee oneself; to foresee oneself amounts to playing a part. You say you no longer know yourself. At least it means you can extemporise your life, make it up as you go along. You ask me who you are. You're beautiful, a cross between a young Virginia Woolf, a gypsy and a twitchy New York psychotherapist. You are clever, with eyes like a mediaeval witch, and sometimes you wear glasses to disguise that. At the centre of you is something restless, and bad, and it is that I love best. You eat too much cheese, and have bad dreams. You still don't tie proper bows on your shoes, and always push doors when they say pull yet you perform a great blow job. (Why blow job? My first girlfriend blew all over me. It was a great disappointment.) You can't sew. There is a touch of arrogance about you. You are loved by me.

Phillip

Dear Susan,

I'm sorry I said I wished you dead. At one time or another I want everyone dead. It's my favourite solution. The tragedy, the spotlight, the grief, all the pain, the longing – gone away. Even me, sometimes I want me dead.

Love,

Phillip.

39

'Why did you split up with Phillip?' said Rebecca.

'Oh – this and that,' said Susan.

'The way he talked about you . . . you know, when he came to breakfast . . .'

Ivana appeared from nowhere, standing in the garden, by Rebecca. 'Could I possibly borrow a little butter?' she asked Susan, who stood up, tall and dark, and brushed the dirt off her hands, and Ivana stepped back a little.

Later Rebecca sat cross-legged, cross-armed on the floor, a pre-teen garden gnome, seeing how many different shapes she could make with her mouth as she watched *Gigi* on the television. Her goldfish mouth worked well, the sexual smile flung up one side of her face lacked a certain authenticity; the sulky baby mouth, in which she thrust out the bottom lip, she enjoyed doing but then it made her feel a little sad, as though something had indeed just gone wrong. A fly buzzed around the room, a pilot out of control. Her mother read a newspaper, clasping it as if she were drowning, huddled at one end of a sofa.

'Weird the way mosquitoes make that noise – like an out of tune violin – in your ears, as if to warn you they're coming, don't you think?' said Rebecca, as she sat on the sofa of the family room, beating off a mosquito who sailed round her. 'They give you a chance.'

'Odd, isn't it?' said Susan.

Rebecca never sat back straight, bottom down, a perfect L, but slouched and wriggled and curved, as if trying to tuck all of herself into one tight little ball. Today she wore a bright pink T-shirt and tight white shorts. But as soon as she managed the tight ball one of her legs kicked out violently as if trying to escape. Right now the battle was taking place on the grubby beige sofa.

Rebecca made a swipe at her long-legged mosquito tormenter. 'How do these creatures manage to appear and disappear like ghouls? I mean one moment it wasn't there at all, the next moment there's the violin playing and then there he is, dragging those legs of his around, waiting to land. Yuk.'

Susan took out *David Copperfield* and gazed at the picture of a sombre child with a big black necktie and white collars like mountain slopes.

The mosquito circled like a glider.

'I think this mosquito is actually enjoying the attack,' said Rebecca. 'I think it might have a sense of humour.' Her face was tilted up towards the mosquito, like Joan of Arc towards God.

'Ugh,' said Rebecca. 'It got me . . . after all that, I let it get me.'

Rebecca lurched forward as the mosquito lurched to one side, and Susan clapped her hands over the mosquito, holding them together like someone praying, then parted them, and on her left hand was a little smudge, such a small bit of darkness.

'Oh,' said Rebecca, and put her head in her hands.

'Rebecca,' said Susan and sat down and put her arms round her daughter's stiff frame. 'I love you. What's the matter?'

Later, lying in the hot bath, Rebecca noticed a tiny spider on the hot tap. It lost its footing and fell, then managed to climb back to the tap. But then it fell again and again, each time saving itself from death.

40

Susan walked round the house, rearranging furniture, as if, were she only to get the layout of the furniture right, the layout of her life would follow. But she put the furniture too far apart and all of a sudden it seemed everyone in the house was living further away from each other, and they began to shout at each other, as if from a great distance.

'Where's Rebecca?' said Jim as he bounded through the front door.

'Out.'

'Oh – that's why you're so morose.'

'I like her to be out enjoying herself.'

'You do and you don't. What about dinner out? What time is she back?'

'Sleepover,' said Susan.

'I thought she hated them.'

'She does. But she thinks she should try things.'

He knelt by her and cupped her face in his hands and kissed her. 'Come out to dinner. Where would you like to go? Where do you want dinner?'

'Somewhere very luxurious and very American.'

'Right,' he said. They dined in the restaurant

where they dined most Fridays and the waiters were so enthusiastic and reasonable Susan tried to feel reassured.

Susan, now, as she sat in the white restaurant, watching the waiters in white, was feeling again the same awful strangeness she used to feel in that flat with Phillip, where she'd felt so stranded. She took off her gold earrings, which were hurting her, and put them down on the white tablecloth. She sipped at the white wine (Jim usually insisted on red, for its health-giving qualities, but as she was upset tonight he made an exception) and it tasted cool and hard.

'I don't understand what it is we're all seeking,' she said, taking a piece of rye bread from the basket, a healthy brown well-crusted chunk. Susan tore the bread to pieces, then left it on the plate.

'Well,' he said, about to discuss the point.

'Well,' she said, leaning forward, her aquiline features somehow more penetrating than usual tonight. 'What do you think?'

'I'm going to have the halibut, although I really do loathe it,' he said.

'Really? But you always have it.'

'It's good for you. The peppercorns help it along a bit.'

'Oh Jim,' she said, as he bent over the menu.

'Well . . .'

She laughed.

She put out her white hand, and he covered her hand with his.

'By the way, I had lunch with Phillip Jordan,' said Jim. 'He said to thank you again for the dinner. He said how reckless you used to be, that you drove faster than anyone he ever knew. He was surprised you'd managed to settle down. I said I was too. He's very friendly, seems genuinely to care about you. The women in the office all adore him.'

'Friendly . . .' she said. 'Did you read that there was a drive-by shooting in the hamburger restaurant next door last week? A woman was killed,' she said.

'Yes,' he said, his face peering up like a periscope over his stiff white shirt and beige jacket. How he managed to keep his rosy view of human nature was beyond Susan, but it was one of the things she loved him for. It was impregnable, somehow, as Rebecca's innocence was impregnable, and it went with a tremendous hopefulness. He would wake upon a rainy morning, sit upright immediately and declare he was sure it would be a lovely day, and often it was; that was the curious thing, his hopefulness was by no means inappropriate.

Today as he sat there, casting glances round the room, taking it all in, she experienced such tenderness for him it quite shocked her and she had to look away. What was so extraordinary about his quality of optimism was that he was perfectly able to suspend it when necessary – when writing a damning piece about the drugs or armaments industry for instance – then take it back up exactly where he left it. Even people he'd exposed in print for unwise deals or decisions, when he saw them he clapped them on the back as though overwhelmed by affection. It was hard not to like him, and few people managed it, although of course there were some who could not forgive the precision of his pen. She supposed that was why he approved of Phillip – he seldom disapproved of anyone. He had almost too much forgiveness.

'Phillip says they still feel a little isolated here . . . particularly Sandra,' said Jim, when they'd eaten.

'Isolated!'

The waitress appeared and offered them coffee.

'Please,' Susan said.

'Large decaffeinated,' he said, splashing a hectic grin at the waitress, who wobbled back a little then nodded affirmatively, as if admiring his choice.

Susan sipped her white wine.

'Where did you eat?' she said in a muffled voice.

'Oh – a Cajun restaurant in Adams Morgan. Phillip knew the owners. They seemed to adore him,' said Jim, leaning back on his chair as if he were the most relaxed and well-adjusted person available.

'Yes. Phillip always knows the owners. You could go to Outer Mongolia and Phillip would know the owners at the local yak restaurant.'

Jim laughed. His laugh was a curious mixture of warmth and a hint of desperation.

'I have to admit I wasn't aware he was quite so well thought of. Except for the war reporting, of course. And his reputation for not ducking. We really do have to be a bit more sociable. You were so tense at that dinner with them. When is the last party we gave?' Suddenly his fingers began to tap dance on the black marble table as if to say that if he couldn't move around, at least they could.

Susan unfolded her napkin onto her lap, and pressed down its strong white creases.

'While Rebecca was little we had every reason not to go out. Remember she hated you going out? But now . . .' he said. 'We should have the world at our feet . . . In the middle of our lives. This should be the time . . .' he said.

'She used to create a three-part tragedy every time I went out,' said Susan dreamily. 'It was all *Romeo and Juliet*. Once she got down on her knees and begged me not to go.'

'And you didn't,' said Jim, elbows on the table, eyebrows up.

'What?'

'You didn't go.'

'Well . . .' she said.

'I went alone. To the Israeli embassy. There was an empty seat where you were supposed to have been.'

Susan drank more wine. 'When I married you, darling, I was not aware I was going to be consort to a kind of diplomat.'

'We should give a party,' he said. It struck her that he seemed a little paler than usual, that maybe he too was finding something unsettling here in this town, which so far had been charmed for them.

'If you like,' she said. 'But I'm not inviting Phillip.'

They walked back hand in hand through the soft, dark night, and every now and again he leapt up to see if he could touch the overhanging branches of the trees.

When they got home they made love.

41

When Susan came down one morning the chess game she'd been playing with Rebecca had been altered. She was sure of that. Her white queen had been next to the knight but now it was by the bishop.

And there were certain clothes she was unable to find, as though someone were coming and taking them one by one.

'They must be at the dry cleaner's, darling,' Jim would say, looking at her curiously.

'One of our spare side-door keys is missing,' said Susan, staring into a kitchen drawer.

'We're always mislaying keys,' said Jim.

'We must always put the alarm on at night,' she said.

'I'll forget and it'll go off. Just relax,' he said.

'You should publish the story – the investigation – about Senator Spalding,' said Susan. 'Now. In case someone has the story.'

'That's what the paper says. I just need a few more

things,' said Jim, flinging open the door of the fridge and jumping back at the sight of all the food.

'Let's all have dinner!' Jim would exclaim. 'Let's all play tennis!', 'Let's all go for a walk!' and he would try to buoy up his family and bounce them off to parks or restaurants or to friends as if they were balloons. And all the time they watched each other, knowing somehow that something was going to happen but not knowing what. As for Susan, she was afraid, for her life and for the lives of those she loved.

The air conditioning had broken down and the air was heavy in the rooms, with the shut windows.

Susan flung a cushion onto the bed.

Even Rebecca was remote and jumpy, and kept going over to Ivana's and returning with a distraught expression. When Susan asked Rebecca if anything was the matter, her little face became grave and pinched.

'Are you planning something?' asked Susan.

'Ivana says she might show me Poland one day.'

'Great,' said Susan, uncertainly.

As for Jim, he didn't get home until twelve.

'How can we sleep with no air conditioning and no windows open?'

Susan spent time polishing and dusting, as though if the house were clean enough whatever it was that was disturbing it would go away. She was afraid to go out much and instead stayed at home, drawing and painting, guarding the house, listening for sounds.

*

In the morning Susan opened the French windows and stepped out into the uneasy morning light, where faint sunlight was throwing itself in patches over the overlong grass, burnt brown in patches. At one side dark green holly bushes stabbed into the sky and the ivy fought its way over the metal fence at the back like prisoners trying to escape. The rose bushes stood stunted and cautious, more suitable for a lush English garden than this empire on a swamp. Above it all, the vast trees spread themselves out, as if turning away, looking out over the country club, with its exclusive membership, its well-tailored lunches, its air of paradise on earth.

She listened to the hum of cars out on Wisconsin Avenue.

She stepped out onto the grey stone of the terrace, and then out onto the lawn. Behind her the house stood sulky with its drawn curtains and early-morning silence.

The dew clung to the blades of grass.

She swung round and went back into the house, and up to the rooms where Rebecca and Jim still slept.

Susan looked up Cologne in a guide book: '. . . its close proximity to the beautiful scenery of the Rhine has rendered it a favourite tourist resort. When viewed from a distance, especially from the river, the city, with its mediaeval towers and buildings, the whole surmounted by the majestic cathedral, is picturesque and imposing . . .'

Sometimes she tried to imagine the boy in Cologne, a middle-aged man now, surely, having a coffee at a café with yellow umbrellas, slightly more thick-set, still with blond hair. But she couldn't imagine him quite. That was normal, she told herself, of course you can't imagine someone you met as a boy as a man. Of course not.

'Throw to me!' cried a squeaky voice of one of the little ones out in the warm summer street. As soon as the children were big enough to toddle, they were out playing in the street, beneath the tarpaulin of leaves. Only Ivana ever drove fast along there. The heat never seemed to bother them, neither did the cold; the young children seemed immune to changes of temperature. Indeed even now sometimes she would touch Rebecca, out on a cold day in a T-shirt, and her skin would be hot, as though the outside world was irrelevant to her, only her own inner temperature mattered as yet.

'Me!' shouted the ecstatic voice of another fat-kneed child only newly out there in the street. 'Throw to me!'

'I've booked our usual table,' he said.

'Ah yes,' she said.

'Run, Mary!' cried a voice.

Susan and Jim left around seven-thirty to walk down to the restaurant, after kissing Rebecca goodbye, and saying goodbye to Maria, who had come to babysit.

Susan found she was looking forward to the dinner; to the sterility of the restaurant with its windows out onto the street, to the repetitious menu, to the endlessly cheerful waiters and waitresses, bounding up like puppies and almost singing out their wares as if they really wanted to be doing this job, and only this job. The salads when they came were abundant, flowing over the sides of the plates, exuberantly hiding bits of celery or apple or tomatoes down underneath the foliage. And she would munch through the salad. Besides, she didn't really like fish or meat; they lay like stones in her stomach, like grey stones.

They strode on, through the sultry air which contrasted with the brisk and wholesome quality of the houses they passed – all newly painted, it seemed, all with plants which shone as if newly polished, with careful front doors, each one painted a different colour.

But when they turned into Wisconsin Avenue there was a fleet of police cars, in their blue and white livery, outside the restaurant, and the area was cordoned off.

'It's a drug raid. We were warned about some deals going on here,' said one of the policemen.

'Phillip's done this,' said Susan, 'to unnerve us. Or maybe Ivana.'

'Don't be ridiculous,' said Jim, kicking at a stone. 'You imagine things. Really. We'll just have something – at the hamburger place.'

But Susan was already walking home.

42

'Honey, please don't go checking my windows. I'm trying to work,' said Jim, as she stood in front of him making sure the clasps were in place.

'Just want to make sure they're secure. That's all,' said Susan cheerfully. 'I'm surprised you can work right in the window with everyone watching you.'

'Nobody has gone past all evening,' said Jim, his shoulders tensed up. 'Look, can you just try and calm down now?'

'Calm down?' she said. 'Why don't you just pull the curtains? It would be cosier. Ivana looks in from next door.'

'I don't mind if she looks in.' He tapped his pen up and down. 'I'm sitting here working. With my books around me. That's what I do. I'm a writer.' He coughed. 'Or rather a journalist.' He scratched his head.

'It's just a feeling, that's all,' she remarked, and moved back, behind Jim, and she could see his face reflected in the dark windows.

'I know. I know. But I'm just not happy with the drapes closed,' he said.

'In the flat I lived in when I was little no one could get in. We were perfectly safe. There was a caretaker. The flat was just a council flat but it was safer than this place, surrounded by grass, open to the street.'

'This is a detached house in a leafy suburb.' He checked his watch.

'I'd like to set the alarm at nights.'

'There hasn't ever in anyone's memory been a break-in in this street. Most people don't even lock their doors. This is a *great* street with *great* people in it.'

Susan shrugged.

The rain pounded at the windows and the lightning cracked the sky. The dip at the bottom of their drive was quickly filling with water, and the street lights shone into the puddles.

Rebecca stood at the window, watching, with pursed lips, and her father's air of condensed energy, holding a tennis ball in her hand. 'I wish we could go out,' she said.

'That wouldn't be sensible,' said Susan. 'You remember how those schoolboys were struck by lightning at the hockey match?'

'But I get tired of being in all the time. Of being sensible. I want something to happen. Nothing ever happens. I just go to school and come back here and do my homework and time passes. When I'm older I might be a dress designer.'

Her mother was staring out with glazed eyes like dark windows. 'Some boys,' said Susan, 'were just playing hockey, just a few miles from here, at the school playing fields. You remember – it was the ones who took shelter under the trees who were hurt.'

The lights flickered again.

'You know never to take shelter under a tree, don't you?'

'Absolutely,' said Rebecca. 'I can't quite remember . . . did anyone actually get . . . killed?' She tossed the tennis ball from hand to hand restlessly.

'A few. A few survived, with terrible burns.'

There was a crash of thunder.

'Will the roads be flooded?' asked Rebecca.

'I should think so.'

'Maybe we won't be able to get to school tomorrow,' she said. 'I wish I was eighteen and didn't have to go to school.'

'An hour ago it was bright sunshine,' said Susan. Her shirt gleamed purple in the half light.

On the other side of the street were tidy houses which at any minute could – and did – lurch with quarrels and divorces. Suddenly, in the middle of a conversation about a vacuum cleaner or a school, Susan would be overcome by the humour of it all – the houses, the well-paved street, the politeness, the wholesomeness, all of which could at any moment be turned by the unpredictable weather from a tranquil street into a nightmare of lightning, floods and thunder.

'The year before we came, Washington was struck by a hurricane,' said Susan.

'The tree fell through the roof of that grey house up the road,' said Rebecca, tapping at the window, 'but nobody was hurt.'

'The hurricane ripped trees from their roots,' said Susan.

Mother and daughter continued to stand at the window watching the rain hurl itself down, the trees shake like madmen, the puddles turn to whirlpools, and the road become a lake.

'I hope we never have to go back to England,' said Susan.

'I just wish something would happen to me,' said Rebecca, turning and throwing the ball onto the sofa then rubbing the end of her round little nose and stooping down to pull up her socks. 'One day I'll go to Poland. It will be an adventure.'

Rebecca often spent time looking into mirrors to see who she might be – adjusting her hair, the tilt of her head, her smile. She practised her signature too – and as she watched the words take shape, she wondered who she was, what person the words contained.

The lights suddenly went out.

Rebecca saw that the whole street was in darkness but they could still see the shape of the houses and the sky above and the pavement and the trees which were black. There was a glimmer of silver and for a moment Rebecca thought it was a ghost. She grabbed her mother's arm. Susan just laughed, as if the darkness was hugging her like some velvet cloak. But then Rebecca realised the silver was only Ivana sweeping up their path fighting with an umbrella in the wind, and wearing a silver mac.

Rebecca's mother sighed.

'Oh, it was so nice, the way everything vanished,'

she said, and slowly moved over to open the door for her neighbour. Ivana closed her umbrella, shook out the rain and walked in, closing the door behind her. She took off the silver sou'wester which matched her raincoat, and shook her hair.

'My dears! What a fearsome night! It's all so primitive here – the way the lights keep going out,' said Ivana. She looked down at Rebecca. 'I brought you something.' From the pocket of her mackintosh Ivana brought out a little yellow plastic torch, with a flourish. Her rings glinted.

'Thanks,' said Rebecca enthusiastically. 'Thanks,' she repeated, switching on the torch, and turning it round the room. It flung patches of light on the paintings of the Madonna and child, on the mantelpiece where Pan chased nymphs, on the carpet with its golden splashes, and into the face of Ivana, who blinked. Ivana had applied fresh lipstick, but not very well. Rebecca liked that about Ivana: even though it was dark, she had put on lipstick to come out to see her neighbours. Then Rebecca pointed the torch down, thinking it was childish to play with a torch.

'I'll go back now,' said Ivana. 'Back to bed.'

And Ivana vanished, as she had come, a silver figure in the night.

'You see how thoughtful she is,' said Rebecca to her mother. 'If ever I went on a holiday with her I'd be fine.'

Susan looked at Rebecca oddly. 'But you won't do anything silly, will you? You know you must always tell me if something is worrying you.'

*

Looking out of the drawing room the next day, Susan saw Ivana totter past with her little dog scrambling along behind her.

There was little sign of the storm the night before apart from a few extra twigs by the side of the road, a puddle of water at the bottom of the drive and a faintly uncomfortable smell in the basement laundry room, where it often flooded.

The sun was out again, declaring it had never been away, and that this was what life was like, this continual, wonderful sunshine which brightened the colours of the trees and made people smile at each other.

The sun dazzled the roofs in the little cul de sac while in kitchens, in bathrooms, in the back yard, people turned sharply away from the ones they loved, wondering how the years had taken them here, to this room, to this view from this room, with this person.

43

Jane Meadows moves the chairs nearer to the sofa.

Later that evening Jim sits there, the windows pouring in light, asking her question after question about her relationship with the senator, and eating the little cupcakes she made for him, and after that the bowls of peanuts and tortillas she provides as if wishing to make him so fat he won't be able to get out of her door. He throws back the pages of his reporter's notebook, filling page after page while the tape-recorder twirls round and round.

Her books are neatly filed in their white shelves.

Meanwhile day after day the distance between her and the senator widens. When she sits down to take a letter, she moves the chair far away from him.

When he talks he moves his plump hands, and she can almost feel their heat and feel his warm tongue running over her gums, between her teeth and her lips, and in her ear too, he used to lick the inside of her ear, and she used to like that. But now even when he is there with her in the room, he is absent, his eyes way back in his skull.

She knew it was dangerous what she was doing,

but she didn't care. Sometimes, for all the years she'd been alive, she had very little to lose, only the boredom of this apartment, with its television set and books, waiting for her every day, and the sadness of spending each day with someone she loved who no longer loved her.

Jim, meanwhile, generated enough energy to power the appliances of her apartment. He dashed to get himself a drink in the kitchen, plunged out into the sitting room, exclaimed on the brilliance of the location of her apartment, told her he loved white, informed her that this story was enormous, in particular as she was implying, but in a circuitous way, that the President actually knew of the senator's involvement and had spoken to him about it, but was keeping it all quiet to avoid scandal.

'Great,' said Jim, smashing his fist into his hand as he stood by the window, while Washington lay below him grey and blurred.

'Is it really so great?' said Jane, pouring out a cup of decaffeinated coffee.

'Why yes,' he said, leaping back to his seat. 'Why of course. But it's great to have . . . discovered it . . . Don't you think? It could cause a political crisis.'

Jane pursed her lips. 'I don't know if I'd like that. I wouldn't like the President to be damaged in any way.'

Jim leapt up again and she watched him pace up and down.

'If he's involved, why not?'

'Surely it would be better if we could go a little further and actually get to the cartel at source rather than mess around here,' she said, lifting her cup to her bow lips.

'Sorry?'

'Go to South America. Do a real story . . . not some little Washington storm in a . . .' she looked down, '. . . teacup.' She looked up and smiled. 'Don't you think?'

'This place isn't a teacup,' said Jim.

The white walls lapped around them.

'You could do a book then,' she said. 'A major book. That seems to be where the careers are really made. When people write major books. But of course I know little about these things,' she continued, bowing her head.

'I couldn't take the time off right now. Besides, I should do what's the best thing . . . you know. Drugs is one of the things that's destroying this place. Maybe the best way to deal with it is from here.'

'Maybe. And you have a lovely house. Such a cosy neighbourhood.'

'Yes.'

'Some men around your age start to panic. I've noticed it. You're lucky you're not like that. They think . . . I'm moving into the danger zone . . . heart attacks, strokes, you know . . . What have I done with my life?'

'No. I don't think that,' said Jim, checking his watch. 'I should be getting back.'

Jane Meadows yawned. 'I'm afraid I do sometimes, even at my age . . . I feel sad sometimes . . . and discontent, you know . . .' She traced a pattern on her sofa, and looked up. 'That it all closes in on you little by little – the house, the possessions, the apartment, until you can hardly breathe and you think, that's what is tiring me, that's what is making me old, if only I could get out of here I won't feel like that any more. And often people do get out and they don't feel tired any more,' she said.

'But often they do.' He stood, hands behind his back, gazing at a poster of a still life of some cheeses. 'Great picture!' he exclaimed. 'I love the blue cloth. The cheese looks as though you could eat it!'

Jane cleared her throat and tidied the magazines on the new coffee table she had bought to make the apartment more welcoming.

The next day, at lunchtime, Jane Meadows took a walk by Susan's house and saw her at the front, her hair falling over her face, with bare feet, a gypsy-looking woman, and when she looked up and stretched it seemed there was a tremendous power about her, as if the house were part of her, and the grass, and the clothes she wore – a purple and blue cotton dress – as if nothing could get to her.

Jane Meadows walked over the carpet of her main room, in her little turquoise Chinese slippers, wearing her high-necked, knee-length, duck-egg blue nightdress, her hair a neat helmet over her head.

She and Senator Spalding used to make love on his desk. She would have to clear it first: move the picture of the three daughters, move his ink blotter, move his dictionary, move his Bible. He would watch her move these things as he stood there, hot and little and overweight in his suit, with beads of sweat erupting over his forehead. Then he'd watch as she pulled down her pants and took them off, and put them in his top drawer with his pencils and pens, and all the time he would keep glancing at the door, although it was locked, as if half hoping someone would burst in. Senator Spalding always made her keep her shoes on, with the high heels he insisted she wear, but sometimes as he pushed into her they would fall off onto the floor, softly onto the deep carpet.

Jim was hard at work on his piece. But the problem was the more he found out, the more he needed to know.

That afternoon, organised by Jane Meadows, he went to interview Senator Spalding about the progress of the finance bill, a perfectly safe topic.

Jane was there to introduce Jim to Senator Spalding. The senator's office was the usual spacious room with plush green carpet, photographs of the senator with various past presidents, his state flag and the stars and stripes shoved together in a brass umbrella stand. Some decoy ducks represented his interest in hunting, a college football photograph displayed his wholesome talents for sport, and a baseball cap signed by various famous baseballers again reminded visitors of his wholesomeness. In the outer offices other lesser beings, including Jane Meadows, moved back and forth bringing messages and cups of coffee while he doled out sincerity. His slightly loose collar suggested an ease of manner as he shook Jim's hand, allowing his face to puff up into warm sausages of smiles while Jane stood a little way back, her head a little bowed, her hands moving around more than usual, stroking her skirt, touching her hair. In the office she was less of a person than at home, thought Jim, which was unusual. Usually jobs gained people stature but this one turned her into an empty figure, with a too-long skirt, scurrying at the corners of things. If it were not for the eyes which had met his when he knocked at the door, he would have thought that she really was nobody much. But her eyes flashed under her pale brows with what could only be called mischief, which he liked in anyone, and daring, which he admired too, for he knew at heart he was not a daring man. He was a clever man, a kind man, a sensible man, a hard-working and energetic man, but he was not daring. But do we have to be what we are or can we choose – make a mental decision – to be someone else?

The shaking of hands with Senator Spalding seemed to go on endlessly and all the while he found himself wondering whether or not they were all fixed where they were, with the personalities they had discovered so far, and for a moment he felt a certain compassion for Senator Spalding, who seemed trapped too, here in these yards of office, with presidents staring at him from their rectangular frames, with the mementoes designed to express personality.

Jane had described making love on this desk here, by the side of which the senator was smiling, and Jim found himself sensing a vulnerability in this man with all his props. Maybe this was why he did it, to try and make himself invulnerable.

'You know all about these seats of power, do you?' the senator was saying in his warm voice. 'Your wife seemed to when I sat next to her. Beautiful woman. Quite beautiful! Take a seat. Take a seat.'

He gestured to a chair. Jim wanted to ask him exactly how he first met the drug runners – could he confirm it was when the Republicans were supporting them against the Communist government of their regime?

The man's pebble eyes examined him closely and Jim wondered if he had heard yet of Jim's inquiries, which had been very, very discreet so far.

'Jane . . . has mentioned you a few times. She seems quite taken with you! Beware!' said the senator, as if he were joking, and Jim repositioned himself, finding the attention now on him. 'Just some advice, that's all,' he said, with a chuckle, as his white fingers drummed over the desk. The desk, like the desks of all senators, was virtually empty suggesting total control over the debris of life, whereas no journalist's desk was anything but untidy, suggesting that all he or she could do was battle against the news, but never win the battle.

The magazine wanted him to produce the story he'd been working on for weeks now, but somehow he didn't quite want to finish it. He felt he needed more meetings and research. His editor had been pressing him to get a confessional interview with Senator Spalding, who was watching him warily now, but Jim felt the time wasn't ready quite yet. He needed more work on the South American angle, more comments from Spalding's friends and foes, who he was contacting now under the cover of doing a straightforward interview. Besides, most weeks Jane Meadows unearthed some new startling piece of evidence, from bank statements to a love letter of Senator Spalding to her, asking her to join him in his house he would build in the Caribbean. It was hard to see how he could be so careless, except there was a certain heaviness about him, as if maybe he didn't care quite as much as he should, as most of these politicians do.

In the outer office, Jane Meadows tidied up some papers, shuffling them into position, her heels digging into the carpet.

44

'Susan!' called Jim, in his fluffy white dressing gown which was too big for him, 'did you leave the back door open last night?'

'No!' she called.

'Someone must have left it open and it blew further open, I suppose,' said Jim, out in the fresh morning, looking round. 'What a wonderful still morning,' he said, stretching.

Susan moved quickly to him and took his arm. 'There's something odd. Someone's been in the house.'

He examined her for a moment. Around him the garden stood back in all its grey morning glory and the insects and birds began to call softly to each other as if testing out their voices for the day.

'What are you talking about? We just forgot to close the door and it blew open.'

Susan strode back, into the house.

'Your filing cabinet's wide open.' Although everything else in his study seemed at a glance to be in place – the photographs, the biographies, the careful disarray of stationery – the filing cabinet had an abandoned air. 'You must have left it open,' said Susan. 'The keys are in the lock.' She tugged her hair back into its scarlet band but it was so heavy bits straggled out and, exasperated, she turned away.

'I didn't leave it open,' he said, hurrying over and nearly sticking his head in. After a moment or two a hush descended on the room.

'The documents are gone. The tapes of my conversations with Jane. Everything.' He turned his head. 'Have you got them?'

'Excuse me?' said Susan, opening out her white hands, covered in rings. Her violet nightshirt dazzled his early morning eyes and he looked back at the grey cabinet.

'I just wondered if you had them,' he said. 'The notes. You know. About Jane Meadows. Could have been a joke of yours,' he said, his voice wandering off as his mind concentrated again on the cabinet, his thin back to Susan, while all around the shiny biographies of men with grey beards – Tennyson and the rest – glimmered and glittered as if laughing at the little figure in white with the bare feet, and the ankles draped in black hairs.

'Why would you think that?' she said. 'That's bizarre.'

A fly landed on the top of the cabinet and began to clean itself, interrupting its toilette every now and again to watch Jim.

'You have copies?' she said.

'Of some of them,' he said. 'I didn't want copies everywhere.'

'I see,' she said. 'Well! Maybe they're somewhere else in the house.' Susan touched a pearl button on her nightshirt. 'Maybe Rebecca moved them. What do you think? We'll ask her! Don't worry,' she said to his increasingly solemn shoulders, and gently touched them, half expecting them to be cold like snow.

'Yes,' he said, straightening, optimistic again. 'Maybe that's it. We'll ask her. Things just don't disappear!' He pounded two at a time up the stairs to where Rebecca was drowsily getting dressed.

'No,' replied Rebecca. 'I don't know about any documents. Should I?' she continued, putting on a pair of semi-matching white socks.

'You didn't leave the door open, did you?' said Susan. But Jim interrupted her as he returned briskly down the stairs; the belt on his fluffy dressing gown had come undone, and the front strip of his body was visible but he didn't seem to notice.

'It's such a big story. I haven't wanted to talk about it. Jane Meadows made me promise not to talk about it . . . you know, all the details. Of course I remember most of it. That's not a problem. Besides, I can ask her to go over anything I'm not a hundred per cent clear on. I don't know why I'm worried.'

'Who knows you're working on it?'

'Other journalists have guessed, I assume . . . I've been seen with Jane Meadows a lot. Besides, I had to brief my editor, and the trouble with journalists is once one person knows, everyone knows. All kinds of journalists have been snuffling around.'

'What was in the files? I mean, how bad?'

'How good, you mean? All kinds of great stuff. I told you.' In the kitchen he wrenched open the door of the fridge and the light illuminated his face; he stood there for a while, as if at a private altar, and then he grabbed a plastic carton of milk in one hand and a doughnut in another.

'I don't know why you buy these things. Do you realise how bad they are for us?'

He began to hum.

Jim bit into the doughnut and slid the milk onto the kitchen table while Susan passed him the corn flakes. He tipped so many into his bowl that the bowl overflowed. He grunted and sloshed some milk on, and sat down and began to spoon corn flakes into his mouth, while turning the radio on with his free hand.

'It could have been Ivana. Or Phillip,' she said.

'Phillip?'

'Or something to do with your story. Surely it could be to do with that. It's certainly not one of the *racoons*. Someone took them. Or you lost them.'

'Maybe,' he said.

'What? Darling. Everything is falling apart and you behave as if life's going on as usual.'

'Life's not falling apart.'

'I don't understand it. I think things happen when they don't. Rebecca's desperate for things to happen and you want nothing to happen at all. Yet you're the journalist. We all seem to be running on different tracks. And what about the people involved?' she said.

'What?'

'Some people are presumably involved in this drug business. Your senator. Other people.'

'Oh – them,' he said.

'Sometimes it seems you don't think real life actually happens,' said Susan. 'If you write about something, it becomes just a story. God, I hope you never write about me.'

'Why?'

'Because then you'll think I don't exist any more,' she said. She went out of the front door to get the copy of the *Washington Post*, which lay in its little plastic bag, in the dew, where the paper boy had thrown it from his van. The street was too still, and she hurried back.

'Do you remember that time you wrote a story about how gold was definitely going up, and it did, but it had never occurred to you to buy any gold yourself?'

Jim sliced a banana up into his second bowl of corn flakes.

'We should call the police,' said Susan.

'I don't want the police involved,' said Jim.

'What is it? Is everything OK?' said Rebecca, standing at the kitchen door.

'It could have been Phillip, though,' said Susan. 'He would have come here, in the night. Phillip.'

'Look,' said Jim. The strap of his watch was tangled with his dark hair. 'It could be anyone,' continued Jim. A spoonful of corn flakes hovered by his mouth. 'Or no one. A mistake. Maria perhaps. God knows. Ivana. I don't know. Some explanation.'

'What is it?' cried out Rebecca, black eyes like damsons, hair uncombed.

'In the study,' explained Susan, 'the filing cabinet was left open. And the back door.'

'A burglary!' yelled Rebecca. 'Did they take any jewels?' she said, dancing from foot to foot.

'We don't have any jewels,' said Susan, repositioning one chair after another around the kitchen table.

'What did they take then?' insisted Rebecca.

'Your father's things – some documents, interviews, that sort of thing – may possibly have gone.'

'Gone!' echoed Rebecca. 'Vanished!'

'If we get the police onto it, we'll have to give details of the documents. We must keep this private. Definitely,' said Jim, after calling Maria, who said she knew nothing of any damn documents, from which remark he assumed she was in bed with someone.

Jim stood, hands lost in the caverns of his pockets, before calling his editor to tell him of the burglary.

'You have copies?' said the editor.

'How could I do that? Everything was secret. I didn't want to run the chance of someone else – some other paper – getting their hands on this material. I knew that was the last thing you'd want. But what do I do now? Do we go straight ahead and publish before anyone else can?'

'Yes.'

'But . . . the only thing is . . . my source was getting me some last vital evidence. I really need that . . .

some details of the exact location of the airports where the drugs are arriving.'

'OK. OK. Get that and publish. I know it'll be good. It'll be great. I trust you, Jim. I have every faith in you. But, next time, use a safe, will you? This paper spends hundreds of thousands on its Washington office. You can afford a safe. Really. Get one. I'll pick up the tab. OK, Jim? A safe.'

Next Jim phoned Jane Meadows.

'Oh well,' she said, in a voice which he thought sounded a little afraid, 'never mind.'

45

'I've been thinking – this ghost,' said Maria. 'Maybe he took those documents.'

'That seems a little far-fetched,' said Susan, holding an old pink rabbit toy by the ears.

'Well,' said Maria firmly, driving the iron down over a white handkerchief, 'I can't cope with it all. I might stop coming here.'

'You're saying the ghost is male?'

'The guy who killed himself,' said Maria.

'Which one?' Susan enquired.

'What do you mean?'

'The father – the atomic physicist – and his son both committed suicide here,' said Susan, 'but the only ghost I know of is the old lady who is still alive in a nursing home in Ohio. She certainly haunts the place as much as she can. Always calling and sending messages through the neighbours.'

Susan had been tidying and Maria ironing in what had been the basement playroom and was now another storage area with scattered remnants of Rebecca's childhood: a red chair which was too small for her even when they arrived here, a pretend kitchen, a puppet theatre, a cardboard box overflowing with soft toys, their legs and arms waving as if asking for help. Susan was piling them into cardboard boxes to be put up in one of the attic cupboards.

'Maria,' said Susan. 'You're not serious about quitting?'

Maria wouldn't look at her. 'I am,' she said.

'And the ghost? You believe in a ghost?'

She nodded surlily.

'There must be another reason,' said Susan into the stillness. A family of crickets lived down here and one chirruped as if wishing to join in the conversation.

'I'll give you proper notice,' said Maria. 'I know it's just a part-time job but I'll still give you notice.'

'Is it the money? Do you want a rise? You know how much we value you.'

Maria forced the iron down over one of Jim's shirts. She was paying uncharacteristically careful attention to the sleeves of the pale blue shirt, the silver arrow-head of the iron digging into every crevice. Beneath Maria's arms, patches of sweat were darkening her orange T-shirt.

It was hard to imagine her intimidated by a fear of ghosts.

The hot water made cranking noises every now and again as though clearing its throat to say something truly terrible.

Maria hung the shirt over the back of a chair then bent down and moved the white plastic laundry basket over to one side. From it, she then took out a large handkerchief.

'Mrs Stewart, you just don't seem so . . . yourself . . . you know . . . you always were so kinda serene . . . and now you're not. You've been a little weird with me. Suspicious somehow.'

And then the dark eyes disappeared and the iron toiled to each edge of the handkerchief, flattening it all out, making the room smell of heat and linen. A soft-toy tiger looked up plaintively at Susan. Susan tried to remember her own toys. It seemed so long ago, and now Rebecca was finished with these dusty toys, her own childhood was finally finished with too; it was all gone, and life seemed to be growing darker and colder. Susan shivered, although it was hot down here, in the basement, because it had been too expensive to fit air conditioning here.

'And I've been offered another job,' said Maria.

Susan threw the tiger back onto the floor.

'I see. What job?'

'Oh, just cleaning. But in an office. You know, there'll be other people around. More opportunities. Companionship. An opportunity to meet other people and better myself while I'm studying for my exams.'

'That doesn't sound like your words.' Behind Maria two small black windows looked out onto two small below-ground wells; windows looking nowhere. 'Who told you that?' she said.

'You're sharp,' said Maria, looking at Susan. 'You are always sharp.'

'Who was it, Maria?'

'Sometimes you look for things that aren't there,' said Maria.

Susan picked out another handkerchief of Jim's from the wash bin, and examined his blue initials sewn in, given to him some Christmas before she knew him.

Susan could feel sweat begin to pour out of her body, and her white T-shirt was damp at the back, and her shorts clung to her legs as though stuck with light glue, and all around her hairline the beads of perspiration seemed to press out as though her insides were melting.

Maria was watching Susan, and she held the iron in one hand. She plunged her hand into the basket and withdrew a T-shirt of Jim's, which she began unnecessarily to iron. A cricket, who always seemed particularly fond of Maria's voice, chirruped from the corner. Maria often sang down here, and one or the other of the crickets would join in. Once, however, a cricket jumped out at her when she was walking over the room and she stepped on him and squashed him.

The T-shirt looked very large splayed out there on the grey shiny ironing board as Maria attacked it.

'And you got that gun up at the top of the house. I don't hold with no guns, Mrs Stewart,' she continued, ironing more fiercely. Some of the tiles had come up here and there, and some were cracked, and there was an ink stain on another. The same family had lived in the house for sixty years, and it had a dilapidated air. Susan liked the quality of imperfection: the cracks in the walls, the tiny kitchen dominated by the avocado green fridge, the missing black and white tiles in the bathroom, the broken ones in the basement playroom, the sadness in the empty bookshelves, the grief in the cedar closets which had once held someone else's clothes.

'I don't hold with no guns,' said Maria.

Later that day Rebecca stood smiling in the doorway with that distant look in her eyes, as if building herself palaces in India.

'What is it?' said Susan, who was attentively cleaning one glass pane of her bedroom window with a tissue.

'My shoes,' said Rebecca. 'I wondered if you liked my new shoes.'

Her shoes were silver and had a little heel. She lifted her foot in the way Ivana always did. Rebecca bent down. 'They fit well,' she said, 'except for the right little toe.'

Susan plucked out another tissue and started cleaning another pane.

'They're a present . . . from Ivana,' said Rebecca, in her yellow shorts and yellow T-shirt and brown arms, a golden girl. 'Is that OK?'

'Really you should not take presents. You should take them back.'

'But I love them.'

'You should still return them, darling.'

That evening Susan got out a tray of beetles and stared at them: at their glossy legs, their agonised eyes, the precision of their design.

She remembered the beginning of *Metamorphosis*:

'When Gregor Samsa awoke one morning from troubled dreams he found himself transformed in his bed into a monstrous insect. He was lying on his hard, shell-like back . . .'

With charcoal, Susan began to draw a beetle, his stiff old man's legs.

Women wouldn't be quite so surprised by such a transformation, she thought; we change far more than men ever do. I sometimes expect to be someone different in the morning. We are selfish, sexual, ambitious young women and then overnight, with the birth of a child, change into unselfish, patient creatures endlessly caring for someone else, people who hardly exist, who vanish overnight.

Now Phillip comes back into my life and sees me the way I was, and the image I have of myself is distorted. I do not know who I am. I don't know if I'm the endlessly loving, carefree, playful mother of Rebecca or the dark vision of Phillip's dreams.

She drew in the antennae of the beetle.

46

Rebecca lay in bed with her eyes closed, imagining she was the Queen of England. Sometimes she executes people, sometimes she bestows great honours. When she was little, British Royalty was her favourite game but no one at the local school had wanted to play it with her except Judy, a gawky girl who played on condition she was a princess. Eventually Rebecca had decided she was better off just playing it by herself so she used to play the game, with all its complex ramifications, at recess, alone. But now she has made some friends.

She still liked to think about history.

Henry VII 1485–1509. She enjoyed thinking about that strange portrait of Henry VII with the clever hands and calculating face – as though he'd personally made up the whole of history.

Even though she liked to play basketball or soccer with the boys out on the scraggy green behind the school, she didn't feel quite comfortable. The boys wore loafers and big T-shirts. They walked with heads down and shoulders up as though brooding on some athletic triumph, for their bodies were all radiantly well-organised, whereas sometimes hers didn't seem to have been fitted together properly. She felt like an earlier, unimproved model. Even their hair was golden, burnished by sunshine.

When she had first arrived at the school the teacher had asked them what they wanted to do when they grew up. Someone said an airline pilot, another a lawyer, another a doctor. Rebecca said she would be a storm.

'Seven is a difficult age,' she had heard her mother tell her father.

Rebecca liked odd facts. She liked to remember that during the reign of Henry VII playing cards were first invented and that his wife, Elizabeth of York, was the model for the queen on the playing cards. Ivana told her that.

Ivana said that the cards showed Rebecca's mother was going to suffer.

Rebecca turned on her side and curled up.

The door was ajar so some of the light from the hall spilled into her bedroom and kept bad thoughts away.

She got up and walked with bare feet over the wooden floor to the tiled bathroom. The shriek of the television carried up the stairs.

She looked down at her white hands, like Henry VII's, and wondered if she could make things happen.

She went to the window and stared out at the blackness. When she was in England the night was an altogether more approachable affair. Here it was black and didn't seem to forgive anything.

She left the black panes of the window and

walked softly into the den off the main bedroom. Some paper lay on the white wicker coffee table. Rebecca curled up on the sofa and began to draw. She tried to draw the face of her sister. Her mother wanted her to have a sister but she didn't know what the sister would look like. Would she be her friend or her enemy? Rebecca gave her a big smile and a mop of curly hair before colouring her in.

She wondered where unborn children waited and in her mind saw a crowd of children jostling and shoving at the sides of a stage, trying to get on while some stood further back listening for someone to call their name, and after all maybe the way is to draw a picture of the child, maybe that's how children really come into the world. Once she recalled long ago she'd asked her mother about how babies arrived and she became flustered, and tidied her hair, and at that time Rebecca had assumed that was because she was embarrassed about not knowing.

Of course, Rebecca knew now that that wasn't so.

Rebecca put down the picture and wandered, in her spotted pyjamas, to her parents' bedroom. Picking up a magazine lying by her mother's side of the bed, she sat on the bed, and flipped through it until she came to a picture of a little girl of her age, and wondered if her sister would look like that. This girl had knowing eyes and a black bun. She turned over more pages, scouring for glossy pictures.

Rebecca put it aside, and sighed. She wished she were nine or ten again. At ten nothing was expected of her. Now she was supposed to know what she wanted from life, who she was, yet she didn't feel any different. The night before her eleventh birthday her father kept looking at her and shaking his head.

'Oh . . . you're not going to be a little child any more,' he said. 'You're nearly a teenager.'

It was as though there would be some kind of awful transformation yet nothing happened, except her mother and father treated her differently, with a new respect she didn't like. They even expected her to be tidier. It was silly, really. She tried to explain it to her father but her father didn't listen. Her father wasn't good at understanding what she said. Sometimes it seemed her father didn't see her clearly, just saw her as a little girl, or rather his idea of a little girl, a sort of mixture of films he'd seen and what he remembered dimly about his own childhood. He was always referring back to his childhood. Often he was too simple. Last winter he was sitting at his desk, which faced the street, and Rebecca came in. Thick snow had fallen in the night.

'When I was your age,' said her father, crouched over his paper throwing papers on the floor, 'I loved the snow.'

Rebecca climbed out of her bath, the water from her body pooling on the broken linoleum floor. A tiny spider danced into the corner of the room and as she dried herself Rebecca watched it try to disappear round the corners of the linoleum.

Later, carefully covered over by her pyjamas, Rebecca crept upstairs to the cupboard in her mother's attic study to watch Sillea, the pale yellow spider with bright orange markings she especially liked. Unusually for a spider living in a house, she made an orb web, dropping her silken strands, sewing her clocks of web, round and round, as soft as dandelion seeds, as strong as steel, intricate as a maze made of silver dew. Sometimes Rebecca would follow each strand and wonder where, if she followed the web, they would lead her.

Rebecca followed a strand; one of the anchors led to the cardboard box labelled 'Personal letters' in bumpy blue biro, another to a black bag labelled 'Rebecca's baby clothes'. This time she didn't look at any of the letters.

She watched a tiny fly catch in the web.

There were black widow spiders (*Latrodectus mactans*) down in the shed, with their flamboyant red markings, but Rebecca didn't tell anyone in case someone killed them.

47

'But why do you have to have him round just because he's Chief Editor?' said Rebecca.

'Editor in Chief,' expounded Jim.

'Mummy doesn't want anyone round. I'm not sure she's well,' said Rebecca.

'We have to. He asked to come round.'

'Can I stay up?' said Rebecca.

'Sure.'

'I'm surprised you're having Ivana round. Sometimes, you know, I'm not so sure Mummy does like Ivana.'

'Ivana's husband, Gustav, is an old friend of my boss.'

'I don't think Ivana thinks he's done really well . . . you know, in life. She thinks all he cares about is his collection of old glass he keeps in his study. He's not an ambassador yet. I suppose she'd like him to be an ambassador,' said Rebecca.

At the dinner an expert on Europe came along who was very depressed-looking and didn't say a word all evening but just ate, very close to the table, with an expression of infinite sorrow about his moustache. Rebecca found he was the only person she identified with, in part because he was rollingly fat and reminded her of Box Hill, an area in Surrey, England, that she had visited with her mother one summer. It was soft and hilly and there was somehow too much of it. His features were tucked away somewhere in his fat so that it was hard to know what he looked like. His pudgy fingers kept grasping the wine and pouring it out. He had flown in from Brussels a few days ago.

Gustav, Ivana's too-handsome husband, ate demurely. It was as though he could be taken apart bit by bit – first the white teeth, then the aquiline nose could come off, then the hair which lay smooth and black. On his hands he wore two gold rings and his suits fitted him perfectly. Beneath the suits shone well-polished shoes. When he spoke all she could see of him was those glinting white teeth, and his polite, half-bowing frame.

Rebecca's mother had said she couldn't manage a dinner party so Rebecca and her father had ordered a meal from a Lebanese restaurant and gone to collect it just about an hour ago. As they had been unable to park, the traffic round Dupont Circle had been held up as they loaded the pots of couscous and the salads and the kebabs and all the other chopped up this-and-thats into the car. The dishes had all been covered over with Cellophane and had been put carefully in the trunk and back of the car but every time it stopped or started on the way back the plates all slipped around.

Each time Ivana took a bite, Rebecca just knew

she would say she recognised the food as from Houmanias (Ivana prided herself on her knowledge of Washington restaurants), and Rebecca hardly kept her eyes off her throughout the meal, as she sat at the end observing the adults, while pretending to be enjoying the food speckled with green bits of herbs.

Rebecca wondered if it was a good idea if she went with Ivana to Poland. There was something about Ivana which fascinated Rebecca – the browning photographs she brought out, with women in high-necked dresses, and small lockets, gazing inscrutably through time – but something that disturbed her too. Rebecca liked to watch Ivana's hands, little ivory hands, and the antique-shop smell of her bedroom.

If she went with Ivana to Poland, she would dress like that too, Ivana had said, in a high-necked satin dress, and walk over the terrace of the old house and into the ballroom with the vast gold-rimmed mirrors. Her mother would let her go because her mother loved her so much. Her mother wanted her to be happy. She knew her mother would let her go in the end if she really wanted to go, although she would worry about her and miss her.

Rebecca loved the names – Poland, Warsaw, Cracow – like the smell of the last sherry-brown slithers of scent at the bottom of a bottle.

Gustav was staring at his glass now, the cold glass. Ivana could have been warmer too, if she had been loved like Rebecca was loved. Instead Ivana had grown into a porcelain figure. Terrible not to be loved, thought Rebecca. So lonely. She smiled at Ivana.

Her mother began to talk too much, perhaps to stop Ivana from saying she knew the food was from Houmanias.

It was hard to know exactly why, but it seemed what her mother was saying wasn't quite right for a dinner party today.

'I read in the *Post*,' said Susan hectically, her elbows on the table, her eyes too bright, her voice too high, 'about a diarist in this area who writes down everything he does, minute by minute, from taking a drink of water to pouring out his corn flakes to peeing.'

The editor in chief coughed, and poured himself more wine.

'But how do you store time?' she continued, turning her glass of red wine round. 'Photographs are only a partial success. Some, I suppose, is stored in other people. Someone steps into a room and brings it all back, with a smile or a grimace or a way of shuffling their shoes or scratching the left side of their nose or of speaking.'

'Yes, how right you are,' said the editor in chief uncomfortably, who had heavy jowls. At the end of enormously long arms his hands pushed his meat around as though mourning the deaths of the animals involved. The jaw was so square and heavy Rebecca kept checking it to make sure it hadn't fallen off.

The shiny knives and forks seemed too bright and the crystal glittered by the candlelight.

'Washington is agog about these missing documents of yours,' said Gustav to Jim.

'Oh really?' said Rebecca's father. 'I thought no one knew.'

Sometimes he seemed younger than she was, like a small child, with his large head, domed forehead and alarmed eyes.

'The person who took them would know they were missing,' said Susan.

'Amazing how news gets around,' said Jim.

'Especially damaging news,' said Susan.

'Not that it matters,' he continued. 'We had copies of it all. It's all fine.' He seized a glass of wine and drank it enthusiastically, then looked round with a grim smile which puckered the corners of his mouth. He leapt up to serve wine to everyone else, and went round the table twice before sitting down.

'They can't just have disappeared,' said the editor in chief, who dug his hand in his pocket and after some while produced a handkerchief and sighed, as if nothing illustrated the simple horror of life more than this search through his pocket.

Rebecca moved her couscous to one side of her plate and began to construct a small mountain.

'Do you want a proper investigation?' said the editor in chief.

'I don't think that would be wise. I want to try and keep this quiet,' said Jim. 'Publicity does us no good.'

The editor in chief blew his nose loudly while everyone waited respectfully.

'Well!' said Ivana once the sound of the nose-blowing had stopped. 'A ghost must have taken them! I always said this house was haunted!'

'Yes,' said Susan. 'You did!' Today Susan's eyes were dark and wary and Ivana seemed made of wire jutting out here and there.

Rebecca wasn't sure she was liking the conversation and the way her father pushed his food around on his plate.

'The situation really is a calamity,' said Gustav about something or other, rolling his perfectly formed words down the centre of the table, each word separately, one by one, as his gold ring flashed and his smile flashed and his super-white shirt shone gloriously.

'Jim didn't mislay them and they didn't disappear. They were stolen,' said Susan. 'What is so odd about that? You journalists spend your life among dramas and yet when dramas happen to you, you try and minimise them. You think,' she continued, again a little too brightly with a smile like a rough sea, 'that life takes place somewhere else. You think stories happen somewhere else not in your own house, but that is where all the real stories take place.'

Susan's eyes were particularly huge tonight, and outlined in black.

Lugubriously, the editor in chief scraped at his plate, sending the last fragments of couscous to one side before being shovelled up onto the fork and plunged into his mouth.

'And who took them, then?' said the editor in chief.

'If they were stolen,' sighed Rebecca's father, 'a

journalist could have taken them, the drug dealers, or even the government.'

'But you said there was no sign of a break-in.'

'A friend then?' said Ivana. 'I hope you don't suspect me!' She giggled like a kettle boiling. 'What about your maid Maria?'

All the men round the table except Jim wore dark colours, church colours, while Jim had on a white suit as if he were a sacrifice.

'They were hidden right at the back of the filing cabinet.'

'You do realise,' said Ivana, 'that some people think you took them? Isn't that amusing?'

Susan turned slowly to Ivana.

'And why would I take them?'

'Someone said you were jealous of the investigation.'

'We shouldn't be talking like this,' said Jim.

A green handkerchief stuck up from Rebecca's father's pocket, and it seemed somehow a tremendously hopeful object.

Rebecca yawned and began to think about swimming tomorrow. Sometimes, when you were tired, swimming was like trying to get a grip on quicksilver, it just slipped out of your grasp when you wanted it to propel you forward through the wall of water.

'I'm devastated the documents have gone,' said Jim. 'The filing cabinet was locked, and the keys were in the pocket of my jacket by my bed. It's almost inconceivable someone would get in, creep up to our bedroom, get the keys and open the filing cabinet.

The keys were left in the lock.' Rebecca wondered if her father really did wonder if it had been something to do with Susan.

Intimately, Ivana leant over the editor in chief. 'I told you, a ghost!'

'Any ghosts in this house are on our side,' said Susan.

It was so peaceful in the water, covered in silver, fighting through the bubbles, but being human was so limited, thought Rebecca.

She wondered if she would see the ghost tonight, and realised she was afraid of going to bed.

'We've had a lot of stress recently, Susan. Are you sure you want to go ahead with our party?' asked Jim that night.

'Yes, OK. We'll go ahead,' she said.

48

In the cat's cradle is the spider waiting to run across and catch the prey and as she watches the spider Rebecca knows that here in the mysteries of the web – in the dance of geometry – is the answer. It seemed, from watching television, that men and women felt the answer was each other – 'I love you', 'You are the one'. But if they could only see that there was something else they wouldn't be hurt so much. Crouched up, hiding, ready to run out and pounce, the spider's beauty was to Rebecca a concentration of the whole, glorious, abandoned world – its shades, its legs, its silken tresses spread across the air. Designs of hammocks, string, ropes to hang people and ropes to raise great pyramids into the air, the spider hides and broods, sending out silken strands to swing down and down.

49

It was odd, thought Susan, drawing a spider up in her attic room, to love such strange creatures, the spinners of webs, dancing like weightless crabs over the face of the earth, hurling out threads, swinging from trapezes, acrobats defying all assumptions.

Here they were, in every crevice, every corner, waiting to dance forwards or backwards, weaving their way, magic and mysterious, into the most ordinary lives. An event can be a small thing, she thought.

50

Although her parents had employed a small catering company which handled some of the British minister's more low-key functions, Rebecca had offered to help serve the canapés at the party. She watched a young man with one earring in his left ear prepare the shiny smidgens of smoked salmon on dry toast, the bits of smelly cheese on biscuits, horrible stuff, she thought. Rebecca wandered off upstairs to see how her mother was getting on.

Her mother did not seem quite balanced, as though she might at any moment tip over in either direction. Her make-up was hectic tonight, rather as though Rebecca herself had applied it. Susan wore an Indian-Raj style silk jacket and black trousers, and her black hair was loose.

'Thoreau wrote, "Beware of all enterprises that require new clothes,"' said Susan, as she tugged up her trousers, and pulled at her dark unruly hair.

Usually Susan was well put together but recently her features had become separated and seemed to wander round her face wondering where to stop, as though playing a game of musical chairs in which the music never stopped playing. The mouth in particular seemed lost, and the green eyes were cloudy and imprecise.

'You should put on more lipstick,' said Rebecca. That way, she thought, it would at least be clear where her mouth was. It was curious how when adults were disturbed their faces changed completely. Hers didn't change much from day to day, but then she was seldom sad.

At any moment, Rebecca thought, her mother would just reach up and take off her pert nose, strip off her hair . . . for she didn't seem real. She was a modern artist's version of herself, decided Rebecca.

Rebecca thought it was probably because this other child hadn't come yet. She wondered if that's what happened if you didn't get what you wanted; you almost ceased to be you.

During some of the party her mother was in the kitchen talking while Rebecca carried round a plate of canapés, ducking under her mother's arm and out into the party where she enjoyed listening to scraps of conversation. Being a child at an adult party was a little like being invisible.

The conversation wasn't shocking but it was exciting, somehow, the way it buzzed and the way the adults kept sipping at their drinks, and the music played, and the way the adults who had been charming to her for the first half an hour now completely ignored her. You could see their personalities: the shy one who made an effort, the person who was confident, the sly one, the boastful one, the one who never listened, the one who kept telling jokes, the boring one . . . Once they'd had a few drinks they weren't much different from the girls and boys at school, only the children at school were rather more fun.

When she had first told her friends that she collected stamps, Mary Evans had frowned.

'Stamps. How weird,' she had said, and then proceeded to tell Rebecca about her collection of pencil sharpenings.

'Pencil sharpenings?' Rebecca had queried.

'You know . . . the bits left after you sharpen your pencil. I have three jars full.'

'Well done,' Rebecca had said.

Another girl collected pencil leads.

Quite a few of the people at the party were English – other English journalists or people from the British embassy. Others were neighbours and there were many American journalists and politicians.

Her father was winding through the party like a blind dinosaur while her mother stood in corners talking, but without her usual calm. She kept looking around and kept tugging at her hair. But she was lovely, thought Rebecca, with her graceful neck, her elongated white hands, the way she moved. She seldom wore boring clothes; there were castles in her jacket, or dragons in a brooch, as though the clothes were part of her thoughts rather than part of the front she put on for the outside world.

Rebecca thought she might live in Morocco and be a witch when she was older.

As Rebecca made her way through the party she noticed how much better put together the American women were compared with the English women who seemed to have been assembled from different packages. The English didn't see themselves as wholes. The shoes sat uneasily on the feet; the legs had an uneasy relationship with the feet; the skirts seemed to be a little uncertain as to what they were supposed to be doing, hanging around the hips, and the blouses covered over the breasts tentatively. As for the hair, it was sketchily arranged, indistinctly coloured, as though the owners of the hair were attempting to project such a tiny quota of personality that, having met her once, no one would recognise her again. The American women, however, had authority and bearing. They would walk into rooms rather as John Wayne walked into saloon bars.

Rebecca decided her father was excellent at parties as she watched him whisper in ears, dart from one side of the room to the other, always be there when the door opened, make every face he spoke to light up.

Ivana stood in the middle of the room talking nervously, wearing a bright shawl, taking off her earrings every now and again while her husband Gustav drifted at the edges like something washed up at sea. Ivana kept glancing softly at Gustav. Rebecca realised that Ivana loved him, but he had no interest in her.

'Chopin!' she heard Ivana exclaim.

'I hate this place. I hate America,' Ivana's voice rang out. 'I hate all this open-plan living!'

'Rebecca,' said Gustav, in his cushiony voice. Today he had that same charming expression wrenched across his face as though fixed in it by a change of the wind. He patted his hair, which was too thick and wavy for a middle-aged man, and his lips were too thick and wavy too. 'I wanted to say – I am glad you can be a friend to Ivana. She needs someone . . . She always wanted a child. I spend too much time with my work and my collection of glassware. I know that.'

'I don't really like things,' she said. 'I don't know why grown-ups do. I mean, I used to like dolls you can play with, and I like clothes but I can't understand *glassware* or furniture.'

'It's because glassware has nothing to do with people,' he said, brushing a fleck of dust from his jacket. 'I suppose that's it.'

Rebecca stepped back into the party but he followed her. 'I hear you're going to Poland with Ivana?'

'Maybe,' said Rebecca.

'It is just a weekend?' he said.

'Probably,' said Rebecca.

'Good,' he said. 'Because sometimes I wonder if she's planning to go there and never come back.'

'Oh no! We're just going for a little holiday and coming back together. That's what she said. I've got to ask my mother though.'

'She's said very little to me about it, you see,' said Gustav, and moved away.

From the other side of the room she saw Ivana watching Gustav. It must be sad to love someone who doesn't love you, thought Rebecca, and went over and lightly touched Ivana's arm as she passed.

'You know they said I had leukaemia?' said a voice. 'Of course I didn't. And subsequently I've found no less than two other women whom the same doctor misdiagnosed. The cost of the tests. You can imagine.'

'I had a birthday party which was like the Last Judgement,' said the voice of a woman with fluffy hair and tiny hands. 'Everyone came back from everywhere in my past and they all paraded in front of me, presumably so that God could decide whether I'd lived a good or bad life. Everyone got drunker and drunker and ended up throwing wine at each other all over the walls. It stained everything and people who'd been in love fell out of love and people who weren't in love fell in love. Everyone said it was the best party they'd ever been to but I hated it. Even my mother was there and one of my old boyfriends tried to seduce her . . .'

'In my twenties I was defined by the clothes I wore. Now it's furniture,' said another woman, examining her nails.

Rebecca meandered on, looking up at the mouths opening and closing, the tilted glasses, the lipstick on the glasses. She heard a man telling a woman he worked on 'the hill' and she had a vague idea that this hill was something to do with government. She had queued to go round the White House. It had been pretty boring. Although it was, well, interesting to be at an adult party, it wasn't as exciting as parties in films because no one was kissing or holding hands or dancing wildly or slapping each other's faces as they did at the cinema or on television when they'd drunk alcohol.

'He's been fighting cancer for ten years. Ten years,' someone was saying.

'I jog every day without fail.'

'Rebecca, this is an old friend of mine, Jane Meadows,' said her father, introducing her to a woman with black square glasses and neat clothes. 'Jane works for a senator.' Jane Meadows stared at Rebecca intently. Jane Meadows had high black heels, a well-pressed blouse, well-filed nails. 'She's helping me with the book.'

'Hello, Rebecca,' she said in an oddly lush Southern voice. 'Are you enjoying the party?'

Rebecca's father stood by moving from foot to foot; the woman had a slow inquisitive smile as if wishing to creep beneath Rebecca's skin.

'Yes I am!' said Rebecca, examining Jane Meadows severely, and moved off, leaving her father and Jane Meadows talking together. She heard the woman suddenly laugh, clearly and rather beautifully. But adults were always behaving like this to each other because they couldn't have any real fun.

Every now and again Rebecca would wander back into the kitchen to get more canapés from the young bartender with the single earring in his pierced ear. The rest of the house had been tidied – fresh flowers poised sympathetically, pictures repositioned – but the kitchen remained wild. A tomato ketchup bottle battled with a salt cellar, a packet of corn flakes lay on its side, an array of paper clips spread themselves to one side of the microwave. It was as though an entirely different set of rules applied there.

Rebecca wondered where her mother was, and wandered round the house, finding evidence of her in various rooms. In her bedroom there was a dent in the bed where she had been sitting. There were more lipsticks out on the dressing table than before. The drapes had been pulled over every window. Even in Rebecca's room, there were signs of her mother's presence; the bedcover had been straightened, the room smelt of her mother's scent.

Eventually, Rebecca went down into the kitchen, and her mother was there, with her back to the door. She didn't seem to hear Rebecca, and Phillip, who must have been aware of Rebecca's presence, didn't look at her as Rebecca softly closed the door behind her. The ugly and unfashionable fridge looked a little like a bodyguard, and gave a threatening murmur every now and again and the radio played some rap music. Phillip Jordan was facing Susan, leaning against the oven. They seemed to be in the middle of some argument, and the smoke from his cigarette filled up the room and seemed in some way to cut them off from her.

'I need to talk to you before things get even more out of hand,' he was saying to Susan, in his soft, clear voice. 'I got your message on the answering machine about Jim – the documents – well, I don't know anything about them.' He took another puff on his cigarette. 'Look, Susan, it's hard to know how to put this but I know you're still . . . obsessed . . . by me. I know that. It's quite clear. The way you look at me. Everything you say.'

Her mother's back was made of steel.

'That's why I think we should just try to be friends,' said Phillip with a funny little smile. 'That's why I came here today to the party, although I know you didn't invite me. But Jim wanted me to come, to see you, and have a talk. I mean, it's beginning to upset Sandra . . . I just want to be friends with you, with your daughter, with your husband. We might be together in this town for years.'

Rebecca could sense the sweat under her mother's arms and down her back and on her forehead. Phillip took a step towards Susan.

Susan stepped back, as if she thought he was about to touch her. 'Excuse me,' she said, tucking stray hair behind her ears, then raising her head as if coming up for air. 'But just because you had a right to do this thirteen years ago, doesn't mean you have one now.'

'A right to do what?' he said, blinking.

'This, Phillip.'

'For God's sake, Susan, I'm just talking to you in a kitchen at your party. That's all.'

'You were going to touch me.'

'Of course I wasn't.'

'I'm sorry then,' she said.

He threw his cigarette butt into the sink and wiped his mouth with the back of his sleeve.

'I went abroad. You probably saw the pieces in the papers,' he said.

'I never read your pieces,' said Susan.

His white face looked down at the ground.

'Or your letters,' she said.

'Look,' he said, 'thirteen years ago it might have

been different but we're talking years and years and years ago, another life . . . You are a mother now . . . You have a life . . . I know you love me . . . you just have to forget it. I should like to be friends, that's all, to be able to take a walk with you now and again, have you all round to dinner. After all, we are part of each other's pasts. Apart from that, you are nothing at all to me now. You have to accept that.'

'Phillip,' she said, after a moment.

'Yes,' he said.

'I don't want you to get to know us better,' said Susan, turning away.

'Hi!' said Rebecca.

Susan spun round. 'Have you been there long?'

'Just a minute,' said Rebecca.

Susan walked away, back into the party, turning to look at Phillip as she passed through the door. It was a sort of cold way of looking which made Rebecca uncomfortable.

'Hi, Rebecca,' said Phillip. He lit another cigarette. 'Are you bored to tears by all these adults gossiping?' His voice sounded uneasy.

She shrugged and reddened and tried not to stare at Phillip, who created some kind of reaction in her she didn't understand as he watched her so slowly.

'Do you like Washington?' she said, to try to make him feel better.

'I find it interesting.'

'It's really quite dull here,' she said. 'Nothing much happens. Well, it's all right for children. We like roller blading and riding bikes. But if you're a grown-up . . .' She shook her head.

'But they plan wars here. That's interesting,' said Phillip.

Rebecca screwed up her nose.

'Well, quite,' he admitted.

Phillip wore jeans and a white shirt with no tie and didn't seem quite like the other people at the party, as she, Rebecca, didn't feel like the other people. He seemed to be coming from a long way away as she seemed to have come from a long way away.

The bartender swung through the kitchen door.

'I'm going to Poland on holiday in a couple of weeks,' Rebecca said to Phillip.

'Oh really?' said Phillip.

'With Ivana . . .' said Rebecca. 'See you,' she remarked as she followed her mother.

Phillip's girlfriend Sandra was still at the party, standing round and talking, but somehow without any enthusiasm. She seemed lonely in her little black skirt and top, with her chin lifted perkily up as if trying to seem happy. She was speaking to Ivana.

Rebecca joined them.

'Yes,' Sandra was saying, 'I believe Phillip knew Susan a long time ago. He was an old boyfriend of hers. Funny, isn't it?'

'Oh yes,' said Ivana, 'I just wondered . . . one watches these things, don't you find?'

The women laughed, although there was no reason to laugh.

'This is Susan's daughter, Rebecca,' said Ivana.

'We met,' said Rebecca.

'Hello,' said Sandra, lifting her head back like a

nervous pony. 'We must go soon. You haven't seen Phillip, have you?'

'He was talking to my mother in the kitchen . . . but she's over there now . . .' said Rebecca. 'Maybe he's still in the kitchen.'

Sandra checked her watch and smiled a watery smile before wandering off.

Soon afterwards Rebecca saw Phillip leave with Sandra hanging onto his arm as though she couldn't stand, and her face tipped up towards him.

51

In the morning, hung over, Jim hurried along the corridor of the press building passing doors labelled 'Voice of Korea', 'Polish State Radio', 'Nigeria Today', each label stuck into a little brass holder on the door, like visiting cards. Every now and again the cards would be replaced by another name.

In his office his secretary, Wendy, greeted him with enthusiasm as she always did, exhausting enthusiasm on a morning like this. Indeed, she seemed to leap from her seat, and her frizzy hair seemed to be even frizzier, as if experiencing a series of electric shocks.

Feet moving rapidly, he hurtled into his office, and stumbled back a little.

'Christ!' he said.

His secretary hovered behind him like a helicopter making a distant humming noise.

'Yes!' he said.

'You had a call,' she said, softly. 'From Jane Meadows. Wanting to thank you for the party. She wants you to ring her.'

'Sure,' he said, and she handed him some coffee. 'Is it decaf?'

'No.'

'Good,' he said, and took it from her. 'Thank you,' he said, more mildly.

He still glared at the room, as if it had ambushed him unexpectedly. The rectangular desk. The windows gazing out, dazed, on the same street scene. Christ, and his head hurt. He swirled decisively round to his chair, sat on it, and grabbed the phone, and stared at that accusingly.

'Everything OK?' said Wendy.

'Not particularly.'

'Matthew – from the White House – wondered if you were free to play tennis tonight.'

'I only play because he's a good contact. He can hardly hit the ball.'

From the desk, Susan and Rebecca smiled at him uncomfortably from a photograph frame, and he frowned at it, feeling that he too was somehow trapped in a photograph frame and couldn't wriggle free. It was time that had trapped him, just the passage of years, each decade nailing another side to the frame which ended up all around you, and however much you beat on the sides of the frame you couldn't get out.

It's why people took drugs, to get out of the frame. But Susan and Rebecca were his solace, he reminded himself.

He slumped back on his chair. The offices of the magazine were divided by partitions, and there were marks on the carpet where other partitions had been before. As soon as anyone left or was fired, their office within the main office was pulled down, and another one erected soon afterwards to suit the prestige and needs of the next journalist to take his or her place.

Sometimes it seemed to Jim that Susan smiled at him from the photograph, a slow, musing smile as though finding him entirely temporary but loving him for that all the same.

Well, what does she want? he thought, shoving one of the green Pentel pens back in the old mug kept for that purpose. He took out a packet of chocolate-chip cookies from his top left drawer, and an assortment of vitamin bottles.

Behind him, the wide window was full of grey: grey sky, a grey office block, grey clouds like smoke.

'Do you know where you can get green tea?' he said to Wendy as she left the room. 'It's a great antidote to free radicals.'

She shook her head. 'By the way,' she said, 'that British journalist Brian came in asking how often you saw Jane Meadows. I said I had no idea. So nosey.'

'Good.'

As a child he had kept a diary and written bad poetry. He had dreamt of writing something which stopped time, which made him remembered for generations. But the best he could do nowadays was keep up with the present. The future was out of the question. Except this story . . . sex, politics, drugs . . . perhaps its sheer vulgarity would make it last. It was dangerous, though. Perhaps he should back off.

Jane Meadows rang again.

'It was great to see your wife again . . . and your daughter is a real beauty. I loved your home. Wonderful you're so settled, somehow, as if you'll be there forever, to your dying day. That must be a great feeling.'

'Yes,' said Jim.

'You know, a contented marriage must be great. None of the hurly-burly.'

Jim wished Susan were not so distant at present.

'Why don't you come over later and we can do some more work?' said Jane.

'I don't think I should be seen round at your place much more . . .'

'I have managed to get some more key documents you may want to see.'

'I'll come tomorrow,' said Jim.

He began to write . . . and that night he took home all his notes, and the tapes he had recorded, as he was beginning to worry that too many people were circling round the office, looking for information.

52

Susan and Rebecca walked through the capacious darkness of their street to the main road, which they ran across, then sauntered up a little turning, by the houses of friends, with bicycles on the porches, passing the funny red wooden houses which served as the town hall, and coming to the bank on the other side of which was Rebecca's school playing fields. They approached the playing fields up some stone steps, with rusty nails, and saw the school stretched out before them in the heavy summer air. Soon it would be August, and the rabid heat would become even hotter, and it would be impossible to step out except to a swimming pool. The community pool was just down the road and the children spent their summers in and out of the pool, wandering through the area by themselves, apparently completely safe.

'Ivana asked me if you were well,' said Rebecca. 'She said you seemed nervy. She seems to care about you a lot.'

'How kind,' said Susan.

Susan and Rebecca crossed the scraggy grass of the playing fields and entered the school by the side door while other children and parents converged on the school from other directions for the once-a-week evening maths club, which took place all the year round except for August. The club aimed to inspire children to see that maths was amusing.

Rebecca, head up, led Susan up the stairs, past paintings on the wall ('I did that,' she said, pointing at a charcoal picture of a clown, as she went by), past the doors of classrooms, past wall displays about John Kennedy and Martin Luther King.

In the classroom where the maths club was taking place, the desks were cleared away to the edge of the room and there were about a dozen maths puzzles arranged around the room – versions of the 'move one matchstick to make two squares' problems.

'They're too easy,' said one of the handsomer fathers, Matthew Fink, frowning deeply and crossing his arms while his daughter Nina talked to Rebecca. 'Just too easy,' he said, frowning even more deeply and taking a step back as if believing that distance might help him solve the problem.

An agonisingly shy man with frizzy red hair was standing by the puzzles putting his hands in and out of his pockets as the children chatted and the parents milled around trying to do the puzzles.

After about fifteen minutes, the red-haired man suddenly plunged into the middle of the room, and stood with his legs wide apart and announced, 'My name is Jeff Rogerson. Dr Jeff Rogerson. To-night I wanted to outline a few ideas of Quantum Physics.'

There was a generalised shuffling in the room.

'One,' said Dr Rogerson, 'is the uncertainty principle.' He seized a pack of cards from his pocket. 'Now, you are uncertain what the top card is, aren't you? But the uncertainty principle goes further than that. *The card itself is uncertain.* The card is not,' and Jeff Rogerson turned it over, 'the four of clubs until it is turned over, until we see it. That is one of the most important points in quantum physics.'

'That's nonsense,' said Nina loudly. 'It's a four of clubs whether we know it is or not. It just is.'

'Another important principle,' said Dr Rogerson, 'is the many universe or multiuniverse theory – which states that every atom, every movement, every choice, has an infinitude of histories.'

'What?' said Nina in a loud whisper.

'You decided to come here in this universe but in another you might have gone somewhere else, to a pizza place . . .'

'I wish . . .' said Rebecca softly.

'And the theory is that at this exact moment in time all the other choices, all the other possibilities are in fact happening. The past is continuing to happen.'

Susan listened intently. Rebecca and Nina began to try to see who could balance one of the matchsticks on her little finger for the longest.

Later, outside the main gates, the children were all running about wildly playing tag while the parents stood to one side.

'Sometimes I feel I've slipped into the wrong

universe. I should in fact be a conductor of an orchestra,' said a father.

'In another of the universes I might be an actress,' said someone else. 'My mother couldn't take me to an audition when I was eleven because she was ill. Everyone said I'd have got it. Perhaps there exists a universe where I did go to the audition . . .'

The children's screams shot through the night and it seemed to Susan that this particular time and place, on a warm summer night, with the fireflies lighting up the darkness, and the children hiding behind trees, and running fast and laughing, was quite a perfect time and place.

At bedtime, Rebecca lay caressing the edge of her blanket. 'I'm not going to slip into another universe, am I?' asked Rebecca, her face pale as the moon.

'Of course not,' said Susan.

'You are really there?' said Rebecca. 'You're not going to disappear? Recently you seem sometimes to be disappearing. You know, like usually you're so warm and cosy like you say your mother used to be, but recently you seem . . . I don't know . . . sort of strange. Ivana says maybe you and Daddy need more time to yourselves.'

Susan leant over and kissed Rebecca on the forehead.

'Sorry. Maybe that's it,' said Susan.

Before Susan went to sleep that night she went around checking every window, every door. Some of the old metal windows had clasps which were difficult to close properly.

'Oh Susan,' said Jim. 'Come to bed, darling.'

'Just trying to get this shut.'

'You should get some boiling oil you could pour down,' he said.

53

After a piano lesson, Ivana took Rebecca up to her bedroom and showed her the flaky, pale brown leather suitcases she had on the top shelf of her wardrobe.

'They were my father's,' she said.

Ivana pulled up a tapestry stool, stood on it, and stretched up to get a suitcase down. Rebecca stood anxiously by her side, fearing the suitcase would fall and snap off Ivana's head, but buoyed up by the mystery of the small, dark room with the heavy curtains and sumptuous small pictures of fruit and flowers, one with an exquisite drop of water on an apple.

'Careful,' said Rebecca as Ivana edged the heavy suitcase forward with her long, delicate hand, white and strange like the paintings in her bedroom, which had no sign of any male presence, although she'd noted a small room with a bed opposite, and a suit jacket hanging over the back of a chair, which she assumed belonged to Gustav.

The suitcase came off the shelf and Ivana managed to grab it. Rebecca stretched out her arms to help and together they placed it on the bed, with its bedspread of damson roses. 'It had some jewellery in it,' she explained. 'Family heirlooms. Quite valuable. And some documents,' she said.

The suitcase smelt sweet and old and dusty – like the back of Rebecca's mother's cupboard, and as she opened it Rebecca leant over to peer in – with an intake of breath at the sight of the glistening treasure.

'This is an aquamarine wrapped in a ribbon of diamonds,' said Ivana, glancing at Rebecca. 'You see . . . it is a ribbon of tiny diamonds . . . and this is a Maltese Cross bracelet made of baked enamel and set with pearls, diamonds and gold . . . and these rings here, well they're not of great value but very beautiful, made of garnets, citrines, amethysts and peridots.' Ivana picked one up and it glistened and she passed it to Rebecca who slipped it on her biggest finger. 'If I had had a daughter, I would have given her that,' she said. 'My tastes aren't for huge diamonds, although there are one or two here, but I think that's mineralogy, not jewellery. This is lovely too – a ruby heart pendant wrapped in a ribbon of pearls. You see, most of these pieces look false so we were able to get them out of the country when the Communists came. My mother insisted they were worthless costume jewellery. But they're real. And when I get back to Poland, they'll help me establish myself.'

'I see,' said Rebecca, puzzled. The jewellery was strewn over the bottom of the suitcase.

'I'll probably have to sell them.'

Rebecca stood and listened, as Ivana kept trying to subdue stray wisps of hair which escaped from her bun.

'Now,' she said, with a smile again, as if this were all a game, 'you can ask your mother about our trip. I gather you've already told Phillip about it?'

Rebecca blushed. 'I tried to tell my mother . . . but she didn't seem to listen. Perhaps I didn't pick the right time.'

'They're so preoccupied at the moment. Both of them. As I say, it just makes my point. They need time alone. It'll be a nice surprise for them – you to have a lovely holiday, and them time to . . . be together. It's one of the things Gustav never gave me. Time. There were a number of suitors I chose from. He was the most handsome, and mysterious . . .' She adjusted her skirt. 'The house has sixteen rooms and huge grounds. I have plenty of money . . . put away in foreign accounts . . . for our stay, you know.'

'Sixteen rooms. That's big,' said Rebecca, moving her face from side to side, dazzled by the silver mirror.

That night Rebecca lay in bed imagining herself in one of the sepia photographs of the house Ivana showed her; in her imagination she was dressed as a countess, with white gloves to her elbows.

Ivana had polished the piano, and it shone like chestnuts. Open on the coffee table were glacé fruits, the taste of which Rebecca disliked. But she liked the look of them as they lay in their paper cots, dotted with crystallised sugar.

'Ah – as you play I wish to see forests, meadows, sunlight, castles ... I want romance! Poland! Happiness!'

'I'm tired,' said Rebecca.

The photograph of Gustav gleamed at Rebecca from the piano top.

'Soon we'll be in Poland! Only a few more days! At the end of the week.'

'I don't think my mother will want me to go. I could only come for a very short time.'

'Why?'

'She'll be afraid of any harm coming to me, I suppose, or maybe my just being away from her. She says I keep her safe.'

'So romantic!'

'No, I don't really think my mother is at all romantic,' said Rebecca.

54

'Hello,' said Susan to Phillip, as she stepped out of the cloakroom at a Washington party. Her voice sounded dubbed; it seemed to arrive a little time after she opened her mouth, as if it wasn't hers.

'Susan! Nice to see you. I didn't spot you,' he said, in a ragged voice, taking a step back.

'Stop following me,' she said.

'Susan, are you OK?' he said, bending towards her.

From the main room Sandra – wearing fawn trousers and gold bracelets – came and pulled him away with a disdainful look at Susan. Soon Sandra was standing on tiptoes talking to Phillip, every now and again glancing round the room anxiously.

Before Susan left, she went over to Phillip, who was accepting some coffee from a waiter, and put her hand over his arm, and he started, and spilt a little coffee out of the green and gold little coffee cup onto the green and gold little saucer. A tiny bit splashed onto his shirt. 'Phillip . . .' she said, and he stared back at her in astonishment.

'I'm sorry. The coffee,' she said.

'Susan . . . I . . .' And he blinked at her, again, then glanced towards where Sandra was watching with lowered brow, and Susan remembered again how very boyish he could look.

'Leave me alone,' she said.

'Phillip's a nice guy,' said Jim afterwards. 'Honestly, darling, we don't need this kind of stress at the moment. I think . . . look, do you want to see someone about this problem?'

'What problem?'

'You . . . you know . . . you're getting a little, why, sort of odd about Phillip.'

She swung round. 'Who said that? Was it Phillip?'

'Of course not, Susan,' said Jim, and put his foot on the accelerator.

Sometimes Susan would see a dark shadow move behind her as she looked in the mirror, and would turn, only to discover it was the leaves outside throwing shadows, or the fluttering of curtains, or the movement of the insects who ruled this curious house.

When they got home she went for a run, her hair scraped back into a rubber band, seeing how night changed it all, made the flowers loll white in the shadows and the people in their lit windows appear to be enacting peculiar little dramas for her interest – the late dinner, the reading of books, the watching of television – although sometimes it seemed strange that as she passed the windows no one ever seemed to be talking to anyone else.

55

Over in Jane Meadows' flat, Jim is standing by a window where in the right-hand corner a spider is making a cobweb. Jane moves towards him, about to tell him she loves him, but she sees the cobweb and stops for a moment to wipe it away with a cloth, and as she does so he turns and moves away to get his briefcase and go. But there will be another occasion, and he stands coyly at the door, moving from foot to foot, puzzled about his feelings.

As for Ivana, unseen by her, a tiny spider scuttles across the room, about to scurry up her window, as Ivana plays clock patience, passing the time.

Poor Sandra, out for a walk, doesn't see the web glistening over a shop front, and the spider, a high-wire artist, making a sudden dash for it. Instead Sandra stares at a hat.

The senator taps at his window. His doctor has just told him his cancer is in fact inoperable and he has only a few months of life, instead of years. There never would be the house in Jamaica, the novels read by the pool. He has not yet told Jane Meadows he knows of her treachery, just as she knows of his.

As for Rebecca, she brushes a money spider off her hand because her mind is uneasy today, thinking about her mother.

But the spider up in the cupboard where the love letters are kept, where the gun is kept, and the old children's clothes, carefully works at establishing the lines of her latest kingdom in the darkness there, sliding down her drag line, throwing out another, measuring with perfect geometry the thin threads of her mansion.

In my father's house are many mansions.

56

Jim called Susan to say he'd be home late, very late. 'It's this story. There's so much to do on it,' he said.

'I see,' she replied.

'It's possible – at the end of this week – I might have to go away for this book.'

'That's when Rebecca wants to go away. Ivana has bought tickets for a holiday to Poland. Apparently they've both talked to me about it but I didn't listen. Rebecca's so excited I haven't the heart to stop her but I don't know. It frightens me. But everything seems to frighten me at the moment. They say it's too late to cancel the tickets. Rebecca cried when I said she'd have to. We'll talk when you're home.'

Susan went round the house, checking and double-checking every window, every lock, keeping the outside world outside. Wherever she went there were mirrors watching her. Phillip used to say her eyes were too deep and that he drowned in them, couldn't breathe when she was near him, how he hated her ability to control him.

Susan walked through, into Jim's study, and picked up the phone which was ringing.

'Hello. Hello,' she said, but there was no reply and her voice hung in the hot stillness of the evening. Sharply, she put down the receiver, and turned, and marched to her bedroom. She took off the red dress she was wearing and threw it onto the bed, where it lay like liquid, full of shadows and movement.

Elsewhere in Washington, over the other side of the Anacostia river, a man wore a red tracksuit top round his waist as if carrying a gun in its folds, as he stood, legs apart, at the end of another cul de sac, where the houses had broken windows and the weeds grew up magnificent. When he frowned at another man, the frown was curiously heavy, like lead, but most menacing of all was the scarlet new tracksuit top draped around his thick waist.

And out in the garden a red cochineal beetle, native to this area, flew close to the spider's proud new web, its wings making a whirring noise like a tiny helicopter.

The weather began to darken, ready for a storm.

Susan watched at her window as over on the other side of this street, in this middle-class cul de sac, June Brown walked in her clapboard house from room to room, appearing at each lit window in turn, an animated advent calendar.

The day slowly subsided, the night sucking the light out of the day and as she watched, her happiness subsided too, and only the thin clouds remained in the sky, stretched too thin, until the day snapped tight.

*

Susan looked out of the window. Sometimes when she woke at night, she would stand in the dark at the window and watch the ambling figure of a racoon cross nervously over their lawn from the golf course towards the dustbins which were usually overturned by the morning. Their other neighbours, a kindly judge and his wife, had told them to try and trap the racoons as they could have rabies.

The garden was usually full of squirrels and birds, each one pursuing a complex agenda, the squirrels dropping walnuts from their trees to crack and break on the wooden outdoor table, the red cardinal bowing over the lawn. But now the garden was silent except for the stirring trees.

Susan went up to one of the attic's closets. When she opened it the smell of cedar soaked into the room as she unwrapped the little gingham dress from its white tissue paper. She carefully folded the dress back into its carrier bag, from a Georgetown baby shop. She still had all Rebecca's baby clothes, packed at the back of this cupboard. The house was full of cupboards – cedar cupboards, dark cupboards, cupboards which led you back and back into the house until you thought you'd never come out. In the next box were piles of her old writing, with yellowing pages and small, earnest letters. The articles seemed to have been written by someone else.

As she read one of them, standing beneath the skylight, she wondered why we kept things, and whether the thinning newspaper cuttings about awards and papers were about the same person as stood here, on the wooden floor, beneath the skylight, now. Why don't I just let it all go, throw away the articles, the letters, crumple them up and put them in the wastepaper bin?

She should have thrown away the letters from Phillip long ago.

From pale green municipal-looking metal files of specimens which stood to attention against the wall she took out one mahogany tray, and the room smelt of mothballs, as Susan carried the tray of dead beetles to her desk where with a microscope she examined a fierce black beetle. She squinted, put on her round glasses, and began to make notes with careful handwriting, not unlike Rebecca's. Next she took out some moths, each specimen lanced with a single pin, and placed them on her desk.

She took out one of her trays of beetles, crouched in rows: the Common Black Ground Beetle with its glossy undertaker's coat; the Black Pine Sawyer beetle, its flamboyant antennae as curly as Salvador Dali's moustache, the stag beetles unchanged day after day after day.

The moths lay pinned to their board, ghostly shapes flying in from another dimension. She examined a tray of scarab beetles with their black armour and dark knight pincers ready for battle.

Because of their soft bodies, spiders were hard to preserve, and had to be kept in bottles. She had a few of these. In one was a male crab spider, a creature who spun a little web, a bridal web, round a female spider he wanted to mate with so that she couldn't grab him and eat him while mating. In another bottle floated the hunting spider who also treated his mate with tact, offering her a present of a silk-wrapped bundle of insects which she ate while mating, though if she finished it too quickly she sometimes decided to eat him too. The things we do for love.

Although Susan had studied at length the qualities which made a successful insect – chiefly being an efficient member of an organisation designed to breed – she still didn't know what a successful human being was. Was Ivana, who appeared to think of herself as a successful member of the species, therefore one?

Susan thought of spiders – their black legs, their apparent lack of emotion, their absolute sense of their own selves and their function. Thinking of them was like opening a door into a quiet room.

She envied spiders their dark dancing legs and uncomplicated loves.

57

In the supermarket the bright lights shone insistently as Susan steered the cart up and down the aisles, past vast bottles of mouthwash as blue as a swimming pool, by endless rows of toothbrushes, shelves of muffins, hanks of meat, the landscapes of purchasing.

A man in a white coat leant over legs of ham tightly enclosed in plastic as if otherwise they would escape.

The fish lay naked among crushed ice, beige and pale pink while, nearby, chickens turned on a rotisserie.

As Susan put her hand up to take one of the chickens already encased in heat-proof bags, another hand came up to take one, and brushed hers, and she at once recognised the hand.

'Phillip!' she said.

'Susan! It's you. I didn't recognise you for a moment.' He smiled easily, pleasantly, like a member of some pappy pop group for pre-teenagers.

'What are you doing here?' she said. 'Look, how dare—'

'Well this *is* my local supermarket. It's just round the corner from where I live. I might ask you that question.'

'I just felt like coming here,' she said. 'Did you follow me?'

A mother of someone at Rebecca's school came by in a white baseball hat and blue tracksuit, swinging her arms like a gorilla.

'Follow you?' said Phillip, screwing up his face. 'Look, I live round here. This is my nearest shop!'

'You could have asked Maria. She knew I was coming here.'

'Maria?' said Phillip.

'My cleaner. You know her. When you hang round the house when I'm not there you must have met her.'

'I don't hang round your house. And I don't recall her,' said Phillip, squinting his eyes as if trying to summon up a picture of Maria. 'Ah well, I suppose I'd better move on,' he said. 'Trying to get some things together for a dinner party. Pity you won't come. Be nice to be friends. You know, be able to meet.'

'I know what you want,' she said sturdily. 'You want to meet me as a friend and then bit by bit try to take me over again,' she continued.

Phillip coughed, and reddened, as if embarrassed, and his eyes were soft and gentle and almost pitying.

'Susan,' he said, touching her on the arm (it felt as if she'd been touched by a sparkler), 'really.'

Susan had her head to one side and wondered if his lips were still scorching, and if the temperature of his skin was always as hot as it had been before, and if his skin was as baby-soft everywhere, and if he still kissed as well as he used to, for his kisses had been five-star events, scooping out her soul, inflaming the corners of her mouth, inflaming every corner of her body. Other boyfriends from the past she had bumped into and had felt nothing at all – it had been like visiting a house you used to live in and finding there was nothing for you there any more. But meeting Phillip, that was like visiting a house you used to live in and finding you were still there.

'You should leave me alone,' she said.

Behind them stood shelves of jello, of oil, of peanut butter, and further down a display of eggs went on and on and on, offering free-range, brown, white, every size.

He swung round, and left the supermarket, but he looked back, she was sure he looked back at her, just as he was leaving, or maybe he was looking back at something else, some cheap offer.

Afterwards, she felt so depressed she could hardly move, and she abandoned the trolley in the aisle, and drove home.

58

Susan tried to imagine the German boy sitting watching television, with a beer in his hand. She tried to make him into a grown man, with a stomach, but he stayed as a young man, with blond curly hair.

She looked up Cologne in the encyclopaedia: 'Cologne, a city and archiepiscopal see of Germany, in the Prussian Rhine province, a fortress of the first rank . . .' – but it was meaningless. In the coffee-table book she had bought, young men and middle-aged men sat around beneath yellow umbrellas in cafés. But none of them looked like the boy. She could picture him so clearly, with his wide blue eyes and his skin like a woman's. Now he is a man, though, she told herself, a man nearing middle age, maybe with children.

But she didn't believe it. I should go there and try and find him, she decided, and began to phone up the airlines to enquire about the costs of flights, then realised how ridiculous she was being.

The house was beginning to seem like some kind of crazy house at a fun fair as she walked around and the walls seemed to lean away from her and the furniture seemed to be taking up positions against her.

Susan went out. She couldn't bear to stay in any more. Of course Jim and Jane Meadows were seeing a lot of each other, she thought. They were working on a story together, that was all it was. Of course Rebecca had to grow up. All this was natural. She had to accept it and not allow old terrors to prey on her. The boy had been fine. No doubt he'd been fine.

As she drove down Connecticut Avenue towards the Smithsonian, she found she was watching cars to see if Phillip was in any of them, and then she saw that the car in front of her was his. It has happened again, she thought, I summon him up.

Everything went very quiet, the air slackened and time seemed to stretch out. The road and the buildings around the road shimmered.

Even that first time, she realised now, she had been absolutely ready to see him, almost needed to. She wiped one hand over her leg, with its short, violet silk skirt. And why, she wondered, am I dressed like this? Perhaps we all just hurtle, appropriately dressed, to our fates. We put on our lipstick and die in a car crash. We adjust the angle of our hats and die of a heart attack.

Phillip was trying to destabilise her life so that he could walk back into it. Or maybe he was going to tell Jim what had happened. Or perhaps he just hated to see her happiness. What was that quote – Iago's about Othello? 'He hath a daily beauty in his life that makes me ugly.' Jim had been such an easy prey – so eager and so ambitious, almost like Othello, thinking he knew so much yet knowing so little. He wasn't really interested in the patterns of the human heart. Phillip had made sure Jane Meadows and Jim got together.

The windows were dirty, shading off the outside world. But the front window was clear enough, with him, magnified, looking back at her through his rear window.

Perhaps, she thought – putting her foot down more firmly on the accelerator, the torn and crumpled map of Washington beside her, roads swirling here and there like a child's scrawl, the circling beltway, the splodges of green – he is always there, except sometimes I don't see him. Perhaps he has always been there. Or perhaps there is one of my lovers in each of the cars around me but they are dressed unusually so I can't recognise them.

Beside her a Volkswagen sped by and as she glanced she was convinced the driver was her first lover, a red-haired young man who'd taken half an hour to come, by which time she had been so bored she'd decided knitting was more interesting than this, and less sticky. Oddly, she'd come rather quickly and enthusiastically, and up to that point had considered the whole procedure terrific.

Behind her, through her rear window, she could see a beaten-up Chevy which for a moment she imagined was driven by Edward, an architect, another old boyfriend, one of those heritage-ridden young men who in memory reminded her of old, but good-quality socks. Every time she passed some building with him, he used to tell her all about it – its date, its architect, his verdict on it. At the time she'd been impressed but depressed too, and would wake up on the days she was seeing him with such a malaise that she didn't want to open the curtains and have the harsh light smash into her face. Susan hoped he wouldn't see her now. She remembered him showing her round the London house he was going to do up and she had heard herself say, to irritate him, 'Why not rip out the old fireplace? Then you can run a line of fitted wardrobes along the wall.'

The dog had pawed at a cockroach.

'We're restoring the house, darling,' Edward had said, 'not destroying it.'

He had smirked a little. He had been good-looking in that absurd British way – tall, with a tweed jacket, as if he ought constantly to be surrounded by hollyhocks. As he stood there in the half light, on the bare boards, he had looked as though he ought not to mess about with the late twenties, early thirties, a family and all that. He ought just to skip right on to being in his sixties, in his country garden with the hollyhocks and a bad back. Being sixty was after all so much more tasteful, so much more English, than being young, than having black, thick hair, than having an embarrassingly long and blank future.

There was no room for blankness in the lives of people like Edward. It was all filled in. The past was thoroughly researched – the type of lights, the type of skirting board, the angle of the light, all the detail. People like Edward distrusted the future because of its emptiness. Susan had wanted to run straight into it, particularly right then, as she watched the dog play with the cockroach and Edward go on talking about cooking implements in the 1890s. She had wanted to run out into the gorgeous, white, empty future and spin around it. When she had looked at Edward again, he had been a long way away as though he had actually retreated into the past, or she had moved into the future, so that one way or another they were no longer in the same time.

'Susan's impatient,' Edward had told his surveyor friend.

'Edward has great patience,' she had said in the same confiding tone of voice Edward had used. She had drawn her initials in the dust in the window.

A few days later he'd said, 'I'd like you and me to marry in the church by my parents' house in Little Missenden. Just a small country church wedding,' he had said.

'Edward . . .' she had said.

'Just a small country church – about fifty friends,' he had said.

She had taken a step back, and there was the lovely Atlantic between them, an immense ocean, and he had swayed over the other side of it and she'd realised all her life people like him had been trying to get her to act in their plays, to belong in their scenarios, although she was wholly unsuitable for their parts. He was slightly unshaven, and she liked that.' He was handsome, with dark sad eyes. He certainly needed looking after, but she was through with all that, or so she thought. Other women at other times had led that kind of life so she could no longer do it, she thought. She was grateful to them.

Let some other self-sacrificing, maternal woman look after Edward, and admire his choice of period lighting.

'But I love you,' he had said, 'very much.'

The house where they had been standing was cold, so cold the damp reached into her bones and as she stood there she'd felt that if she stayed she'd become like that house, with damp, dry rot, cockroaches. Above them sprawled a plasterwork ceiling. Of course, beauty was there too, in the detail of the ceiling, along with decay.

'I just want to get out,' she had said.

'Is there someone else?' he had said.

She had shaken her head. Even then as she stood, in her black beret, a brightly coloured shawl over her black coat, she longed to punch her fists through the window and let in some fresh air. She had wanted to hear the violence of the cracked glass. She had wanted to break it all up. It was what, later, drew Phillip to her and her to Phillip. This anger, and desire to break out, this strength and violence.

And on the other side, she overtook a slow car she had no doubt contained a sweet young man called David, now masquerading as a scrawny businessman, and she felt sad for what she'd done to poor David, who had loved her so, she realised now. Every time he'd come into her room at college, he'd kind of hovered at the doorway, as if entering her sanctum was almost too much to expect. His hair had been frizzy, and his sexual technique boyish, but he'd been gentle and funny and she had lost interest in him, just drifted out of interest with him, and never told him, just left him hovering there, day by day, losing colour, losing personality until she'd heard a few months later that he had left the university. There always seemed to be men knocking at her door. Sometimes she would lock it, and switch off the light.

But Phillip, in front of her on the highway, there had never been anything boyish about his technique. He was one of those men able to know the very shivers and movements and longings of another person's skin. He would caress the palm of her hand like spinning a web, like spinning roads round a city, creating momentous patterns. The moth's kiss of his lips on the back of her knees, on the inside of her thighs, his face watching her. That was it, she supposed, it was the way he watched her. The others had been little boys snatching at sex, but Phillip . . .

Susan sped up and as the car in front drove faster she drove even more quickly, shunting her way out into the fast lane, going up to eighty, and finally managing to push the car containing Phillip off the road.

She wondered if he were dead whether she'd still see him.

Phillip got out of the car. For a moment she was shocked to see it was actually him, rather than some simulacrum, some laser roadshow of her imagination. There he was. The shirt unbuttoned at the neck, the texture of the shirt, something soft like childhood sheets, and his mouth, wider than most men's mouths, the beige trousers so much more louche than any other journalist would wear, and his long, white, beautiful hands clutching his car keys.

'What the hell do you think you're doing?' he said.

Behind him naked mannequins gestured like robots in the window of the department store.

'Damn it, Phillip. Stop it!' she said, getting out of her car. 'Just stop it. Everywhere I go, I see you. People never stop talking about you. Ivana! Jim! Just stop it. What are you doing? You're trying to take over my life.'

'Christ. I was just driving along Connecticut. You could have killed me. I can't understand how anyone can be so unreasonable. What are you playing at? I could have been killed. You could have been killed. You were driving like a lunatic.'

She took a step forward. 'You were following me.'

'Following you?' He swept his hair back. 'Christ. You were behind me. How can I be following you?'

'You track me. You know my every move. Someone tells you, doesn't she? Ivana perhaps. You can be so charming. Or is it Maria?'

'It's not true,' he said.

'And you were in the supermarket!'

'I was buying food. It's where I shop.'

'You knew I was going there. That's why you went there just then,' she said.

'Just pull yourself together,' he said.

He was looking at her mouth the way he always used to look at it, as if he were drowning. 'Look, Susan . . .' he said gently, and for a moment she thought, Give in, Susan, let it go, and she moved towards him.

The traffic roared past them.

She stepped back.

'We should talk about the German boy,' she said quickly. 'Just tell each other the truth and then all this madness will stop.'

'The German boy?'

'Yes. You know, Phillip. Stop it.'

'I don't know anything about a German boy.'

She frowned. He seemed quite genuine.

'You know, Phillip. There was blood everywhere. The cat licked up the blood with its little tongue. What happened to him, Phillip? I need to know.'

'I don't know what you're saying,' he said, in that warm, tangled voice, and he was still watching her lips, and she wanted him to kiss her but she stepped back still further, into her car, and he watched her go. His kisses had always been so tender.

When she got home, she slept, and afterwards woke up feeling much more peaceful.

If only I were pregnant, she thought, lying on the bed. If only Jim had a son none of this would be happening. Jim wouldn't be so obsessed by this story. I would be stronger. And besides, Phillip wouldn't even be here.

59

'I saw you take the files, you know,' says Senator Spalding to Jane Meadows, as he signs a letter, without looking at her. Around him his office is suddenly a kind of waiting room, and Jane Meadows wonders at what moment it lost its vitality. Not long ago it had been a bombastic room, with the photographs of presidents gleaming from the frames, with the state flag, with certificates parading his awards and achievements, but today it is just a series of unlinked objects with a small man sitting in the middle of them as if he might be selling them all off.

'I informed . . . certain friends of mine . . . I thought about it, what to do.' Senator Spalding swivels a little on his chair. He sniffs, and takes out a white handkerchief with which he wipes his brow. He coughs, still not looking at her. His hands, once quilted with fat, are thinner now as he drums his fingers on the table. Jane Meadows stands up in front of his desk, her hands hanging limply by her side. She notes there is a mark of coffee on her sleeve, and wonders how that could be, she is usually so meticulous.

She feels afraid, but she doesn't know whether she

is afraid for him or for herself. She moves closer to him.

'Sam . . .'

He takes off his glasses, and begins to polish them up. He then looks at her, with his narrow eyes, and she thinks how very sad he is nowadays and then she hears his voice come out hard and clear. 'You are at risk, you know, you and your boyfriend . . . If I were you, I would get out of here . . . ideally today . . . I . . . my friends . . . they're killers. They won't want him – or you – talking. '

He sighs.

'Sam, he's not my boyfriend.'

He continues to polish up his glasses.

'I'm sorry. I haven't been well . . . I'm tired . . . I . . .' He fumbles in his drawer and takes out a little silver box. 'I bought this for you . . . just to remember . . .'

'Look, Sam, are you OK? I mean, are you well? You—'

He closes his eyes. 'Just take the box, Jane, please,' he says, opening them. 'Just take it and go,' he says. 'But take care.'

'Of course,' she says.

'You know what I mean. You have a reckless streak. It could get you into trouble.'

'You liked that reckless streak . . .'

He looks at her with eyes bare as lightbulbs. 'You know I'm not alone in this. My advice to you is to vanish. Both of you.'

'You arranged for the documents to be taken?'

He nods.

'I thought so,' she says.

'But you went on . . . you knew you were in danger . . .'

She unfurls a smile. 'I liked that. You should know. I like that.'

She wipes her damp hands on her skirt. Beneath her her black high heels tower up but she is weary somehow and wishes suddenly to take them off and curl up somewhere.

'Are you having an affair with him?'

'No. I told you.'

'But you intend to?'

'He might not have me. Like you, he might not want me,' she says. 'He has a wife and a child.'

'Yes.'

'Remember you tired of me. You didn't want me . . .'

Sam Spalding coughs. 'I'm a little tired now,' he says. 'I might rest a little.'

'I'm sorry. Look . . .'

'I must rest now,' he says.

60

Phillip's girlfriend Sandra turned up at Susan's front door in tight jeans and a T-shirt, and Susan let her in, moving backwards, as the girl walked in, in a pre-rehearsed march, as if refusing to be intimidated by Susan. Sandra tossed her butter-blonde hair but it hardly moved. Her surly eyes became points of steely light as she pursed her lips.

'Come in,' said Susan distantly, wiping her hands on her old cotton dress.

'Look, I just want to say, Phillip's told me everything,' said Sandra in a high voice.

'I'm sorry?' said Susan, turning round, wishing she and Sandra could just dissolve into the house. It was hard for her to think about what had happened that last night with Phillip, but she remembered thinking that she wished they could all disappear – the young boy, Phillip and her – and that it would be strange and suitable if the flat had been left there, with its white walls and grey carpets, having absorbed the people passing through it. Instead the people staggered on, leaving blood on the walls, on the floor, the marks of burning cigarettes in the carpet.

'Why, that you're in love with him, of course. And won't let him be. That's why he's so scared of you. Recently he's seemed quite upset. He nearly got run over by a car – walked straight out into the road. And he nearly smashed the car into a tree yesterday – I had to grab the steering wheel.'

Sandra stood with legs slightly apart, hanging onto her little black handbag with her left hand as if about to swing it at Susan, who stood near the door, in bare feet.

'Would you like some coffee?' said Susan.

'Decaf please,' said Sandra, pouting, as if Susan had played another unfair move in the chess game of sexual relationships.

'Do take a seat,' said Susan, and heard her voice emerge swaying, laconic, while Sandra stood there with jumbled emotions, much younger in every way. Susan walked to the kitchen, and found the cups.

Sandra crouched over her coffee and as she did so made an 'S' – S for Sandra, thought Susan obscurely, remembering the chart around the kindergarten wall at her very first school, her mother waiting at the window, plump and smiling, waiting to take her home.

Susan was aware of how far all the objects were from one another – the chairs from each other, the sofa from the coffee table. If only I'd thought to move the furniture closer, none of this would have happened, Susan thought. Maybe Phillip would never have come back. We make the layouts of our lives here at home – the separated furniture, the wrong colours. Like witches, the women at home control their loved ones by moving furniture, changing colours, adjusting physical realities to alter emotional ones.

'Look, I can see this anxiety about not having another child could have bad effects,' said Sandra, studying the contents of her coffee cup as if examining a crystal ball, while Susan sat opposite. 'But you can't let your irrational feelings destroy other people's lives. I mean, we were happy until we came here, Phillip and I. But now he jumps every time the phone rings, fearing it's going to be you. Of course he's fond of you – you had a great thing going in the past. But that was the past. He wants you to let him go now.'

Susan poured some more coffee, black liquid from a white pot.

'Yes,' said Susan to Sandra, 'it was a long time ago. Years ago. We should both forget all about it. Tell him that. I agree. We should both forget all about it.'

Sandra, a little surprised, repositioned herself on her chair.

'Good,' she said. 'I'm glad it's been useful to have come here . . .'

One reason, Susan thought, that the drawing room was so lacking in cosiness – apart from the position of the furniture – was that there were too many openings, too many ways out. The front door led very nearly straight into the drawing room and from there one pair of French windows led into a breezeway, and a doorway into the dining room.

Curious that a feeling of safety was created by not having too many ways out.

'You see,' said Sandra. 'I want a life with Phillip. We were happy together. If you can learn to forget the past and just live, you know, side by side here, it would be great. I know it's a small town. Of course it is. But still. You can try, as you say.' Sandra moved her handbag from her left side over to the right. 'Phillip's not an easy person but if he's willing to make the effort . . . he's fond of you, you see. And what about poor Jim? I think it's affecting him – your behaviour. I'm sorry to say it. I didn't want to. I've kept away all this time hoping it would all die down. But people are talking. You know what it's like.' All the time she spoke she didn't look at Susan.

'Phillip's so morose and difficult,' continued Sandra. 'Just so different from how he used to be. When we heard he was coming here he was just so excited. You know, a new challenge. But now he's terrified of meeting you. Wherever we go, he looks round to see if you're there. Or people talk about you. You know – Susan Stewart. Beautiful Susan Stewart. And Jim – darling Jim. Why, everyone likes Jim. You know. Phillip's an attractive man. I can understand why you are so . . . obsessed by him. But you're married, and you have a child. What happened between you was a long time ago, when you were young.'

Susan smiled obliquely.

'He said after you two split up you had a mental breakdown,' continued Sandra, 'and had some weird fantasies about a German boy you picked up.'

'He said I'd picked up a German boy?'

'He said you said you had. He didn't seem to know anything about it. He said it was some fantasy.'

'A fantasy?'

'He said you were clever, and could twist anything . . . He can be like that too. That's how he knows, I suppose. I think you should move out of Washington. Leave him in peace. He'd like you to leave him in peace. After all, Jim's made a mess of things – losing the documents. Maybe it's time to go.'

Sandra clasped the cup of coffee to her like a mug of hot chocolate on a cold night, and looked up at Susan with mangled hatred.

Sandra's cup was stained with lipstick.

Sandra frowned. 'Why won't you let him alone? Is it to make your life more interesting? I know . . . being a mother must be limiting. I mean, someone like you, who was so wild. It must be hard for your self-respect. Or perhaps you need the fear. Some women get off on that . . .'

Sandra tried to push her buttery hair behind her ears, and her mouth set into a sullen line. Susan found she was listening for the whisper of Phillip's feet on the stairs. For a tall man, he trod softly, especially over the velvety carpet of the flat where they used to live together.

Sandra stood up, brushing herself down as if she'd just emerged from a dirty shed, and tried to replicate the way she had marched in as she marched out.

'Sandra,' said Susan.

'Yes,' said Sandra.

'Leave him. You'd be better to. He's destroying you.

Certain people do. He's just playing with you ...' Susan stood up and took a step forward.

'How dare you!' said Sandra. 'He's just a little disturbed at present.'

'He's always disturbed. He's not your problem.'

'You want him. He told me you wouldn't let him go.' Sandra slammed the door as she left.

Afterwards, Susan went outside, where violet clouds seemed to be pulled from a point as a silk scarf is pulled through a ring. At least there was some wind today and not just that interminable stillness.

She wondered how long it would be before he came.

61

Rebecca lay in bed listening to the rowdy gossiping of the insects outside, through the open window. She liked the sense of another life going on in the garden and the house, represented by the occasional appearance of some vast tropical insect staring up or down at her from a wall or floor.

She liked the house itself. It had an air of stopped time, as though while she and her mother and father lived in it nothing would change – the dust would maybe accumulate in the dark wooden alcoves, termites would maybe try to tunnel further into the walls, but by and large there would always be a stillness here. Even the dust hung without movement in the sunlit air of the drawing room whose long windows looked out onto the cul de sac where they lived, where children played on the streets and rocking chairs swayed on porches of yellow clapboard houses.

She turned on one side and then to the other. There was a knock on the door and her father opened it, letting light shoot into the soft blackness. She murmured, still half asleep, and put her arm over her eyes.

'Rebecca,' whispered her father. She murmured again.

'Rebecca,' he said more loudly.

She peered at him.

For a minute, she decided she was dreaming his daytime figure hovering at her doorway in the middle of the night, and she closed her eyes.

'Rebecca,' he repeated.

'Yes,' she murmured.

'I want to talk to you.'

'Yes,' she said, sitting up.

He sat at the end of her bed. 'If I were to have to go away for a while on a book, would you be OK?'

Rebecca squinted at her father.

'Why are you coming in in the middle of the night to ask me this?'

'I just wanted to talk to you alone. I never seem to see you alone. Your mother says it's fine if I need to work on the book abroad. She doesn't want me to go, but she understands.'

A little murmur of anger shot through Rebecca. Why did she, Rebecca, always have to be the reasonable one, the adult one? If she'd had a brother or sister she could have been unreasonable with them.

It was curious, she thought, how at moments like this your room stays the same. I mean, she thought, the wardrobe doesn't move politely away, and bow its head like a Disney cartoon character, the walls don't rupture, snakes don't start to dangle from the ceiling. All these thoughts go on in our heads and yet nothing happens. The world goes on. The newspaper arrives.

In her bookshelves her childhood books stood, mixed with her older ones: Hans Christian Andersen fairy tales, Dodie Smith's *I Capture the Castle*, a copy of *Jane Eyre* waiting for her to be older, waiting for her to reach the age when she would read this. 'You have to read things at the right time. If you don't read them at the right age you lose them forever,' her mother had said.

Her father was talking about the important investigation he was going to do which would help to damage the drug culture throughout the States.

'I need to get to sleep now. I have camp tomorrow.'

'Yes. I know. I just wanted to get a sense of what you felt about it.'

'What I felt about it? I don't know.' She tucked her black hair fiercely behind her ears, and repositioned herself on the bed, plumping up her pillows.

Rebecca caressed the soft ribbon edge of the cot blanket she had had since she was just a month or so old.

After her father had gone, Rebecca stepped out of bed and padded, in bare feet, over the wooden floor of the upstairs hall and down the sweeping staircase with its wrought-iron railings curved into the shape of flowers. Although she loved the house, it did not have a comforting quality, it had a strangeness which embraced unhappy as well as happy things. She walked through the half-darkness to where the wide sky threw the light of night into the drawing room where her mother lay on the sofa.

'Oh,' cried out Susan, waking up from having fallen asleep on the sofa.

She half wanted to kiss her mother but didn't quite dare to hug her, fearing whatever was crumpling up her mother's face might be in some way catching.

'I had a bad dream, Rebecca,' said her mother, rubbing one hand over the skin of her bare arm. 'But I'll be fine. Go back to bed now, darling.'

Rebecca opened the front door, and stood there, in her bare feet, breathing in the complex sound of the nighttime insects and the smells of a warm summer night.

She stood for a while on the doorstep. The lights were off in all the houses – the windows were all just dark patches. A lamp shone on each of the porches. The night isn't really all that dark, she thought, looking up at the sky, at the few stars scattered around.

The cry of the cicadas grew louder.

She closed the door.

For all the next day everyone seemed dazed, stumbling about the house. Even Ivana seemed odd. Her mother said that's how spiders were before a moult, dazed.

'I won't go with Ivana to Poland – if you don't want me to, if you'll be lonely. Will you be lonely?' said Rebecca.

Susan frowned. 'Will you be . . . comfortable . . . with Ivana? You like her that much?' said Susan.

'Oh yes. I really do. She's always so kind to me. With you, she can be a little . . . false . . . but with me she's great.'

'I see. '

'I'd be sad not to go though. It would be an adventure.'

'I . . . it's true I feel I don't want you to go. But I suppose that's just because I want you with me.' Susan managed a smile. 'I suppose in a way I don't really want you to be independent, but I should.'

'Can I tell Ivana I can go then? Please? I want to so much. You said I'd worked hard this semester. We'll go and see where her family once lived. I'd remember it all my life.'

'I don't know.'

'It would be exciting,' said Rebecca.

'It's exciting here,' said Susan.

'Oh no. This is just home.'

Susan sighed. 'If you're absolutely sure you want to . . . of course, I want you to be happy. I've been so confused recently . . . I don't know whether to believe my instincts, or whether my instincts are just playing tricks with me . . . and maybe Jim and I should spend more time alone.'

'Trust me,' said Rebecca, putting her arms around her mother. 'I'll be fine. Ivana's just odd with you because she's jealous of you. She's fine with me.'

62

Ivana unlocked the door of Gustav's study and inside it the cabinets of glassware shimmered bright and cold.

When she thought of Gustav it was always there that she saw him, among the glasses, holding one by its stem, his eyes bright and cold.

The glass had surrounded him all this time. For a moment she thought she could see his face trapped in one of the bowls, staring out at her.

She went to the cupboard and took out the bowl and smashed it.

Ivana had been up until two folding her silk shirts between tissue paper, polishing her shoes, arranging her jewellery in her small brown leather case to take on the plane. The lights had been dimmed so Gustav wouldn't wake in the guest room. On the kidney-shaped glass on the dressing table sat a sepia photograph of the old grey house in Poland, with its wide terrace, and the lawns stretched down to the lake.

Ivana drummed her nails on the glass of her dressing table.

In the morning she had got Gustav his breakfast – wholemeal bread, honey, a bowl of chopped fruit. His cuffs gleamed white as usual, carefully clipped together by cuff links.

He combed his hair in front of the mirror, his hair shiny as satin, his suit perfectly cut. He frowned, smoothing down his hair.

She examined her face in the mirror; what thin lips you have, Ivana, her mother used to say.

For the journey she had put on an aquamarine shirt.

'Please don't go,' he said, in a far-off voice.

'I'm sorry, Gustav. I've made the arrangements.'

'I noticed the smashed vase,' he said wearily. 'Of course I didn't say anything about it.' He brushed a speck of dust from his jacket.

'Of course not,' she said.

63

After she had waved Rebecca and Ivana goodbye Susan went back to the house and found it full of shadows. I can't stay here, she thought. She walked into Rebecca's room, where towels and clothes lay strewn on the floor and a teddy Rebecca had considered taking was left forlorn on the bed, its arms outstretched. Rebecca had been so proud of her 'travelling outfit' – beige trousers and a new black shirt with white collar and cuffs – but then had begun to cry when she kissed her mother goodbye.

Susan wondered if Jim had made love to Jane Meadows.

Susan checked that she'd locked every window and door, got into her car, and drove off, past detached houses that were so relaxed it seemed they'd just drifted there onto the deep green lawns where trees rested, their languid branches providing an arch over the road, and shadows everywhere.

In the car Susan passed the Washington cathedral area, filled with huge houses, wrap-around porches and people talking to each other in the street, which used to be where smart people built their country houses in the nineteenth century because it was on a hill and cooler than central Washington. Eventually she came down to Georgetown, driving up the cobbled streets lined with doors standing to attention in their liveries of scarlet, green and blue, with antique shops nudged between. Now this, she thought, will calm me down. I'll just wander around. Her car backed into a space and she stepped out and locked the door, thinking how could she possibly ever consider returning to England. She walked briskly, then suddenly stopped, still, the sunlight on her, as looking back at her from a junk-shop window was the grinning head of a puppet, jutting out from a chipped vase.

Susan moved quickly on.

Susan took a short cut to the bank and noticed that it was the street where Jim had told her Phillip and his girlfriend lived. Number 56, she remembered him saying, and she glanced at the little Georgian house and stared for a moment. She walked on, slowly. The cobblestones underfoot made it hard for her to walk properly on her high heels when she crossed the road.

I shouldn't have come here, she thought, I should have stayed safe at home guarding the house. But she found she feared going back to the empty house (where even now Jim was trying to ring her). Besides, she had waited, afraid, for long enough.

As she queued in the bank, she had a curious feeling, warm and cold at the same time, her heart pumping, wondering why she was having this perverse reaction to queuing at a bank. In front of her a squat man stirred restlessly. A child took a green lollipop from a clutch of them on a table. Some personal bankers sat at desks and on cushioned chairs to the left of the cashiers behind their prison-visiting bars. One drummed his fingers on the desk while smiling pleasantly at a customer. The thin green carpet was worn in places, and the air conditioning was on so high she shivered.

An arm went round her waist and lips pressed against her neck.

'Chilly?' said Phillip's voice and she spun round and he was smiling as she jumped back, knocking into the squat man with the too-long trousers, who apologised. Phillip was looking down at her but she found somehow she couldn't see him properly.

'Why aren't you always in bank queues?' he said in a velvet voice like the step of a cat. 'Rather a long way to come to the bank, isn't it?' he continued.

She was aware of the outlines of her body – the magenta checked shirt curving into her small waist, the shape of her bottom with the creases of her skirt running down on either side.

'I needed to come to this branch. You live near here, don't you?' she said.

'Yes, as you know, Susan. I saw you walk by the house, and stop, and look at it. So I came after you here. I thought that was what you wanted. Were you thinking of knocking on the door?'

He was standing close to her.

'Did you expect me to be in?' he said. 'Did you know I was? We used to know all kinds of things about each other.'

'I don't think I can wait here much longer,' she said, feeling him kissing her forehead in the past, tiny traitorous kisses, and then his tongue in her ear, everywhere, stealing over her, robbing her. She wondered if for one moment in the past she had actually liked Phillip. Her headache was growing worse. He pushed back his hair. There had been blood on his hand – but that was long ago.

The cashier called her forward, and she wrote out a cheque, all the time aware of him watching, and then in a minute or two he was called to the next till and side by side they took out money, and as soon as she had it she hurried away, and he called out to her, but she hurried on.

'Susan!' he called.

She turned into a drugstore to get some headache pills. Inside were the usual brightly coloured goods – markers, iridescent nail varnish, orange lipstick. The bold packaging had the usual array of superlatives and exclamation marks, suggesting perfect energetic worlds – New Glamour! An Enticing Shade of Red! Discover the Magic of Avocado Soap! – while the fan in the far corner continued with its hopeless task of trying to cool the room.

Two shop assistants stared at her as she walked along the long aisle, past nail scissors and emery boards and equipment to mend broken nails, to the area selling antiseptics and pills for pain. She reached down for a red and blue packet.

'Can I get you something? A cup of coffee perhaps?' said Phillip, and she started.

'I have a headache,' she said.

'You can't just walk out like that. It's not even polite,' he said, smiling. 'Come on, we're virtually neighbours.'

He seemed a long way from her, very tall, his wiry hair greying, and his skin ashen, his face thinner and more sculptured than before. He put a peppermint in his mouth and smiled. The smile carved into his face yet was tender too, stealing under her skin. His legs were out of proportion to the rest of his body, great stilts covered over in jeans. He was in a creased linen jacket with immense pockets.

How charming he is, she thought, with his deferentially teasing air. But she remembered the other side of him, when the gentleness went out of his grey eyes. She remembered when every movement of his seemed exquisite to her.

'Come on,' he said.

'I didn't mean you to follow me,' she said.

'Of course not,' said Phillip.

She remembered his letters . . . 'At one time or another I want everyone dead.' The violence had always been there, just as her behaviour was part of her, the desires that had made her leave their little flat and go to cafés, bars, seeking trouble, events.

If only Rebecca hadn't gone away. If only Jim had been around more. And Ivana, watching her out of the window, trying to steal her happiness.

A little black boy with a perfect cherub's face watched them one after the other, as they spoke. Behind Phillip stood a tower of plastic toys, and to his left a range of different bleaches.

'I need some bleach,' she said, and strode past him.

'Christ, Susan,' he said. 'You're so *weird*.'

She stretched to take a shampoo for dry hair off the shelf.

'Do you know,' she said, 'drugstores hold the story of people's lives: first the nappies and the baby food to keep you alive, the vitamins for childhood, then the creams for preventing spots, then the lipsticks and eyeshadows and depilatory lotions to help attract the opposite sex, then the dyes for greying hair and the endless rows of medicine.'

'Dry hair?' he said softly. 'You used not to have dry hair.'

'Well I have now,' she said, and she knew her voice was too soft. 'And if you come down here you'll see the light powder I buy to conceal the shadows under my eyes. That's time too. Sometimes I find grey hairs and then I put a colour rinse on my hair, so you see I'm not the same person at all, not at all.'

'It was years ago, Susan. Years. Please. Can't you just be normal and pleasant? Can't you at least pretend like everyone else does. You were always so angry. Are you still so angry?'

'I don't know what you mean, Phillip,' she said, and marched to the cash register, and felt him standing by her.

It was as though everything that was happening was happening underwater, very slowly. The girl at the counter, with her dark hair tied back in a plait, the cigarettes behind, the sense of Phillip moving slowly behind her, it was all happening in another dimension. Through the dirt-smudged window she could still see her black Volvo outside, and it seemed extraordinary that it was still there, a kind of time machine taking her from one life to another. The girl sighed as she piled the bleach and the pills into a carrier bag and handed it to Susan with a half-smile.

'Your daughter,' said Phillip. 'Rebecca. She looks like you.'

'That's what people say. But I don't know. I can't see it,' and the sound of the familiar words, so often said to her, comforted her a little. 'Yes,' she said, repeating herself like a mantra as she heard his breathing behind her. 'I can't really see it at all.'

'You look much the same,' he said.

'Thanks.'

'That's not necessarily a compliment. People should change,' he said.

Both women at the till were watching Phillip as women had always watched Phillip.

There was a cut on Phillip's cheek, as if he had cut his cheek shaving. She wanted to touch it.

He dug his hand in the pocket of his jacket and got out a packet of cigarettes. She noted his hand was shaking as he struck a match and held it to light the cigarette.

The little black boy's mother called him. 'William, will you just come on over here!' The boy grinned, and left, turning his head back as he went.

Susan tried to check her watch but it took forever for her head to lower to see the hands of the watch, and anyway the time didn't matter. There was no one at home. It seemed there hadn't been anyone at home for some while.

The happiness in the house had been so radiant before but now it was all packed up in boxes, the furniture was draped in mourning clothes and the rooms had grown larger and larger until no one could see each other any more.

Meanwhile the darkness blew in like dust, spiralling into the corners of rooms, drifting through the air, up and up the stairs to her studio whose white walls had always startled her with their brightness, up into the cupboards where the trapped insects lay pierced with pins, forever alive and forever dead. Phillip and she had wanted everything to be so momentous, but they were younger then and hadn't understood that small things can be momentous – a play of light, a shadow, the touch of a child's hand. They had wanted so much, and had got it all, too much, far too much, so much that that grey flat high up above the streets had cracked apart, opened up, and thrown them both out into the ensuing years. Years and years. Years and years. Phillip's face had all the years in it – the lines on the forehead, the casualness in the eyes.

His face was all locked up, as if locked up in that flat with the boy sprawled out naked on the floor, his body so thin and childish and Phillip even then older and angrier, a huge figure fighting his demons.

Phillip opened and closed his hands. Years and years released.

'I need to go,' she said, standing there, watching the hands opening and closing.

'You've been fine then, on the whole, have you, Susan?' asked Phillip gently. It was the gentleness that was unbearable. She could always cope with his rages. It was always his gentleness she couldn't stand. His voice sounded similar to what it had been, but not exactly the same. It was as though he were propping up his words.

'You keep using my name. Don't use my name,' she said.

She could feel sweat over her back.

He was watching her intently and she sensed him swallowing, trying to speak clearly.

'I heard you had an abortion,' he said.

'Oh did you?'

'Yes. I learnt that quite recently. Just a week or so ago.'

'Really?'

'From Ivana. Your child mentioned it to her. She'd read some letter of yours to me that you never sent and eventually ended up confiding in Ivana. The letter just said you had an abortion. Or that's all your daughter remembered, and I wondered if you could tell me, was it my child?'

She turned and walked out to her car, and felt Phillip watching her through the window.

His car followed hers and she pulled off at the supermarket and went in, her heart racing. The fish lay in its casket of ice, a maiden surrounded by white jewels. A little ribbon of blood trailed from the fish's mouth and the man behind the counter sliced the head off a trout, opened it out, and started to take out the bones for a woman with huge pale eyes and sleepy lids, a little like one of the fish she was buying.

For a moment, when the man behind the counter turned away and then turned back, she thought he was in fact Phillip.

She walked up and down the aisles, checking the biscuits, staring at the slabs of cheese white and bland, reminiscent of mortuaries. She wondered if the German boy had ended up in a mortuary.

The packets of biscuits had an air of revelry about them – chocolate chip! digestive! She picked up a jar of maple syrup. She found herself over in the meat section.

If only I had had another baby, Phillip wouldn't have come back. There would have been four of us then – the four walls of a house, fighting from the parapets.

When I had the abortion, the baby was tiny, like a little piece of meat.

When Phillip came towards her she closed her eyes for a moment because she thought she was seeing herself, with her black hair and dangerous eyes.

'Susan,' said Phillip. 'You don't look well. I should get you home. And you didn't answer my question.'

She leant against the meat counter. There was too much blood here – dripping over the counter. The cats had lapped up the blood. The dead baby. The dead boy.

'Susan, really,' he said. 'I'll take you home.'

Her personality was losing shape, as she stood there, yet something in the centre of her knew exactly what she wanted, what would make everything all right.

The aisles spread out before them, endless lines of aisles, as if dividing up the whole world into breads or cereals, fruits or fish, meat or cheese, an immense game which someone had already played.

She once went fishing with him and saw him knock the fish hard with his bare fist, and there had been blood over him afterwards and he wouldn't wash it off. He had hit the boy and the boy had screamed then fallen.

Phillip stooped down by her. 'Look, I should take you home,' he said. 'You look ill. You're wavering. You're grey.'

She focused on him for a moment, took in the eyes like hers, the hair like hers, the lanky body.

'I'm OK,' she said. 'Perfectly fine.'

Behind them pots of noodles and rice stood in rows. Just add water!

'The top button of your shirt is undone,' said Phillip softly.

He bent forward and began to do it up.

'It's cold here. We should go,' he said.

'No,' she said.

She liked all the straight lines, and the way most of the food was packaged, transformed, turned into something else, into cubes and jars and cones and squares. Phillip put his hand on her arm and as it lay there she could see through the skin to the muscle and blood underneath.

'Susan, I must take you back,' said Phillip.

'No one will be at home when we get there,' she said. 'Maria's gone. Rebecca's gone. Jim's gone. You can't come in.'

'I know. We'll go in my car. You're in no fit state to drive,' he said.

'How *efficient* you are,' she said.

The doors opened for them. Behind them, on the back seat, was the laptop computer, a briefcase, a tape recorder, all the paraphernalia of his life.

'You know, Phillip, I'm OK. I'm just a little weak. I've had a few shocks recently.'

'Perhaps,' he said.

'You still drive too fast,' she said, huddling down and watching him. Now he had threads of grey wire in his hair.

She laughed.

'Bye,' she said, as she got out of the car, when they reached her house.

'I want to come in,' he said.

64

In her apartment block on Connecticut Avenue Jane Meadows moves around, tiny feet in tiny slippers, over the carpeted floors of her life, adjusting the angles of the books in her bookshelves, the magazine by the telephone, getting everything straight. She told the senator she was ill today, but he must have known she was going to work with Jim on the investigation.

The phone rings.

'Jane. You have to get out right now,' said Senator Sam Spalding. 'My friends ... they're not happy. You'd better call off the story. They don't like it. Nobody likes it. You'd better tell your friend. Otherwise they say one of you could easily get killed.'

Her lips set firmly as she thinks of him. Although he looks overweight and ordinary, he has hot, clever skin, full of treachery and desire.

She misses him.

Jane Meadows packs her bags and as she does so the window closes in on her, staring at her, and the furniture too watches her. The whole apartment has turned against her, the place of sanctuary turned inside out, and even the clouds in the sky observe her as she flings her passport and her jewellery into a brown leather bag.

Her forehead is lined and her skin as pale as bone, as she wipes her hands on her pleated skirt while all the straight lines and clean surfaces of her apartment distort, as if all along they have had no outside reality at all. Her little pictures of sailing boats scream at her now.

Jim rings the doorbell, and strides in, with one of his wavy smiles, and the gust of good nature which blows in whenever he enters a room, and she stands there a long way away, a little person, very frightened, very lonely, as she wipes her hands on her skirt once again.

'I think Sam Spalding's sick,' she says. 'I think he's dying.'

'Christ, Jane,' says Jim. 'You work with him every day. Don't be histrionic. Of course he's not suddenly dying. You'd have noticed.'

'You think nothing ever really happens.' She swings round. 'I'm packing. I think we should get out.'

'Everything will be fine,' he says.

Jane shakes her head and continues to pack.

'I know Sam. He'll do anything to stop this story now. He wants the fucking President at his funeral. He doesn't want to ruin him. He'll do anything. His reputation. We have to get out.'

'Where?'

'Somewhere safe. We've had a death threat, Jim. This isn't a game. It's not just newsprint.'

'My paper will protect you . . .'

'Your paper won't protect anyone. This is big stuff, Jim.'

'I'll file the story today. Once it's done we'll be safe.'

'I'm going, Jim.' She picks up her bag. 'I called a cab. Come with me. Please. You're in danger. I want you to call off the story. You have to. He's warned us.'

'I can't do that. I don't want to do that. Your lipstick's smudged. You never smudge your lipstick,' he says in an uneven voice, and she moves towards him, but he turns away.

65

Under one of the bridges of Washington which carries traffic to the Kennedy Centre, a tramp has covered over a table with a white sheet he has found, and is laying out his scraps of scavenged food like a banquet for kings and queens.

Down in Georgetown, a lady with a black bun two feet high sits on a cane chair, surrounded by lavender bushes. Out of her antique-shop window, a puppet's head glares at her from a vase.

Elsewhere in Washington, on the junction of P Street and 9th, little more than a mile from the White House, an elderly tourist from the Cotswolds is being mugged in an area of barred doors and liquor stores with armoured glass, and litter eddying about in the wind. The Metro section of the *Washington Post* reports such murders (the old man subsequently dies) rather as a local paper reports church fêtes, in a small column without much detail but with a certain affection, as though the familiarity of the event makes it reassuring.

66

At his office Gustav sits with his head in his hands. He reaches out for one of his glass ornaments of a swan which sits on his desk, clear as ice, and flings it onto the carpet. He picks up the phone to call the airport, to try to speak to Ivana so she doesn't leave him but he stops and instead gets up to crouch down over the cold swan with the broken neck.

His shoes shine like ebony.

As Rebecca and Ivana waited at the airport, Ivana didn't seem the same person as she had been, and Rebecca realised she had never seen her out of the cul de sac. Here she was smaller, more fragile, and her left hand constantly fiddled with a chunky ring on her right hand, as she stood in the sea of her suitcases. How thin and wrinkled the skin on her hands is, thought Rebecca, yet when Ivana's fingers opened out on a piano they plunged into the notes drawing out all kinds of sounds – young sounds, old sounds, nostalgic sounds, all kinds.

Ivana kept looking round like a frightened bird, and Rebecca wondered what she was afraid of.

Maybe Ivana had been hiding in the cul de sac for the last years; the lights in the airport were bright, and Ivana kept blinking as if unused to the light, and Rebecca realised she had always seen Ivana in the half-darkness.

'I'm so pleased you came,' said Ivana suddenly. 'I needed your help to get out.' Her eyes blazed at Rebecca. Rebecca began to shiver, and she took a step back. 'You're such a comfort to me,' continued Ivana.

Flight announcements shrieked out, and everywhere people darted about, again like birds, little urgent figures with frightened eyes. At any moment they might all fly up to the high ceilings.

Ivana, as she stood at the check-in desk, dabbed at her nose with a powder puff, and seemed like someone from an old film, with no connection to all the bustling diverse people all around. Her face was over made-up and her suitcases swelled out all around her, as the announcements cried out their messages, and people trudged by, and Rebecca fingered the smart white collar of her shirt.

Ivana was bundled up in her fur coat. 'I'll need it when it's cold,' she said. 'It's too bulky to pack.'

'But it's summer even there, isn't it?' said Rebecca.

'Not all the time,' muttered Ivana, and re-applied pink lipstick. Even here, Rebecca could smell her perfume. In the cab it had been overwhelming.

Rebecca bent down and picked up her brown case for comfort. She took her ticket from Ivana's hand, and examined it.

'It's not a return, is it?' she said.

She found herself moved backwards, away from Ivana at the check-in desk.

67

Beneath the sky of unremitting blue the drowsy neighbourhoods of north-west Washington laze around, each one splendidly dressed in tall trees, wide streets, the cry of cicadas and a scent of summer; the hidden cities of a town better known for its marble-columned monument and its enthusiasm for murders.

Over in Georgetown, camp waiters pirouette from table to table, receiving late orders with smiles of appreciation as if now, finally, they had met someone who really knew how to order a meal.

While various journalists and their contacts finish a meal the large windows span out on a Georgetown street scene, with sulphureous yellow cabs speeding by, their exhausts spewing out fumes, messengers from hell.

In Anacostia a young boy of fifteen aims a gun at his best friend because his friend owes him $100. When, later, a policeman asks him if he requested the money back before killing his friend, the young boy will reply, 'Naw. I just shot him.'

The restaurant guests are sipping at the last of

their coffee, and the eerie notes of Traffic's *Dear Mr Fantasy* wind through the air, tightening their grip on those who come to restaurants like this to be part of the present, and then find themselves in sudden agony at the loss of the past as a poignant old track seers through them.

The lobbyist for bottled water, for instance, sits straight-backed, the fan whirling above him, and realises he never meant life to be like this. In the past, he was going to be a sailor in the future, and just sail and sail around the world.

Sam Spalding, the senator, stands at the window of his office, looking out.

In Rock Creek Park, which lies in the centre of Washington and separates the north east from the north west, spiders climb over vast canyons of leaves, others fight giant ants, and some give birth here, in the warm undergrowth, protecting their egg sacs with their lives, part of a world that isn't for anything, a world that is just there, the spiders tend their future, their genes.

Meanwhile the statues of men all over Washington stand or sit, arm resting on hip, arms crossed, arm holding helmet, or just resting on the arm of the chair in which they sit, for these are all men of action who look about to spring up and come up with another political statement or battle plan.

General Andrew Jackson rides through Lafayette Square. Rear Admiral S.F. Dupont stands firm in

Dupont Circle and George Washington rides through the Battle of Princeton in Washington Circle.

In the hospitals babies cry out as they are born.

And in the White House, in his oval office, the President shuffles through some papers, then leans down and scratches the sole of his foot.

68

Phillip closed the door behind Susan. The drawing room was shadowy, with closed curtains.

'I've thought about this, ever since I was staying in your house that night,' he said, 'fucking Sandra and thinking of you down the other end of the house with your marble white skin like some kind of Washington memorial.'

He moved the hair from her face, and kissed the side of her nose, and her closed eyes, and her cheeks, and his hands strayed down over her breasts and he undid the buttons of her shirt. The texture of his skin was rougher than it used to be and his eyes had lost some of their polish. He had a little less hair, just a little, but there was still that power, way back behind the eyes. His hands were as warm as ever. He was more desperate, that was all. Whereas most people become less desperate with time, he had become more so.

Even his gaiety and his charm seemed emptier than before.

'I tried to keep away from you.'

'Did you send Sandra here?'

'No. She was distraught. I'd told her it was all over. She knew it was to do with you. She came of her own accord. It was a last attempt to get you out of my life. She told me about it. She said you'd been rather courteous, and that she'd found herself liking you.'

'Where is she now?'

'She left last night. She's gone home.'

'Tell me, did you intend to tell Jim?' she said.

'About what?'

'The German boy.'

'What about him?'

'What happened. You know.'

Phillip smiled. 'I thought about it. Often I nearly told Jim. He thought you were so perfect. He didn't know about all your little secrets.'

Outside, the other side of the closed curtains, June was picking out weeds with their warm wet roots and a man with a dog glanced at the darkened house. Further down the road, the elderly couple were preparing themselves a sandwich lunch.

'I used to talk about you to him. He liked that. He adores you,' he said.

He undid her skirt and let it fall to the ground. 'You aren't any fatter,' he said, shyly touching her belly. 'You know, some people after having a child get plumper ... and you still wear the necklace I gave you.'

Susan stood in the shadows, her shirt loose, her skirt concertinaed on the floor, with his eyes flooding her face.

He smiled quickly, a lopsided smile which reached

up to the right side of his face as if trying to get out. That was at the heart of Phillip, the desire to get out. He was always trapped and looking for a way to escape. Even his features were only just held together by his face: the nose, the chin, the mouth, the eyes were all stronger than the lean face which held them together.

'You should have stuck with your wars,' she said. 'You shouldn't have come here.'

'I came because I was offered the job,' he said softly, 'but once I was here I . . . Wherever I went I saw Jim or you. I tried to get you to hate it here, to want to get out, so you'd leave me in peace.'

'No, you wanted to show your power over me. Just as you used to like to,' she said.

'Maybe . . . I was playing a little,' he said.

'I haven't been playing,' she said. 'I have a child and a husband. You should get out.'

He put his lips over hers. She made an attempt to push him away but it seemed the scene had already been written, and for once it seemed Phillip was actually in it rather than at the edge of things, trying to get out, looking for exits.

'You used to say,' he said, 'that all that mattered in the world was passion – you had some line about fierceness mattering. We made plans, you know, but you have forgotten them all: lofts in New York, a yacht on the high seas, living in Chicago in a top-floor apartment . . .'

'I've had plenty of passion – for my child, my husband, my house.'

'But, Susan, what about me?' he said.

'You've always been there. You know that. You just shouldn't have come back.'

'You used to undress in front of the bedroom window, knowing I was out there, hiding in the garden,' he said, his hands running over her breasts.

'That's not true.'

'Wasn't it enough to have me pinned in your memory like one of your moths, kept away from the air? If you kept me there I could never age, never fall out of love with you. I often thought of killing you for much the same reason. So you'd never change, never leave me. But in fact you turned the tables on me and I was the one who became unable to live.'

She took a step back but he held her arm.

'I'm sorry if that happened. That wasn't my doing. I just got on with my life. I kept a few memories, naturally.'

'Your thoughts kept me trapped,' he said.

'You were always unhappy, Phillip. From the beginning, you were never happy.'

Susan remembered how conclusive Phillip's smiles had been, announcing there was no more to say, that the world had been sorted out according to his given dimensions. But with time she had become more and more sure that there was nothing behind Phillip's certainty, only a chasm she didn't want to fall into and that all that was keeping him from falling was her, Susan, and her arms were growing tired of holding him. Not that he saw the chasm; only Susan seemed to, behind his eyes, and she didn't want him to take her with him when he fell. But all the while the emptiness made him more dazzling, more charming, so quick and funny and wicked. And his love-making was cataclysmic because then, and only then, did he include his sense of emptiness.

The night before she left him Phillip had held her neck so tightly she had been afraid he would strangle her. When she screamed for him to stop he had hit her. She had told Phillip she wanted to leave him.

'I'll never let you leave me,' he had said.

69

In south-east Washington the heat is intense, as if eager to persecute this area. The sun blazes down on the dry street, making people take shelter in doorways, taking the colour out of the scene.

In Anacostia, an addict is trying to find a vein to inject some of the heroin the senator helped import. If he misses the vein the arm will swell up. Outside the apartment, a child of eight is playing among the used needles. He trips and falls and the palm of his hand digs into one. When he screams, no one comes, so he pulls the needle out himself.

And all the time, the senator walks the corridors with his thick-soled shoes and thick-lipped smiles beneath the dome of Congress, sparkling in the sun.

Jim drove in his old gold Thunderbird car back to the house. He drove slowly, trying to work things out as he went. He couldn't abandon the story because it was dangerous.

Jim remembered how, only a few weeks ago, Rebecca had lain tossing and turning with a fever, with Susan and Jim sitting by her bed.

Around the room had been evidence of Rebecca's creations – half-strung beads, a vase made of papier-mâché painted blue with curious white shapes, a picture frame in which Rebecca had put quotations from Shakespeare – 'Lord, what fools these mortals be!', 'Sleep thou, and love'. There had been a swimming certificate, and a certificate for having achieved a personal best at running in the last sports day; personal best was a phrase they had laughed at, as it usually meant coming in last, but still she had kept it fondly on the top of her chest of drawers with its bright green handles. The chest of drawers had served as a counter for changing Rebecca's nappies when she was a baby.

There were photographs too.

Susan had dabbed Rebecca's forehead with a flannel as Jim had stood at the door.

'Shall I get her some more paracetamol?' he had said.

'Yes, a little more. Can you get the fan from upstairs? It might bring her temperature down.'

But the next day, as is the way with childhood illnesses, Rebecca had been fine, although quiet, and Jim and Susan had been close, closer than they had been for some time, since Jane Meadows arrived in his life with her creamy white skin and certain smiles.

Through the window, when he stopped at a traffic light, he listened to the sound of doves cooing somewhere, the hum of the distant traffic, the way the air seemed to gather up all the sounds of the day and swaddle them gently before letting him hear them; each one muted, resonant, making him think of bees and daisies and summer, and of those first halcyon days he, Rebecca and Susan had spent together, as if they'd walked into some dense description of happiness, the grass scratchy on his back, the sky soft and deep and blue.

He thought how peculiar happiness is, how it separates out each thing it sees and makes you look at it and wonder at it. He passed a one-storey house of some friends of theirs, and outside, the children's bicycles leant against the porch and the sight of those round wheels and the tilt of the bikes, clearly left there by careless children, busy to do the next thing, the sight of them was like the feeling of finding old fireworks in your pocket and thinking, Oh yes, I remember that night; the bonfire, the children, and happiness real and hard like a jewel.

It was essential to fight for that, but not just to protect your own happiness and that of your family, for the sake of other communities too. He couldn't just turn his back on the story, but he was afraid for his family because of the threat he'd received. Perhaps the threat was real. If happiness was real, horror might be too, real and hard like a jewel.

His hands were sweating and he could hear his heart thudding as if trying to get out of the cage of his ribs. He tried to smile, failed, and began to hum. He was aware of every detail of the inside of the car – the road map of the Washington area with its torn pages, the half-empty bottle of seltzer water, a pair of Susan's sunglasses lying on the floor of the passenger seat, the smell of her in the car, a packet of Rebecca's favourite bubble gum. He turned on the radio, and it told him of a drugs-related shooting in Anacostia. He changed the channel to a rock music station and told himself what a bright afternoon it was. If he got out of this he'd take everything more seriously, grasp it all. He called Susan from the car phone but there was no reply in the house. She should be at home, he thought. She said she would be. He pressed his foot on the accelerator.

For a while when he and Jane had worked together he had thought he wanted to escape the emotion in his house but now, as he drove back to his house and child and wife, he knew how urgently he needed them.

'I want to get out,' Jane had said.

'You don't want to see him being disgraced,' Jim had said.

'Maybe,' said Jane, looking at him directly. 'Maybe. Plus I don't want to die. You should get out too.'

'I'll publish the story tomorrow,' he had told her. 'It's an important story. I have to do it, don't you see? We aren't in a vacuum, just protecting ourselves and our immediate interests.'

Jane had turned sharply away.

70

It was odd to Susan that the street was continuing as usual, as Phillip pushed his tongue deep into her mouth; the last of the azaleas were dying down, browning at the corners, the cars were packed attentively in the drives, the sun beat down, pouring out its rays on the grey tarmac and the still trees.

She kept her eyes shut tight.

While Phillip had been away from her all these years, he had been in wars. His newspaper articles had been good, full of detail – the swagger of torturers, the way their mouths were more fluid than other people's, the crumpled handkerchief a killer took from his pocket, the way the rain made even the toughest men look tender and vulnerable. And meanwhile she had been on another journey, in another direction. She had been through the female version of war, giving birth. She had been there at the beginning of things, touched by life and death at the same time while the silly little details of life went on – the gynaecologist's tummy rumbling as he watched the baby emerge, the nurse scratching her nose, a door creaking down a corridor. She had not known if in the end she would be brave or cowardly as men don't know whether they will be brave in war or not, and maybe no one can quite know who they are until they know that. In birth as in war, death was possible, a quick death, alive one moment, and dead the next. Horror was there too – the dead baby, the pain. She wanted birth again. She wanted the screaming again. She wanted the slither of the bloodied baby on her stomach. She wanted the fear as she watched a needle showing the baby's quivering heart beat. She wanted the fierce reality of it all, the way it led you to what you really were, showed you that all that time before was just a patch to this reality, just a meander, and what you were and what you always had been was this woman bending over this baby, amazed by the fierceness of love.

His kiss was gentle, this time, at first, for a while his fingers caressing her ear, his tongue inside it. He ran his tongue down the curves of her face, and began to repeat the same old patterns over her body. 'This is it,' he murmured as he buried himself in her neck, and it seemed to cover him over, dark and slumberous.

It had been silent as she lay on the floor with the German boy. It was odd how silent it had been, as though all the traffic in the street outside had stopped. Then one of the cats had miaowed, and at the time she'd thought the cat was complaining about the boy's presence, although the boy was just watching her with an intensity she hadn't wanted. Perhaps the cat knew Phillip was on the way home.

71

'Rebecca!' said Ivana. 'Come with me.'

'No. You'll be OK now,' said Rebecca as she drew back.

'Rebecca!' Ivana said, a little figure in a fur coat surrounded by her suitcases. 'You'll miss the flight.'

'I'm not coming!' called out Rebecca. 'I don't want to. I'm going home. You carry on.' Ivana gave a funny terrified smile, and more people joined the queue and seemed to engulf the little woman as she was carried forward to the desk.

Rebecca turned and walked off, towards the taxi rank, but on the way she stopped and bought herself a magazine, a woman's magazine, and when she came out she waved to Ivana whose head was still watching her from the group waiting to check in for the Warsaw flight.

There was a peacefulness about Ivana's expression Rebecca hadn't observed before.

As she waited in the queue for cabs Rebecca was suddenly, wildly, jubilant. She was on her own.

72

Around Phillip and Susan, who stood in the middle of the drawing room, circled her various possessions – the blue velvet rocking chair, the early Victorian sofa with its beige upholstery, the frameless print of a snow scene, the dark photographs in their glittering frames. I thought the things I had would barricade me, she thought, but here they are just watching me and him. For a moment she could see the room as it was that first day, with its scrolls of carpet wrapped in thick brown felt, and the mantelpiece bristling with candlesticks, and June and her husband standing at the door holding the gift of a cyclamen and some cookies.

She started when the phone rang.

'Don't answer it,' he said.

She did up the buttons of her shirt.

'Phillip is such a reasonable person,' Jim had said, 'so considerate.'

'He's an actor,' Susan had replied.

Maybe there was the casualness in his eyes now which helped make him seem older. There was something in his eyes she had never liked, a kind of bleakness far back. When she tried to move to the phone, he held her arm. There were soft lines in his face now, like rivulets in sand, but his hand had the same tight grip.

Downstairs, she could hear the cricket singing. The washing is piling up down there, she thought vaguely, I really must sort it out . . . She thought of the way the fluff from the dryer clung to the walls. As he kissed her, his smell brought back the smell of him that day, at the flat, a kind of mixture of anger and desire and some smell which only he had. She remembered how she used to go through his clothes, his huge jackets with their dark warm pockets, the softness of his frayed collars where they had rubbed against his neck.

She tried to think of the street outside, the other side of the curtain, but the street had become a children's theatre with paper figures moving back and forth and all that was real was that room in their flat all those years ago.

'What happened that night, with the German boy?' he said. After she had left Phillip, she was unable to remember Phillip's voice. Occasionally she'd hear a tone of it in one person or another, but the voice itself had left her completely.

'I never made love to him, you know,' she said.

She had asked the boy back for coffee. He'd approached her at the Natural History Museum and asked her questions about spiders. The boy was about nineteen, with a carved face and blue eyes. For a moment, life had seemed a simple matter. When she said she had a good collection of books on spider's webs, the boy seemed riveted. Anyway, he came back with her. They were laughing and talking and somehow he began to kiss her and at that moment she thought, I don't have to stay with Phillip and be unhappy, I could get out. She let him undress her. It had all seemed normal enough until Phillip came home early.

She found she could think about what had happened in a way she hadn't been able to for years. She knew that somehow it was imperative she did so.

The boy whispered things to her in the silence and the stillness and of course it came back, the silence and the stillness, but that was later. She looked up and saw Phillip there, standing over them. His movements had always been those of a cat, stealthy and silent, and he was there like one of his cats, and for a moment she had thought he was one. That day he was dressed all in grey and the odd thing was he looked at her with the calm of a cat.

The boy had seen Phillip. Perhaps it was the beauty of the boy, or the delicacy, or something else which was beyond him, because all of a sudden Phillip's face cracked open and his mouth roared and the boy cowered back and Susan screamed.

Phillip picked the boy up by his blond hair and smashed him in the face. The boy fell back, holding his face, but then moved towards her as if to try to protect her, but that seemed to madden Phillip more, and he lifted the boy up by the shoulders, and smashed his face again, and the boy reeled back, and

Susan caught him in her arms, and she felt the warm blood then.

'Phillip. Stop!' she said. (She remembered now: she had said that. She had at least tried to stop it. She had guarded him with her body.) But Phillip pushed her back and hit the boy again and again and again as Susan tried to fight him and then, all of a sudden, Phillip didn't hit any more and the boy was still, his face the colour of clay, an expression of surprise on his face. Blood from his mouth slid onto the grey carpet and one of the cats walked cautiously over and put her nose in the dark blood, and afterwards her nose had blood on it, a clown's nose. The cat purred as it rubbed against Phillip. Susan sat with the boy's head on her lap. The boy lay there, his limbs crumpled up, and blood running from his mouth.

'Get an ambulance. What have you done? Get an ambulance,' she said.

But when she looked at Phillip he wasn't seeing the boy. He was still angry, and his whole body was trembling.

The boy's white T-shirt lay on a chair by the window.

'Get away from him!' Phillip said.

'No,' she said, frowning. 'Get an ambulance.'

He grabbed her arm and hoisted her up, then flung her over to the other side of the room, as if trying to hurl her far away into the next life, and she remembered thinking that she had no idea he was that strong before she banged her head against the edge of the glass coffee table.

When she came round, there was no one there except the cats – no Phillip, no boy. Her head hurt. She put her clothes quickly back on – a dress, a pair of white pants, sandals – and then she realised they were sprayed with blood. There was dark blood splattered on the white walls and the cats were licking it off. They had scarlet tongues.

On her hands and knees, with bowl after bowl of water and a sponge, she tried to clear up. She tried not to panic. It was important to stay calm. Her hair kept falling over her face and her knees hurt her.

There was too much light in the room, she thought. If only it were dark.

She feared he'd go to prison for what he'd done unless she cleared up every bit of blood. There was so much blood. She was afraid he may have stabbed the boy – by mistake, of course, by accident, in a moment of rage. She checked the kitchen knives. There seemed to be one missing.

Susan took her splattered clothes off, put them in the washing machine, added the boy's shirt, and turned the machine on. I'll wash everything away as if it never happened, she thought.

In the walk-in wardrobe of the room she and Phillip had shared – with the television jauntily projecting on a bracket from the wall – she chose a yellow tailored dress to regain control.

Phillip's car, a black mini, had gone from its parking place. She wondered what would happen if she called the police. But she didn't call them. She sat on the grey sofa and called every hospital she could think of, one after the other, to find out if a German boy had been brought to the accident department. No, she said, she didn't know his name.

As she waited on the phone she was puzzled that the noises of the fight hadn't somehow remained in the room. The smell did, of lust and fear, and the taste in her mouth of iron, of blood. Beside her on the table lay a red book with Shakespeare's dark outline on the front.

The books lined up on the walls, a painting of the sea hanging on the pale wall, all the efforts to fill up a room, to give it enough life to stop this kind of thing ever happening – a few shells on a shelf, a piece of driftwood, some photographs of him and her, arms round each other too tightly as if clinging to each other rather than just standing, him always at the side of every picture, only just there.

A pair of Phillip's shoes, expensive brown brogues, lay in front of the sofa. On the coffee table still lay copies of the Sunday newspapers, slightly curled at the edges, but all the same evidence of normal life. His cigarette ends lay in the ashtray and she put down the phone, went over and put her lips to one.

Next she climbed the stairs to their room, passed the bed, still unmade from last night, the sheets tangled, and she stretched to get a suitcase from a shelf in the wardrobe. Susan flung in a few clothes, the jewellery which mattered to her, her make-up, and all the time she felt she was robbing him.

But I am not his, she told herself. I belong to myself. I cannot be robbing him. These are my things.

It isn't easy, this, she thought, as she pushed her

possessions down in the canvas suitcase, almost wishing he would return.

Love is not always on our side, she thought. It has its own agenda. I have mine.

She walked round the flat one last time as the day grew into evening but all she could see everywhere were dark stains like those still just visible on the carpet downstairs. I must get out, she thought. She walked along the corridor, down the stairs, her hands hurting as she dragged her suitcase.

It didn't happen, she told herself, closing the front door behind her, none of this happened. I shall forget it.

A taxi came by. She called it. For months afterwards she would make taxis take detours to pass by the flat, on the top two floors of the building, to be near him for just a moment.

She took the taxi to Bayswater, to a cheap hotel.

Outside, the moon melted into the dark sky.

He can't find me here, she thought. He can't find me then destroy me here. She wondered what he could have done with the body if the boy had died . . . perhaps he took it to the sea, out on the coast of Wales, where he was brought up.

And so the rest of her life started up again.

There was no mention anywhere of the boy's disappearance so maybe, she persuaded herself, he had recovered. Or else he was already someone on the edge of life whose parents had already lost him.

She suspected he didn't try harder to see her because of what had happened, and that he was afraid of her.

*

If only she'd gone to the police at the beginning, that first evening.

'You say you never made love to the German boy?' he said, a distant voice, still holding her arm.

'No. You were crazy.'

'You were in each other's arms.'

'It was nothing. Phillip, I called up the accident departments of all the London hospitals. None had received a German boy,' she said.

'You were trying to leave me, Susan. I could see that. I took him to a hospital on the Fulham Road. He was fine. A little dazed but fine.'

'When you lie, Phillip, which is often,' she said, 'your right eye quivers a little. Did you know that?'

'Look, it was years ago and this is now,' he said.

'You and I don't exist now. We're back in that room. We always will be unless you tell me the truth.'

'You're lying to me too,' he said.

She shook her head.

He stood back and slumped on the sofa, lighting a cigarette.

'We never made love,' she repeated, standing there, as he watched her, his long legs stretched out, his collar soft against his neck. The sight of his lips made her feel almost drowsy.

'Do you have a drink?' he said in a low voice. 'No, don't go,' he said, as she moved away. 'Sit down,' he said. 'I don't want you running away again.'

'No, Phillip.'

The smoke from his cigarette filled the room so

that all its dimensions seemed hazy and changing, almost as though they were back in the past in London.

He got up and pushed her down on the sofa opposite him.

'You used to do what I said.'

'I got out of that,' she said.

'I've imagined this so many times,' he said. 'Open your legs.'

'No. You took the key to the house when you stayed the night and came here, and moved things around,' said Susan.

'That's right. This should have been my life, you and me and a child. I liked coming here when you were out, and watching the house. I wanted you no longer to feel safe. Women need their homes to be safe . . . if they're safe everything else is OK but if they're not the rest starts to sway and wobble. Isn't that right? I said open your legs.'

'I said no.'

'I love you,' he said.

'Get out, now,' she said. 'Already it's getting too late.'

'It is too late,' he said, and stubbed out another cigarette.

'The boy died, didn't he?'

'Of course not,' he said.

'You befriended Maria then offered her a job to get her out of this house.'

'That's right. I wanted you to be alone, as you are now.'

'You put petrol on the roses.'

'That was just a joke – to scare you. I thought you'd suspect Ivana. Your neighbour.'

'She adored you,' said Susan.

'I told her things she wanted to hear.'

'You rang that restaurant about a drug scare.'

'Yes. I didn't like your cosy dinners with Jim. I wanted to . . . damage your relationship.'

'You left the door open so the documents could be taken – or you took them yourself. You wanted to damage Jim and make me mad.'

'Someone asked me to help them out. I did it as a favour. I had the key to the front door so I merely took the key to the filing cabinets from Jim's pocket while you and he slept. You know how quietly I move. I kissed you while you slept but you didn't wake.

'I gave my friend the documents, and I told him the layout of the house in case one of his acquaintances needed to come back.'

'You helped Sam Spalding.'

Phillip shrugged.

'You suggested to Ivana she take Rebecca to Poland,' said Susan.

'Correct.' He smiled, and now the smile didn't seem to be trying to escape. 'I even bought her the tickets. I wanted to see you alone. I believe Jim is going away too, if he has any sense. He's been quite brave over this story. I wouldn't like him to die. I've got quite to like him, in spite of everything. Open your legs. I want to fuck you.'

'You should go,' she said.

'I didn't know you never actually . . . That it was my child. It makes a difference. That it was my child.'

'I couldn't have coped, Phillip. We couldn't have. The violence. How could we have had a child?' she said.

He stood up and walked over to her.

'This would have been our life here. You took it all away,' he said, and slapped her face.

This time, she stood up and hit him back and they began to fight, like cats, her fingers at his collar, burying her fingers in the heat of his neck, dragging her nails across his face, the blood on her nails, as he tore open her shirt and pushed down her pants then gathered her up for a moment in his long arms as if she were some demented flower before lowering her down on the floor and raping her, one hand over her screaming mouth, watched by a photograph of her, Jim and Rebecca, standing proudly in front of the Grand Canyon.

73

'Can you hurry?' said Rebecca to the driver, as they drove from the airport, leaving Ivana. Every time they went round a corner, the driver's sunglasses slid along the dashboard.

She sat at the front of the seat, her magazine on her lap, the little suitcase with the wheels and handle, which she and her mother had packed so carefully the night before, on the seat beside her. She placed her hand on the suitcase's rough material to steady herself as the cab rocked from side to side and the radio cried out a rap. She swallowed tightly, as if her throat were narrow.

Already, when she thought of her house, it was almost in a dream, at a distance, washed in sunlight, resting by the side of the street, as if it had floated there and could float away at any time – the grey door, the stone walls, the ivy on the walls, it was all so unlikely, such a fantasy place, as unreal as any Polish palace, and it could become so, if she didn't love it.

Rebecca had a sudden sense of the reality of life, behind the stories and the dreams, and that that reality was something more dangerous and delightful and damaging than any talk of Polish counts and countesses, than any dream-like letters of long-past love affairs and dead babies, and that it was all in the house, waiting to crumble, to become a dream, if she didn't return in time.

74

'You planned this just as carefully as I did,' Phillip whispered, and pushed her black hair from her face with its red swollen mouth. In recent weeks her skin had taken on an almost translucent quality.

'That's not true,' she said, looking round for her clothes. Her torn blouse lay nearby, and her white pants, and she put them on but couldn't do up all the buttons on the blouse because some had been torn off. It was a cotton checked blouse, and he helped her do up the buttons, kissing her red swollen lips as he did so. She was too exhausted to resist.

'Go,' she murmured.

He ran his tongue over the edges of her ear.

'You don't mean that,' he said.

'I'll go when you show me the attic,' he said. 'I want you to take me to your attic,' he said, 'the high place.'

'No,' she said, remembering the phrase.

'The fortune teller told me one of us would die in a high place. If you were dead you'd stop haunting me,' he said.

Upstairs, in the attic, the beetles shimmered in their boxes and the butterflies spread their blue wings.

I have the gun there, she thought. I'll get the gun and order him to go. Then everything will be fine.

But when they reached the attic, he made straight to the cupboard and took the handgun from the hiding place.

'Maria. She's very talkative,' he explained.

She lurched forward to take the pistol from him and as they struggled one of her glass-topped mahogany trays fell and smashed, leaving wings of blue butterflies like dead leaves over the floor.

The little blue bits of wings shimmered all over the floor. I'll collect them up afterwards, she thought. I'll be able to put them back together.

He took her arm and pushed the blouse off her shoulders. He began to kiss her again.

On her table lay one of her drawings of spiders; the spiders fought together, the female rearing up above the male.

He had left the cupboard door open and she could see as he held her shoulders the old cardboard boxes and bulging black bags piled in the coal-dust darkness, cargo in a ship. To one side were stacked mahogany trays of insects – locusts yellow like old gentlemen, beetles so black it seemed they'd been polished and polished, beetles shiny and iridescent, jewelled homages to a universe perfect in its details.

As Phillip held her, he was far too big for the room, some dinosaur from another age, out of period, with his long-legged faded jeans, his black belt which wasn't done up, his soft blue shirt. Close up, she could see his face clearly – the high cheekbones, the slightly sunken cheeks, his strong jaw, and the eyes which always seemed to have just seen her after a long absence.

His lips were thin but when they touched hers they seemed wide and thick and engulfing. She'd always found him too attractive to see him clearly. It was a pity really. She'd never really known him. They might have got on if she and he hadn't been swamped by desire the second they saw each other. Susan felt immensely weary, and sorry for him, and for this passion of theirs which had weathered all these years.

Above them the skylight let in the repetitive blue sky and through another window she could see the chimney which had had to be repaired soon after they came.

Around them were the white sloping walls, a few chairs, the skylight above pouring down blue sky and sun although somehow the room remained cool and grey.

'You know, I feel much freer now. Much happier. I've been trapped for so long. Love is a terrible thing. You look the same,' he said, gently, 'except you have a grey hair here and there. The curious thing, when we were together, was that I always loved the idea of you getting older.

'I've known I should be living another life for years. I think a great deal of people have it – the feeling that someone else is living their life, or that their real life is happening somewhere else. I felt it for years – my real life is with you.'

'Put that gun back, Phillip,' she said.

'People miss out on the life they should have,' he said. 'They take the wrong turning down a street, leave a party a minute or two early, decide not to attend that wedding. And their lives carry on without them while they're left in some cul de sac of existence, some railway siding, with weeds growing over them.'

'That hasn't happened to you,' said Susan. 'You've had a remarkable life. A war correspondent! You're famous for not ducking. Now put the gun away.'

'I'm a minor figure. A really very minor figure. And I haven't even been happy.'

Phillip was watching Susan now intently, just as the German boy had done, absorbing every shadow of her face.

'You shouldn't have had an abortion,' he said. 'This should be my life. When I was looking at your house that first time,' he said, 'when I stayed the night, I thought that really it should have been mine, that in some way Jim had taken what should have been mine. You know – the child, the house, the sunlit garden, and that atmosphere. I've never been anywhere like that, so extraordinarily happy. When I thought the baby may have been the German boy's, I didn't mind so much . . . but to think it was yours and mine . . .

'I felt it for years – that my real life is with you. But I struggled against it. I felt after all that had happened we couldn't go back. But as the years passed it began to seem that actually I was just missing the life I should have had, and that if I wanted to make any shape of things at all I had to come and see you and sort it all out finally. Even here, you know, in this house. I'm comfortable in it. This is where I should be. You must have got the feeling sometimes, a kind of emptiness. It should be me there with you, not Jim. The fortune teller said you'd have my child. Rebecca should be my child.

'You see, that night I came to stay I couldn't sleep,' he continued, 'not with you down there. So I got up and went down the stairs softly, and down to the drawing room with those photographs of you and Jim and Rebecca in silver frames. Such a lovely girl, Rebecca, just like you, but with the sweetness you used to have, when I first met you, before you began to grow up. And him with his arm around you both. It did seem odd, that that man should have his arm round you and her. I didn't really like it. And then I went into his study and saw an ugly little card – made up of newspaper clippings – she had given Jim on Valentine's Day and the green dinosaur with the chipped leg and I was puzzled and hurt because I felt she ought to be mine.

'I remember you in that bookshop like an apparition, and I thought again how very much I love you, the way you move, the twitch of your upper lip, the way when you're nervous you play with your necklace, the fear always at the back of your eyes. And then at that dreadful embassy party, there you were, scattering out of the building like Cinderella, and when I entered the room it was so lonely without you and I realised I'd been lonely all the time, every moment, since you left me.'

Through the frame of the window overlooking the garden the blue sky shone like a newly minted stamp; the colour rich compared with the airy white and high spaces of this attic room.

And in the cupboard, sensing the movement outside, seeing with all its eight eyes, the spider scrambles over the letters of Phillip inside the cardboard box: *Sometimes I have wanted to kill you, because only by killing you could I possess you. But, of course, even that is false. You'd be even more separate then, in another world, only at least the memory would be intact, and you'd never leave me, and you wouldn't make love to other men. You'd be like one of your fine insects, pinned down in the box of my memory . . . At one time or another I want everyone to be dead . . . all the pain, the longing – gone away. Even me, sometimes I want me dead.*

'Darling,' she said, her heart beating fast, 'after what happened . . .'

Outside the garden roared green and lovely and the walls of the attic slid down white and bright all around them, and there seemed to be no way out, only the walls all around them, moving closer.

On the easel, worms of colour sat trapped in their tubes; reds, oranges, greens. A case of turquoise and sapphire butterflies glimmered in a glass-topped case on the wooden table in front of the window.

'It seems,' said Phillip, 'that at the centre of things . . . there is a kind of ruthlessness, a neutrality, as if love has nothing to do with it . . . and it is the ruthlessness which matters.

'Odd, to keep a gun in the house,' he said. 'I thought happiness was enough to protect you. I thought what you had here would defend you.'

'Yes. I thought that,' she said.

'I intended to kill you then myself,' said Phillip. 'Possessing each other forever. Doomed lovers, you know. The spotlight. The drama. The wonderful finality. Sort of adolescent. But appealing. Certainly more appealing than anything else. But now, you know, I don't know if I do want to kill you. You see, I rather like Rebecca and Jim – he's a good man, with courage, and she is a remarkable little girl, like you were, a long time ago. I don't want to annihilate them. What I'd really like you to do,' he looked up, 'is to shoot me.'

Susan felt the air leave the room. She could imagine Phillip's body burst open and the blood spurt out, crazy and red like his scream. The boy had opened out, had his blood pour out through his mouth. The boy's white shirt had been left behind. She wondered what Phillip had done with the body. Susan closed her eyes tight. Curious that such a tall man, with such broad shoulders, couldn't take the weight of his life. If only the boy hadn't died, thought Susan.

'I shan't do that,' she said.

'I think I might make you,' he said. 'Take it.'

'No,' she said. 'No. I shan't.'

75

In the back of the attic cupboard, a spider skims up the air-conditioning unit – the black shape of the spider on the silver of the air-conditioning unit, over the boxes buried with letters, with the curves and lines of loving words, over the black bags, loving the black silk darkness . . . Generations ago her forefathers dropped threads as she does, sprawling in the swamp that was Washington, before the Capitol rose up, before the White House was built, before the roads were laid down as P Street, Q Street, R Street – all wonderfully alphabetical and well-organised although as you slip down letters in an easterly direction, things change and the streets grow dangerous. It isn't far before things get dangerous, just a few streets, just a few wrong turnings.

Austere, supremely beautiful, neutral and both careful and careless, the spider plots the strands of her empire.

Rebecca's cab drives fast towards her mother. Jim, too, drives towards the house where they had been so happy for so long. Two men drive to the house also, sent by one of Sam Spalding's friends. Jim Stewart was a brave man, they'd been told, who couldn't merely be threatened.

Ivana, over at the airport, blinks away her tears.

Maria works at her new job, at Phillip's office, dusting a desk and wondering why.

As he drives, Jim thinks of Susan, and presses his foot hard on the accelerator. His article is nearly complete. It just needs a little more colour. These last weeks he, like Susan, has been caught up in a torpor like a spell.

Susan and Phillip hear a noise downstairs as they face each other in the high white room.

He gives her an odd little smile.

76

The two men who broke into the house had been sent to kill Jim Stewart. June Brown, the neighbour from the house opposite, saw the black car stop outside the house and the two men get out and slip around the side of the house. There was something about the way they moved, almost gliding over the grass, which concerned her, and she called the police, but the police were slow, and it was a while before they came, putting on their guns, lumbering over in the direction of the old grey stone house.

The gunmen smashed the kitchen window, and opened it, and climbed in, past the huge fridge which shook and rumbled as they passed by, through to the drawing room where the furniture was set back, far apart, and they walked up the curving wooden stairs, past the statue of a woman in an alcove, towards what sounded like voices at the top of the house. It was as though the house, with its arrangement of chairs and pictures, was leading them up there. Clearly, Jim Stewart must already be home, the killers thought.

There was a still, languorous quality to the house, though these men didn't notice it. When they reached the hall at the top of the stairs, a bathroom door opened onto an old black and white tiled bathroom, and next to it was another dark door, with a wooden carving on the front, which was half-open. The men passed softly through the door, carrying their guns, and up the stairs to the attic room where a tall, half-naked man stood with a dishevelled woman beside him.

'You Susan Stewart?'

She nodded.

'You her husband? Are you Jim Stewart?' said one of the killers.

The man smiled, and nodded. 'Yes,' he said. 'Yes I am. I'm her husband.' It was curious the way he smiled, the killer thought afterwards. The killer aimed and shot the man neatly in the heart.

The man crumpled, his legs buckling, his body crashing down like some vast statue. The woman cried out.

A child's voice yelled up, 'Mummy, I'm home!' and as they were, for a moment, distracted, the woman at once grabbed the small pistol out of the dying man's hand and shot at them but already they had stepped down, down the steps, down through the house, through the patterns of furniture, twisting and turning, leading them out, past the scrawny child with damson eyes, past a man stepping out of a golden Thunderbird who called out at them to stop, past an officer stepping wearily from his car.

Jim took the number of the car and remembered the faces.

Phillip held Susan. Her hand was over his heart, as she knelt by him, kissing his face. But all the life was draining from him, all the colour, all the reality, and soon he was slumped against the wall, fading into the past, into memory. She remembered how the boy had fallen back in that other high white room. She screamed, and then fell silent. She could hear Jim's footsteps on the stairs and his desperate voice. 'Susan!' he shouted. 'Are you OK? Susan! Christ, Susan!' A spider from the cupboard ran out, over the floor, and seemed to watch the scene for a moment – the dishevelled woman, the thin man in her arms – before the whole room began to shake with the footsteps of people.

77

The baby who was born nine months later was much loved, a very happy child, very happy although a little wild, and spent all his childhood in the curious grey stone house adored by the man he called his father. The child's eyes were like Phillip's, but they had no bleakness in them, only a dancing amusement. These ties of ours are far stronger than we think, and draw men and women over oceans, round corners, through doorways, called by the past and called by the future.

'Phillip's death – the whole thing – I can't believe he died instead of me. I feel responsible,' Jim used to say, pacing up and down. 'It was the story. I was too involved. Never again.'

But of course he went on being too involved in stories, taking risks, passionate in his own way, still innocent.

Only Rebecca really changed. She loved her little brother and enjoyed the stillness which had come over the house and her mother, freeing Rebecca to move forward, out into the sunlight as the seasons folded over them all, the beetles shimmering, the spiders weaving their extraordinary, glorious patterns.